MW01253749

All Through the Night

All Through the Night

Barrington King

Five Star
Unity, Maine

Five Star First Edition Romance Series.

First Edition, Second Printing

Published in 2001 in conjunction with the
Kidde, Hoyt & Picard Literary Agency.

Set in 11 pt. Plantin by Al Chase.

Printed in the United States on permanent paper.

Library of Congress Cataloging-in-Publication Data

King, Barrington.
    All through the night / Barrington King.
      p.   cm. — (Five Star first edition romance series)
    ISBN 0-7862-3287-0 (hc : alk. paper)
    1. World War, 1939–1945 — Underground movements —
France — Fiction. 2. France — History — German
occupation, 1940–1945 — Fiction. 3. World War,
1939–1945 — Women — Fiction. 4. Americans — France
— Fiction. 5. Women — France — Fiction. I. Title.
II. Series.
PS3561.I4728 A79 2001
813′.54—dc21
                                       2001023121

For Sarah, as always

Part I

The Coming of the Night

Chapter One

Elizabeth surveyed her desk strewn with papers. What a week it had been! Her own graduation from college, Leonore suddenly deciding to go to France in August, despite the talk of war, and, according to Jaime, Leonore's daughter Paula arriving unannounced in the middle of the night. Then there was the pile of correspondence to be dealt with, and each day brought more. She spread out the morning mail, picked out a telegram and opened it. Well, that solved one small mystery. The telegram was from Vassar. The dean wished Leonore to know that her daughter had once again left college without permission, and this time there could be no reprieve. Paula was expelled.

"Haven't seen my pipe, Elizabeth, have you?"

She looked up into the kind, sad face of Eustace Warden.

"The curvy meerschaum one?"

"That's it."

"On that little table over there, under the portrait of your father."

"Thanks. I hear Paula came in last night."

"That's what Jaime says." Elizabeth handed Eustace the telegram.

"Has Leonore seen this?"

"She's not up yet, as far as I know."

"There'll be hell to pay."

"Yes," Elizabeth said, "I imagine there will be."

9

She watched Eustace shuffle off in his dressing gown and slippers. Elizabeth turned back to the mail, sorting it in piles of decreasing interest. On top of the first pile was a letter from Peter Warden, in an embossed envelope of the American embassy in Paris, where he served as political officer. No one had been surprised at this choice assignment for the grandson of Augustus Warden. She missed Peter. She took the letter to Eustace in the library, where he was reading a book.

Next, Elizabeth turned to her calendar. Before she dealt with the correspondence, she had to go down to Laurel Hill to select flowers for a big dinner Leonore was giving that evening. On the way to Laurel Hill she would save someone else a trip by stopping at the train station to pick up Leonore's New York newspapers. She lifted the receiver of the house phone and called down to ask that the Ford station wagon be brought out to the rear entrance.

Elizabeth descended the back stairs that led from the upper floors of Beaulieu to the kitchen and pantry and the garage below. At the pantry door she paused for a moment to look at herself in the full-length mirror, where those who served the Wardens at table were to inspect their appearance before entering the dining room. She was not the same young woman who had looked out from a piece of mirror nailed above a kitchen sink on that day that had ended her old life and begun her new existence.

Then she had looked younger than her nineteen years: dark brown eyes, dark arched eyebrows, hair in shades of wheat and straw. Now that thick long hair was pulled back in a tight bun, and in her fashionable suit—handed down, along with much else, from Leonore, with whom Elizabeth happily shared the same dress size—she looked older than her twenty-two years. What had not changed was that she still had no life of her own, still felt almost as suffocated, after more than two years at Beaulieu, as she had as her father's housekeeper and Amos Leach's assistant.

Elizabeth drove fast and skillfully down the narrow road that wound past the college to Laurel Hill, arriving at the station just as the train from Washington was pulling out. Leonore's papers would be carefully put aside in the station master's office. As she marched quickly down the platform, her heels clicking on the wooden boards, she saw that the morning express had left off two men. They seemed lost.

One was of her height, and she was tall, with reddish-blond hair and a roundish, almost angelic face; the other was even taller, dark-haired with olive skin, his long narrow jaw unshaven. Both were very good-looking in their very different ways. She guessed their ages to be between twenty-six and twenty-eight, and she had the impression that they were foreign.

"Excuse me, miss," the blond, almost-angelic one said, "could you tell me how we might reach Beaulieu estate?" The accent was French.

"You . . . have some business there?"

"We are expected by Mrs. Devereux."

Of course. "Then one of you must be Monsieur d'Aubigny's son."

"But how did you . . ."

"I am Mrs. Devereux's secretary, and you were expected a month ago."

"We decided to see the Grand Canyon, instead," and the blond young man smiled unapologetically. "Better late than never, as you say in English."

We'll see about that, Elizabeth thought. Paula Warden expelled from Vassar, and now two Frenchmen showing up a month late and unannounced. Well, it would have to be dealt with.

"My name is Elizabeth Vail," she said, holding out her hand to the blond one.

"I am Marc d'Aubigny," and the young Frenchman grazed the back of her hand with his lips, "and this is my friend, Jean-Luc Cabanasse."

"Enchantée de faire vôtre connaissance," she replied. French came easily to her now. Leonore Devereux had seen to that. "Well, come on then. You can ride back to Beaulieu with me, but first we have to pick up some flowers."

And so she drove the two Frenchmen up to Beaulieu, more slowly this time, so that they could pass, as though it were the usual way, through the grounds of the prestigious institution from which she, Sarah Elizabeth Vail, the first of her family to attend any kind of college, had just graduated. Marc d'Aubigny sat in the front seat with her, and the other one, with the Spanish-sounding last name, in the back with the flowers.

"Laurel Hill College for Women," Marc read from the bronze plaque on the massive stone gate. "It was founded by the Wardens was it not?"

"Yes."

"A school for rich girls."

"I'm an exception." She could hardly leave it at that. "You see, until my last birthday I was Eustace Warden's ward."

"You are his relative, then?"

"No, I'm just a country girl from Laurel Hill."

"Ah, oui?" He was clearly baffled. "And now that you have finished college you will continue as Leonore's secretary?"

"No, that's about finished."

"So then, what are your plans?"

That was, indeed, the question. "For now, I suppose I will go back to the job I had before I went up to Beaulieu. I worked for a portrait photographer. But he's not well, and I would sort of manage the business. At least that's what he's offered me."

"Have you ever considered a career as a fashion model?"

She took her eyes off the road to look at the smiling young Frenchman. "Why would I do that?"

"I would have thought it obvious."

"Bah," said the dark one in the back seat, who had been silent until then, half-buried in lilies. "Modelling is not serious. Photography is art—at least it can be."

They were silent then, and as they drove up into the hills, Elizabeth had the feeling that, for the first time in her life, things were about to happen to her that were not just part of her role in the lives of others.

She took the two men up the back stairs, they carrying their bags and she with her arms filled with lilies. She had avoided the front stairs so as not to run into Leonore. It was best to forewarn Leonore of anything unexpected.

She put the flowers down on the pantry table where the butler sat on a high stool polishing silver.

"Jaime, this is Mr. d'Aubigny and Mr. . . ."

"Cabanasse," the dark one finished.

"They will be guests for . . . a while. Can you find them rooms?"

"Oh, sure, Miss Elizabeth. No problem."

"Where's Mrs. Devereux?"

"In her apartment with Miss Paula." The diminutive Filippino grinned. "Door's been closed a long time."

She turned to the two young Frenchmen to find them both staring with that look that men tended to give her. They would have been surprised to know, behind the surface polish that Leonore and Laurel Hill College had given her, how innocent she was. Besides a crush on Peter at age fifteen, and almost losing her virginity to a boy at the resort hotel where she worked in the summer months when Leonore was in Europe, nothing. She had stopped the boy in a panic. She was beginning to suspect that she was a frigid woman, or at least that is what a book she had consulted in a quiet corner of the college library had suggested.

"Well," she said, breaking an awkward silence, "why don't you let Jaime show you to your rooms. After you've freshened up, if Leonore hasn't made an appearance, I'll take you on a tour of the house."

As she passed the door to the library on the way back to her desk, Eustace called to her. "You don't happen to know where the *Almanach de Gotha* is do you, Elizabeth?"

"You mean the book that lists European royalty?"

"That's it. It seems Peter wants to marry one."

She felt a sharp pang of regret . . . for what? He was bound to marry someone. She rolled the library ladder to where the reference works were kept, climbed it and brought down a small red volume.

"Well, they're in here all right. Prince and Princess Jan Ravitsky. They live in Warsaw. Title's Lithuanian. Goes back a long time. Hm. Wife's from California. Daughter Natasha, the only child. She's just Peter's age. He says in his letter that she's a fashion editor at French *Vogue*. That's all right, but before that she was a Paris mannequin. Leonore won't like that. Wouldn't like it either Peter marrying a Pole or whatever, except her father's a prince, so I guess that's all right."

"Eustace," Elizabeth said, exasperated, "Peter's your son, not your sister's."

"Well, Leonore makes such a fuss about things, and you know me. Peter's of age, and I wouldn't stand in his way about anything. Not like my father did with me. . . ."

They had grown quite close, this immensely rich man and

the daughter of his estate manager, whom he had accidentally killed in a hunting accident. He had taken her into his own home afterwards—and it had not been easy for either of them at first—and seen that she got as good a college education as money could buy. But her pride would not let her give nothing in return, and so she had become Leonore Warden Devereux's social secretary—and Eustace Warden's friend.

"I should mind my own business, shouldn't I?"

"Oh, that's all right, Elizabeth." He smiled. "I wish Leonore would move back to New York. . . . Well, I think I'll have a canter before lunch, if you wouldn't mind calling the stable and ask them to saddle my horse."

She went back to her desk, made the phone call and stared at the unopened mail. At age fifteen, when Elizabeth and Peter had ridden horses together on the Warden estate, and taken picnic lunches and lain in the grass and kissed, and even a bit more, she had had this idea that she and Peter . . . How naive she had been. Wardens don't marry the daughters of their estate managers. They marry women who have Polish princes for fathers, and mothers, no doubt rich and beautiful, from California.

She looked up to find the two Frenchmen standing in the doorway. The dark one had shaved.

They went first through the reception rooms, quiet and sunny, where a maid was dusting, and stopped beneath John Singer Sargent's portrait of Augustus Warden, Eustace's and Leonore's father.

"He was ambassador to France," Elizabeth said in her role as tour guide.

"Yes, I know," Marc d'Aubigny said. "He knew my family well and visited our château quite often. Eustace and Leonore used to play on the grounds as children. Eustace once, they say, got lost in the forest, and all the servants and huntsmen and farmhands were sent out to find him, and only late at night with lanterns did they."

"I once was lost in a forest, near my father's village in Roussillon—that is on France's border with Spain," the dark one said, until then silent, "a very wild area, but no one came looking for me. Still, I had a piece of cheese and some bread, so I spent the night in a cave and the next morning found my way home. It was a fine adventure."

People my own age, Elizabeth thought, who have lived very different lives, not like the willfully ignorant boys from Laurel Hill or those dreadful young men who came down from New York with their rich parents to visit the Wardens; but in a few days both of them would be gone. I wish . . .

The dark hall on the floor above was lined with the heads of moose, mountain sheep, lions and tigers, all the trophies of Augustus Warden. After he had transformed a large inheritance into an even vaster fortune and used it to acquire the ambassadorship to France, he had taken up big game hunting, she explained, and had made a great success at it.

"Of course, with enough money," Jean-Luc Cabanasse said with a shrug, "one can succeed at anything."

The billiard room was filled with light, the walls lined with guns and fly rods in glass cases.

"*Très sportif,*" Marc said. "Whose are all these guns, Eustace's?"

"His father's, mostly."

"Eustace is not a hunter, then?"

"He once was, but he gave it up."

From somewhere came soft female laughter. Elizabeth turned. A pale plume of smoke rose from the sofa at the end of the room in front of a Renaissance fireplace that Augustus Warden had had sent over in pieces from Italy. Paula Warden rose from the sofa, a cigarette in one hand.

"Sorry, Elizabeth. I didn't mean to laugh, truly, but it was just *so* grotesque."

She came toward them, flicking ashes on the Persian carpet, quite pretty, with pale skin, coal-black hair and green eyes in which there was a hint of all the trouble she could cause.

"And who are you two?"

"Marc d'Aubigny."

"I thought so. I pushed you in the pond at the Tuileries Gardens when I was eight years old."

"I remember . . . Paula."

"And you?"

"Jean-Luc Cabanasse, a friend of Marc's."

"Ah. Marc d'Aubigny, did you know—I only found out recently—that my grandfather and your grandmother were lovers?"

"I have heard that, yes."

"What are you doing here?"

"We were invited. Your mother . . ."

"For how long?"

"Well . . . when is Leonore going to France?"

"Not till August this year," Elizabeth said.

"That is if she doesn't change her mind again," Paula said. "She doesn't know who to believe about whether there's going to be a war in Europe. In any case she's taking me with her—at least she thinks she is—and you're going to be invited too, Elizabeth . . . as I'm sure you know."

"Me? No, I didn't know."

"Graduation gift, she said. Anyway, how long are you two chaps going to be around?"

"We leave for France from New York on Wednesday."

"Well, there you are. The four of us might have some fun

here in the meantime—if I can stay out of my mother's way. I thought she was going to kill me."

They all had lunch together: Eustace, Leonore, Paula, Marc, Jean-Luc and Elizabeth, and the conversation quickly switched from English to French. Paula said hardly a word during the entire meal, presumably not wanting to attract any more attention from Leonore, who for her part completely ignored her daughter. But with the two young Frenchmen Leonore was at her most charming, brushing aside their apologies for arriving a month late and unannounced.

After nearly three years of working for and living in the same house with Leonore, her mercurial changes of mood still surprised Elizabeth. In the world that she came from, if a person was mean or generous or just plain odd, they could be counted on to act that way pretty much all of the time. Among the very rich, it seemed, one behaved the way one pleased when one pleased.

"So, messieurs, tell me about yourselves," Leonore said, helping herself to the *filet de sole, sauce parisienne,* according to the menu card in silver holder before each place setting. Two maids served them under Jaime's watchful eye. "Now that you have had your tour of America, presumably you will have to go back to France and *do* something. What are your plans, Marc?"

The young man with the golden-red hair and pale blue eyes turned his angelic—but also, Elizabeth thought, calculating—gaze on Leonore. "I would like to fly a plane around the world and write poetry but, as you know, my elder brother perished in the Great War. I will be under family pressure to take over management of our estates."

"And will you be the obedient son, or will you rebel?"

"Probably a little of both. I will manage the farms for the

time being, I suppose. My father is not well. But for a couple of years, after graduating from the Sorbonne, I worked as secretary to Pierre Laval. He has offered to launch me on a political career—if he becomes Premier of France again. Should that happen, I would probably go into politics."

"Good for you. If people of your kind fail to take an interest in politics, the same thing will happen to France that is happening to us. Thank God you got rid of that dreadful man Léon Blum, as bad as Roosevelt, who is ruining this country!"

"Oh, I don't know, Leonore," Eustace ventured. "Something had to be tried. The country was in rotten shape in '32."

Leonore ignored her brother's remark. "And you, Monsieur Cabanasse? Should I know your family?"

"I would be surprised. One grandfather was a Catalan shepherd, and the other ran a small hotel outside of Antibes."

"That is nothing to be ashamed of."

"I am not ashamed," the dark-eyed young man said quietly.

"And your father, what does he do?"

"He is no longer living. He had a shop—in Paris—where he sold antiques."

"Greek and Egyptian antiquities, I suppose you mean. You see," Leonore said triumphantly, "I do know your family. The name Cabanasse is quite well-known among collectors of important art, and your mother is, I believe, an opera singer who rather took Paris by storm."

Jean-Luc reddened and was at a loss for words, but only for a few seconds.

"However, I, too, am interested in politics. I am a journalist. My paper, *Le Populaire*, sponsored my visit to America. I am writing a series on how Americans view the situation in Europe."

Elizabeth caught the exchange of glances between the two

Frenchmen, which led Marc to cover his mouth with his hand in suppressing a laugh.

"Is there something amusing that I am missing?" Leonore asked sharply.

"No, not at all, Leonore," Marc said, unruffled. "Jean-Luc has good conservative connections as well."

"For instance."

"Well, de Gaulle, for instance."

"I have never heard of any de Gaulle, and I know French society extremely well."

"No, I suppose you would not have heard of Charles de Gaulle. He is only a colonel in the French army but, according to Jean-Luc, if the French generals would only listen to him France could defeat Germany in the war to come."

"And what do you think, Marc?"

"I think that nothing can save France, because dry rot has eaten away at the fabric of our nation until there is nothing left to save."

"I see."

Elizabeth looked at Jean-Luc, who looked down at his plate.

"My goodness," Leonore said, switching back to English, clearly not interested in pursuing a conversation she could not dominate, "I'd almost forgotten that we have a new graduate of Laurel Hill College at table." She threw an unpleasant look in Paula's direction. "Well, Elizabeth, what are *your* plans?"

"I really don't know."

"What did you study?" Jean-Luc asked.

"My major subjects were drama and French."

"Why?" A little jolt of electricity passed between them.

"I took drama because I was told it might help me overcome my shyness," Elizabeth said with a directness that only living at Beaulieu—and having been on stage—could have allowed her, "and I suppose it has helped some. French because . . ."

". . . because I bullied her into it," Leonore interrupted. "My dear, what you need is some time to think over what you want to do with your life. I want you to come to France with me this summer—and I should have spoken to you of it earlier. There you can see a larger world and think out what your future might be. Will you?"

Although she had known for two hours that this was going to happen, Elizabeth had not been able to focus her mind on what her response would be. But what were her alternatives if she cut her ties to the Wardens? Surely not taking portraits at Amos Leach's studio for the rest of her life. Teaching? Marriage to a local man? She looked around the table. The eyes of Marc, Jean-Luc, Paula and Eustace, as well as those of Leonore, were upon her.

"I would be delighted to accompany you to France," she heard herself saying in a steady, confident voice. "You are most generous, Leonore." Not Mrs. Devereux. Leonore. Now Elizabeth felt electricity flowing from her all around the table. She had done it! An exaltation grew within her. She knew, as one knows only a very few things in life, that this had opened the possibility—for better or worse—of her shaking the dust of Laurel Hill from her shoes forever.

"Bravo," Eustace said. "Wise choice."

"Then we'll all be in Paris this summer," Leonore said with feigned enthusiasm.

"Not me," said Eustace, "but I would like to contribute something to this occasion. What's for dessert, Jaime? I can't even read the bloody menu without my glasses."

"Raspberry tart with cream, sir."

"Then have a couple of bottles of Château Climens, a good year, put on ice."

"Yes, sir."

"And I would like to offer you young people the cabin on the lake for the weekend. You don't want to be hanging around here with all these boring types from New York and Philadelphia that'll be drifting in this afternoon."

"Eustace, really, I don't think . . ." Leonore began.

"Well, I do, Leonore."

Chapter Two

As they climbed the mountainside on that Saturday morning along an old road newly-mown and fresh with the smells of Virginia in early summer, it was Elizabeth who led the way and told the two Frenchmen of the origins of the cabin on the lake, where she had spent many summer afternoons alone with a book.

It had all begun when Augustus Warden had ridden to the end of the railroad line that he had bought a few years earlier to try the trout fishing, and deciding when he had seen it, that this was a place where he could "get away from it all." He had bought a vast amount of mountain land and had a stream dammed to create a little lake with a fishing cabin.

Next came the main house built of limestone blocks quarried in Tennessee and finished up on the spot by stonemasons brought all the way from Italy. It was not so grand as the Vanderbilts' "Biltmore" in the mountains of North Carolina, "just in better taste," Augustus is supposed to have said. He had named it Beaulieu, after the town on the French Riviera where he already owned a vast villa to which he was much attached. Beaulieu was positioned to look down upon the site of the women's college that was to come next, and its first building was constructed from what remained of the slightly pink limestone used for the building of Beaulieu. . . .

And as Elizabeth rambled on about this spot she loved, they came out into the little clearing at the edge of the lake where a rowboat, newly painted, was tied to a rough stone dock. She had not told the two Frenchmen that the large cabin, made of logs and field stone, was on an island in the lake. Cattails grew around the edge of the lake; and as they stood there a kingfisher plunged straight down into the still, dark water, and came up with a fish in its beak.

"C'est magique," Marc said.

In Elizabeth's world men did not cook, at least not beyond bacon and eggs for breakfast or a trout fried on a fishing trip. But here were Marc and Jean-Luc engaged in animated discussion on the fine points of preparing the Provençal meal that Jean-Luc proposed to serve them on the terrace.

"Why do you laugh, Paula?" Marc said, looking up from the chicken he was turning over on a homemade grill set above a wood fire. "Food is a serious matter in France, too serious to be left to women. And if I were not here to restrain Jean-Luc's heavy southern hand, we should have everything reeking of garlic and thyme and olive oil."

"That is," Jean-Luc said, "reeking of azure skies, the deep blue sea and the sun. Whereas in the north of France they smother every dish in gray sauces made of eggs and butter and cream and eat them on gray days, in the rain."

"But in Paris, and not in some hut on a mountainside covered with goats. It depends on one's taste."

"Indeed it does," Jean-Luc said, squatting beside the fire, turning over halves of tomato, green pepper and onion sizzling over the fire.

Elizabeth took a sip from her glass of wine, lay back in the canvas chair, watched the fluffy white clouds sail lazily by in a clear blue sky. She was having her first taste of paradise, a place where no one talked of serious things, where the men were handsome and witty, where the important thing was to have a chicken cooked to perfection and the wine chilled to just the right degree, where a lifetime of possibilities lay just over the horizon. . . .

After lunch, which was such a great success that Paula crowned Jean-Luc with a wreath of vine leaves, the two men left for Beaulieu. Paula, who declared that she had no intention of camping out, had given them a long list of things to bring back. As the rowboat pulled away from the dock, Paula leaned back in her canvas chair and lit a cigarette.

"Well, what do you think of our two Frenchmen?"

"They seem . . . very nice."

"They teach them manners over there, Elizabeth. Don't confuse that with nice."

"Of course, you know France well."

"We used to go every year, before things got impossible with my father. The family still has the place on the Riviera, but mother doesn't like to go there. Bad memories. God, be glad you don't have a family. Sometimes I felt like I was going to suffocate."

"You can suffocate without a family. A small town in Virginia can do that to you."

"Then get out. You know that after France Leonore is not coming back here?"

"No, I didn't know."

"I guess enough time has passed since her divorce—with all that scandal—that she can face the social scene again. She's reopening her house in Manhattan this fall. She could do things for you. You'd have to put up with a lot, but you already know that."

"And what will you do?"

"What Leonore would like is to get me married off. I can tell from the way she looks at Marc d'Aubigny, that she's considering whether that would be a good match. I expect he would jump at the chance."

"You think he is attracted to you?"

"I think he is attracted to you, and so is his friend."

"Attracted to me?"

"You aren't exactly plain, Elizabeth."

"Oh, that." Beauty. "But Marc would jump at a chance to marry you?" As soon as she had said it she realized how naive the question was.

Paula lowered long black lashes over her green eyes and smiled indulgently. "The d'Aubignys were once very important people in France, and they still have lots of land and a château in the Loire valley, but I guess they're finding it ever harder to live in the style to which they became accustomed many centuries ago."

"Would you marry him?"

Paula shrugged. "Maybe. Or someone like him. There are worse lives than Paris—I would have to have an apartment there—and a château in the country. But not now. I want to have fun. Not that you can't keep having fun after you're married, but I don't want to be tied down. Not for now."

"What about love?" Elizabeth asked timidly, as though this was a subject she was not qualified to discuss; and she wasn't. That's why she wanted to find out things.

"Love? I don't know. If you mean sex, I'm all for that. But love? I'm not so sure I'm capable of it."

Among the articles on Paula's list was a windup phonograph and some dance records. After supper the terrace was turned into a dance floor, hung with Japanese paper lanterns found in a cupboard; and Elizabeth saw that there was no escape from having to dance. In high school her father would not permit her to go to dances, and by the time she entered college she was ashamed to admit that she didn't know how, so she always managed to find some excuse for not attending dances. It was not only that. The only boys she knew were from the town, and they would not have been comfortable in the atmosphere of the college—probably wouldn't have come even if invited, and if they had, wouldn't have been made to feel welcome.

Then she found herself being held by Marc, one of his hands encircling her perspiring hand, the other firmly placed in the small of her back. The music was slow, and she managed to step back when he stepped forward, and forward when he stepped back, without treading on his toes; and within a couple of minutes she had the rhythm of it. Why, there was nothing to it!

"You dance very well," he said.

"*Merci, monsieur.*"

"Dance is part of your drama training, I suppose."

"No, I've never had lessons."

"Then you are a natural. Very few women dance really well."

He held her closer, pressing her body lightly against his, and Elizabeth made another discovery. Being held close by a man could be a pleasurable experience, but it was also too intense. She groped for something to say to relieve her skittishness.

"Tell me, Marc, what did you find so funny about Jean-Luc saying he worked for that newspaper . . . what was its name?"

"*Le Populaire.* What's so funny is that the paper is more or less the organ of the Socialist Party, which is headed by 'that awful man Léon Blum', as Leonore called him, who writes for it—along with my friend Jean-Luc Cabanasse."

"Yes, I remember now that Blum was Premier of France

not too long ago. And you were secretary to another Premier, Pierre Laval. I don't think I know him. Where does he stand politically?"

"At the opposite end of the spectrum."

"But you and Jean-Luc are still friends."

"To let politics affect your choice of friends is bourgeois, Elizabeth."

"Wine's ready," Jean-Luc called from the dock, where he had pulled up a bottle on a cord from the lake.

"*Superbe,*" Marc pronounced, after rolling around the straw-colored liquid in his mouth, "but our stock is dwindling fast."

"Get some more from Eustace's cellar anytime you want," Paula said.

"But shouldn't we ask?"

"He'll never know the difference. There are more bottles of French vintage wine down there than he and his guests could drink in a hundred years, and every time he goes to France he buys more."

"In that case . . ."

"I'm sure you'll find the key to the cellar where I found it when I was fourteen, in the pantry hanging on a nail behind the refrigerators. You see, grandfather had a rule that Warden children were not allowed to drink wine until age sixteen, boys could not smoke until they were twenty-one, and Warden women could not smoke, period. And no one would think of changing a rule laid down by Augustus Warden."

"After that, we bought a boat and floated for several days down the Mississippi, like Huck Finn and Jim, sleeping on the bank at night. What a vast river, and just as Mark Twain described."

Jean-Luc paused, and Marc resumed the story of their travels. "When we grew tired of that, we sold the boat and bought an old car, but that was not such a great bargain. In Kentucky it stopped running, and we did not have the money with us to get it repaired. I decided that the time had come to visit the Wardens, and so we took a train . . ."

"And as we were standing on the platform of the Laurel Hill station," Marc continued, "wondering how we would get to Beaulieu, this beautiful, tall blond woman approaches . . . and the rest is history."

Elizabeth laughed. She was not used to men who talked like this. The two Frenchmen spoke with a kind of studied innocence, a frankness that assumed you were sophisticated. They treated her and Paula like comrades, but at the same time they never let you forget for an instant that you were a woman. She enjoyed this treatment and was flattered by it.

More wine was drunk; and they danced until they were all perspiring. Paula, who had included bathing suits on her list, proposed a swim.

Then Elizabeth found herself with Paula in the little dressing room at the end of the dock, lit by a lamp taken from the terrace, and experiencing another new sensation. There was no choice but to disrobe for the first time in front of another person, even though a female. That was another thing that she had managed to avoid. The girls at Laurel Hill swam nude in the heated indoor swimming pool that Augustus Warden had donated just before his death—the last of his many gifts to the college—but Elizabeth could not bring herself to do that.

Paula took off her clothes in a leisurely fashion, while Elizabeth tried to get out of hers and into the navy blue wool tank suit as quickly as possible. Even in the process she could not help looking at Paula, all creamy-white with a luxuriant triangle of dark hair above her thighs.

"I might have known," Paula said with a low laugh, staring unabashedly at Elizabeth struggling to get the bathing suit over her full breasts.

"What?" she said, feeling her face redden.

"A figure to drive men crazy, graduated *cum laude* from Laurel Hill, sweet and innocent, and calm as lake water. You have it all, don't you?"

Finally getting the straps of the bathing suit over her shoulders, Elizabeth said, "Paula, I not only don't have it all, I haven't even done anything."

"Consider yourself lucky," was the reply, and Paula slipped past her and out the door of the dressing room. Seconds later came the splash, as Elizabeth followed her out the door, of Paula diving into the lake.

Elizabeth stood barefooted on the old, half-rotten dock that still shook from Paula's vigorous dive. She shivered in the chill of the June night, despite the rough wool bathing suit that she had been barely able to squeeze into. On the island the candles in the Japanese lanterns had guttered one by one, until only three of a dozen were left alight.

The two men came out of the cabin in bathing suits like, she thought, two Greek gods. Marc, as he passed through a pool of candlelight, his golden-red hair set alight, was Apollo; Jean-Luc, tall, dark-haired, olive-skinned, was . . . which god? Hermes, she thought—fresh from a course in the classics—the quiet dark one, the thief in the night. What strange ideas she was having!

Marc broke into a run and dived gracefully from the end of the dock into the lake with hardly a ripple, coming up beside Paula, who had just emerged to the surface from her noisy, deep dive.

"Shall we?" Jean-Luc said, coming up beside Elizabeth.

She turned to face this male presence, this lean body like a Greek statue, she thought, caught up in the image she had created.

"Swim? No. Now that I'm all dressed for it, I don't want to."

"Dieu merci. C'est pour les Esquimeaux."

"And if I had said yes?"

"Then honor would have required me." He smiled, and his dark eyes offered no threat. She was both excited and re-assured by this small exchange.

They looked down on the bobbing, laughing heads of Paula and Marc in the lake, and a shiver ran through her body.

"You're shaking," Jean-Luc said. "Why don't we go up on the terrace, and I'll get you a wrap."

"Yes."

Then, as they turned to go, he took her hand in his.

"You're also freezing," he said.

"Yes."

Jean-Luc's hand on hers was warm and very masculine, and she shivered again, but this time with a thrill of sexuality, an erotic feeling that she kept deeply suppressed, for she knew that she had great difficulty controlling it when—rarely—it did come.

They sat in canvas chairs on the terrace of rough field-stone, Elizabeth with a blanket thrown about her like a cloak, and looked up at a sky filled with stars, now that the last Japanese lantern had gone out. A single lamp burned at the end of the dock. Marc and Paula had swum to the opposite shore of the lake and vanished in the darkness.

"We won't see them for a while, I suppose," Jean-Luc said and laughed.

What did he mean by that? She remembered what Paula had said that afternoon about sex, which had shocked her. Is that what he meant? She had difficulty even imagining what the act was like. No, he couldn't have meant that.

"What do you mean to do with your life, Elizabeth?" Jean-Luc said at last, breaking the long silence.

"Not stay in Laurel Hill, that's all I know for sure. I never imagined I would get away from where I was born, but I'm spoiled for this place now. I knew that for certain for the first time yesterday at lunch."

"Yes, I could see that. But here or somewhere else, as Leonore said at lunch, you have to *do* something."

"What will I do with my life? Truly, Jean-Luc, I've no idea."

"Well, at least you can tell me what you will do with the time in France that Leonore has offered you."

"If there's any time for doing anything, between all the chores Leonore will be giving me. I know why I'm being invited to accompany her to France. I'll think about my life, of course. The time's come for that. I may have had a life in which not much has happened so far, but that just leaves more for the future, doesn't it?"

As she spoke she realized that she had just put into words what had been on her mind for weeks, even months. The chalk was poised above the *tabula rasa* of her life, and she was both eager and afraid to see what would be written there.

"Will I see you in Paris?" he said.

"If you would like."

"May I kiss you?"

"If you would like," she said, too startled to think of any other reply. Besides, it was asked so nicely that it seemed to her it would have been rude to refuse.

He leaned over in the dark and kissed her lightly on the

lips. Then to her surprise he said, "Act for me."

"What do you mean?"

"I would like to see you act."

"All right," she said, once again finding no good reason to refuse.

She got to her feet and recited a particularly dramatic speech from Ibsen's *Hedda Gabler*, in which she had recently played the lead. When she finished she found that she was trembling with her character's emotions.

"That was very good. When you said, as you did at lunch yesterday, that you took up acting to cure your shyness, I knew right away that you were an unusual woman."

"I'm not unusual, Jean-Luc. I'm a very ordinary person."

It was actually more complicated than that. She had said that she had taken up acting to try to overcome her shyness. But in fact, that is what her faculty adviser had suggested, an upper-class, embittered New England woman, who had treated Elizabeth as a case for a social worker. Elizabeth had acquiesced to this analysis because she had had the presumptuous idea, for someone of her social station—and they were expert at Laurel Hill College in making you understand your place—that she could become a real actress, or at least carve out some place for herself in the world of art. . . .

"No, you're wrong. I predict that you will lead a very extraordinary life. Years from now you will look back on this night and realize how right I was."

They were silent for a while, lying sprawled on the wooden dock. The sky was crowded with stars, and from the woods on the shore opposite two owls called to each other. Their glasses of rosé wine glowed in the candlelight.

"We have talked about ourselves all evening," Marc said at last. "Now it is time for the women to reveal themselves.

What interesting things have you done while we have been roaming your great country?"

"Asked to leave Vassar six weeks shy of graduation," Paula said matter-of-factly, flipping a glowing end of cigarette into the lake.

"For what reason?"

"I went to New York for the weekend with a friend, without permission."

"But that is absurd."

"The friend was not another woman."

"Even so . . ."

"Ah, Monsieur d'Aubigny, you still have much to learn about America. . . . And nothing even happened. It wasn't a man I cared about."

"Why, then?"

"I was bored." Paula Warden licked her thumb and fore-finger and pinched out the candle flame. But before she could extinguish the light Elizabeth saw the tears welling in her eyes. "And what of you, Elizabeth Vail?"

She could not see Jean-Luc, could not see anything. She felt alone and naked in face of this question—her question always—and she was still no closer to finding an answer. She had once wanted so much, and her chances of finding it had been so slim; but now she had for three years moved in a world that she could once only have dreamed of, and that world now seemed, despite all the Wardens' money, rather ordinary.

"I've done nothing but work this last year," she said, shrugging in the dark for no one to see.

"Always for Leonore, not for Eustace."

"Yes."

Jean-Luc was the one who, besides playing the game that goes on between men and women, constantly seemed to be searching for facts. She had decided that if Marc was the poet Jean-Luc was the scientist.

"God, let's go to bed," Paula said with a yawn. "I'm exhausted."

The candle was relit, and they made their way across the damp grass, into the musty-smelling main room of Augustus Warden's cabin, up the stairs; and there they parted, the two men going into one bedroom, the two women into the other. Paula threw herself down on one bed, its covers turned back by a maid who had come with linens, and went instantly to sleep. Elizabeth undressed, put on her nightgown and slipped between the sheets. She, too, was physically and emotionally exhausted, but she held off sleep for a while to savor the knowledge that she had this day known a taste of freedom for the first time in her life.

Chapter Three

Elizabeth awoke at dawn, as she almost always did, got out of bed and dressed silently. Paula slept deeply, entangled in a blanket, as though she had passed an unquiet night. No sound came from the other bedroom.

She went down the creaking stairs, started a fire in the little wood-burning stove and made a pot of coffee. Then she went out onto the dock with a cup of black coffee and sat quietly, skirt hiked up, shoes off, and played in the cold lake water with her toes.

She was perfectly at home in this place, early morning mist lying on the water, in the distance the cawing of crows moving out from their roosts, as they did every morning at dawn. This comfortable, familiar life would not be hers much longer. She had chosen to dare, to open herself up to a larger world, and there was no turning back.

Would she awake one morning years hence, in some foreign city, a sleeping man, whom she had not yet even met, beside her? Would she then lie in bed, bitterly regretting that she had not stayed in Laurel Hill, married a local boy, had children, and grown old in a place she knew and understood. Perhaps, but she had made her choice, and she would not now turn back.

"Bonjour, Elisabeth."

She started so that hot coffee sloshed out of her cup onto

her bare thigh. She pulled down her skirt and turned. Jean-Luc, a cup of coffee in his hand, stood over her, smiling.

"Where did you learn to move so silently?"

"I come from a long line of smugglers. No, I really do. My family has always lived on the border between France and Spain, and most of my ancestors made their living smuggling goods from Spain to France or vice versa. May I join you?"

"Please."

Jean-Luc lowered his tall body to the dock and sat down beside her. Seeing her feet dangling in the water, he took off his shoes and let his feet down into the lake beside hers.

"Very cold."

"Not like the Mediterranean?"

"No, not even in the middle of winter."

"To be there," Elizabeth said, "I've always thought, would be like paradise."

"That depends. I think to be here is very much like paradise."

"Yes, I can see that. The lake, the cabin on an island . . ."

"*C'est très beau,* but that is not what I meant exactly. As Marc said, this is all magical. We end up a very exhausting tour of America, in which we forced ourselves to the limit, as is the French custom, with the obligatory, and most unwanted—by me—visit to the very rich American friends of his family. Yet what happens? We are met . . ." Jean-Luc did not finish the sentence that Marc had. "And then at lunch this little shy man, Eustace, stares down his dragon of a sister, and we find ourselves in paradise."

Elizabeth turned then and regarded Jean-Luc's profile, the dark hair, too long to be acceptable in Laurel Hill, the very dark eyes, the narrow nose, the long jaw. He looked out across the lake with an intensity that did not seem to include her, and a shudder ran through her body. She dared not ask any questions about what paradise meant to him.

"You and Marc, I suppose, are old friends?" she said instead, and immediately regretted the banality of the question.

"We are friends . . . and enemies."

"Meaning?"

"That we have the same feelings about some things, but our views are very different."

"Yes, I know. Politics."

"That, but more than that."

Best to change the subject. "Marc said . . ." and she paused, taking a sip of coffee. The kingfisher had flown into a tree across the lake, ready for another day's fishing. ". . . said that if he could do what he wanted, he would fly a plane around the world and write poetry. What about you?"

"If I could do what I wanted—which is not likely—I suppose I might fly around the world, too. That is what we have in common. Marc and I met at the university flying club, which keeps an old plane at Le Bourget, where Lindbergh landed. But poetry? I do not think Marc will write poetry, at least not good poetry. He says so only because he has a famous ancestor who was a poet and lost his head to the guillotine during the French Revolution."

"But that is a poetical idea, isn't it, to finish what one's ancestor began?"

"Yes, I suppose it is." Jean-Luc turned his intense gaze on her. "You are very beautiful, you know."

Elizabeth said nothing. He said this in such a clinical, detached way that she could not even take it as a compliment. At last, to relieve the tension, she said in a soft voice, "Go on. You have more to say."

"Yes. You will go far, but beauty, while it is a great gift, *et très très rare*—my father said this, and he had reason to know—is also a curse. It will open all doors for you, it will bring you rewards that you have not earned. You will not have to strive for things. They will fall into your lap. So, be careful of . . ."

"How old are you, Jean-Luc?"

"I am twenty-eight."

"And I am only twenty-two, but perhaps a little old to be lectured to."

He laughed. "You are right. That was quite arrogant of me."

When they returned to the cabin they found Paula and Marc sitting at the kitchen table, talking and laughing.

"Bonjour, Elisabeth," and Marc got up and kissed her lightly on both cheeks, in front of the others, as though it were the most natural thing in the world, although they had known each other for only forty-eight hours. Well, why not?

"Jean-Luc, we've made you *chef de cuisine* again today," Paula announced.

"Well, I don't mind that," Elizabeth said with enthusiasm, "if it's anything like yesterday's lunch."

"A man of many talents and great knowledge." Marc laughed.

"What about you?" Paula said. "Would you believe, Elizabeth, that sitting on the dock at the landing place last night, he gave me an hour-long lecture on French history, why there's going to be another war in Europe, and on and on."

"I told you last night, Elizabeth, we wouldn't see them for a long time. Anytime Marc gets someone sympathetic alone he gives one of his lectures. As Paula said, they go on and on."

Elizabeth felt a twinge of guilt for thinking Paula might have . . .

"But they're interesting lectures," Paula protested. "Marc has some fascinating ideas."

"Reactionary ideas," Jean-Luc said, "but at least Marc and I agree on one thing. There's going to be a war in Europe. It's only a matter of time. And in the end America will be drawn into it. In writing the series of articles for my paper, I found that hardly any Americans believe that. Or maybe they just don't want to believe it."

"But that's in the future, Jean-Luc," Paula said. "What's for lunch?"

"You were right, Paula," Jean-Luc replied. "Late last night, while you were all asleep, I walked down to Beaulieu. The key to the wine cellar is still hanging on a nail behind the refrigerators. I also stole a loaf of bread—real French bread— and I thought I would make some sandwiches, and we could have a picnic today. *Ca vous interesse, mes amis?*"

"Sandwiches?" Paula said and wrinkled her nose.

"As we make them in the south of France."

"Ah. But if we are going to have a picnic, we must go somewhere." There was real enthusiasm in Paula's voice, not the bored cynicism that Elizabeth had become used to on Paula's visits to Beaulieu. "Where does one go in Vail County on Sunday, Elizabeth?"

"On Sunday?" Elizabeth laughed. "Nowhere, except church."

"Let's climb that mountain," Jean-Luc said, pointing to the peak above the lake covered in mountain laurel that gave Laurel Hill its name.

"We live like gods," Marc said lazily, his back leaning on Paula's shoulder, hers leaning against the trunk of an ancient oak tree. "On a mountain top, looking out over all Virginia, after—even I must admit—an excellent lunch, *grâce à* Jean-Luc—in the company of beautiful women, is that not to live like the gods?"

A shiver ran down Elizabeth's spine. That was exactly what she had been thinking, if one substituted beautiful men for beautiful women.

"Except that the gods are immortal," Jean-Luc said, leaning against the tree, his head close to Paula's other shoulder, "while this company of mortals will be disbanded tomorrow morning. Our paradise will be no more. Elizabeth will drive us to the station, a train will take us to New York, a ship will take us across the gray Atlantic, and then we shall have to work, grow old and die."

"*Hélas,*" Marc said, his eyes now half-closed.

"No, don't say that," Elizabeth blurted out. They all looked at her, sitting apart from them in the grass, her skirt tucked under her crossed legs. "We'll all grow old and die, but . . ."

"But what, Elizabeth?" Jean-Luc said gently.

"We're young, we have lives to live, many wonderful things can happen to us, like today. . . ." She was too choked up to say more.

Bees were buzzing in the clover around the oak tree, and no one spoke. A sentence had been written on the almost blank slate that Elizabeth in her mind held out to her new friends: it said that the bonds of friendship were forged without the need for words. Paula and Marc napped.

"A little walk?" Jean-Luc whispered to Elizabeth.

"Yes."

They walked aimlessly through the fresh grass laced with wildflowers, and Jean-Luc took her hand, almost absent-mindedly—or so it seemed to her.

"It seems impossible," he said, "that we'll all be together again in Paris soon."

Would they? She was very used to Leonore's friends saying to one another with the utmost insincerity how they

41

absolutely had to get together again soon. Would these two young men find Paula and her, particularly her—Paula was rich—all that interesting when they were not in this unnatural isolation, and starved for female companionship, but on the Champs-Elysées, thronging with fashionable young Parisiennes?

"You doubt it?"

She started. He had read her mind.

"You'll find back in Paris that I don't have much to contribute to intellectual conversation."

"Who said anything about intellectual conversation?"

"Then what?"

"What's wrong with just being friends?"

"That would be great. I like all of you a lot and," she blundered on, "I want friends. I've never really had any."

"We all need friends. Who isn't lonely most of the time?"

She looked up into his eyes. "You?"

"There's a writer of yours, his name is Thoreau, who said that most men lead lives of quiet desperation. . . . Sorry, Elizabeth, I was about to start an intellectual conversation wasn't I?"

They smiled at each other and he squeezed her hand. "Talk to me, Elizabeth. Tell me about yourself, about Laurel Hill. Why are you and the county named Vail?"

She was surprised. No one ever asked her to talk about herself. And what could you say about the tacky little town of Laurel Hill?

"Vail County was named for an ancestor of mine. He was one of the first settlers. The family's come down in the world since then." She laughed. "Or maybe we never amounted to much. Anyway, at first Laurel Hill was called Fort Vail."

"There was a fort here?"

"To guard the pass against the Indians and the French.

Your ancestors." She laughed again. "Nothing much happened after that, except for some cavalry skirmishes around here during the Civil War. It might have become more of a town if the railroad had gone on over the mountains into the West, but Laurel Hill was the end of the line, and still is.

"That's about it. It's like most other Virginia towns around here. There's a red brick courthouse with a Confederate monument out front, a big water tank up on stilts, the train station, a library given by Andrew Carnegie, and, of course, Laurel Hill College for Women."

"How do people feel about that?"

"They're sort of proud of it, but they distrust it. It brings in money, but it's northern money."

"They haven't forgotten the Civil War?"

"Never."

"And all the people here are descended from the original settlers?"

"Almost all, and almost all Scotch-Irish. There are a few German families, but they mostly changed their names. Or if they hadn't already they did during the Great War, when Germans weren't too popular around here. There's a Greek who has a restaurant across from the train station, and two Jewish brothers who run a department store. Their father came here peddling pots and pans."

"Will you miss it? You've got deep roots here."

"Miss it?" She considered. "No, I won't miss it."

"I will watch with the greatest interest how you and Paris react to each other."

"You say I'm going to have an extraordinary life."

"If you dare."

"Standing here, now, talking to you in the Virginia countryside, I would say yes, I will dare. But I've never been any farther from home than Washington, and then I didn't see

43

anything because I was accompanying Leonore. When I get
to Paris I may be as timid as a mouse."

Jean-Luc laughed, took both her hands in his and looked
into her eyes. Goodness, she thought, he's handsome.

"You're refreshing. You say exactly what's in your heart,
don't you?"

"You mean I'm naive."

"I mean you're refreshing. Don't change. You'll love
Paris, and you *will* dare."

"Except Leonore will take up all my time, and we sail for
home at the end of October."

"Stay on. You don't have to return to America with
Leonore."

"Jean-Luc, I don't have any money. Not a cent."

"Become a rich man's mistress."

She laughed nervously. "Don't tease me."

"Then get a job. There's always a way if you really want to
do something. I know lots of people. My girlfriend Bettina
can help. You'll like her."

His girlfriend. Her heart sank. But why? He had offered
her friendship and she had been happy with that.

He must have seen the brief look of dismay on her face, because he leaned over and kissed her on the cheek.

"Bonne chance, chère Elisabeth."

They walked back in silence, but Elizabeth's mind was
working furiously. With only a few more hours left, she did
not want the web of friendship that had been woven to simply
unravel when they parted. She had never had many friends,
and without these new, very different friends, she would
never be able to make her way in the world beyond Laurel
Hill.

Paula and Marc were still sitting at the base of the old oak,
but now Paula was cradled in his arms; and they made no

move to separate. There was a trace of lipstick at the corner of Marc's mouth.

"Well," Marc said, "did he give you one of *his* lectures?"

"No, just some advice."

"Was it good advice?"

She looked into Jean-Luc's eyes. "I think so."

Paula stood up, stretched, yawned and brushed grass from her skirt.

"Paula, are you still thinking . . ." Elizabeth said, "about staying on in Paris after Leonore returns?"

"Haven't decided yet."

"If you do, I will too."

"Really? You would? Well . . . well, sure, why not. What else have I got to do?" She kissed Elizabeth on the cheek. "Good for you. It's what you should do. Get the hell out of Laurel Hill and don't come back. But for God's sake don't breathe a word to Leonore or she won't take you with her."

Elizabeth was speechless at what she had done. What a long way she had come since lunch on Friday. She had now been kissed by all three of her new friends, and one had already kissed her twice.

Elizabeth stood in the middle of Leonore Warden's spacious dressing room, four open steamer trunks positioned around her like the points of the compass, checking off items on a list attached to the clipboard she held. Three maids, at her direction, brought clothes from the closets that lined the room, and other articles from other rooms. The list was a decade old at least, modified by Leonore each year in blue ink in her small neat hand, occasionally to delete an item, but almost always to add yet another article that she couldn't get along without in France.

Well, space would be no problem, either on the ship or

traveling to New York. She had understood, of course, that they were very rich, but nothing had quite brought it home to Elizabeth as much as calling Washington to ask that the Wardens' private railroad car be taken out of the shed where it was kept in the rail yards outside of Union Station and brought to a siding at Laurel Hill.

"Almost done?" Paula inquired, sauntering into the room, smoking a cigarette and flicking ashes on the rug. Elizabeth was convinced that Paula did this as a way of symbolically destroying Beaulieu and all that it stood for. Freud had been very popular at Laurel Hill College and Elizabeth had been carried away on the tide of enthusiasm, though she was careful not to look too deeply into her own psyche.

"Almost done, I think."

"Well, you're going to France, but remember what what's-his-name said, 'Be careful what you ask for, because you may get it.' "

That thought had already occurred to Elizabeth. It had bothered her a little at first, but now not at all. Any life, whatever sorrows and trials it might bring, was better than an existence in Laurel Hill.

"I suppose Marc and Jean-Luc will have about forgotten us by the time we get to Paris."

Paula gave her that ironic smile Elizabeth had been trying to avoid, a smile which meant that only naive, anxious girls asked questions like that.

After lunch brought to her in her room where she struggled with how to get her own things, mostly hand-me-downs from Leonore, into two suitcases, Elizabeth took an armload of files out to the vine-grown summer pavilion at the end of the long terrace. There there was fresh air, a magnificent view of the Blue Ridge mountains and peace and quiet, away from the turmoil that ran all through Beaulieu whenever Leonore was about to arrive or was preparing to depart.

Sitting at the rough wooden table in the pavilion, she methodically made her way through the remaining paperwork, tied up the loose ends of Leonore's social life in America. Whatever the future held, it would not be a return to this. God, how good it was to be alone! Particularly when your whole life was changing, and there was so much to think about. However, just at that moment Eustace Warden emerged from the conservatory, and came toward the pavilion—where she had thought herself hidden in the dappled shadow of lattice-work and vine leaves.

"Hullo, Elizabeth."

"Hello, Eustace. Is there something I could do for you?"

"Would it be all right if I just sat here for a few minutes?" said the owner of this vast estate to his sister's social secretary.

"Of course," she said, and lifted her fingers from the keys of the Underwood portable.

Eustace lowered himself onto the cushioned bench that encircled the pavilion, reached into a jacket pocket for a pipe that was not there, cleared his throat.

"You're going tomorrow."

"Yes."

"I'm sorry. No, actually I'm glad. But you know that."

"Yes."

"It's, well, I just wanted to say goodbye properly, that is without a lot of other folks around."

What he meant was without Leonore around.

"I'll miss you, Eustace."

"Will you, really?"

"Of course."

"I'll miss you, Elizabeth. You've meant a lot to me. I hope

47

I've been of some help to you."

"Of course you have." She knew, without any doubt, that what Eustace Warden was asking was whether in the end he had done the best he could to make up to her for her father's death. "You've meant a lot to me, too."

"You'll be seeing something of Peter in Paris, I suppose."

"I don't know. He must be awfully busy."

"He'll have time for you," Eustace said matter-of-factly. "You'll keep an eye on him for me, won't you?"

"He has a fiancée now to look after him."

"Don't know her. Hope she's got some spirit. The boy's too serious."

"Determined, I'd say."

"You'll like Paris."

"I expect to."

"You might even want to stay a while longer. . . . You see, Paula told me that . . . Anyway, here's a little graduation present." He handed Elizabeth an envelope. "You don't need to open it now."

As she took the envelope she squeezed his hand. "Thank you, Eustace, but thank you most of all for what you have done for me these last three years."

When he had gone she did open the envelope. It was a check for five thousand dollars. She quickly put the check into a pocket of her linen jacket. She had been expecting something like this, and she had already decided that it would not be possible to refuse whatever Eustace might offer her as a graduation gift.

She had also decided that she would not take it with her to France but put it in a local bank, in case things didn't work out and she had to come back to Laurel Hill and earn a living. With that amount of money she could buy out Amos Leach, the house where he had had his studio for twenty-five years, the photographic equipment, everything. There would be a comfortable living for her she knew.

Stop it! she told herself angrily. Things *will* work out. They must. But the vision of a gray-haired woman portrait photographer wouldn't go away.

Her final task was to sort the morning mail—for the last time. There was one telegram. She tore open the envelope and unfolded the yellow Western Union form bearing just two pasted strips of white tape, on which were printed in purple block letters:

ELIZABETH = ALL PARIS & ALL FRANCE AWAIT YOUR ARRIVAL STOP BON VOYAGE ET A BIENTOT = MARC & JEAN-LUC.

Her eyes filled with tears of joy and relief. This message of encouragement and friendship, arriving out of the blue at just this moment, was all that she needed to turn her face finally away from Laurel Hill and the past and toward whatever future fate had prepared for her.

Chapter Four

Paris
August, 1939

The Hôtel Meurice had sent its own porters to collect Leonore Devereux's trunks, a boy in gold-braided gray uniform and pillbox hat to run any errands she might require on the spot, and a dark-suited assistant manager to escort her to the hotel. He and Elizabeth occupied the jump seats opposite Leonore and Paula in the limousine, and the man from the hotel carried on light conversation with Leonore as they sped down the Rue La Fayette. Leonore's French was really impeccable. Elizabeth was a bit frightened. What would be required of Leonore Devereux's social secretary in Paris would be nothing like what she had learned in Laurel Hill, Virginia, and that had been difficult enough.

The hotel manager and two other assistants, these in winged collars, cutaways, and striped pants, escorted Leonore and her party from the elevator to her suite, where a maid was already in attendance. The maid curtseyed as though Leonore were royalty.

"I hope everything is to your satisfaction, Madame Devereux," the manager said, including with a sweep of his hand the antique furniture, the gilded molding of the high-ceilinged room, the flowers in vases, the silver bucket holding chilled champagne, the view across what Elizabeth supposed to be the Tuileries Gardens.

"Everything seems quite satisfactory, Monsieur Bruant."

"We've had the personal articles you stored with us placed about the suite as best we could remember, but Violette, who will be your maid during your entire stay, will rearrange them as you wish."

"I suppose I have messages."

"Quite a few. You will find them on the escritoire. Also, there are three gentlemen below who would like to pay their respects to you when you are settled in, your nephew, the young Marquis d'Aubigny and a Monsieur Cabanasse."

Leonore laughed and handed her hat to the maid. "I imagine the latter two rather want to pay their respects to these young ladies. You can tell them they may come up now."

"Charles," the manager said to one of his assistants, "would you call down and have the gentlemen escorted to the suite."

Elizabeth, taken by surprise, looked at her image in the mirror. She had been given a short and very smart haircut in New York. Leonore had insisted upon it: Paris was no place for hair tied up in a bun. How would Jean-Luc find her in his own environment: stiff and gauche? That was how she felt. And her heart was pounding when they came through the door.

The two Frenchmen, whom she had first seen in plaid lumberjack shirts with their corduroy pants stuffed into hiking boots, were transformed. Marc wore a navy blue blazer with a paisley handkerchief tucked in the breast pocket, Jean-Luc a gray flannel double-breasted suit that made him seem even taller and leaner. These were two young men of the world very much at home in their surroundings. That this was so sent a shiver of excitement through her body, though she could not have explained why.

"Elizabeth!" Marc cried and crossed the room. She had

51

known that it would be he who came to her. "You are more beautiful than ever." He took her by the shoulders and turned her around. *"Quelle belle coiffure!"*

Then the others came, except Leonore, who remained by the windows, sipping from a glass of champagne and looking out at the Tuileries. Jean-Luc kissed her on both cheeks, in the French fashion, and just as lightly as that first time he had asked permission to kiss her. Peter held out his hand to her— he had grown a mustache—and Paula stood to one side, smiling like a stage director who has arranged a scene and finds it to her liking.

"How good it is to see you," Peter said, still holding her hand. "I would never have thought to see you here, in Paris. . . ."

"It's good to be here, Peter."

Only then did Leonore turn from the window and give them a long assessing look. "Now you young people get out of here. I've some private phone calls to make. The Meurice serves a nice tea. Well, go on, go on."

They stood in the doorway of the large, dimly-lighted room, the frescoes on the vault above barely visible. Elizabeth knew about *le five o'clock*, the French expression for afternoon tea, even about *le thé dansant;* but this looked nothing like what her French teachers at Laurel Hill had described. Couples twisted and turned on a small dance floor to jazz played by a Negro trio. Cigarette smoke swirled upward in the soft light projected from alabaster torchères. Every table was filled.

"Ne vous inquietez-vous pas, monsieur," a white-haired waiter with starched apron down to his ankles said to Marc. "I'll have a table brought. It will take only two minutes."

As they waited Elizabeth looked at herself again in the

large mirror on the silk brocaded wall opposite. She really did look good in one of the more glamourous of Leonore's hand-me-downs. People were staring; but she looked again in the mirror and saw that they were staring not only at her but at five good-looking, very well-dressed young people.

"I really don't think I can stay," Peter said, glancing at his watch. "There's a telegram to Washington that I must send out tonight."

"Oh, don't be silly," Paula said. "Mr. Hull and Mr. Roosevelt can wait until tomorrow for your wise counsel."

"It isn't that. The ambassador . . ."

"Well, he can wait, too." Paula linked her arm in her cousin's. "You're going to have a drink with us."

"All right, but I can only stay a few minutes."

They were shown to a table that had been wedged into a far corner of the room, and they fitted around the table so tightly that shoulders and legs rubbed together. It was cozy and nice.

"Messieurs-dames, you desire?" the waiter asked.

"Champagne?" Marc suggested. "It is, after all, a special occasion." Everyone agreed that it was.

"Who are all these people?" Elizabeth asked of no one in particular. "They don't look like hotel guests, and hardly anyone's taking tea, but cocktails and drinks, though it's barely five o'clock of a Thursday evening, when I was told everyone in France would still be at work."

"This, *ma chère*," Jean-Luc replied, "is the idle class of France. They have no offices to go to, no work to perform. Marc probably knows most of them by their Christian names."

Marc laughed, looking his most cherubic. "Quite a few. For instance, there is, on the dance floor—the blond in the green dress—the mistress of the head of a major manufacturer of automobiles; and at the table just opposite us, in the red dress, his wife. The two are said to have agreed on rules for sharing the great industrialist."

"I also recognize a few politicians," Peter Warden said. "The National Assembly's just across the Place de la Concorde from here, and a lot of deputies have gathered in Paris, thinking they'll be called into session. Things looked so bad a few days ago, with Hitler threatening to invade Poland, that I started to cable you not to come, but by then you had already sailed. Now, however, it looks as though Chamberlain and Deladier may have called Hitler's bluff by saying that military action against Poland means war with England and France. Still, the situation in Europe looks ominous."

"As it has for years," Jean-Luc responded, "for those who were willing to face the truth about Hitler."

"Including yourself, of course," Paula said with her ironic smile, "and what are you doing to save the situation?"

"I try to warn people in my articles in *Le Populaire*. Whether the readers pay me any attention I don't know."

"Well at least one of us is gainfully employed," Paula said.

"What about me?" Peter asked with a frown.

"I don't count people who work when they don't have to."

"It doesn't make the work any easier."

"You know perfectly well, Peter, that Augustus Warden's grandson will get ahead in the foreign service whether he works or not."

"That's just why I do work hard, and I damned well don't appreciate your sarcasm."

Paula winced but then leaned over and kissed her cousin on the cheek. "Don't be such a grump, Peter. I'm sorry."

"You know I don't take teasing well."

"No, you never did, and I could never resist teasing you." She laughed. There was an awkward silence around the table.

The champagne arrived along with a gorgeous plate of canapés, and everyone began to speak at once.

"Would you like to dance, Elizabeth?" Peter asked.

"Well . . . sure."

Although she had danced on only one evening in her life, she felt no hesitation in throwing herself into the frenetic beat of the jazz. That was one fear she had put behind her; if she could only conquer the others as easily.

To her surprise serious, reserved Peter was an excellent dancer. Probably in the diplomatic life that was a requirement. Then the saxophone slipped into a lower key and the rhythm of the drums slowed. Peter took her in his arms.

"I'm sorry about that little scene."

"It wasn't your fault."

"I shouldn't let Paula get to me like that. She's done it for as long as I can remember."

"But why?"

"She's bored and unhappy. She leads an idle life, and she resents anyone who tries to accomplish something, particularly if that person is a Warden and doesn't have to."

"Why does that upset you so much?"

"I'm not upset, I'm just telling the truth. You asked. I guess I sounded like a stuffed shirt, though, didn't I?"

"Eustace says you're too serious."

"But don't you see, Elizabeth, my father is why I'm serious. I could end up like him, wandering around in that big house like he's half-lost, starting something and not finishing it, then starting something else, and always, always, avoiding responsibility. But enough of that. I do work hard, but my weekends are usually free. I would like you to meet my fiancée Natcha. We could go some places together."

"I'd love to."

"That is, if your Frenchman leaves you any time."

"He isn't my Frenchman. Marc is here as a friend of your family. . . ."

"I didn't mean Marc."

"Jean-Luc came along with him when he visited Beaulieu. They're just showing good manners by calling on Leonore."

"I see." Peter smiled. "In case you're interested, Jean-Luc carries a lot of weight in Paris for someone of his age. That's why I've got to know him. *Le Populaire* may be a socialist paper, but he has solid connections all across the political spectrum."

"Such as Colonel Charles de Gaulle."

"You've heard of de Gaulle?"

"Of course," Elizabeth said, savoring her first small social triumph in France.

By the time they returned to the table, a second bottle of champagne had already been opened, and the little storm between Paula and Peter had been forgotten.

Just as Peter was helping Elizabeth into her chair at the back of the crowded table, the blond young woman in the green dress floated off the dance floor, leaned over Marc and kissed him on the cheek.

"Good luck tomorrow, Marc."

"We'll certainly need it, Arlette. You'll be there?"

"Bien sur, chéri," and she moved on to another table without allowing herself to be introduced.

"Tomorrow?" Paula inquired.

"The races at Longchamps. We—father—has a horse running. He won't be there, though. He's boycotting Paris these days. I was about to ask you all if you would like to join me in our box."

"Top hats and tail-coats required, which I don't happen to own," Jean-Luc said.

"Nobody tells the d'Aubignys what their guests will wear," Marc said with an aristocratic hauteur.

"In that case I'll be there." To Elizabeth's surprise, Jean-Luc looked at her expectantly.

"May I bring Natcha?" Peter asked. "She'd kill for a box seat at the opening races."

"You may all bring anybody you want. And you can tell Natcha she may bring her sketchbook and camera as well. As I said, you are my guests."

"You can count on Elizabeth and me to be there," Paula said.

"I'm not so sure about me," Elizabeth ventured. "Leonore may have things for me to do."

"You leave Leonore to me," Paula said. "She's not having you over to Paris as a 'graduation present' and then making you work seven days a week."

"I always thought you were afraid of your mother," Peter said to Paula with just a hint of sarcasm.

"I am . . . a bit. But then she's sort of frightened of me. You'll be at the races tomorrow, Elizabeth."

"Well then, *à bientôt mes amis*," and Peter left.

"He's a nice boy," Paula said. "I don't know why we don't get along."

Marc laughed. "Let's dance, Paula."

"So, you made it," Jean-Luc said to Elizabeth, as though they were in some conspiracy together. It was nice to be alone with him. Things were so supercharged when the others were around, and then there was this feeling about him that seemed to be growing with every minute.

"I made it." She smiled at him. He filled her glass with champagne.

"And you'll stay?"

"I can't promise. I may lose my nerve. Although I haven't

even been out of the hotel yet, I can already see Paris won't be easy for someone like me."

"Just don't let Paris know you're scared. That's the secret."

"But you are all so sophisticated."

"I would say that it is you who is sophisticated. You know who you are. Most of the people in this room don't."

"Does Marc?"

"He knows his place in society, which for the old aristocracy is all you need to know about yourself."

"Do you?"

His dark eyes looked into hers. "Yes, I know who I am, and I know where I'm going. You know who you are, but you don't yet quite know where you're going. You'll find out soon enough, as long as you don't let these people you call sophisticated convince you you're something you're not." He smiled. "I'm lecturing again, aren't I?"

"You are, and you're also being arrogant."

"As when I warned you on the dangers of being beautiful."

"Yes." Then he did remember. Was that what she had wanted to be sure of?

Elizabeth awoke the next morning with a throbbing headache from having drunk too much champagne. Throwing back the curtain to the round dormer window, she found that a steady rain was falling: the races at Longchamps with her friends, which she had so looked forward to, would surely be cancelled. And if that were not enough, a note from Leonore had been slipped under the door. There was much correspondence to be answered, including telegrams that could not wait another day. Oh, damn! Elizabeth returned to her bed and went back to sleep.

She was awakened by the phone ringing. Oh, God, it was

Leonore. What time was it?

"Hello?"

"Elizabeth?"

"Yes."

"For Christ's sake, what are you doing in your room? You were supposed to be downstairs half an hour ago."

It was not Leonore's voice but Paula's.

"I was?"

"The races. Remember?"

"But it's pouring down rain."

"It was. The rain stopped nearly an hour ago. The races are on."

"Oh." She was still not quite awake. "But I've got some urgent work to do for Leonore."

"I told you I would take care of Leonore, and I have. Are you coming or not?"

"I'm coming."

It was one of those days, Elizabeth would soon learn, of aqueous blue skies in which the softest of white clouds floated, for which Paris was famous. From somewhere Paula had acquired a dark green runabout, its tan canvas top turned back; and they sped up the Champs-Elysées, careened around the Arc de Triomphe and headed out the avenue Foch to the Bois de Boulogne. From the day that Leonore had given her the chance of accompanying her to France, Elizabeth had devoured guide books and maps; and there was not a monument along their route that she did not recognize. Nothing, however, was quite like what she had imagined. It was so much more beautiful.

"*C'est jolie, n'est-ce pas?*"

"Paula, *c'est magnifique.*"

"*Il n'y a qu'une Paris.*"

There is only one Paris. . . . Was it at this moment that

Elizabeth Vail set alight the bridge that led back to Laurel Hill, Virginia? She didn't really think about it at the time, she was so busy looking at everything around her; but later she rather thought that this was the moment. And later she would understand that it was not actually Paris that had set that bridge alight.

At the entrance to the stands at Longchamps, one young man in racetrack uniform took over the green runabout from Paula and another led them to the tree-shaded paddock where the owners of the horses running in the next race and their guests were gathered: the men in gray top hats, frock coats and striped pants; the women in dresses that Elizabeth knew instantly, from Leonore's wardrobe, to be by Chanel, Lanvin, Patou and the other great names of French *couture*. She was herself wearing a somewhat let-out, two-year-old Patou of Leonore's.

As if this were not enough color, the elegant crowd mingled with jockeys in bright silks, while fine thoroughbred horses, bays, chestnuts and grays, led by exercise boys, circled the paddock.

"Quelle beauté," Marc said coming out of the paddock and taking each of the two young women by the hand and leading them back with him. In his formal wear, with the sun playing in his golden red curls it was he who was the beauty, Elizabeth thought. And then she caught sight of Peter and . . . Jean-Luc, and it was enough male beauty to take your breath away.

"This is Natcha, who says she's going to marry me, though I don't really believe it yet," Peter said, as though he really could not believe his luck.

"I have heard much from Peter about you both," the very beautiful young woman said. She wore a pale blue flowered gown, a Schiaparelli Elizabeth guessed, and a little hat of feathers with a half veil that just covered her gray eyes. She had high cheekbones, ash blond hair and a perfect summer tan. One could indeed imagine that she was the daughter of a Polish prince and a California beauty. Her accent was pure American.

"The only way I could get her away from the office today was for her to cover the races for *Vogue*."

"As you see, I have been working," and Natcha flipped open a sketchbook with her pencilled impressions of the crowd. Beautiful and talented too. In the distance a hunting horn sounded.

"Post time," Marc said, "and this is our race. You got here just in time. We had better go to our box."

"First let me get a picture of the golden youth of Paris together," and Natcha took a Leica from a bag she was carrying.

Paula and Elizabeth formed a group with the three men, and Elizabeth thought to herself that it was true: six young handsome people without any real cares and all monied except for her, and for now anyway she could live as though she were. Her first day of perhaps what she had always wanted.

As Natcha adjusted her camera, Elizabeth turned to Jean-Luc. "I was rather hoping you would bring Bettina. I want to meet her."

"Bettina?" Jean-Luc seemed puzzled.

"Your girlfriend."

"Did I say that? We were speaking English as I recall, and perhaps I did not express myself well. She's a friend, that's all."

The sun came out from behind a cloud and showered gold through the trees. It was indeed what she had always wanted, and now Elizabeth could admit to herself that she was perhaps in love with Jean-Luc Cabanasse.

"You've heard the news, of course."

"What news?"

"No," Marc said, "no news until after the race. Now we have to concentrate on getting Nestor across the finish line first," and he pointed to a bay gelding that was being led toward the starting gate.

Many binoculars strayed from the race that day to the three young women in the d'Aubigny box. Elizabeth had never felt so excited, and by the time the horses came down the stretch they were all on their feet screaming for Nestor and she was holding Jean-Luc by the wrist. And then Nestor moved out of the pack and crossed the finish line first and they all embraced.

After they had calmed down Marc suggested they go to the club house for champagne.

"At least there's one thing we can celebrate on this awful day."

"What do you mean by that?" Paula asked.

"You really don't know?"

"No," Elizabeth replied.

"You and Paula must be the last people in Paris to hear. Hitler invaded Poland at dawn this morning."

"Oh, why, why did this have to happen to us?"

All eyes turned to Natcha whose eyes were filled with tears. She turned her head away. "I'll be all right in a minute. It's just all so bloody terrible."

Peter awkwardly put his arm around his fiancée and led her away.

"Where are her parents?" Paula asked.

"In Warsaw. I wondered how long she could keep up appearances," Marc said. "I should have cancelled the party."

"What happens now . . . for France?" Elizabeth couldn't believe what she was hearing. Leonore had come to France, after much hesitation, because she had been assured by her most influential and well-connected friends that it would never come to this.

"France and England are almost certain to declare war on Germany," Jean-Luc said.

She turned to Marc.

"There's no other way out now. The stupid politicians. I expect to be called up."

She looked at Jean-Luc, but he said nothing.

"Well, anyway, let's have some champagne," Marc said. "We did win the race."

"I'd better get back to the hotel before mother has a chance to do something foolish," Paula said. "She'll be trying to book herself on the next ship home."

"Yes, I think I'd better be going too," Jean-Luc said.

"Can we give you a lift?"

"No, I'll just walk across the Bois and catch the Métro."

"Well, I guess champagne wasn't such a good idea," Marc said. "Let's all go. Natcha shouldn't stay here, and Peter has to get back quickly, in any case. He only took off a couple of hours so he could be with Natcha and try to cheer her up. They are working around the clock at the American embassy."

And then to Elizabeth's surprise Jean-Luc said to her, "Would you like to walk across the park with me? I'm going to take the Métro. You can get a taxi at the Métro station."

"Would you mind, Paula?" She wanted to go with Jean-Luc very much.

"I'm a big girl, Elizabeth," Paula said with her ironic smile. "I can find my way back to the hotel alone." She had seen what was beginning to happen.

Chapter Five

Elizabeth and Jean-Luc walked beneath the trees of the Bois de Boulogne in a silence punctuated by the occasional beginning of a sentence left unfinished. He did not take her hand in his, and his mind seemed far away. It was the war, of course, and it was his country that was in danger. But then why had he asked her to accompany him?

It was only when they reached the Ranlagh Métro station on the edge of the park, where they were to part, that he stopped and turned to her. "I'm sorry I've been rude, but I was lost in thought."

"There's much to think about. If you have to go into the army . . ." And just when—she realized as she spoke—I've fallen in love with you. Another sentence was left unfinished.

"That was not what I was thinking about. I was thinking that the dreams of millions of people—people like you and me—were shattered today . . . all those dreams that now will never be realized. . . ."

Her heart beat a little faster. He looked so serious. Two women passed by and stared appreciatively at the tall handsome young man in rented formal clothes amid the crowd of workmen in blue overalls filing into the subway entrance.

"Yes. Poor Natcha. I hope her parents are all right."

"Will you be going back to America now?"

"I . . ."

"The reason I've been so quiet is that I was debating with myself whether it was fair to say to you what I felt."

"I don't understand what you mean." But she knew what she hoped he would say, and she knew already what her answer would be.

"Tell me what you feel," she said.

"I feel that you should not go back to Laurel Hill, Virginia. It would be a great waste. You were meant for greater things."

"Why would it be unfair to tell me that? It is a fine compliment . . . especially from you."

"Because war is coming to France."

"You can't know that, but in any case I've already decided to stay in Paris." She hardly dared admit to herself that she was staying only because he was in Paris.

"Then I needn't feel guilty?"

She laughed. "No you needn't feel guilty." Suddenly the war didn't matter anymore.

The tenseness went out of his face. "I think I won't take the Métro. Will you walk with me?"

"Where are you going?"

"To my father's old office. There are some papers I want to look up."

"I should get back to Leonore." She desperately wanted to go with him, but she had to be sure that this was what he really intended.

He smiled. "Let Leonore take care of herself for once."

"All right. I'll walk with you."

Then he did take her hand lightly in his, as if he were taking the hand of a friend. He had said nothing about the two of them, had put everything in terms of her future. She didn't care. She had never been in love before, and there was no hurry. It was enough for now to know they would be in the same city. She would wire for the money that Eustace had given her.

They strolled up the Avenue Mozart, and Elizabeth, who a short while before had been so eager to see Paris, saw nothing. Now as they walked his words poured out, but all the while her mind was on how to get loose from Leonore, on how she would live in Paris. . . . What had he just said?

"I won't be going into the army."

"But surely . . ."

"I'm not a French citizen. We Catalans live on both sides of the border, and my village is right on the frontier. I was born in a hospital in Barcelona."

"Oh, how . . ." She had been about to say "how wonderful". "I could volunteer for the French army . . ." Her heart sank. ". . . but I can do more in other ways. I've been thinking about it for some time."

"Yes, I remember when we first met you said war was inevitable."

"And France's defeat is inevitable. Then you'll *have* to leave. I don't know what I was thinking of in suggesting you might stay."

"Remember that it was my decision to stay. Besides France may not be defeated."

They had paused beneath the Arc de Triomphe with its frieze of ancient warriors charging into battle. The eternal flame at the tomb of the Unknown Soldier flickered in the early evening breeze. She gazed down the Champs-Elysées. Would there still be light-hearted, romantic times there?

"Once again we go to war, after only twenty years . . . Yes, France will be defeated. Hitler is not the Kaiser. This time it will be total war. This time . . . I've seen German planes dive bombing Spanish villages, German planes strafing civilians on the road—just for practice—leaving a trail of corpses of men, women and children."

"You were there?" She was astonished. He had never once mentioned this.

"My father had organized a shipment of medical supplies for Catalonia and had accompanied it to Barcelona, where he was trapped when the city was besieged by Franco's forces. I was going there to see how I could get him out, but Barcelona fell just as I crossed into Spain. The next thing I knew I was caught up in the Republican army's retreat toward France, firing a rifle—very inexpertly—from behind boulders and olive trees. When we finally made it to the pass at Perthus, the ground was covered with thousands of rifles thrown down by Republican soldiers as they entered France. I threw mine down with the rest. The war was over."

"But that was only this January. I didn't realize your father was still alive then."

"When Barcelona fell he was one of many executed by Franco's men after so-called trials."

"I'm so terribly sorry." She was stunned, barely comprehending.

He shrugged. "After that there was nothing more to be done, so I returned to Paris, and talked my paper into sending me to America. And so here we are."

"And your mother?"

"She and my father were divorced years ago. She's remarried, to a very rich Argentinian and now lives in Buenos Aires. I have no family at all in France, which may be just as well."

They walked on in silence for a while. How very different things looked with the passage of a few hours. Such was the man she had chosen to fall in love with and on such a day. While everyone else was urgently making arrangements to return to America, she was planning to stay in France and to withdraw from her Laurel Hill bank the money that would have assured her a comfortable and safe life there.

"Will you tell me what you are thinking?" he said at last.

"I was thinking that what has been missing from my life— what is so conspicuously missing from the lives of the Wardens and all of their rich friends—is the unexpected. They arrange their lives so that there are never any surprises. And if you work for them, as I did, you start to think like that."

She stopped and took his hand. "Jean-Luc, I want surprises, risks even, perhaps even danger. It has taken today to make me see that."

"Well, you have certainly chosen the right time and place for all of those. But at some point it won't be possible for you to go back. It was painful for me to speak of Spain, but I wanted you to know what war is really like. Elizabeth, are you sure you know your mind?"

"Better than that, Jean-Luc, I know my heart." That was all that she could say, because this wager she had made on the future was based on her new-found love for a man whose feelings she could not fathom. He seemed very attracted to her, but his words were cautious. There was certainly something he was not ready to tell her. But surely he would come to love her. He must.

Flushed with emotion, she looked up at a blue-enameled sign on a wall. "Rue du Faubourg St. Honoré. Isn't that where all the fanciest shops are?"

"Many of them, including my father's," Jean-Luc said, pointing to a darkened window with "Cabanasse" in gold letters on it. "It is mine now, though I don't know what I will do with it. I don't have his knowledge of paintings and sculpture and antiquities. And that elegant pile across from it is the Elysée Palace, the residence of the President of the Republic. Lots of comings and goings there this evening."

She turned. Long black cars, carrying middle-aged men in

dark suits, were being waved in and out of the palace gates by guards.

"Everyone looks so grim," Elizabeth said, "and I suppose they have good reason."

It was twilight now. The sidewalk in front of the palace was blocked by armed guards, and they crossed the street to the Cabanasse gallery. Jean-Luc took a key from a pocket, unlocked the door and they stepped inside.

When he turned the light switch Elizabeth started with surprise. It was like a stage set. A dozen or more small shaded lights illuminated groups of paintings, gilded medieval sculpture, Greek vases and ancient Egyptian artifacts: seated pharaohs carved in stone; a painted human figure with the head of a jackal; a piece of plaster from a wall, on which lithe women in diaphanous gowns danced; a small ceramic figure of a hippopotamus; several mummy cases with wide-eyed, staring faces, one opened to reveal the intact mummy inside.

"Do you remember what Marc said when he first saw the lake and the island in the Virginia woods where we spent that weekend together? He said *'C'est magique'*. That's the way I feel now."

"My father was something of a magician. He had an eye for art and he had a way with rich people. That's how he met my mother, and she's the one who got him into the business of antiquities. Unfortunately, he also had a conscience, which cost him his life. I've thought about him a lot today. We wouldn't face up to Franco, so now we must face up to Hitler."

Jean-Luc turned another key in a lock and opened a door that led into an inner office. Then he turned on an overhead, green-shaded light and dialled a combination lock on the door of a safe.

"It *is* here," he said, laying on a carved desk a much-used leather notebook, which when opened revealed detailed colored maps backed with linen, lists of names and addresses, and page after page of notes in a tiny, meticulous hand.

"What is it?"

"All the information he compiled on the border passes between France and Spain, on those persons on both sides of the border who opposed Franco and were ready to risk their lives in the cause of freedom, on those in the police and the secret services who were most to be feared, and those who could most easily be bribed. . . ."

Elizabeth felt herself moving, second by second, from the safe world she knew so well to a dangerous world that she had so carelessly said attracted her.

"And what will you do with this notebook?"

"Perhaps even avenge my father."

There were tears in his eyes. She came close to him and stood straight and still, offering herself, and the offering was accepted. He put his arms around her and drew her to him. At this moment she knew for a certainty that she, who had always depended wholly on others, was for the first time in her life a source of strength for another. Was this what love—which had so baffled her—was all about?

"Come," he said, putting the notebook back into the safe, "let's go get something to eat. Are you hungry?"

"I haven't had anything to eat," she said, realizing it for the first time, "since tea yesterday at the Meurice. What a day this has been."

"There's a *brasserie* around the corner."

"I'd love that."

As they came through the swinging doors of the *Brasserie du Cirque* Jean-Luc's arm was around her waist in a way that was not anything like the way he had held her hand an hour before. The waiters knew Jean-Luc; the maître d'hôtel cast an appreciative eye over Elizabeth in her Patou gown, and showed them to a corner table; and they were soon dining on oysters on the half-shell and a *choucroute* of sausages and smoked ham and sauerkraut. The vast room was filled with people and smoke and light flashing from mirrors. That Hitler had invaded Poland at dawn simply couldn't be true; at least for this evening, the happiest of her life, it wasn't true for Elizabeth Vail.

"Tu es contente?" he asked, striking one of the big restaurant matches with his thumbnail and lighting the Gauloise she had accepted from him.

Tu? She lowered her eye in confusion, trying not to inhale any of the smoke from the French cigarette made of yellow paper and tobacco as dark as tar. If you weren't related or old school chums, Madame Regnier, the French professor at Laurel Hill had said, then a man and woman don't use the familiar form of "you" unless they are very close. The girls in the class knew what *that* meant.

"Très contente," she said. "I know these are difficult times for you and for . . . both your countries. But I cannot help feeling happy tonight."

"I take that as a compliment."

She raised her eyes and looked directly into his. She could see that, despite everything, he, too, was happy. His dark eyes, the slight smile on his long lean face, the way that he slumped back in his chair, still in his rented formal dress, now much rumpled, drawing on his Gauloise, all showed it.

"You're definitely staying in France then?"

"Yes, definitely," she said, continuing to hold his eyes with hers. "That's decided."

"Well, then," and he reached out and removed the little glass filters atop their cups that had finished draining the coffee, "it's a new chapter isn't it?"

"Yes." Her heart was beating fast again as she waited for what he would say next.

"Whatever happens, you can count on me as a friend."

"I know. I . . . I wouldn't have considered staying in France if I hadn't been sure of that." It was almost like a declaration of love, and to her surprise and delight that was the way he took it.

"Il y a, donc, Mademoiselle Vail, la possibilité de quelque chose plus que l'amitié?"

She paused for what seemed ages, but was probably only seconds. "Yes, Monsieur Cabanasse, there is the possibility of something more than friendship. I will need a little time, that's all."

"Naturellement."

She reached out and put her hand on his. He had declared himself without being gushy or solemn but in a light sophisticated fashion that pleased and flattered her enormously; and he had done so before having, in any but a friendly way, kissed or even touched her. He had understood that beneath her surface polish she was a shy person, an innocent woman and even frightened by the idea of physical love.

"What an elegant way to begin, Jean-Luc," she said in all sincerity, giving his hand a squeeze.

Chapter Six

Elizabeth awakened slowly, a vivid dream escaping her as her eyes opened, leaving behind only a feeling of contentment and yet excitement. And then she remembered: *"Il y a, donc, Mademoiselle Vail, la possibilité de quelque chose plus que l'amitié?"* She would never as long as she lived forget those words spoken in a low voice with the accent of the south of France, the look in those dark eyes. No wonder she awoke feeling both content and excited.

The phone was ringing. She opened one eye and looked at her travel alarm: five past eight. Surely Leonore didn't have work for her this early on a Saturday morning. She was probably going to be chastised for attending the races and then disappearing. She picked up the receiver of the upright French telephone.

"Hello."

"Good morning. Did I wake you?"

"Jean-Luc. Is there anything wrong?" she said, instinctively feeling that something threatened the first happiness she had ever known.

"No. Everything is fine, just fine." He laughed softly.

"Then . . ."

"I just wanted to hear your voice."

"Oh." She raised herself up on one elbow, wide awake now. "How sweet of you."

"You don't regret last night, do you?"

"Regret what?" Had she misunderstood his meaning?

"Regret the things we said to each other."

She hadn't misunderstood, but she wasn't taking any more chances. "Jean-Luc, you can forget what I said last night about needing a little time."

"What are you saying?"

"I'm saying that I love you."

There was a long silence. "Jean-Luc?"

"Sorry. I was a little . . . I hadn't hoped to hear those words . . . so soon. I love you, Elizabeth."

There. The irrevocable words had been spoken. "Oh . . . oh . . ."

"When can I see you? Elizabeth . . . I am leaving for a few days, but I must see you before I leave."

"Leaving? Oh, no! For where?"

"To the south of France. I've urgent business to attend to. If I had known what was going to happen between us last night . . . but I've made commitments I must keep."

"I understand," though she didn't. "When must you leave?"

"As soon as I know what Britain and France will do. The British Parliament is meeting tomorrow or the next day, and then we will know. Whatever the English do, France is bound to follow suit."

"Then you think they will declare war on Germany?"

"Most probably."

"Promise me you won't do anything dangerous, Jean-Luc."

"What I have to do is not dangerous, I promise you, but it is something that must be done quickly. When can I see you?"

"I don't know. I haven't seen Leonore since the day we arrived." Was that only the day before yesterday? "She may already have booked passage home."

"You won't let her . . ."

"No, Jean-Luc, nothing can change my mind now. I'm staying in France. . . . Our timing wasn't so good, was it?"

"Who knows, Elizabeth. If it weren't for the war, perhaps you and I would have passed in the night. Maybe we're lucky."

"All I know is that this morning I consider myself the luckiest woman in the world. . . . I'll call you as soon as I know when I can get away from Leonore. I have some obligation to her, but I *will* get away. Jean-Luc, I don't even know your telephone number."

"Balzac 77-39. Make it soon, darling."

"Yes. *A bientôt. Je t'aime.*"

Elizabeth slowly hung up the receiver, realizing for the first time that in loving Jean-Luc she had assured herself the life of surprises and risks and even danger that she had said she wanted. She still felt content and excited but also a little frightened.

She quickly got out of bed. She would get dressed and start preparing Leonore—and Paula and Peter—for what she was about to do. She pulled her nightgown over her head and paused to look briefly at her naked body in the mirror. Now she had some reason to be glad for her beauty.

When she entered Leonore's suite, Paula was standing by the window and Leonore was talking on the telephone.

"What do you mean you can't go with us? I know war is likely to be declared in a day or two. That's precisely why three women can't travel alone across France. There may be bombs falling everywhere. . . . Well, why isn't it likely? Peter, I don't care what your ambassador says. This is your family. . . . What do you think your father would advise you? That you should stay at your post? Well, then I suppose there's nothing further to say. . . ."

Leonore slammed down the receiver, paused and then picked it up again. Paula winked, and Elizabeth crossed the room to her.

"What's going on?" she whispered.

"For the first time mother's been unable to get exactly what she wanted when she wanted it. It's been worth watching. She demanded that the hotel manager book us immediately on a ship sailing from Le Havre. Of course, everything is reserved, particularly if you're not prepared to travel less than first-class.

"Finally, Monsieur Bruant got so exasperated he told her that she wasn't the only person in the world who had money and influence. So did the people who were holding the reservations, and they weren't about to give them up. In the end he did get us on a ship sailing from Nice on Thursday at midnight, so we'll have to take the train south. There was the devil of a time even getting train reservations. Everybody wants to get out of Paris. I think Bruant pulled a lot of strings just to get rid of mother."

"And she wants Peter to go with her to Nice."

"You heard the conversation. Of course he's not going. If he walked away from his job just as Europe was going to war, the name Warden wouldn't save him from being fired on the spot by Ambassador Bullitt, who's a good friend of Roosevelt's."

"Paula, I'm not going back to America. I'm staying here in Paris."

"Oh, how wonderful! I've decided the same thing. Well, I guess it's not wonderful, but I'll sure be a lot less scared if you stay too. But for God's sake don't say anything about my staying to mother until I get her on that ship, or she'll make life living hell for me from now until Wednesday. My only problem is money. . . ."

"*You* have money problems?"

"Sure I'm rich, but mother has control of my money until my next birthday, and that's months away."

"I could help you. I'm going to wire for money."

"That won't be necessary, actually," Paula said with an enigmatic smile. "I've come up with a very neat solution."

The phone was slammed down again. Leonore turned in her chair and gave Elizabeth an angry look. "So there you are. Where were you all day yesterday when I needed you?"

"I told you, mother, that we were going to the races."

"I wasn't speaking to you, Paula. And afterwards, Elizabeth? I called you until ten o'clock last night, and there was no answer."

"I went out with Monsieur Cabanasse and we had dinner," Elizabeth said in a quiet controlled voice.

"Without informing me. You knew a war had begun, you knew . . ." She was at a loss for words. She twisted the strands of pearls at her neck with a hand on which a large emerald glittered. Suddenly, Leonore seemed much older.

"Stop it, mother," Paula said, with that dangerous edge to her voice that even Leonore feared, the signal that she was about to cause someone serious trouble. "Save your energy for what's important. There's still a lot to be done, tickets to be picked up, telegrams to be sent, and we don't yet have hotel reservations in Nice."

"Nor do we have anyone to accompany us there, with war about to break out here. Peter should be . . ."

"You can stop worrying. Marc d'Aubigny will escort us."

"Are you sure?"

"I haven't told him yet, but, yes, I'm sure."

"I thought he was being called up in the army mobilization."

"His father got him off. The family estates that he manages produce a lot of food that France is going to need."

"Then I suppose that will be all right. Elizabeth, you'll take care of all the details, won't you?" Leonore said with a slightly apologetic smile. "Now, I'm late for an appointment to have my hair done," and she picked up her handbag and went out the door.

"Isn't she something?" Paula said, shaking her head. "I've always feared becoming like her."

"Just as Peter fears becoming like Eustace."

Paula looked at her closely. "You understand, then. People think money is a blessing, but in fact it's a curse . . . and people think war is a curse, but maybe for some of us it will be a solution."

Elizabeth was not yet ready to tell Paula that she might be one of those; nor was she ready to tell her that she was seriously in love. Her love was too new and precious to be spoken about.

At nine o'clock on the evening of September 2, 1939, with Europe poised on the brink of war, Elizabeth finished the last of her duties for Leonore Warden Devereux, discharged whatever debt she might have had. Only then did she pick up the receiver of the phone in her little room and call Balzac 77-39.

"It's me," she said, her heart overflowing with happiness.

"You had me a bit worried, *chérie*," but from the pain in his voice it was clear that he had been more than a little worried. "I thought perhaps something had gone wrong . . . that perhaps you had . . ."

"No, nothing has gone wrong, and nothing will. It's just that I couldn't bring myself to call you until I could tell you that I was able to come to you. Jean-Luc, I have all tomorrow off and . . ."

"And it's a Sunday. Can we meet early?"

"The earlier the better."

"Have you yet ridden the Métro?"

"No."

"Then it's time to start, if you're going to live in Paris. I'll be waiting for you at the Cité Métro station. Now here is what you do. . . ."

Puzzled and amused, she wrote down his directions.

"I may get lost. Why not just meet at the Meurice?"

"You told me you wanted a life of surprises," and now there was joy and not pain in that melodious voice from the south of France, "and I am about to start you out on such a life. And from now on we will speak only French together."

"D'accord, cher ami." She liked that. If one was going to take a French lover, then one should go all the way. She felt terribly sophisticated—and terribly scared.

The next morning she passed through the doors of the Hôtel Meurice almost exactly twenty-four hours after Jean-Luc had called her, when everything that had been complicated had suddenly become simple. It was a perfect morning with just a hint of fall in the air. She turned left and within a few steps saw the Art Nouveau entrance, in green bronze, of the Tuileries station.

She descended the white-tiled stairway into the subway, bought a pack of green cardboard tickets, and remembered to take the corridor with the name of the last station on the line in the direction she wanted to go. She successfully changed trains at the Châtelet station, and now the next station was Cité. She got off and climbed the stairs from the dark labyrinth of the Métro into the bright light, her heart beating fast again, and was surrounded by birds: hundreds and hundreds of brightly-colored singing birds of all kinds, in cages large and small. Beyond the birds were banks of flowers. And then she saw Jean-Luc.

They came toward each other. She felt the reality of his body hard against hers, his arms around her, the long and tender kiss. This was the reality that she had longed for; so much so that the day they spent apart had seemed as though it would never end.

Now he was kissing her on the ear and on the neck as though he would devour her. To think she had said that she would need a little time. To think that she had been afraid of love. She had never felt less afraid of anything in her life. He was kissing her on the mouth again, and she responded passionately.

Finally their mouths parted and for a while she let her head rest on his shoulder. She was breathing hard and she could feel his heart pounding. Their kissing had attracted not the slightest attention.

"The happiest moment of my life has come," she murmured, remembering to speak French, "and no one even notices."

"This is Paris, *chérie,* and we are just doing what a man and woman—a beautiful, tall, blond woman—are expected to do." He held her out at arm's length and examined her lovingly.

"Where are we?"

"At the flower market on the Ile de la Cité. Birds are brought here to sell only on Sunday mornings. It's been done for a very long time."

"What a wonderful surprise. And what a wonderful place for lovers to meet for the first time." She wanted there to be no doubt about that. Her one abiding fear had vanished like the phantom that it was. She already considered that she was his.

"Then you were surprised."

"Yes," she said, as she reached out and touched the olive skin of his face and felt the stubble of his beard. It made her shiver. "But the greatest surprise will always be that between the time I saw you in the paddock at Longchamps and the time we were having coffee after dinner in the evening, I had fallen completely and hopelessly in love."

"It is called *le coup de foudre*: when lightning strikes two people. You will find that the French have words for everything that concerns love. I knew what was happening to us, and I wanted to speak, but I was struggling with the idea that I had no right to keep you here in danger. By the time we were having coffee, and you said that you would not have stayed if you had not been sure of my friendship, I knew I must speak. It was going to happen no matter what my ideas might be."

"And when you called the next morning," she said, a lump in her throat, "I had to tell you immediately that I loved you before something—I had no idea what—could come between us."

And now she took him by the shoulders and held him at arm's length, gazed at his long lean face, the prominent narrow nose, the dark hair falling over one of his dark eyes.

"My God, Jean-Luc Cabanasse, *tu es beau.*"

She would always remember what he was wearing on this day: checked pants, a navy-blue pullover and a shirt open at the throat.

"Have I overdressed?" she asked anxiously. She wanted everything to be perfect.

"What does it matter? What does anything matter?"

"You are right. What does anything matter? I just want this day to last forever. Where do we start?"

"Have you had breakfast?"

"No."

"Neither have I. Come on."

He took her hand in his, and they walked hand in hand through the flower market. They could not keep their eyes off each other, and every few moments one would look at the other and they both would smile at their happy secret. Their life together had begun.

They crossed one of the bridges from the Ile de la Cité to the Left Bank. There was a café at the end of the bridge with a view of Notre-Dame, and they sat on the terrace in the sun and had café au lait and croissants and he talked of Paris and all the things that he would show her.

Afterwards they crossed back over the bridge and wandered around the island for hours, talking constantly of everything and nothing. They finally ended up in a little park at the very tip of the island, with trees and shrubs and park benches. There on a bench, in semi-privacy, they kissed hungrily and felt with longing each other's bodies beneath their clothes, while tourist boats passed only yards away. Soon the morning had melted away, and lunch was beginning to be served under awnings on the boats.

"Hungry?"

"Ravenous."

"There is a little square right in the center of the island, tree-shaded and quiet, where there is a modest restaurant with a terrace. The food is not bad."

"It sounds wonderful."

"And afterwards, we have the whole afternoon to do whatever you want."

As they got up from the park bench, she said, "I have just realized that I do not even know where you live." If he wanted to go to bed with her that afternoon, she wanted to give him the opportunity. It did not have to be today, but it did have to be soon.

"I have a studio apartment on the quai, not far from here, very small, up among the roof tops, with a view of the Seine in one direction and of the Eiffel Tower from a little terrace on the back."

"It must be wonderful."

"Six flights of stairs to walk up, though. No elevator."

The little square was just as he had described it, and on the awning of the restaurant was painted, "La Rose de la France".

"What a sweet name," she said.

"Nothing grand."

"Grand is the last thing I want today."

They were seated on the terrace, under an old plane tree, and the young woman who seated them greeted Jean-Luc by name. Her hair was short and very dark, her oval face shaped much like Jean-Luc's, her skin had the same olive coloring, and there was a slight trace of mustache on her upper lip.

"What a striking woman," Elizabeth said. "Not pretty but . . ."

"They are Catalans. The father does the cooking, the mother and Marie wait on table. You will like them."

"They are Catalans like you? Then of course I will like them."

"It is said that Catalans make passionate lovers," and he blushed a little and she laughed, "but fierce enemies."

"Then I have nothing to fear and much to anticipate."

Could anything be better than this? she thought, as they ate and drank and laughed a lot through a long meal, until for the second time coffee was dripping down into their cups from little glass filters.

"And now what? There are still hours of afternoon left."

She could see the longing in his eyes, the same longing that she knew he must see in hers.

"I am going to let you choose," she said, taking a Gauloise from him, and this time inhaling just a tiny bit.

"Would you like to see my apartment now?" he asked in a tense voice.

"I would love to," she said, looking him directly in the eyes. She wanted to begin, to learn about love-making, to spend nights with him, to awake next to him naked in bed. What a difference two days could make.

"Then I will call for the check."

The owner, with a dark face as round as a moon, arrived with the check and stood over them as Jean-Luc glanced at it.

"Is everything satisfactory?" The man looked as though he didn't think they had enjoyed their meal.

"It was excellent," Elizabeth said with enthusiasm.

As Jean-Luc took some bills out of his wallet, the owner said, still looking gloomy, "Jean-Luc, it has happened."

"You mean . . . war."

The man nodded his head silently.

"When?"

"Just as you were sitting down. I thought I would wait until you were finished. I did not wish to spoil your lunch."

"The British?" Jean-Luc asked.

"Yes. It was on the BBC. The British Parliament is even now meeting, on a Sunday. Prime Minister Chamberlain has just announced that as of eleven o'clock this morning a state of war exists between England and Germany. France will declare war before the sun is down, that is for sure.

"Oh, Mon Dieu!" the restaurant owner cried, "why did it have to come to this? The stupid politicians." Marc d'Aubigny's very words, she remembered, coming from a very different part of the political spectrum.

After the owner had returned inside, they stared bleakly at each other. They both had for the entire morning deliberately

84

avoided speaking of war.

Jean-Luc looked at his watch. "We have been together in peace for exactly five hours."

"It counts for nothing," she said, "war or peace, we will have each other."

"Are you able to believe that?"

"With all my heart."

"Then you make me very happy. We have done the right thing."

"We have done the only thing. Shall we go to your apartment now?"

"I wanted it to be perfect, but now this imminent declaration of war is pressing down on me like a heavy weight." He looked at her imploringly. "Elizabeth, I . . ."

"I understand. Let's not go to your apartment this afternoon. I can wait . . . but only a little while," she said, in a husky voice, blushing a little. "You will be going south now."

"Tonight would be best. Elizabeth, just this one thing I must do. I beg your forgiveness."

"You do not ever have to ask my forgiveness. All you have to do is come back to me safely. How will you travel?"

"I will drive. There will be no places on trains leaving Paris."

"It concerns the leather notebook in your father's safe, doesn't it?"

"Yes, I want all of them to know that I have replaced my father, and that if the French-Spanish border becomes important again they can count on me, and to know that I can count on them. You can only do this with these people by looking them in the eye."

"When will you be back?"

"I will drive all night. Four or five days to do my business—I will call you every day—and I should be back by Saturday, or Sunday at the latest."

"And then I come to your apartment?"

"Then you must be in my apartment." He looked at her with a desperate longing that made shivers run down her body. "To stay, if that is your wish."

She put both of her hands on top of his on the checked tablecloth. She was so happy she could not speak. Finally, she said the only thing that seemed to make any sense: "I love you, Jean-Luc Cabanasse."

Chapter Seven

Once again Elizabeth stood in the middle of a room, this time the salon of a suite at the Hôtel Meurice in Paris, directing maids in the packing of Leonore Devereux's trunks. Her life seemed to be moving at ever-increasing speed. She thought constantly of Jean-Luc and lived from one telephone call to the next. On Monday he had called her from Perpignan, the largest town at the Mediterranean end of the French-Spanish border, on Tuesday from a smaller town, with an unintelligible name, somewhere up in the Pyrenees mountains that divide France from Spain, and now she was awaiting his last call before Leonore left—without her. She dreaded the scene that would follow this announcement.

The first thing Paula said when she entered the room, a cigarette in one hand and a drink in the other, was, "Well, have you told her?"

"No, I'm a coward."

"What can she do? Have they wired your money?"

"Yes, it's already in the bank."

"You're staying because of Jean-Luc Cabanasse, aren't you?"

She turned to face Paula. She had just as well get it over with. "Yes. I'm very much in love."

Paula flicked ashes on the Aubusson carpet. "Well, you could have done worse. Where is he, by the way? I know you spent Sunday together."

"He had some urgent business in southwest France, around Perpignan, the area he comes from. He's driving back to Paris on Friday or Saturday."

"That will leave you all alone in Paris after mother and I take off tonight. Where are you going to stay? You certainly don't want to pay the Meurice's rates."

Just as well get the whole story out, Elizabeth thought. Paula will find out soon enough. "I have a key to Jean-Luc's apartment."

Paula took a sip of scotch, shook her head and laughed. "You certainly move fast for the shy, retiring girl I knew in Laurel Hill."

"Love does that."

"I guess so. They also say that people in love don't think clearly. You have reservations on the Train Bleu with mother and me and Marc this evening, don't you?"

"Yes."

"And we're going to the Midi, and that's where Jean-Luc is?"

"Yes, I guess you could say all of the south of France is the Midi."

"Well then, why wait here all alone in Paris? When he's done with his business you could meet him somewhere in the Midi and drive back to Paris together. Now isn't that romantic? Also that way neither of us need tell mother that we are not going back to America until it's time for her to sail."

"Oh, Paula, it never occurred to me. And you could come back to Paris with us."

"Now, that's not very romantic. Besides, I have other plans." The phone rang, and Elizabeth quickly crossed the room and picked up the receiver. It was not Jean-Luc.

"Elizabeth? It's Peter. I'm at the front desk. Is my aunt there?"

"No, she's out shopping . . . all day . . ."

"That was Peter," Elizabeth said, putting down the receiver and turning to Paula. "He called from downstairs. He's coming up."

As soon as Peter Warden came through the door Elizabeth knew something was wrong. His face was pale and his expression grim.

"Peter, what's wrong?"

"Natcha's parents. They've been killed."

"Oh, no!"

"The Germans have been constantly bombing Warsaw. Their apartment building took a direct hit. A friend of mine at our embassy there got a message through to me."

"Oh, Peter, I'm so sorry," Paula said and put her arms around him. It was the first time Elizabeth had ever seen Paula show affection to anyone.

"The Germans had no need to bomb Warsaw," Peter said. "The Polish army is already as good as beaten. It's Hitler. He wants to demonstrate to others what happens if you oppose him."

"How cruel, how sickening," Elizabeth said. "How is Natcha?"

"She's in a state of shock, of course. She's at my apartment. The doctor's with her now, and he'll stay until I get back. I thought that if you and Paula could come over . . . it might help her to have some female companionship for a while. You see, I have to return to the embassy. I know it sounds callous, but it's just because Hitler is what he is that I can't let the ambassador down. There is so much to do."

"I can't go, Peter," Paula said. "I can't handle emotional things. It's something that was left out of me. You know that."

"I'll go with you," Elizabeth said. "Paula can stay here and finish supervising Leonore's packing. That still has to be done."

She wanted to ease the strain on Paula, who was telling the truth when she said she was emotionally deficient. She remembered Paula saying to her that morning at the cabin on the lake that she didn't know whether she was capable of love. How awful that would be. She hoped Jean-Luc didn't phone while she was away.

"I live on the Rue Boissy d'Anglas," Peter said. "It's only a short distance from here."

As they walked down the Rue de Rivoli and past the American Embassy, Elizabeth told Peter that not only was Paula staying on in France, which he knew, but so was she.

"Despite the war? I think I understand Paula's motivation, but you?"

"I'm in love with Jean-Luc Cabanasse."

"Ah, so. I can understand how that might happen. What will you do?"

"I was planning on travelling with Leonore and Paula— and Marc d'Aubigny—as far as Nice, and perhaps even meeting Jean-Luc in the south of France, where he is for a few days. But I could stay here to be with Natcha."

"No, Elizabeth. You have your own life to live. There are plenty of friends of hers, and mine, who can help look after her. It's only the first few days I am concerned about. She's strong."

As they rode up to Peter's apartment in the tiny iron cage of a French elevator, Peter said, "Our world's coming apart, Elizabeth. Unluckily, Natcha's parents were among the first, but it's only the beginning."

"I know, Peter, but I'm staying anyway."

Natcha was lying on a chaise longue, with a glass of water

and a pillbox on the table beside her. Her eyes were red and swollen, but even this could not mask her extraordinary beauty. While Peter stepped into the hall with the doctor, Elizabeth sat down in the chair vacated by the doctor.

"We have only just met, Natcha, but I have known Peter all my life, and I want you to know how my heart goes out to you both."

"It was good of you to come. I've never had any tragedy in my life before today. Everything's always gone just as I wanted it. And now . . . but they were both still so young. . . ." She began to cry again.

"I lost my father in an accident. It's not like losing someone to illness. I understand the terrible shock. . . ." She wasn't putting it very well.

"My heart should be full of grief, Elizabeth, but I'm afraid grief has to leave some room for hate. If ever I can do any harm to the Nazis . . ."

When Elizabeth returned to the hotel, the trunks had been taken away. Paula had poured herself another drink.

"This vacation didn't turn out quite like we expected, did it? I'm sorry I couldn't make myself go to be with you and Natcha, but I just couldn't."

"It's not important."

"How is she?"

"She's taking it in a normal way, according to the doctor. Peter says she's strong, and I think she is."

"Jean-Luc called while you were out. I told him you were going with us to Nice, but I didn't think it was my place to suggest he might meet you in the Midi. He said he wouldn't be near a telephone for the rest of the day. . . ."

"Oh, no, and we're leaving tonight. . . ."

"Elizabeth, they have telephones on the Riviera. I told him the train gets into Nice early tomorrow morning and that we were staying at the Negresco. He'll call you there."

How different the atmosphere was in the vast train station from that on the day of their arrival. Then the passengers on the boat train from Le Havre had all been in high spirits, noisy, eager to begin their Paris vacations, shutting out of their minds that these vacations might be brought to an abrupt end by war. Now the crowd was subdued, but there were many more people boarding trains, with piles of luggage, as though they were prepared to be away for a long time.

"Wouldn't you know," Paula said with a laugh, "that mother would end up escaping back to America on the poshest train in the world?"

"It is?"

"Le Train Bleu? Oh, my dear. The Orient Express is shabby in comparison. And the liaisons that have taken place aboard Le Train Bleu. Oh la la!"

Elizabeth looked down the length of the sleek blue train. Stewards in blue and gold uniforms stood in doorways, waiting to help passengers aboard. A chef in a tall white toque leaned out of the galley window. All the women boarding the train were dressed in traveling suits and hats and gloves and stockings. Further down the platform Leonore was engaged, with the same assistant manager of the Meurice who had met them, in overseeing the loading aboard the train of crates containing the spoils of her day-long shopping spree.

"She certainly made up for not being able to stay, didn't she? With all that loot you would think she had been in Paris for five months instead of five days."

"Five days? I can't believe it, Paula. I feel as though more has happened to me since we've been in Paris than in all the rest of my life."

"That may just be. A major love affair, a European war and now a break with Leonore when she least expects it, which may equal in intensity the first two events."

So Paula thought she and Jean-Luc were lovers. Well, if Neville Chamberlain's announcement to Parliament had been delayed for a few more hours they might have been. She had been so passionate and eager on Sunday, but now that Jean-Luc was far away she felt once again a little timid and frightened at the thought of making love with a man.

"I feel bad about what I'm doing to Leonore."

"Don't. Believe me, it's the only way. You don't owe her a thing, anymore than I do." There was a hard cold look on Paula's pretty face that was not attractive. "Ah, here come Marc and Peter."

"You don't think Peter's going to Nice with us after all?"

"Heavens, no. He's just doing the proper thing by seeing his aunt off. Now let's see how he is received."

Leonore greeted Marc with some warmth and allowed Peter a kiss on her cheek, but after a few words with him she turned back to the loading of her purchases.

"You see. Leonore never forgets and never forgives."

The two men approached Elizabeth and Paula, and after the usual kissing on the cheeks—although Elizabeth noted that Marc added a kiss to Paula's mouth—Peter took two calling cards out of his vest pocket and gave one each to Paula and Elizabeth.

"If either of you have any trouble, you are to call me. I have put down my number at the embassy, the duty officer's number, in case I'm not there, and my apartment number." He grinned. "I figure Marc can take care of himself. . . . I don't think the Germans are likely to turn on France anytime soon, at least not until they have finished off the Poles, but you never can be sure with Hitler."

"How is Natcha?"

"She's doing OK. I can only hope that with time . . . We've decided to get married soon. We had planned our wedding to suit her parents' schedule, but now . . ."

"So, you are going to stay with us, too, Elizabeth," Marc said.

"Yes, I've decided to stay in France."

"Good."

Marc looked at her closely, but said nothing more. She was sure he already knew about her and Jean-Luc.

"Are you confident you can get Leonore aboard her ship tomorrow night?" Peter asked Paula.

"Oh, yes. She's scared to death that the Krauts are about to march into Paris. She's sailing on a Swedish ship. The Swedes are neutral, so she won't have to worry about being torpedoed by the Germans, and she has the number one suite, so she won't be able to complain about comfort. Oh, she'll go all right, if not in the best of humor."

There was a whistle blast, the acrid smell of an engine getting up a head of steam, a last few stragglers climbing aboard a train, several tracks down from them, that was already beginning to move.

"Mostly rich Jews," Marc said. "They aren't taking any chances that the Germans won't move right away against France. They'll flee to the Mediterranean and stay with relatives until they see how things play out. I don't blame them. They aren't exactly well-liked in Paris."

Le Train Bleu hurtled through the night at, to Elizabeth, an astonishing speed. Their luxury train passed arrogantly, without even slowing down, through small towns announced by their names on plaques lighted by enameled goose-necked lamps, passed, slowing only slightly, through even large towns, as they sped past crowded station platforms, where anxious travelers awaited other trains to take them south, away from the Germans.

A steward entered the compartment that Elizabeth and Paula shared. Leonore had her own, of course; but the best they had been able to do for Marc was one of the tiny cabins with a narrow bunk intended for the personal maids of ladies incapable of traveling without them.

The steward put down a tray containing two scotch whiskeys in heavy crystal glasses, some nuts and olives, and starched linen napkins embroidered with a floral design.

"Cheers," Paula said, lifting what Elizabeth reckoned was about her sixth drink that day.

"Cheers." Elizabeth didn't care for whiskey, but after five days of turmoil, a strong drink seemed not a bad idea; and with a few sips she did feel calmer.

"Well, we've done it, haven't we?" Paula said, looking out into the blackness of the night.

"You're happy about it, aren't you?" Elizabeth replied, looking down at her glass, and finding to her surprise that half of the whiskey had disappeared.

"Yes. I don't really care what happens to me as long as I'm not bored. Well, I'll care if something terrible happens, I suppose, but I've been so bored sometimes I could have killed myself. I guess a war will take your mind off that."

It was then that Elizabeth understood that at some point, probably at Vassar, Paula had tried, or at least thought about, suicide.

"You're right. War takes your mind off the mundane. You know, when we were up on that mountain in Virginia, that last day, I thought how wonderful it is to have friends; and now here's Peter again, and now Natcha. We'll take care of each other, Paula."

Paula was looking out into the night again, and Elizabeth knew that she was framing a reply; but then there was a knock on the compartment door, and another steward entered with cards assigning them their table places for dinner.

"I'm seated with mother," Paula said. "She has some things to say to me—probably for the last time—so why not. You'll have to entertain Marc."

"I don't mind," Elizabeth said, putting down her empty glass.

"Aside from trays brought to me in my room or Leonore's suite at the Meurice, the only meals I've had in France were in a *brasserie* and a little *bistro* on the Ile de la Cité. . . ."

"Both with Jean-Luc."

"Yes, Marc, both with Jean-Luc." Something told her that from now on what passed between her and Jean-Luc was none of Marc d'Aubigny's business. Perhaps it was that remark about Jews. "So, this is the first really *haute cuisine* meal I've had in France." Her French professors and Leonore—and Eustace—had tutored her about French cuisine.

"The cuisine on the Train Bleu is the equal of the best restaurants in Paris, that's true."

"The *quenelles de brochet* melt in your mouth, and the *sauce Nantua* is a perfect accompaniment."

"Yes," Marc said, a little taken aback, pouring more of the white burgundy—a Montrachet—into her glass.

He had expected the girl he had danced with on the terrace of the cabin on the lake at Laurel Hill, but she was gone forever. Elizabeth knew that she was a little drunk, but she didn't care. She was on—what had Paula said?—the poshest train in the world, headed at great speed for the south of

France, the Midi, as the French said, where the sun shines straight down, headed, she hoped, to Jean-Luc Cabanasse.

"You and Jean-Luc have become close?" Marc asked, a portion of fish mousse poised on his fork.

"Yes."

"He and I are friends, but we disagree about many things. Now, it seems, we disagree about everything. So, who knows what may happen between us in the bad times that are surely coming."

"Marc, what are you trying to say?"

She was surprised at the seriousness of expression on Marc d'Aubigny's cherubic-cynical face beneath the golden-red curls. She was beginning to suspect that there was much about Marc she did not understand.

"What I want to say is that whatever happens between us there is one thing I will never deny. Jean-Luc has great courage."

"Which is to say?"

"That you should know this, that's all. You need never have any doubt about it."

His words were, she felt, a kind of chivalric gesture from someone who knew they might soon be enemies.

Chapter Eight

When she awoke sun was streaming under the curtains. She raised them to see palm trees speeding by in a blur. The sea was a blue that you saw only in paintings. The houses, amid vineyards and orchards of olive and orange trees and clumps of dark spiked cypresses, were all roofed in red tile. So this was the Midi. No wonder Jean-Luc loved it.

"Well, good morning, sleepy head."

She turned over in the bunk. Paula was standing in the open doorway of the compartment in pajamas and a dressing gown. Between Elizabeth and the door was Paula's bunk, which had not been slept in. She had left Paula and Marc having a drink in the bar about eleven in the evening. She looked up at Paula, who gave her one of those familiar ironic smiles.

"Well, it was the least I could do, Elizabeth."

"What do you mean?"

"Marc and I are getting married."

"So that was your neat solution."

"That was it." She stretched and yawned. "Have you ever tried to do it on a maid's cot in a closet?"

Elizabeth did not reply. She had not made love anywhere, and when she had she would never speak of it to Paula or anyone else. However, she found Paula's comment neither shocking, or even surprising—for Paula.

"This is the most fantastically beautiful country I have ever seen," Elizabeth said instead.

"It's paradise, *chérie*. Too bad our villa at Beaulieu is all tied up in mother's mind with the breakdown of her marriage, or we could have stayed there. But the Negresco is not bad digs."

"I can't wait to get off the train and see everything."

"Well, we'd better get dressed. We are coming into Cannes. After that it's only a few minutes to Nice. I've ordered some breakfast brought to us in the compartment."

Soldiers with bored faces, in steel helmets and with fixed bayonets, were posted at intervals along the platform of the Nice train station. Leonore, greatly alarmed, asked if the Germans had invaded France.

"No, madame," the baggage porter said, a Gauloise bobbing up and down in his mouth as he spoke, "just a precaution. That *sale type* Mussolini might try to take advantage of the situation to grab a piece of France. Nice is just thirty kilometers from the Italian frontier, you know."

Leonore did not find this information reassuring, nor was her state of mind improved by the fact that the car they had asked the Negresco to send was nowhere to be seen. Finally, Leonore departed for the hotel in a taxi, taking Paula with her, and leaving Elizabeth to arrange for the delivery of their trunks. The station was in turmoil, with the baggage of those who had fled Paris piled everywhere, and it was an hour before Elizabeth was in a taxi herself.

She paused on the steps of the turreted Hôtel Negresco for a moment and looked down the palm-lined Promenade des Anglais that hugged the long curve of the Baie des Anges. The temperature was perfect, the sea beyond the pebble beach the deepest blue, the mountains behind Nice a pale lavender, and everywhere there were flowers. All that was lacking for it to be paradise was the presence of Jean-Luc; but at the reception desk there were no telephone messages for Mademoiselle Elizabeth Vail.

As she rode up in the elevator she suddenly felt drained. Too much had happened to her too fast. The Germans could invade France at any moment, and she had no idea where Jean-Luc was except somewhere in the wild Pyrenees mountains. Possibly he had not been able to get to a phone, or more likely the phone lines were all busy because of the war. Yes, that was it. It was only with the greatest difficulty that she kept from crying.

As soon as Elizabeth opened the door to Leonore's suite she forgot about her other worries. Leonore and Paula were sitting at opposite ends of the room glaring at each other, both smoking cigarettes.

"So you are deserting me, Elizabeth?" Leonore said coldly.

"You told her?" Elizabeth said, turning to Paula.

"I figured it was best to get it all over with at once."

Elizabeth turned to Leonore. "You don't need me anymore, Leonore." Suddenly she realized that whether Leonore created one of those scenes she was capable of—and which she had so dreaded—no longer mattered to her.

"Why do you suppose I ever needed you? I think what you two girls are doing is extremely foolish, so don't expect any financial support from me. Oh, you'll do all right, Paula. Marc d'Aubigny will be glad to support you till your birthday, when he can get his hands on your money."

"How charmingly you put it, mother." Paula had changed to pink silk slacks and a flowered blouse and looked stunning. She was obviously enjoying the situation.

"But what about you, Elizabeth?" Leonore said, ignoring

Paula's remark. "How are you going to support yourself?"

"I'll get by." Clearly Eustace had not told his sister of the large check he had given Elizabeth.

"Well, so be it, then," Leonore said quite calmly, and it occurred to Elizabeth that she was actually glad to be rid of them. She and her daughter thoroughly disliked each other, and as for Elizabeth's role, once aboard ship Leonore would be pampered by the crew. Then it would be a limousine from the New York dock to her Fifth Avenue mansion, where servants would be waiting.

Elizabeth's hypothesis was confirmed by Leonore's next remark.

"Well, now that I'm rid of my two chaperones, I may just have a little shipboard romance. I'm in the mood for that sort of thing. By the way, where is this ship?"

"It doesn't arrive from Genoa until six this evening," Elizabeth said.

"And doesn't sail until midnight. I'll go aboard as soon as it arrives. You needn't accompany me. Now, you two go have lunch with Marc or something. I want to be alone."

Once again Elizabeth was drinking filtered coffee on a café terrace, smoking a Gauloise cigarette of which she actually inhaled a puff or two. It was a ritual meant to recall Jean-Luc's presence; and it was then that she realized, almost in a panic, that if one has known a man only a very short time, when he is absent it is difficult to recall his image. The only solution, surely, was to be with him for a very long time, so that his image would never leave her.

"Elizabeth, what is it?"

She blinked away tears. "Jean-Luc. I don't know where he is. He hasn't phoned. Europe suddenly is at war. All of that."

Paula reached across the table and took Elizabeth's hands

in hers, and that too was a remembrance of Jean-Luc. Twice that had happened between them, when their hearts were so full of emotion that they had had to reach out to each other in a crowded restaurant.

"You love him very much, don't you?"

"Yes."

"And so quickly."

"Yes. Jean-Luc said the French call it a *coup de foudre*. The lightning strikes."

"Don't worry, *chérie*. He will come to you. You are a very lucky woman to be loved by such a man."

"You have Marc."

"But I do not love him. He is convenient to me, that is all."

"I don't believe that, Paula."

This time Paula's ironic smile quivered a little, and there was a trace of moisture in her eyes.

"He and I are a lot alike. It may not be a bad marriage. Who knows? I might even learn to love him. That is nothing unusual in Europe. Marriages are arranged, and it's the job of the man and wife to grow into love. Only, in this case," and Paula laughed, "I arranged the marriage. Isn't Leonore totally impossible?"

"Yes," Elizabeth said, freed now of her inhibitions with Paula. "She's the most selfish person I've ever known. You are wise, I think, to choose Marc. You two are suited, I believe." Since when had Elizabeth Vail, virgin, become an authority on such matters? She blushed. "What is this mysterious errand you have sent Marc on?"

"To Beaulieu, a small town just down the road, a posh suburb of Nice really, where my family's villa is—and where we have lots of influence—to see if we can cut through all the French red tape, so that we can be married right away in the mayor's office. I wish you and Jean-Luc could both be there."

Elizabeth's eyes filled with tears again.

"Sorry, old friend. Look, the flowers are coming in."

Elizabeth looked across the big empty square, and from every street emptying into the Cours Salaya carts loaded with flowers were emerging, big market umbrellas were being raised, prices were being chalked on pieces of slate. Soon the square was filled with flower stalls. There were not only flowers but stalls of vegetables, ranging from mushrooms the size of a soup plate to golden squash blossoms to bins filled with dozens of kinds of olives. It reminded her of that magic moment when she had emerged from the Paris Métro into the flower and bird market of the Ile de la Cité and glimpsed Jean-Luc. Everything, it seemed, reminded her of Jean-Luc. Where was he? Where *was* he?

Leonore was as good as her word. She said goodbye to Paula and Marc and Elizabeth on the steps of the Negresco, almost cordially, and departed in a hotel car, once again accompanied by an assistant manager, for the boat dock. The big Swedish liner, packed with passengers fleeing Europe, lay just offshore.

That evening Elizabeth excused herself from exploring Nice at night, as Paula certainly knew she would. She did not want to be away from the telephone, and besides, Paula and Marc would want to be alone. It might not be love, but there was certainly plenty of mutual attraction.

Elizabeth had her meal served in Leonore's suite, which she had inherited. As she ate dinner she looked around the empty room and thought how the rooms of the most expensive and most famous hotels were all alike, and how boring that was. No phone call came, and she went to bed but could not sleep. Finally she got up. The lights curving down the Promenade des Anglais were like a string of pearls laid on a tray of dark velvet in a jeweler's window. She watched until the Swedish ship, ablaze with lights, disappeared over the horizon. The early life of Elizabeth Vail had come to an end.

The phone was ringing. The heavy hotel curtains were so tightly closed that it was impossible to know whether it was still night; and there was no clock. Elizabeth raised herself in bed, turned on the light and picked up the phone, her heart beating fast.

"Hello?"

"Bonjour, *chérie.*"

"Jean-Luc. Oh, thank God! Where are you?"

"In Nice."

"In Nice? In Nice? Where?"

"In the lobby of the Hôtel Negresco."

"Oh, mon Dieu!"

"We seem to have dramatic telephone calls," he said.

"What time is it?"

"Ten past nine."

"Give me fifteen minutes and I'll be down." She did not want him to come to her room, not yet.

Elizabeth got up and threw open the curtains. The sea seemed even bluer, if that was possible, than the day before. People were lying on the pebble beach. Pulled by a speedboat, a young woman on waterskis was tracing an arc of white in the blue Mediterranean. The new life of Elizabeth Vail had begun.

The dark mahogany interior of the elevator had three oval mirrors, to the sides and to the back, illuminated by a soft white overhead light. This was, Elizabeth understood well from her time as Leonore Warden's secretary, so that those who served could verify their appearance before entering the presence of their masters. It was no different from the full-length mirror on the back of the dining room door in the Wardens' estate at Laurel Hill, except that those who rode this elevator would walk out like actresses onto a stage to meet their rich and powerful husbands or lovers.

Oh, you cynical young woman! she said to herself, but you are not one of those. You are descending into the presence of the most wonderful man in the world, who has not and never will make any claim on you. Then why, said her large brown eyes with their dilated pupils, set in an ashen face, are you so frightened? Too much, too fast, was all the response that she could muster.

She saw him the instant the elevator doors parted, and she felt the color rush back to her face. He had not yet seen her and she paused to absorb the vision of him, tall and lean, dressed in rough country clothes, unshaven—almost his trademark. He was wrapped around a gilded chair upholstered in pink velvet, until he almost engulfed the puny thing.

"It's a wonder they didn't throw you out," she said, as she came toward him, laughing to steady her nerves. "You look disreputable."

"They were about to until I mentioned the Warden name."

The sound of his voice sent a thrill through her body. Their hands met then, but she suppressed the desire to throw herself into his arms. It was one thing to do that in the flower market in Paris and quite another in the pretentious lobby of the Hôtel Negresco.

"Come," he said, "let's get away from here. Every tail-coated clerk in the place is ogling beauty and the beast."

She took his arm and he led her away, and she thought he looked almost exactly like that first time she had seen him on the station platform at Laurel Hill, except that his face was older, his gaze more intense, even somber. Well, she would cure the somberness!

The sweep of red carpet funnelled them into a great oval room, where beneath a glass dome, inset with panels of nymphs and clouds, little marble tables were set for breakfast.

"Coffee and croissants?" he asked hesitantly, as though he might be imposing on her.

"Yes, please," she said, almost in tears in her relief in seeing in his eyes that nothing had changed. That was what had showed on her face in the elevator mirrors: the fear that a flame that had had only twenty-four hours of her presence to feed on might in her absence have begun to die down.

"Elizabeth," he said, taking her hand, "I thought of you every minute. I tried to phone you dozens of times, but I could never get through. I think the military must have taken over the phone lines. Finally I just got in the car and came to you, hoping you had not given up on me and gone back to Paris. I drove all day and all night to get here."

"I might have left if I had not heard from you today. We have luck with us, do we not?" She regarded the thick black stubble of his beard. "Leonore sailed for America last night, and I have her suite until check-out time at least. Come up there and shave and shower. And then . . ."

"And then?"

"I could put out the 'do not disturb' sign . . . if you would like."

"Yes, I would like that . . . before something else intervenes." They looked into each other's eyes longingly. "But what about Paula and Marc?"

"Did I hear someone take my name in vain?"

They looked up to find Marc d'Aubigny smiling down on them.

"So you made it, Jean-Luc, and just in time. You were all that was lacking."

"Hello, Marc. What do you mean, I was all that was lacking?"

"All we lacked was a best man, that is if you agree to be Paula's maid of honor, Elizabeth."

"Congratulations, Marc," she said with some uneasiness. "When is the wedding to be?"

"This afternoon at four. Paula just went up to look for you."

Elizabeth gazed imploringly at Jean-Luc, but there was nothing to be done. They were to be frustrated again.

"Of course I'll be Paula's maid of honor, but how did you arrange things so quickly?"

"Despite dancing most of the night, Paula and I arose early this morning and went over to Beaulieu and called on the mayor at his home. He was still having breakfast. Given the war, the long attachment of the Warden family to Beaulieu, etcetera, etcetera, he agreed to waive all the usual formalities and marry us this afternoon. Actually, what did it was Paula reminding him that her grandfather was married by the then mayor of Beaulieu. I don't suppose you brought formal clothes with you, Jean-Luc?"

"Not even a suit."

"Come on then, you can shave and shower in my room," Marc said cheerily, "and we'll rent you a proper outfit."

"I'll go find Paula," Elizabeth said, somewhat dazed by the speed of events. It had been constant motion, constant surprises from the moment she had stepped down from the boat train in Paris.

"Oh, there you are," Paula said putting down the phone and picking up a cigarette from a massive crystal ashtray. "You've heard?"

"Yes. Jean-Luc's here and we just saw Marc."

"Oh, great. Then we have a best man."

"How do you feel?" Paula looked pale and tense.

"Knot in my stomach. Things are happening so much faster than I expected, all for the best, I suppose. Get it over with. There's a lawyer coming in a few minutes with some papers. It seems a law was passed in 1927 that says marrying a Frenchman doesn't give you citizenship unless you declare your intention before the marriage takes place."

"You don't have to become a French citizen."

"I'm a coward, Elizabeth. If the war comes to France, I don't want to leave myself the possibility of using my American citizenship to panic and flee home like Leonore."

"That doesn't sound cowardly, Paula. It sounds brave."

"Or stupid."

"You'll go back to Paris after the wedding or to Marc's family's estate?"

"We are going to take a wedding trip to Switzerland first. I've just booked a compartment on the evening train to Geneva. We'll stay a couple of weeks. If the war takes a nasty turn, if the Germans start bombing, for example, we'll stay longer. In any case, the French government is likely to fall now. Depending on what kind of government we have next, Marc may be asked to take a position in it."

"That's really why you're taking out French citizenship isn't it, Paula? If Marc enters politics he'll need for his wife to be French."

"I don't want to talk about it, Elizabeth. I don't know why I'm doing some of the things I'm doing." She turned away and looked out the window, drew on her cigarette, exhaled smoke. "I'm not even sure why I'm getting married."

Chapter Nine

The marriage of Marc Antoine Louis Marie Joseph d'Aubigny and Paula Warden Devereux took place at four o'clock on the afternoon of Friday, September 8, 1939, and was recorded in the marriage registry of the *mairie* of Beaulieu, signed by Jean-Luc Cabanasse and Sarah Elizabeth Vail as witnesses. Jean-Luc explained that all of Marc's names were meant to recall the deeds of noble ancestors, and Elizabeth explained that Paula's single middle name was meant to remind that whomever Leonore may have married she was by birth a Warden.

When the ceremony was over, the mayor of Beaulieu, a rotund, polished little man, made a brief speech to the guests. Some had connections with Marc's family, others with the Wardens. The Prefect from Nice was there, having locked up his confidential files and taken the afternoon off to lend the prestige of his office to the marriage of a Warden—the second, as the mayor recalled—in this same office in Beaulieu. The Prefect even attended the reception at the Villa Warden, driven there in his black official Citroën flying the tricolor of France.

"I've not been here before," the Prefect said to Elizabeth, examining the opulence of the Villa Warden's main reception room with a wary eye, and then adding, lest it be assumed that he did not move in the same social circles as the Wardens and d'Aubignys, "but I've just arrived from Paris. Who was the other member of the Warden family married here?" The tall florid Prefect was missing information that someone in his position should have had at his fingertips, and it annoyed him.

"The bride's grandfather, Augustus Warden."

"Ah, yes, American ambassador to France some years ago." The Prefect looked Elizabeth up and down, in her hand-me-down Balanciaga suit. He had the air of someone who has found a saving grace in an onerous duty he has been obliged to perform.

"And you are a relative of the bride's, mademoiselle . . ."

"Vail, Elizabeth Vail. No, I am just a friend." She tried unsuccessfully to catch Jean-Luc's eye across the room, but he was dancing with Paula.

"Tell me, mademoiselle, did not the bride's mother sail for America last night? I had meant to pay my respects."

"I know it seems curious, *monsieur le Préfét,* but she and her daughter are not on the best of terms," Elizabeth said to forestall further questions.

"Ah. You will be staying long in the Nice area?"

"No."

"You will be returning to America, I suppose, with the war . . ."

"No, I will be returning to Paris, where I live. Excuse me, please."

Paula had at last released Jean-Luc, and Elizabeth went straight to him. "Can we go out on the terrace? I am suffocating."

From the terrace steps wound down to a boat dock, and she led him down until they were out of sight. Then she turned and pressed him against the wall with her body and raised her lips to his.

After they had kissed a long time she released him.

"There, that's better. I thought I would drown in there."

"What is wrong?"

"Wardens. Warden money, Warden clothes, Warden social events, Warden houses. I've come to like Paula, but look what it has done to her. I just want to get away from them, but they will not let me go."

"The reception is almost over. Then I am taking you to Paris. We can even start for Paris tonight, if you want."

"Just tell me what to do and I will do it. But let's not go back in there until the last minute. The guests will have to start making their goodbyes soon. Paula and Marc's train leaves in an hour. Where did they find all those people? And the band and the caterers and banks of flowers and the champagne, all arranged in a matter of hours."

"Marc can be very efficient when he wants to be."

"Paula says he may go into politics if there is a new government."

"If there is a far-right government. Marc's father is well-connected in reactionary circles."

"I know so little about French politics."

They sat down on the steps then, silently holding hands, and watched the sun sink over the Villefranche roadstead dotted with yachts of all sizes, until she overcame her shyness and spoke.

"Jean-Luc, let's not start off for Paris tonight. I want to spend the night here, somewhere in Nice, somewhere—" her voice trembled "—where we can be alone."

He answered by kissing her gently. "There does seem to be a conspiracy to keep us apart."

Motor cars began to start up at the entrance to the Villa Warden, and they rose.

"At last," Paula said as the door closed on the last guest. She turned to Elizabeth and Jean-Luc. "Thank you for everything. I know it was an ordeal, but it was my way of saying goodbye to my family. A farewell ceremony you might say."

"Paula has a finely-developed sense of irony," Marc said.

Paula laughed. "Anyway, sit down. Let's have a final glass of champagne. I don't want to get on that train until it's about to pull out of the Beaulieu station, and when it starts moving it's all over. I'm free forever of my family."

Elizabeth looked at Jean-Luc. She and Paula were moving out at the same time with the same feelings, except that Paula was one of the richest young women in America, and she was . . . in love.

Paula leaned back in the overstuffed sofa and kicked off her shoes. "Well, there's irony enough, I suppose. You know how Augustus Warden acquired this place? By the time he was thirty he had added so much to the family fortune—including several banks and railroads, and a seat on the Exchange—that he felt he could afford to get out of New York for the worst part of the winter, and he came to Nice and put up at the Negresco. And what should he find but that the Madison yacht was anchored at Villefranche that winter.

"The Madisons were even richer than the Wardens, and so Augustus used that winter to woo and win shy young Martha Madison, and they were married in Beaulieu, before old man Madison could have second thoughts. Augustus rented this place from a Belgian industrialist and eventually bought it from him, and turned it into the finest property on Cap Ferrat, completely invisible except from the sea, with this magnificent view of Villefranche.

"Grandpapa held on to it, and by the time mother and Eustace were safely away in Swiss boarding schools and Martha was deeply involved in good works, he had acquired a mistress—Marc's grandmother. What better place to bring her discreetly than here?"

"Paula," Marc said, looking at his watch, "you had better go change. Your farewell ceremony will be quite spoiled if we miss the train."

"All right, I'm going," and she filled her glass with champagne again. "But first, it's customary to give the maid of honor a little present." Paula reached into her handbag and brought out a small rectangular package. "But you're not to open it until we leave."

Elizabeth and Jean-Luc saw Marc and Paula d'Aubigny off beneath the big lantern, just turned on, that hung over the entrance to the Villa Warden. They watched until the red taillights of the Hispano-Suiza disappeared into the umbrella pines that shielded the house from the outside world.

When they came back into the main room, now growing dark, Elizabeth picked up the little package that Paula had given her and unwrapped it.

"What is it?"

"A set of keys," she said, reverting to French, the language of their intimacy, "and there is a note. 'Stay as long as you like. There is a couple who live in a cottage on the grounds, but they will not appear unless you ring for them. I will think of you often, and keep your fingers crossed for me. Paula.'

"The final irony," Elizabeth said. "We are alone at last— in one of the Warden houses."

"But does it matter?" he said, slumped back in the sofa cushions, pulling off each shoe with the heel of the other, revealing silver-gray silk socks matching his tie, pulled away at the opened collar and revealing the dark silky hair covering his chest.

"No, it does not matter," she said from the depths of an overstuffed chair opposite, where she was ensconced like the mistress of a castle under siege, her own shoes thrown out on the sea of oriental carpet. "Being alone is all that matters."

"More champagne?"

"Oh God, no. Do you suppose there is something honest to drink?"

"I will see," Jean-Luc said, getting up and stretching. He picked up the two half-empty bottles of Tattinger from their silver ice buckets and turned toward the swinging doors that led to—oh, how well she knew—pantries with cupboards of piled linens, stacked china, rows of crystal wine glasses.

"Jean-Luc."

"*Oui?*"

"Rumpled formal clothes suit you. Do you remember the last time?"

"Every detail."

As soon as he had passed through the doors to the pantries she got up and crossed over to the sofa, curled herself up next to the depression made in the cushions by his body.

"What could be more honest than this?" he said, coming back into the marbled, mirrored room. "A simple Côte de Provence, like that drunk in every bar up and down the coast." And then he realized he was addressing an empty chair. "Elizabeth, where . . ." He turned and saw her curled up in the sofa cushions, her sparkling eyes looking up at him. He could not know that behind her provocative pose she was still a timid girl who shrank from what this evening was bound to bring—and which she so much desired.

"Ah," he said, plunging the bottle of white wine down into one of the empty silver ice buckets, "there you are. In twenty minutes it will be at just the right temperature, and the lights will be coming on in Villefranche."

"We have all evening," she said, opening her arms to him as he slid down into a confusion of cushions and a Balanciaga gown riding up over silk stockings and garters and Elizabeth's deep sighs and wet warm lips. Now there was no turning back! But then she realized they were not entirely alone.

"Wait, wait!" she whispered huskily, her dress half-stripped from her, her body pressing against him as taut as a coiled spring.

"What is it?" His voice was as tense as her own.

"The couple that lives on the grounds. They could come in, to turn on the lights or . . ."

"They will not come in, Paula said, unless they are summoned, and you do not plan to do that do you?"

"But all the same . . ." Now that she had hesitated, she felt herself shrink back and she sensed he knew.

"Do you remember," he said gently, "what you said to me on that famous walk of ours from Longchamps?"

"I said so many things that day."

"You said that you wanted surprises, risks, even danger. I cannot offer you much, Elizabeth, but I can offer you all those things."

He was looking intently into her eyes, and she felt her breath coming faster and faster.

"I must dare, you mean."

"Yes."

"Oh, Jean-Luc, yes, yes." And with those words the struggle was over.

He bent over her then, undid her brassiere and kissed the taut nipples of her breasts, while she half held him back with one hand grasping his long hair and fumbled to undo his shirt buttons with the other.

In the semi-darkness of the formal room, the last light of day reflecting from the mirrored walls, Elizabeth lay naked at last amid the sofa pillows, held the nude form of the man she had so desired, felt the strangeness of his entering her. The sharp stab of pain was no more than a reminder that they were now one flesh, and after a while came little waves of pleasure, where his lean hips moved between her thighs, little waves that spread in ripples through her entire body.

She seemed to float compassless in warm waters except for the two anchors of her hands, one fiercely holding the back of Jean-Luc's neck, the other gently following the rising and falling of the small of his back. The shudder that suddenly ran through his body and transmitted itself to hers made her cry out in surprise and delight as she rose to meet him in rapid delicious strokes. As their motion finally slowed and stilled, her body gradually returned from warm waters to the crumpled sofa pillows. She ran her hand through Jean-Luc's damp hair. She had never guessed at such pleasure. It had taken her completely by surprise.

Elizabeth opened her eyes and saw waves of light, reflections from water, moving across the ceiling, and for a moment she imagined herself in the cabin on the lake. But it was the Mediterranean that lapped the rocks below a sun-drenched terrace. Could it have been only three months ago that two young Frenchman arrived at the Laurel Hill train station? It seemed incredible, all that had happened to her seemed incredible.

"*Qu'est-ce que tu pense, Elisabeth?*" a warm male voice said.

"Oh!" She turned over. "What do I think? That it is true."

"That what is true?"

"You and me, last night, everything, Jean-Luc. I have not been dreaming."

"You are as beautiful as an angel."

She looked down at her nakedness and was surprised to feel no shame. She smiled and even let her eyes run with frank interest over his long, lean olive-skinned body.

"What was I thinking? I was remembering meeting you at the train station. How much has happened since then, how much I have changed. I was so afraid of leaving Laurel Hill. I was afraid of many things, of life, of change, certainly of sex. . . ."

"And now?"

"And now?" She sighed. How could she explain? "Even last night, as much as I wanted you, I was afraid. And then you took me by surprise, and I took myself by surprise. I had always thought I was not a passionate person."

"Mon Dieu," and he rolled his eyes in the French fashion. "You were like a tigress last night. Whatever gave you the idea you lacked passion?"

"I have always been naturally timid, and then the way I was brought up, I guess. Before she died—I was twelve—my mother made my father promise that I would be raised in the way of the church she belonged to. No smoking or drinking or dancing. . . ."

He laughed. "Or that other thing people do."

"Yes, at least until you are married, and then, I guess, a woman is not supposed to like it. If I had not decided to go to Europe—and it was because of you, although I did not understand that at the time—I could have ended up a dreary old spinster running a photographic studio. . . . Jean-Luc, what is it? There are tears in your eyes."

"It just came over me very powerfully that only a whole series of chance happenings brought us together." He reached over and touched her face as though to assure himself of her presence. "It could so easily never have happened. For a second I had a vision of life without you. . . ."

"Oh, darling, do you not see that it was fated? You will never have life without me. I am yours for keeps." She took him in her arms. "Make love to me again, Jean-Luc. I want to

117

be absolutely certain that I was not dreaming."

"Paula thought of everything. She even had the refriger-ator stocked with food," Elizabeth said, coming out onto the terrace. She put the tray of scrambled eggs, hot croissants and coffee down on the umbrella-shaded table. "Hungry?"

"Ravenous."

"Me too. What a beautiful day. What a beautiful setting. The colors of the sea, the handmade tiles of the terrace, those big clay jars overflowing with geraniums, even that little lizard there on the wall. Yesterday, I saw nothing, my mind was so occupied." She poured café au lait into two cups. "Today I feel *alive,* alive like I have never been before. And all because of us."

"And every day there will be us. Think of that, *chère* Eliza-beth."

"Oh, Jean-Luc, who would have thought, that weekend at Laurel Hill, that by September both Paula and Marc and you and I would be on our honeymoons."

"Except that we are not married."

"Well, no. . . ."

"Would you like to be married? I will be the same to you either way, but if you would like . . ."

Elizabeth leaned across the table and kissed him. "No, I do not wish to be married. I am turning out to be a different person than I had always imagined, a very different person. For now," she said, avoiding the word war, "I would just like to live with you and love you. You will find me very affec-tionate."

"Tigresses are not usually described as affectionate," he said with that crinkling around his eyes when he smiled that she so liked.

"I will be both those things to you."

Later, while she washed their few dishes in the kitchen sink, he casually turned on the little radio on the window sill.

". . . According to both German and Polish sources, the Fourth Panzer division has entered the outskirts of Warsaw, from where the Polish government has already been evacuated. . . ."

With an irritated gesture he turned off the radio. They looked silently at each other.

"Oh, Jean-Luc, can we go home?"

"Home?"

"Have you forgotten that you invited me last Sunday to share your studio?"

"I thought you meant . . ."

"I will forgive you this time," she said, looking directly into those dark eyes, "but you must believe me when I say I am yours for keeps, and I will go where you go. No matter what."

Chapter Ten

Life with Jean-Luc was even more exciting than Elizabeth had imagined, and her expectations had been high. If she was a far different person, she had unloosed something in him that he had not known was there: a sense of light-hearted fun that filled their days with adventure; and she saw that their nights brought that combination of passion and tenderness that she had promised him. Even war, always just over the horizon, did not come. After Hitler's rapid conquest of Poland, an eerie quiet fell over Western Europe. The French called it the *drôle de guerre,* the odd war; the Germans, *sitzkrieg,* the sit-down war; the British and Americans, the phony war.

It was a crisp evening, the first of November. Roasted chestnuts were being sold on Parisian street corners and truffles had come onto the market. Elizabeth climbed the six flights of stairs with her string bag of groceries and unlocked the door just in time to answer the telephone that was ringing. It was Paula.

"Hi, Elizabeth, and congratulations."

"Hi, Paula. Congratulations for what?" It was nice to speak English every now and then, coming up from the ocean of French culture for a breath of air.

"*Vogue,* silly. I picked it up at my hairdresser's in Tours this morning."

"Oh, you mean that little photograph of me in the back pages."

"Simply bursting out of a little black dress."

"That's what they said at *Vogue*," and Elizabeth laughed. " 'If you want to move up front, you're going to have to lose fifteen pounds.' I don't think I can do it. Tonight I brought home a single truffle—that's all I could afford—and a bottle of cream and . . ."

"You're happy, aren't you?"

"More than words can express. And you, Paula?"

"I'm not so strong on domesticity, Elizabeth, but I guess I can stick it out here in the country until Marc gets some position in Paris. How's Natcha?"

"Fine. She got me the assignment at *Vogue*, of course."

"The reason I'm calling is . . . do you think that the political situation would allow us all to get together again? There's a big horse show at Château Aubigny this weekend. Marc's father does it every year on St. Hubert's Day, that's day after tomorrow."

"St. Hubert's Day?"

"The patron saint of the hunt. Don't laugh. They take this kind of thing seriously here. They start out with a St. Hubert's Day mass on the grounds, blessing riders and horses and hounds—you'll want to miss that—and then there's a lot of horse stuff for the rest of the day. I think Peter and Natcha would come. After all it's his job to mix with all political persuasions, but . . ."

"You mean, would Jean-Luc come?"

"Yes. I really want to see you two."

"Of course he would . . . if I ask him . . . and I will."

There was soft laughter at the other end of the telephone line.

"What is it, Paula?"

"It's just too much, that's all. I have become a young French matron, Peter is married just as properly, and you, the

121

quiet Virginia country girl, my mother's unassuming social secretary, are living in sin with perhaps the most desirable Frenchman in all of Paris."

What could she say? It was true. What she said to cover her embarrassment was, "We'll be there."

"Great. It doesn't get interesting until after lunch—when I intend to show them we know a little something about horses and jumping in Virginia. You and Jean-Luc could have a picnic on the way down."

"*Chérie,* what are you thinking?" Jean-Luc said lazily.

"That is what you asked me the morning I woke up in bed with you in the Villa Warden in Beaulieu—a long time ago—and I told you . . . what?"

"That you were thinking of the morning we met on the platform of the Laurel Hill station . . . and now?"

"And now?" Elizabeth said, putting on her underclothes and stockings, pondering her answer. "Now, I just live in the present, for the present. When I think at all it is never of the past, only of the future."

She lay back on the blanket on which they had made love, turned her head away from him, for a while watched the slow flow of the wide river Loire.

"What do you call those high clouds?" she asked, rolling over on her back. "We call them mares' tails and mackerel scales."

"We call them *queues de chat* and *ciel pommelé,* cats' tails and dappled sky."

"In America you see them at this same time of year, when there is often a week of weather when you can, if you find a secluded picnic place like this, lie naked in the grass . . . before winter comes. We call it Indian summer."

"We call it the summer of St. Martin."

"And will the Germans come in this summer of St. Martin?"

"If they do not move in the next few weeks, it will not be until next spring."

"And then we would have months and months yet to live and love."

"Yes."

"But the Germans will certainly come in the spring?"

"Yes." He looked down at her in such a way that she knew that he knew the truth and would not spare her the truth.

"That is a long time away, Jean-Luc. Tell me about Marc's family. Will they laugh at me, at my French?"

He put her head in his lap, stroked her hair. "I do not think anyone French could have made a better chicken with truffles than the one we just devoured; and you have a way with words in French . . . They will find you *ravissante*."

"Marc's father is an ogre, isn't he?"

"That is for you to judge. I am set against him and all that he and his kind stand for . . . but he is certainly charming. Eleven hundred years of breeding, Elizabeth."

"Eleven hundred years?"

"Marc can trace his ancestors back to the reign of Charlemagne."

"*Mon Dieu!* And yours?"

"Well, mine were probably smuggling goods across the Pyrenees for about that long."

The lithe young woman in riding costume came across the sweep of lawn, still green on this early November day, her black cap in one hand, a silver trophy in the other, behind her the dramatic white limestone backdrop of Château Aubigny, half-encircled by a pond reflecting autumn foliage.

"I told you I would do it to them. La Comtesse de Noailles

had to eat second place and is absolutely livid."

"Paula, you look smashing." It was the first time the two women had been able to have a few words alone. Jean-Luc and Peter Warden were off walking in the woods; Marc and his father were riding to hounds with their guests; and Natcha, as the daughter of a prince, was having tea alone with Marc's aunt.

"My looks? Just good grooming. It's required of d'Aubigny horses and women, Elizabeth. Twice a week I go into Tours for hair, facial and nails, the works. It's a big bore. When I come into my money at Christmastime, I'll have the hairdresser and the others out here."

"And what a handsome outfit." Paula was wearing highly polished boots, fawn breeches and a black velvet riding coat, impeccably cut, with white silk stock.

"That has to be just so, too, as I discovered. The old aristocracy are sticklers for dress and protocol and codes of behavior." She laughed. "It's not considered in very good taste to be too fond of your husband either. Young married women are expected to take a lover. Maybe I should have married someone else, and then I could have taken Marc as my lover."

"You're happy, then."

"I suppose so . . . in most things. I want to get out from under the d'Aubignys though, but we're stuck here. We have to dine with Marc's parents every night—and we dress for dinner. Not tonight. I've made reservations for the six of us at a country inn, where they have a superb chef. D'Aubigny *père* will be so taken up with his horsey friends that we can slip away. And what about you, Elizabeth? You look radiant. Your new life obviously agrees with you."

"I'm very much in love, Paula. I had no idea . . ." She stopped and felt herself blushing.

"Good sex, you mean?"

"Well . . . yes . . ." She would not deny it, but she wasn't going to talk about it either. "Paula, if you're not happy here . . . You're soon going to have a lot of money. Why don't you and Marc move to Paris?"

"Move to Paris? If only I could figure a way. Marc loses his exemption from military service if he stops managing our farms—we produce a lot of food—and his father isn't about to risk that. You know that Marc's elder brother was killed in the last war, and if anything happens to Marc the d'Aubigny name will die out."

"After eleven hundred years."

"As I'm so often reminded. If Marc could get a political appointment—they carry a military exemption—we could move to Paris. But that's not possible until there's a right-wing—I mean really right-wing—government. Then his father would be able to use his influence. According to the old man the last six governments in Paris—left to right—have been controlled by communists and Jews."

From the forest came the baying of hounds and the rich sound of a hunting horn. Red and brown leaves spiraled down from the great oaks that surrounded Château Aubigny.

"Jean-Luc thinks the phony war will end sooner or later," Elizabeth said, "and then Germany will defeat France in short order."

"A lot of people in the d'Aubigny circle wouldn't be that unhappy. Then they could install a government like the one in Germany—well, maybe not quite as crackpot as Hitler's—but they're always talking about discipline and authority and crap like that."

"Does Marc feel that way?"

"He's conservative, of course. How could he be anything else? But he's not a fanatic like his father. That's why I want to get him out from under the old tyrant's thumb. Marc doesn't have a lot of strength of character, you know."

"I hope things work out for you, Paula."

"And you, what do you do with yourself in Paris, aside from the care and feeding of Jean-Luc Cabanasse?"

"I think I'm going to try to make a career for myself. I can't just stay home in that little studio all day. I've done some modeling for French *Vogue* . . ."

"And you don't need to lose fifteen pounds."

". . . and I'm also taking up photography again. I'm learning fashion photography by working as an assistant to one of the really top-notch people that *Vogue* uses."

"Good for you. I wish I could do something, but in my social world women don't work. They ride horses and give dinner parties for the same people and fuck their friends' husbands."

"Paula!"

Paula laughed and shook her perfectly-coiffed black hair. "No, seriously, I'm going to have to get us out of this environment one way or another. And couldn't we have fun in Paris? . . . Ah, here they come. The hours' long pursuit of some small animal is over. Now you'll get to meet His Nibs."

From out of the oak and chestnut forest twenty or more men and a half-dozen women on horseback emerged, like tall ships in a sea of dappled foxhounds.

Armand d'Aubigny dismounted his horse, an animal, Elizabeth saw at once, of exceptional quality. He was helped by a groom in livery, who whispered something in his ear.

"So, *ma fille,* you have trounced them all." He was a small, wiry man, older than Elizabeth had expected, with a neatly-trimmed beard that had once been the golden-red color of Marc's hair but was now turning white. *"Même La Comtesse de Noailles."*

"Even the Countess of Noailles, Papa."

"You are an ornament to the family name." The elder Aubigny screwed a monocle into his eye and turned to Elizabeth. "Mademoiselle Vail, without question."

"Yes, sir."

Marc's father bowed and kissed her hand. "I'm not too fond of your country's politics—particularly those of Monsieur Roosevelt—but I can but stand in awe at the beauty of American women," and he made a slight bow in the direction of Paula. "Even the princess, I understand, is half-American. Would that every ancient family in France could renew itself with the blood of such extraordinary women."

St. Hubert's Day and the summer of St. Martin ended together with a squally cold rain that drove a hundred guests in their elegant hunt clothes off the great lawn and into the château. In the confusion three young couples made their escape in an antique limousine normally used to take guests of the d'Aubignys to and from the Tours railway station. Marc drove, with Natcha beside him, and in the back Elizabeth sat on Peter's lap and Paula on Jean-Luc's; and, despite their slow progress down back country lanes in driving rain, they arrived at the *Auberge du Vieux Moulin* more than an hour before dinner would be served.

They trooped into the dark bar in their damp clothes, Marc and Paula still in their riding habits, the rest in the kind of tweedy dress that one wore to country weekends. A few words from Marc produced a bottle of red and a bottle of white house wine, and when glasses were filled, Marc raised his.

"I propose a toast to friendship. *A l'amitié.* Whatever happens, let us not lose that."

After a surprised silence, they all raised their glasses and clinked them together. *"A l'amitié."*

And then, it seemed to Elizabeth, they all retired into their own thoughts on what Marc had meant. To her it seemed an appeal for understanding for things he might be obliged to do, but also, perhaps, a pledge? . . .

"Well," Paula said, looking uncomfortable, most unusual for her, "let's bring ourselves up to date. It's been two months since we were all last together . . ." and then she caught herself and looked at Natcha.

"At the Longchamps racecourse," Natcha finished, "on the day that war began. Since then I have lost my parents, and now my country, but that is my private sorrow, and I ask you not to think of it when you speak. *L'amitié* demands frankness . . . it . . ."

To Elizabeth's relief, Jean-Luc, always calm and steady, intervened.

"Then I'll both bring you up to date and also be frank. First, I continue to write for my . . . left-wing," and he smiled and nodded his head toward Marc, "newspaper, even though it is probably too late now for what I have to say to make any difference. Second, I'm reopening my father's gallery. And third, as you already know, the center of my life has shifted. . . ."

"As it has for all of us, Jean-Luc," Peter said. "In two months two marriages and . . ."

"An understanding," Elizabeth finished, not in the least uncomfortable with her different situation. She was growing day by day into that new self she had not anticipated. "You all know what I'm doing, a little photography, a little modeling, nothing spectacular. . . ."

"Until today," Natcha said, and while the innkeeper's pretty young wife put a plate of hot hors d'oeuvres down on the scarred oak table, she drew an envelope from her handbag, unfolded a sheet of paper, and laid it out on the table. "A proof of the January cover of French *Vogue.*"

"Oh, my God," Elizabeth said, looking down at her own face in three-quarter view. "*Merde,* now I really will have to lose fifteen pounds."

"It's time you were launched, Elizabeth. You have everything it takes . . . and we may be running out of time."

"Running out of time?" Natcha was probably three or four years older than she and Paula, but since that day at Longchamps she seemed to have grown yet older, her delicate beauty intact, but now almost of another generation, like an elegant, worldly aunt. "You mean the war?"

Natcha shrugged, as though it might be more complicated than that.

"And how about you?" Paula asked, turning to Peter.

"The war has changed things. Ambassador Bullitt wants to surround himself with his own people, which does not include the grandson of an ambassador to France appointed by a Republican president, however long ago. If I manage to stay on at all at the embassy, it won't be because my name is Warden."

"Touché, cousin," Paula said with a smile, apologizing in her own way for her taunting of him that first day in Paris at the Hôtel Meurice.

"Now it's your turn," Peter said to Paula.

"Well, I've a little surprise. I've bought an apartment in Paris, just off the Champs-Elysées. If Marc and I can't live in Paris . . . yet . . . at least we can have a pied-à-terre for weekends. We look forward to seeing you all there. Now enough confessions. Let's talk about other things."

Paula looked into Elizabeth's eyes, and Elizabeth thought she recognized an acknowledgment that already a chasm was opening between them. Paula was about to inherit an immense fortune, but she was trapped in a way that Elizabeth was not.

Chapter Eleven

"All right, Max," Elizabeth said, and pulled the gown over her head. "I'll do one more, but that's it. It's past five o'clock, it's Friday evening, and I have Christmas shopping to do."

"And I have a deadline to meet," the chubby little photographer said, adjusting the angle of his Rolleiflex.

She ignored his remark and went over to the full-length mirror, wearing nothing but her panties, to check her hair and makeup. At first it had bothered her to undress in front of male photographers, even when she kept on her bra. Now she thought nothing of it. Certainly no one else did.

"One more," she said. "So, which shall it be?"

Max sighed. "The Chanel, then."

Elizabeth put on the checked suit with braiding and turned in front of the mirror. "It's a perfect fit. It won't even need pinning." It was a perfect fit because she had lost twelve pounds and was hungry all the time.

"It's a knockout on you." Natcha had walked into the studio. "Why don't you wear it home? You can bring it back after Christmas."

"Oh, could I? Jean-Luc and I are going to have dinner at the Café de Paris tomorrow night and then the theater. It's perfect for that."

Elizabeth walked under the floodlights and struck a pose.

"Chin up," Max said, "and turn your left wrist so the braid

shows more. . . . OK. Now, I've got to change film."

"What are you and Peter doing over Christmas, Natcha?"

"Going to a dinner party every night. God, will I be glad when New Year's has passed. But that's how you find out what's going on. Peter's working very hard, and Ambassador Bullitt is beginning to see the advantage of having an officer with good connections on the French far right. Oh, and we are going to the big charity ball at the Plaza-Athenée on the twenty-sixth. I'm borrowing that gorgeous blue Schiaparelli gown for the occasion. There are certain advantages to working for *Vogue*."

"You'll be a sensation, Natcha."

"I want that. I want Peter to be proud of me. I want to make a new life. But this damned war always pursues me. What's worse is that nothing happens. You know it's going to, but you don't know when. Maybe I'm lucky to work all day and go out every night. I don't have any time to think about it."

"OK, I'm ready," the photographer said. "Let's try one in profile and let's see a bit more *cul*." Elizabeth stuck out her behind. "That's good. One more shot seated and I'll let you go."

"Thanks, Max. I'll make it up to you next week."

Elizabeth walked quickly down the Rue Royale, a few months ago ablaze with lights, but now dark. Once war was declared, Paris was Paris only until the sun went down. The City of Light was no more. Heavy curtains covered windows and cars moved slowly, headlights painted blue. During the day things weren't all that different: there were hardly any young men on the streets; the statues in the Tuileries gardens were covered with sandbags; and the most famous works in the Louvre, like the Venus de Milo, had been moved to safer places. But the cafés along the Champs-Elysées were as busy as ever, and the food stores remained full.

She went into the most famous of them all, Fauchon's, and bought some foie gras, a pineapple, bitter chocolate, candied orange peel. The woman at the cash register, with whom she exchanged a few words, didn't even realize she wasn't French. Moving fast, moving far, Elizabeth Vail, she thought.

She crossed the square and paused before the entrance of La Madeleine. From inside the dark church, built in the form of a Greek temple, came the sound of music, the faint glow of candlelight. An oratorio was being performed. She returned to the Rue Royale, turned up the Rue du Faubourg St. Honoré. It was only a short walk to the Galerie Cabanasse. Opposite it the presidential palace, the Elysée, was as dark as all the rest of Paris.

Elizabeth trained her pocket flashlight on the lock and turned her key in it. Once inside, amidst the smell of antique things, she could make out a dim light behind the frosted glass door of the office, where Jean-Luc would be.

She tapped on the glass and opened the door. Jean-Luc was seated at his desk opposite a man she had never seen before, and they seemed to have been poring over a map that was hastily being folded up.

"Er . . . excuse me . . . I was just leaving," the man said, as though he were the intruder. His dark brown hair was cut short, his mustache neatly trimmed.

"My fiancée," Jean-Luc said.

"Delighted. Well, I must be going." His eye fell on a Russian icon of a bearded, angular saint. "I will have to think about it," the man said. "The price seems rather steep. With all the refugees from Eastern Europe, there are lots of icons on the market."

"Not from the thirteenth century."

"Still . . . Well, I must be going," the man said again.

Jean-Luc saw him to the door and out into the darkened street. Elizabeth put down her string bag of Fauchon purchases and hung up her raincoat.

"Where did you get that suit?"

"This little Chanel? No cause for alarm. It's on loan to *Vogue*. Isn't it a beauty?" She put her arms around his neck and kissed him hard. "How do you like the slimmer me?"

"You were sexy enough before. What are you trying to do?"

"Drive you mad. I am just filled with lust for you." It excited her to talk to him like that.

"Then let's go straight home."

"Hm. Yes, I would like that. . . . But first we are going to have a little talk."

"Oh?"

"That man speaks French very well."

"Yes."

"But he is not French. English?"

"Yes."

"And he was not here to look at icons. Why did you call me your fiancée?"

"I had to say something. You know the English. They think that all Frenchmen keep mistresses."

"Well, does not that old-fashioned word rather describe our relationship?"

He laughed.

"Jean-Luc, I had a chat with Natcha just before I left the office. She looks exhausted. She and Peter lead a hectic social life, but I think it is mostly nerves, waiting for the war to come to France, as everyone knows it will."

"It is getting on everyone's nerves."

"Just the point I was going to make. I think it would be

easier for both of us if you confided in me fully."

"You know, in general terms . . ."

"I know in general terms that you are preparing for some kind of underground activity if Germany defeats France—as you are convinced will happen—and that the Galerie Cabanasse is more of a front for your activities than a legitimate business. But that is not enough. I want to help you, and to do that I have to know the specifics."

"The specifics could cost you your life one day, Elizabeth."

"Jean-Luc, I told you that first morning after we became lovers that I was yours for keeps . . . and you are mine. Whatever happens to you happens to me. Those were my terms then, and those are my terms now."

She could tell from the look in his eyes that he knew she was deadly serious. There was a long silence.

"I guess I would do anything not to lose you," he finally said, "even let you risk your life."

"A passion as grand as ours is surely worth such high stakes," she said, her voice light and easy, to cover that it was nearly breaking with joy and relief.

He nodded his head silently, and she knew that he was as much overcome with emotion as she. Now nothing could come between them. She wanted to take him in her arms again but was afraid she would burst into tears. That was not the kind of help he needed.

"Who was that man?"

"A colonel in the British army. He is putting together a clandestine organization to aid British soldiers and airmen in evading the Germans if they overrun France. We were discussing escape routes. If we have everything set up in advance, we will have a much better chance of success."

"Then that is why you went down to the Spanish border

right after war was declared."

"Yes. That was the beginning. I have recruited a dozen people since then."

"Well, as of tonight you have a new recruit."

"I am glad of it. You were right. It was no good trying to protect you by keeping secrets from you. This relieves the tension."

"Now we can go home, Jean-Luc, and I will show you my own special technique for relieving tension."

When Elizabeth awoke the next morning, feeling deliciously bruised, Jean-Luc had already left. A misty Paris winter rain was falling. On an impulse she phoned Paula.

"Nothing special, Paula. I just thought it would be nice to talk."

"Glad you called. I'm taking the three o'clock train to spend Christmas in Aubigny-sur-Loire. Are you free for lunch?"

"I sure am. Jean-Luc has got some business in Neuilly today. I wasn't looking forward to a rainy Saturday alone."

"Meet you at Prunier's at twelve fifteen, then? We can start with raw oysters, followed by sole in some hideously rich sauce."

"Yum. I'll go off my diet for that."

By the time the taxi pulled up in front of Prunier's, the misty rain had become a steady downpour, and a doorman in galoshes ushered her to the entrance beneath a big black umbrella. It was bright and warm inside and Paula was already seated on a red velvet banquette in a corner. Elizabeth slipped in beside her.

"What a treat. I'm so glad I decided to call you this morning. I was beginning to feel depressed."

"Everybody's got the blues, Elizabeth. In half an hour this

place will be full, with people who want to get away from the rain and cold, the blackout curtains at night, the anxiety about what's going to happen. The only consolation of this wretched winter is that—if it goes on like this—we won't have to worry about a German offensive until next spring."

"Please, Paula, let's not talk about the war."

"Sorry. So, how is it with you, aside from now being the most beautiful woman in the Western world? How did you manage that?"

"I've lost some weight, of course, and they really teach you how to use makeup if you work for *Vogue*. That's about all. You look pretty good yourself, by the way."

"I've carried good bones, good grooming and expensive clothes about as far as they can go. From now on it'll be down hill. Yesterday was my twenty-third birthday, you know."

"I knew it was just before Christmas."

The headwaiter handed them large menus in leather folders.

"Could you manage a dozen oysters?" Paula asked.

"I sure could."

"Two dozen *fines claires*, then, and afterwards . . . we could have the sole in cream sauce with shrimp and mussels or . . ."

"Don't go any further, Paula."

"The *sole dieppoise*."

"Yes, madame. And to drink?"

"Elizabeth?"

"You choose."

"A Muscadet with the oysters and a really good white Burgundy with the sole."

"Thank you, madame."

The headwaiter left with a flurry of instructions for waiter, busboy and *sommelier*.

"What news, Paula?"

"The obvious. Yesterday I met with my Paris lawyers for nearly two hours, signed a bunch of papers. Now I am free of my mother . . . of all the Wardens . . . except Peter, but him only as a friend. And, of course, I am very rich."

"And happy?"

"For the first time the possibility, at least, is out there. But first I have to break Marc loose from *his* family. That's where money will help. I've pretty much got the plans for the Paris apartment I bought *en train*. The decorators should be done by the end of January, and then gradually I'll begin to wean Marc away from Château Aubigny, if . . ." But they had agreed not to speak of the war.

"You have plans for children?"

"That's the problem. I don't give a damn about the continuation of the eleven-hundred-year d'Aubigny line. Marc's parents think I'm trying to get pregnant, but I'm doing everything possible to prevent it. Can you imagine me a mother?"

"How does Marc feel?"

"He goes along."

"But how does he feel?"

"I'm not sure. . . ."

A silver tray bearing two dozen transparent greenish *fines claires* oysters was delivered to their table with a flourish. The two women fell upon them as though they were starved— Elizabeth, at least, was—downing them with lemon juice and brown bread and sweet butter, drinking the liquid out of the shells.

"And your news, Elizabeth?"

"I'm working pretty hard. I think I'll eventually make a good model—forget that *Vogue* cover, which by the way is out today. That was just a fluke, with lots of help from Natcha. But what I'm really interested in is photography. The man who takes most of the pictures of me, Max Bonnet, is really good. I help him develop and print, and he lets me do a little bit of shooting myself."

"What about the important part of your life?"

"Jean-Luc? What can I say? He is everything to me."

"Marriage?"

"No. I'm not the person I thought I was."

"You're not the person *I* thought you were. I wish I knew what your secret is."

The word "secret" caused Elizabeth to stiffen. She had persuaded Jean-Luc to reveal everything to her as they walked from the Galerie Cabanasse to their apartment. He had said that that knowledge might cost her her life one day. She knew it could cost him his. Neither Paula nor anyone else would ever have a hint from her of the secret life that she and Jean-Luc now shared. As a child she had learned well to keep her thoughts, her aspirations, hidden from others. She could never have guessed that one day lives might depend on that talent of hers for secrecy.

Chapter Twelve

"I hate you, Elizabeth."

"You should love me, Max," she said, and laughed. "You taught me everything I know, and if this show is a success you deserve the credit." She had not told him that she had worked two years as a photographer's assistant in Laurel Hill, Virginia, and had already known most of the tricks of the trade.

"The only thing you could have learned from me is how to take pictures of skinny, neurotic women in clothes they could never afford themselves . . . but these," and Max Bonnet waved a plump hand at the walls of Paula d'Aubigny's elegant apartment, "I could never . . ."

"Cécile, may I present the author of these photos, Mademoiselle Vail," Paula said, with the old ironic tone in her voice. "Elizabeth, may I introduce the Duchess of Nevers."

"I don't understand how you did it, my dear," the tall, thin woman with white hair and black eyebrows said, "and you're not even French. But these persons you have caught in the streets, under bridges, in the fog, lying in the grass of the Bois de Boulogne, they are, why, they are Paris itself."

"Thank you, madame."

"I hate you," Max said again, as the duchess was steered away by Paula. He kissed her hand and veered off to where champagne was being served. Good old Max!

She looked around the high-ceilinged room papered in

crushed bamboo fabric, and her silver-framed photographs of Paris, taken with the Leica that Jean-Luc had given her for Christmas. And then she saw them. How and when had they slipped in? They had certainly not been invited. It was no doubt part of the game. Alain was at one end of the room, examining one of Elizabeth's photographs; Nicole, at the other end of the room, was looking at another. She did not know their real names and probably never would. All she knew about them was that they both claimed to have English fathers and French mothers. They certainly spoke both languages perfectly. Could they be husband and wife . . . brother and sister?

"Félicitations," Marc said and kissed her on both cheeks. He still smiled, still had his golden-red curls, still feigned a kind of nonchalance. But caught between his aristocratic family and his immensely rich American wife, between the reality of a European war and his own poetic dreams, Marc d'Aubigny's cherubic look had—in the less than a year that she had known him—begun to fade.

"What next, Elizabeth? Your face on the cover of *Vogue*, your photographs admired by *tout Paris*. . . ."

"The first thanks to Natcha, the second thanks to Paula."

"You are too modest. But what next?"

"I suppose it depends on that man Hitler," she said. She wanted to know what Marc thought, or at least what he would say.

Marc shrugged. "The war seems to have gone elsewhere. The Russians have conquered the Finns, we and the British are fighting with the Germans over Norway. . . ."

"Then you don't think the Germans mean to invade France?"

"Not if we use our heads."

What did he mean by that? "And what about you, Marc?"

"I would like to get off the farm. But you know my situation. The government has finally changed, but now, instead of Deladier, we have as Premier that pro-British Paul Reynaud, egged on by his military adviser, Colonel de Gaulle, who is determined to see that we do fight the Germans. My father is in a constant rage."

She hadn't meant to say it but she did. "Marc, what do you care what your father thinks?"

Before Marc could answer Peter Warden was at her side. That was the way it was at receptions and cocktail parties. No conversation ever gets finished.

"Hello, Marc. Congratulations, Elizabeth."

"Thanks, Peter. Haven't seen you in a while. Where's Natcha?" As she turned toward Peter, she sensed Marc walking away. Was there something between him and Peter?

"Home sleeping. She's exhausted."

"You two should let up. You look pretty worn out yourself."

"There are times when you have no choice, Elizabeth."

As Marc had lost his look of a poetic cherub, Peter Warden, with whom she had petted in the grass at age fifteen, had lost his look of pampered innocence.

"No choice?"

"We've got to make Washington understand. . . ."

"You're happy, aren't you, Peter?"

"Happy?"

"To be dead tired, to be doing something really useful for your country. . . ."

"That is, not having every way smoothed for me by Warden money?"

"Yes, I guess that's what I meant." A year before she would not have dreamed of speaking to a Warden in that way.

"You know, Elizabeth, there was a point—I won't tell you

when—that I seriously thought of defying my family and asking you to marry me."

She gasped. "You, what . . . ?"

"But I think that things have turned out for the best for both of us, you and Jean-Luc, me and Natcha. . . . By the way, where's Jean-Luc?"

"He had some business to attend to. He'll be here shortly . . . I think."

"Then why don't you come out on the terrace with me for a minute. It's not often that you get such a beautiful day as this in Paris in April, despite what the tourist office says."

Peter put a hand firmly under her elbow and guided her through the French doors onto the wide terrace, which was lined with big vases of newly set-in hothouse plants and looked down on the Arc de Triomphe. It was indeed a beautiful, warm spring day, but that was not the point.

"What is it, Peter? This talk, out of the blue, of having wanted to marry me . . . you're squeezing my arm, you know."

"Sorry. It's only a matter of weeks."

"Peter, what is only a matter of weeks?"

"The Germans are about to attack France. All of our best sources agree on it. You must return immediately to the United States. Take Jean-Luc with you. I know he's involved in certain things. . . . I can arrange a visa for him."

She stiffened. "Why should we? What about you and Natcha?"

"I have diplomatic immunity. Nothing's going to happen to us. But . . ."

"Ah, there's Jean-Luc now," she said, waving to him through the glass, greatly relieved not to have to continue this conversation that she did not know how to handle.

★ ★ ★ ★ ★

"It is time we had a little talk, Jean-Luc," Elizabeth said, lighting one of those tarry Gauloises she was becoming accustomed to.

He laughed. "You mean like the time you caught me with the British colonel."

"What is his name anyway?"

"I have no idea."

She was silent for a while, not sure how to proceed. As they sped down the narrow road bordering the Seine, lights were beginning to come on at country inns and weekend cottages along the river's edge. Jean-Luc drove his old Citroën with the same calm competence he did everything he put his hand to. It was the same car, she remembered with pleasure, that had brought them back from Beaulieu to Paris in September. They had taken three leisurely days for the journey through the beautiful French countryside in early autumn—and three nights of introduction to the gentle ways in which a Frenchman—a Catalan he would say— makes love to a young woman.

"No more than you know Alain's and Nicole's real names?"

"That's right."

"If they need that kind of protection, they must be facing real danger."

"They are with British intelligence, Elizabeth. If the Germans overrun France they will need all the protection they can get."

"That is just what I want to talk about. Peter says his embassy believes the Germans will attack France in the next few weeks. He offered to get you a visa so we can go to the United States."

"That is the one thing I cannot do."

"I was sure you would say that, but Peter also said that he

knows you are involved in something."

"*Merde!* We have not even got organized and already there has been a leak."

"You can trust Peter."

"That's not the point. Someone has been talking. The day may soon come when any leak could be fatal. Elizabeth, are you sure you want to continue with this? Because after tonight it will be difficult to turn back."

"You could turn back, too," she said softly.

"*Pas possible.* "

"Why not?"

"I saw what was coming early on. I have made preparations while there was still time. I have got the contacts to make this work. Also, fascists murdered my father. I could not live with myself if I turned back now."

"I accept that. So then, there is no question of my turning back. You know what my terms are. I go where you go."

He turned to her with a pained expression on his face. "I apologize. I owed you more respect than that."

"The male wanting to protect the female from danger is perfectly natural, and I understand." She stroked his leg. "But with you and me it is different. I knew that from the first day. I also told you that first day that I wanted a life that included risk, even danger. Living dangerously with you would be, for me, living at the highest pitch. What more could a girl ask?"

He laughed. "You are amazing. You have been in France less than nine months and you have succeeded as a model, a photographer, and now you want to become a secret agent."

"Look at it this way. For the first twenty-two years of my life I did nothing. I am making up for lost time. But you forgot my greatest accomplishment."

"What is that?"

"Virgin from a small town in Virginia beds the most desirable man in Paris." That was the way Paula had described Jean-Luc, and Elizabeth wanted him to know it.

He laughed again. "I was taking myself too seriously."

"A bit."

"And you are not afraid of risk, are you?"

"Oh, I will probably be scared as hell when the time comes, but I will make you a good agent. I have steady nerves and am secretive by nature. By the way does this organization of yours have a name?"

"It is called the Orchard Net. Each member has a fruit as a code name, and mostly people in the net do not know each others' real names."

"Do I get to choose my own name?"

"Bien sur."

"Then I will be Peach. Just think of something that is delicious and sweet and just hanging there waiting to be plucked anytime you feel the urge."

"I will keep that in mind."

"Tell me, what were Alain and Nicole doing at my show today?"

"To see me and agree on a time to meet tonight, and for me to get directions to where we are going."

"And where are we going?"

"They have rented a summer cottage on the Seine, right on the water, surrounded by forest. There are no neighbors. They will train my people there in the technical side of this business we are about to get involved in."

"They seem awfully young to be experts at anything."

He smiled. "Our age. The Colonel tells me they are among the best people he has."

By the time they reached the cottage at the end of an unpaved road through the woods, the Seine was aglow with the gold and red of the sunset. Smoke rose from the chimney of the cottage against which leaned some fishing poles. A flagstone path led to a little dock where a rowboat was moored. It all looked very innocent.

"What we will try to do tonight," Alain said, "is to show you what we intend to teach your people. How many are there?"

"There are sixteen of us in all," Jean-Luc replied. "I could have had twice that number, but I will not take anyone I am not absolutely sure of."

"You're right about that," Nicole said. "Unless security is very good indeed, you will soon be out of business."

Alain paced the room as he talked. Nicole was sprawled in a leather chair by the fire, her legs dangling over the arm. They both wore turtleneck sweaters. He was small and pale and intense, with a short neat beard. She was also small, with large dark eyes and her hair in a boyish cut. Elizabeth had the impression they might have both been teachers at upper-class English schools before the war.

"How many of your people are women?" Alain asked.

"Eight, including Elizabeth. Half and half."

"That's good. It is essential to have a fair number of women. There is always a suspicion in wartime of young men in civilian clothes."

"Also," Nicole said, "women are better at some things than men, such as setting explosive charges. But your group will not be doing any of that, I suppose."

"No. My agreement with the Colonel is that we are available exclusively to smuggle allied military caught behind enemy lines back to their units."

"And we consider that damned important," Alain said. "If the Colonel had his way we would send you some fully-

146

trained people from England to augment your group. But as you can imagine, not everyone in London is convinced that the Germans will defeat France. So until that actually happens, about the most he can do is to send Nicole and myself to repeat some of the lessons we have been taught."

"And remember that Adolph Hitler is not Kaiser Bill," Nicole said. "What your people have to understand is that the Nazis are beasts. We now have plenty of information on what happened after they conquered Poland. They murdered thousands of innocent Poles, intellectuals and others, who they judged might have become the focus for resistance to the German occupation."

"So, rule number one is," Alain said, "do not get caught. If any of your people are caught they should know as little as possible about the identities and activities of others in the group. If they are arrested by the Gestapo, you can expect them to be tortured to extract from them what they know."

"Hardly any of my people know each other," Jean-Luc said. "I have recruited them separately, and they will know each other only by code names."

"Good. You have the right approach. You will also want to break your people up into teams of four or five. Good communications are essential. Each team should include a wireless operator."

Alain opened a large suitcase and took out a rectangular metal box covered with dials. "This is a transmitter-receiver for morse code messages. With it you can send from anywhere in France to London, as well as communicate with each other. This is a set of crystals, each cut to send on a different frequency. If one changes frequencies often it helps avoid detection. This is a one-time pad for encoding and decoding messages. It gives you an unbreakable code."

Then he drew an ugly looking weapon out of the suitcase.

147

"Belgian automatic pistol. Pistols are not very accurate beyond fifteen or twenty feet, so just keep firing with it until you hit something."

"I do not know if I could use a pistol," Elizabeth said. She had actually been a fairly good shot. But after her father had been killed in the hunting accident, she had never touched a gun again.

"You will have to learn, Elizabeth," Nicole said. "*C'est la guerre*. We all are learning things that we wish Herr Hitler had not obliged us to learn."

"I want to do what I can to help."

"There is a lot to learn. If you are going to be smuggling soldiers and airmen out of France, hardly any will speak French, so somebody will have to accompany them. You have to learn how to spot someone who has you under surveillance, how to evade the enemy, how to make up stories to get yourself out of tight scrapes."

The session with Alain and Nicole lasted until midnight. "Well," Jean-Luc said, as they drove back along the Seine, "what do you think?"

"It is scary, very scary, but it is also exciting. We are going to have to be very careful from now on, aren't we, very professional?"

"Yes, very."

"So what is your code name, *cher ami?*"

"Mango."

Chapter Thirteen

She was awakened by the wail of a siren. Air raid alerts were nuisance enough at any hour, but why in the middle of the night? Or was it the middle of the night? She turned on the bedside lamp. Five a.m. The siren's scream descended in pitch, faded away. Jean-Luc slept on. No one actually went to the air raid shelters, particularly if you lived up six flights of stairs. She turned off the light and went back to sleep.

Elizabeth was next awakened by the phone ringing. Now there was enough light seeping through the curtains to see the face of the clock: a quarter after six. Jean-Luc was speaking over the phone in cryptic monosyllables. The conversation was brief.

"Well?"

"That was Mademoiselle de Fraise."

"Huh?"

"Strawberry."

"Ah, Nicole. And?"

"What date is it today?"

"May 10."

"May 10, 1940. Well, mark it in your diary. *Les jeux sont fait.*"

"The bets are placed? Sorry, I am not quite awake."

"The Germans have invaded Holland and Belgium. So much for the Maginot Line."

"France is next, you mean."

"Of course. The Low Countries are of no interest to the Germans, except as a big broad highway leading to Paris."

"I am sorry, *chéri*. I am sorry you were right." She touched the dark stubble of his beard. How she loved it, to feel it rubbing against her cheek and neck as they made love.

"Well, at least it has begun. It is better than waiting."

"Did Nicole say anything else?"

"That she and Alain have received orders not to try to return to England. They are to stay and work with us."

"I am glad. It gives me more confidence."

"Tu as peur?"

"Of course I am afraid. I am not a fool. But I will be a good soldier. You will see."

She sat up and pulled her nightgown over her head.

"What are you doing?"

"What does it look like?" She took him by his shoulders, turned him on his back and covered his body with hers. "Now, just lie there and let me do the work. I am feeling very frisky this morning."

Afterwards they lay quietly for a while, and she knew that his thoughts, like hers, were on what would happen to them now that war was a reality.

"Jean-Luc, when did you first want me?"

"That weekend at Laurel Hill."

"And what did you think of me then?"

"That you had not dared to live and that if you would only break loose . . ."

"Well, you were certainly right there. All it took was the courage to come to France, and you gave me that. Now I wake up every morning just glad to be alive. Suppose I had changed my mind?"

"Then I would have come back to America for you."

"You felt that strongly even then?"

"Yes. I was not about to live without you."

"I do not need to tell you my feelings." She turned on her side and looked into his dark eyes. "But it is also nice to be able to respect the man you cannot help loving. Jean-Luc, I am very proud of you and what you are doing, and I will be at your side. But both of us, darling . . . we must stay alive."

"I understand you. I will take no unnecessary risks."

"Good. Now go have a shower while I make coffee. You have a busy day ahead of you."

After she had put on the coffee, Elizabeth went out on the little back terrace, with its arbor framing the Eiffel Tower. It was a perfect day, not a cloud in the sky. Soon the news would be on the radio. All over Paris, in thousands of apartments, women would be thinking of their men and wondering, will he come back to me?

And then she cried a little, because she wanted that over with. After all, she was one of the lucky ones. She did not have to wait at home, not knowing. What she would have to do she did not know nor could anyone say. That was being decided two hundred miles away under a beautiful spring sky. . . . The phone was ringing again. It was Peter.

"Have you heard?" His voice was as taut as a violin string.

"Yes, we've heard." She tried not to let the tension show in her voice.

"Natcha tells me you are doing some fashion shots this morning."

"That's right, although it now seems sort of pointless."

"Could I see you for a few minutes afterwards?"

"Sure. I should be finished by eleven-thirty, if Max doesn't get artistic-temperamental on me."

"How about the Crillon? It's just across from the embassy,

151

and I can't be away for more than a few minutes. You understand my situation."

"I understand. I'll meet you in the Crillon bar." She wondered if Peter was up to the pressure that he would now find himself under.

In fact, Max was very artistic-temperamental that morning, and who could blame him? Who could blame anyone for how he acted on this morning when the world was falling apart? Who could blame her for stamping out of the studio in a rage at a quarter till eleven? She walked down the Rue Royale, her heels clicking angrily, still wearing the dress she had been modeling, turned into the Hôtel Crillon, went into the bar. According to the clock above the long mirror it was just past eleven.

The bartender looked up from polishing glasses, arranging the tools of his trade. Although the bar opened at eleven, there were few customers before noon, when the two waiters arrived. The bartender's eyes narrowed. Good-looking young women who arrived early and unescorted in the bars of fancy Parisian hotels were generally of a certain kind.

"A double cognac," she said, sinking down into an overstuffed chair, daring the bartender with her eyes to question her in any way.

"A double whiskey-soda," Peter Warden said to the bartender. "I don't usually drink like this before lunch, but I need to unwind. I haven't been to bed at all. Ambassador Bullitt gave a dinner last night for Prime Minister Reynaud. Dorothy Thompson—the journalist, you know—was there, some British air marshal, and, can you imagine, Dautry said . . ."

"Peter, I don't know who Dautry is."

"The French Minister of Armament . . . he said that he

was convinced Germany would not attack France during 1940, and he was basing the production of weapons for the French military on that assumption. Even as he was speaking, German tanks were moving toward the Belgian and Dutch borders. . . ."

"How bad is it?"

"It seems very bad, though the Germans have the advantage of complete surprise. Maybe tomorrow or the next day the British and French can regroup . . . or maybe not."

"And if they don't?"

"The Germans could be at the gates of Paris in two or three days. . . . That's why I need to talk to you, Elizabeth, to say some things in private before Paula shows up."

"Paula? What is it you need to keep from her?"

"She's a d'Aubigny now, and you . . ."

"Ah." She understood.

"I have family obligations—and I consider you family—that I won't have time to attend to if events continue on their present course. For the first time in my life I'm in a position to do something for—what?—my country?—I'm not sure, but my work must come first."

"I understand, and I'm glad for you . . . and proud of you."

"Thank you." He looked at her gratefully. "But what I wanted to say is that I felt that I had to warn you—what I hinted at that day on the terrace of Paula's apartment—that if the Germans gain control of France, Jean-Luc is a marked man."

"Oh, dear. How did you find out what he is—we are—doing?"

"So you are involved too."

"I soon will be."

"Be careful, Elizabeth."

"We won't take . . . any unnecessary risks. That's all I can promise. But how did you know?"

"From the British. They have an informant in the German government. He told them the Nazis have a list of people working against them who are to be detained if they conquer France. Jean-Luc is on that list."

Suddenly she felt sick. And the Germans might be at the gates of Paris in two or three days.

"Thank you for telling me, Peter."

"If I learn anything more I will let you know."

"I know you will." She didn't want to talk about it anymore. "Natcha wasn't at work today. How is she?"

"She was up all night, too. She has a splitting headache. The Nazis, you know . . . her parents . . . the thought that the Germans may enter Paris."

"But she is protected as the wife of an American diplomat, isn't she?"

"Certainly . . . unless bombs start falling. That's what she has nightmares about. She saw some German newsreel footage of Warsaw being bombed . . . she saw . . ."

"What, Peter?"

"The building in which her parents lived being hit."

"Oh, my God."

"Now it's Paris's turn."

"I can't conceive of Paris being destroyed."

"No, but then the Nazis themselves are inconceivable. But there they are, like some hideous dream come to life. . . . Ah, there's Paula."

"It's almost a relief, isn't it?" Paula said, sitting down and taking off her hat and gloves. "The make-believe is over. My friends have been saying all week that Mussolini was negotiating a settlement with Hitler, that Roosevelt was, that somehow peace was going to be saved. No fairy godmother this time. You look tired, Peter."

"I was up all night, and I have to go back to the embassy in just a minute. Are you going to remain in Paris?"

"I'm on my way right now to catch a train for Aubigny-sur-Loire, while it is still possible to get on one."

"Have you considered going home to America?"

"No. I've made my bed and now I must lie in it."

"Shall I send a telegram to your mother letting her know that you are all right and where she can reach you?"

"No, Peter. It would just be hypocritical. She doesn't care about me, and I don't care about her."

A blond young man approached their table.

"Hi, Peter. No, don't get up."

"Chris Welles, Associated Press. You know my cousin Paula, and this is Elizabeth Vail."

"Hi. Care to swap war stories, Peter?"

"I don't have any. We've lost contact with our embassies in Brussels and The Hague."

"Then you can have mine free. I was just talking to a French general. Things are going to hell in a handbasket. The Dutch have opened the dikes and flooded their country, but the Germans anticipated this and have dropped thousands of parachutists around Rotterdam. Well, that's all for now. Stay tuned. Can I drop around to see you tomorrow, Peter?"

"Sure."

After the AP man had gone Peter stood up. "Well, I'd better get back. You both know how to get in touch with me if . . . you should need to." He leaned over and kissed Paula and Elizabeth on the cheek. "Good luck."

"Good luck to you, Peter."

They watched him move away and then turned to each other, two women alone.

"I'm glad you were here, Elizabeth," Paula said. "I want you to take the key to my apartment. I've told the concierge that you can use it whenever you want. Who knows what's going to happen? It may come in handy."

"But won't you be coming back to Paris on weekends, at least . . . that is, as long as the worst doesn't happen?"

"You mean the Krauts goosestepping down the Champs-Elysées?"

"Yes."

"No, I won't be coming back in any case. Old man d'Aubigny has taken to his bed with his heart ailment and turned over the family's destiny to his son. It seems to have had a profound effect on Marc. He called early this morning to tell me in no uncertain terms that I am to retire to the country for the duration. And you can see how quickly I obey my lord and master."

Elizabeth looked incredulously at Paula.

"Surprised? So was I. And what a relief. As soon as I put down the phone I realized what had been wrong all these years. I wanted to be dominated. But with my money and my will and my sharp tongue, nobody dared. What I really wanted was to find someone who would make me obey. Maybe now I can actually be happy. Elizabeth, your mouth is hanging open."

"I'm flabbergasted, that's all."

"Don't misunderstand. When I say domination I don't mean the tie you up and spank your bare behind kind. I mean that it is possible that my real nature is to be an obedient wife."

"Well!"

"And as long as I am baring my soul, as I imagine a lot of people are doing this awful day, I know that you've never liked me. . . ."

"That's true only up to that weekend at the lake on your family's place in Virginia."

"And then?"

"Then I felt sorry for you. But since we've been in France we've been friends. . . . At least I hope you feel that way."

"Thanks, Elizabeth. We're going to need friends. What's coming will not be easy . . . for either of us. Just remember one thing. From now on you can count on me as I know I can count on you, for help when the going gets rough. And I don't mean money . . . though you can call on me for that as well. I think I am beginning to pull myself together. But being the obedient wife does not mean that I have to share the politics of the d'Aubigny family. Just remember that."

Elizabeth saw Paula off outside the Crillon in a taxi headed for the Gare d'Austerlitz and a train to Aubigny-sur-Loire and her destiny. Then she turned and walked quickly across the Place de la Concorde and up the Champs-Elysées. The weather was superb. She drew up a chair to one of the scores of outdoor tables at Le Colisée and ordered a sandwich and a glass of red wine, tried to sort out all the impressions of this turbulent morning of the first day of war for France. If others were doing the same it was not apparent. The crowded sidewalk café was filled with lively talk and laughter.

She brooded for a while over Jean-Luc and the appalling news that he was on a Nazi wanted list. As for the others, Peter and Paula and Marc had made their decisions. That left Natcha. And this reminded her that she was wearing a dress that had to be returned to Balanciaga in the evening, and that her own clothes were hanging from a hook in the *Vogue* offices' dressing room. And then she should, at the least, go back to the office and apologize to Max for losing her temper—though he should apologize to her as well!

At *Vogue,* the dressing room had a strong female smell like, Elizabeth thought, the Laurel Hill College gym locker room. Two of the Russian models were playing cards in their underwear, smoking Sobranie cigarettes. Most of the models were from Russia or Eastern Europe, tall with high cheekbones. Hardly any Paris models were French. These two were stunningly beautiful, but what their lives were after they left the *Vogue* offices she had no idea.

"Max in?"

"Not back from lunch," one of the models said in a heavy Russian accent.

"Probably drunk," the other said. "Who would blame?"

Elizabeth changed into her own clothes and took the Balanciaga gown down the hall to the reception desk. To her surprise she found Natcha there giving instructions to a delivery driver who was loading cardboard boxes onto a cart.

"Max is very upset with you, Elizabeth," Natcha said, smiling to show that it was not a serious matter.

"I am very upset with him, the little . . ." and she used a word that she had certainly not known when she arrived in France.

Natcha laughed. "I guess everyone is upset today."

"What are you doing?"

"Sending off everything of value in the way of photographs and sketches and records," Natcha said, switching, with a glance at the deliveryman, into English. "Paula has agreed to store them at Château Aubigny until . . . what? Until the war is over? Then France will probably be a province of Germany like Poland."

"No, Natcha," Elizabeth said forcefully, "that's not going to happen."

Natcha said a few words to the deliveryman, and he wheeled the cart laden with boxes out to the elevator. Elizabeth closed the frosted glass door behind him and leaned back against it.

"No, Natcha, that's not going to happen because if it did,

the world wouldn't be a fit place to live in. We're going to fight, you and me, Peter and Jean-Luc, and millions and millions of others."

Natcha shrugged. "What can I do?" There were bluish bruises under her eyes from fatigue and lack of sleep. "I'm not strong."

"Then you have to become strong. You more than any of us know what the Nazis are."

"I know, I know. But I was not made for this kind of struggle. A model and fashion editor?" She laughed.

"None of us were made for this kind of struggle."

"And Peter?"

"America is neutral so far, but just by making sure that Washington knows the true story of what's happening . . . As you know, I just had a drink with him at the Crillon. He depends on you, Natcha. That may be all you need to do . . . just be there."

Elizabeth was astonished at her presumption, even arrogance, in lecturing someone who was among the first to know in her own being the tragedy of this war. But she was compelled to say what she had said . . . because it was the truth. Thank God, at least that was on their side!

A few streets after she had left the building that housed the *Vogue* offices a small dark-haired woman fell in step with her. It was Nicole.

"I've had a phone call from Jean-Luc. He's run into some problems and won't be back in Paris tonight as he had planned. He said to tell you it may be two or three days before he can return."

"Two or three days!" In two or three days the Germans might be in Paris. "He has to come back now, tonight. Where is he?"

"He didn't tell me."

They had reached the little park where the Avenue Matignon meets the Champs-Elysées. Anything they said would be covered by the splashing of a large fountain. Elizabeth stopped and glared at the diminutive young woman.

"Is he going to phone *me?*" She would get him back tonight.

"As from today, the phone in your apartment can't be used for security reasons."

"Who says so?"

"We do."

"You and Alain?"

"Yes."

"Who gave you the right . . ."

"Elizabeth, there is a war on."

"Yes, there is, and the Germans may be in Paris any day now, and Jean-Luc doesn't know he is on a Nazi list of persons to be arrested."

"He knows. He's traveling with a false identity card."

"Oh." The very first day of danger and he had held something back from her. There had to be a good reason, she told herself.

"Listen, Elizabeth, we must take every precaution. I know your feelings. I am in the same situation."

"You mean you and Alain . . ."

She nodded her head. "We are lovers. It's even recommended—in an oblique sort of way—in the training course. In our line of work, if you have an emotional attachment it assures you will take every precaution to see that your partner stays alive."

"Yes. . . ."

On the horizon several small planes wove a pattern in the clear sky. It was, she suspected, her first glimpse of war.

160

Chapter Fourteen

Elizabeth had not rebuked Jean-Luc when he returned two nights later, exhausted, for keeping from her that he had known he was on the Nazis' wanted list. Nicole's last chilling words to her had stuck in Elizabeth's mind. She must do all that was in her power to see that Jean-Luc stayed alive, and that included not adding to his worries by rebuking him for anything. From her he must have only unfailing support and love. That he would have and her body. She could tell by the fierce, almost desperate, quality of his lovemaking when he returned to her, that her passionate response was the proof of her support and love that he most needed.

Now she was saying goodbye to him for the fifth time in a month, and they both knew that this time might mark for them the end of any semblance of normal life. The German armies, having defeated the British and French—however many of them might have escaped from Dunkirk—at long last had turned toward Paris.

"*Garde-toi.*"

"*Toi aussi.*"

It was all they allowed themselves: a promise to take care. And then she stepped forward and kissed Jean-Luc passionately, ignoring the young British airman in ill-fitting civilian clothes. She was long past caring about appearances.

"I have packed you a change of clothes and some sand-

161

wiches and a bottle of wine," she said, handing Jean-Luc the small valise which also contained a Belgian automatic pistol, a code book and a set of radio crystals.

"If I am not back by Thursday you know what to do," and he flicked a glance at the British airman, "and do not wait until it is dark. Move while there is still light."

She nodded her head. "You are not to worry about me. You can be sure I will do exactly as we have agreed."

"Thank you, ma'am, for everything," said the tow-headed boy smuggled to them from where he had landed in Normandy in a parachute from his burning plane. "I can never repay you for what you've done for me."

"If you get safely back to England to fight again that will be payment enough," Jean-Luc said. God, how she loved this man who was strong and wise, yet sensitive to those who needed support.

As soon as the door closed behind the two men, Elizabeth threw herself on the sofa and burst into tears. The time of real danger had begun. Then she dried her eyes and went to the window in time to see Jean-Luc's car pull away from the curb, headed for a farmhouse on the road to Tours, the first stop for the young Englishman—if all went well—on a journey to Marseille and a ship home. "*Garde-toi*, Jean-Luc," she said to herself.

Elizabeth awoke the next morning, alone in a cold bed, with a vague feeling that something was wrong. An acrid smell permeated the bedroom, as though someone had been burning trash. She got up and opened the shutters. A heavy pall of smoke hung over Paris. She listened for the sound of bombs or gunfire, but it was eerily quiet. Now there were no cars at all on the streets. She made herself some coffee and drank it with a croissant. Then she called the American Embassy. It was only seven in the morning, but she knew that at the embassy they were all working around the clock, sleeping in snatches on sofas in their offices.

"John Ellis."

"Hi, John. This is Elizabeth Vail. Could I speak to Peter?"

"I was about to call you. Peter asked me to let you know he's gone to Tours with the government."

"What government?"

"The French government."

"The French government has moved to Tours? But Reynaud said only a couple of days ago that they would stay in Paris and fight to the last man."

"That was a couple of days ago. Ambassador Bullitt and some of us are staying on in Paris to see—seems unlikely to me—if we can help ease things for the French when the Germans move in, us being neutrals and all. Peter and some others have been sent down to Tours to keep in touch with the French government . . . if they can find it. Each government ministry is moving into a different château. They're spread over half the Loire valley."

"John, you said 'when the Germans move in', not 'if'."

"That's right, Elizabeth. You ought to get the hell out of here."

"How long before . . ."

"Four or five days, if the French try to defend the city, and if they don't, a day or two."

"Oh, dear."

"You wanted to talk to Peter, didn't you? Is it something urgent? If it is we do have radio communication with 'our' château in the Loire."

"No, John, it's just all this smoke made me wonder if something bad wasn't happening."

"Could be, but nobody knows. Some think that the Germans have laid down a smoke screen to cover an attack on Paris, others think the French have set fire to oil reserves to keep them out of German hands. In any case, you ought to get out of here. You do have a car, don't you?"

"Yes," she said, and after a few more words ended the conversation. She could not discuss her real situation. She decided to get dressed and go out to see for herself what was happening.

She walked down the quay along the Seine toward the Gare d'Austerlitz from which trains for Tours, Bordeaux and points south departed, and from which she would leave on Thursday, if Jean-Luc had not returned by then.

The quays were empty except for an occasional person on bicycle or hurrying along on foot with a valise. Shops were shuttered, windows painted blue to conform with blackout regulations, and crisscrossed with brown paper tape. There were not only no cars but no boats on the usually busy Seine. But from the distance came the sound of many voices, rising and falling like that of a crowd cheering at a soccer match.

When Elizabeth came out onto the Place Valhubert she found herself on the edge of a vast shouting mob that surged against the locked gates of the Gare d'Austerlitz, behind which policemen, looking more frightened than menacing, brandished rifles. Clearly, she would not be leaving Paris by train. She turned and started back down the quay, tying a scarf around her head to keep off the soot that was now raining down from the smoke-laden sky.

She wished that she could talk to someone, but all her friends were gone, even those at the *Vogue* office. Natcha had been put aboard a train for Bordeaux three weeks before, along with the other wives and children of American diplomats in Paris. The Russian and Polish models were not about to be found in town when the Germans arrived, and Max

Bonnet, who it turned out was Jewish, had disappeared as well.

She walked as far as Notre Dame where she encountered another crowd, but this one strung out along the Boulevard Saint-Michel where it crossed from the Left Bank to the Right Bank. Normally the sidewalk cafés of the Boule'Miche would have been packed with university students. Now their shutters were drawn, their tables stacked and chained together.

Down the Boule'Miche came an extraordinary crowd, moving slowly and stretching as far down the boulevard in either direction as she could see. Old people and young, men, women and children, trudged along silently, with bundles and parcels and suitcases. Some pushed wheelbarrows containing their possessions, others led ponies pulling overloaded farm carts. Every type of conveyance had been commandeered: a hearse, a village fire truck, ancient horse-drawn carriages. A farmer drove his cows before him. There were many soldiers in the procession that passed, in dirty uniforms, some wounded. Where were all these people going? They could not know: just heading south, away from the German army. For the first time Elizabeth felt fear.

She went back to the apartment, very depressed, and waited for something to happen. What this would be she did not know, any more than the refugees fleeing south knew where they were going. She tried to call Paula but was told by the operator that for security reasons calls outside Paris were no longer permitted. It was Tuesday, and she was to wait for Jean-Luc until Thursday afternoon. Suppose the Germans arrived first? She could not be found in the apartment, which the Gestapo would certainly know was the first place to look for Jean-Luc. But how could she flee? She didn't even own a bicycle.

The next morning, after a night with little sleep, she went out early to look for food. No sooner had she stepped into the street than she saw the notices posted on walls: Paris had been declared an open city and would not be defended. Elizabeth expelled the breath she had been holding. The Germans were free to march into the city and could do so at any moment. Her fear and indecision were swept away by the exhilaration of knowing that now she could act, must act.

Back in the apartment she more or less calmly—her hands shaking a bit—packed a small valise with clothes and toilet articles. Then she pried up one of the squares of parquet flooring and took out the stack of large-denomination French banknotes. They represented the $5000 Eustace Warden had given her as a graduation present. She had had the good sense to withdraw the money from the bank a week before. Now, no doubt, the banks would be closed. This was the money with which she had once contemplated buying Amos Leach's photography studio in Laurel Hill, Virginia. Good God, what a strange direction her life had taken since!

At a quarter till nine Elizabeth, wearing a raincoat and carrying her valise and handbag, crossed the Seine over the Carrousel bridge, away from the stream of refugees. She walked up the Champs-Elysées, normally one of the busiest streets in the world, without seeing a single car. By the time she reached Paula's apartment building it was nearly ten. The big wrought iron and glass front door was locked. She rang the bell repeatedly. Finally, the concierge appeared.

"Well, Mademoiselle Vail," the stout woman in bedroom slippers said, "why haven't you beat it like the rest?"

"What about you, Mathilde?"

"Why should I? And where would I go? I have no place in the country, like all the rich swells who have apartments here. And let me tell you, there is not a one of them that has not

166

gone to their country place. You know what is going to happen to these fancy empty apartments? The *Boches* will take them for their generals and officers. But they will need a concierge too." The woman shrugged. "You going up?"

"Yes."

"You will have to use the stairs. The elevator has been shut off."

Once in the apartment, Elizabeth went straight to the bedside table where Paula's car keys were kept. Then she went to the kitchen and filled a shopping basket with canned food and some bottles of wine. These and her valise she took down the servants' stairs. Paula's little green runabout with the tan canvas top was the only car in the garage. She was lucky someone hadn't stolen it—and that there was a full tank of gas. She quietly opened the garage door, not at all sure the concierge would permit her to take Paula's car. It started almost instantly, and she drove out of the garage. A window opened.

"Hey, where do you think you are going with Madame d'Aubigny's car?" Elizabeth did not reply or even look up but roared out into the street.

Now Paris was almost completely deserted, and the only cars she passed that were not in the stream of refugees were police patrol cars. She drove through red lights for fear that if she stopped someone might try to take the car away from her.

An hour later she was nearing Versailles, driving along an unpaved farm road. Had she done the right thing? All she knew was that she had to reach Jean-Luc by whatever means possible. If he could not come back to Paris, they had agreed that he would stay where he was at the farmhouse in the Loire valley owned by a member of the net; and she would come to him. This she would do, no matter what the obstacles, no matter what the risks.

167

★ ★ ★ ★ ★

She drove along back roads, avoiding the clogged highways, for what remained of the day, stopping only to consult the road map. Clearly, by nightfall she would be nowhere near the village where—she hoped—Jean-Luc waited for her. What then? Travel by night would be all the more dangerous for a single woman—driving an expensive car and carrying $5000 worth of French francs. France was effectively without a government, and law and order must soon break down.

At dusk Elizabeth found herself on a narrow road that was about to join Route Nationale 20, as packed with refugees as it had been at the gates of Paris.

She was about to turn the car around when out of the sun came what looked like three giant birds. With a roar the birds became three planes, three German fighter planes, flying so low that she could see the black and white crosses on the wings, the silhouette of a pilot's head. People along the road were screaming, running off into the fields. The planes banked and turned away, but then they turned again and passed over once more. And this time, to Elizabeth's horrified disbelief, spurts of orange flame came out of the front of the planes' wings. They were machine-gunning the people on the road!

Within seconds the highway was empty except for a few cars, the abandoned carts and wheelbarrows and baby carriages—and the bodies of those who had been killed. The rest of the refugees lay face down in the fields, but the planes did not return. Instead German armored vehicles came speeding down the road, knocking aside cars and carts and anything that obstructed their way. On either side of the highway German tanks rolled across the fields, heading south.

One tank passed within feet of where Elizabeth sat stunned in her car. The man in the tank's turret looked

168

straight ahead, not a trace of pity or any other emotion on his face. They were not interested in the refugees. Having been handed Paris on a platter, the Germans were now pursuing what remained of the French army; and machine-gunning was just a quick and efficient way of clearing the road for their armored cars.

The refugees were getting to their feet now, and a woman came running toward Elizabeth's car dragging along a girl of about five.

"Madame, madame, please take my daughter. I don't care about myself. But please, take my little girl to safety." Tears were streaming down the woman's face. The wide-eyed girl had her thumb in her mouth.

"I have no idea that I'm going to get to safety myself," Elizabeth said, putting into words what she had until then not articulated to herself. "You would be better off going to the next village. Maybe you can find a room."

"I am too tired to walk anywhere. We have not eaten all day. I have not one sou to buy food with, let alone rent a room."

"All right then, both of you get in. The girl will have to sit on your lap. I will drive you to the next village and give you some money." God knows, she had plenty of that to spare.

On the horizon a church spire was silhouetted against the evening sky. She drove toward it.

"Bless you, madame, for helping us. I do not know what we would have done."

"Where is your husband?"

"He was at the front. For all I know he is dead or captured by now. The filthy Boches."

After she had left off the woman and child, Elizabeth found a *boulangerie* that was still open and was able to buy two *baguettes*. Then she drove a few kilometers out of the village to a forested area, found an old logging road, and went up it as far as the car would go. Sitting on the ground she ate some of the bread with a can of sardines taken from Paula's pantry and drank wine out of the bottle. Then she lay on her back, smoked a Gauloise and looked up at the peaceful star-filled sky.

Well, Sarah Elizabeth Vail, you've done it, she said to herself. You are now in Nazi-occupied France, and if not tonight by tomorrow so will be the only man you've ever loved. She hoped the British airman was well on his way to Marseille. And then she realized with a shudder that helping an airman return to England would become under the Germans a crime carrying the death penalty.

She sighed. There was no point in feeling sorry for herself. She and Jean-Luc, Paula and Marc, Peter and Natcha, Nicole and Alain had been born at the wrong time. The older generation had not stopped Hitler when it was possible, and now her generation's blood must be spilled to do it.

She would do what she had to do, and that meant continuing on her journey to Jean-Luc. She had already sworn that no obstacle or risk would prevent her from being at his side, and there she would remain for better or for worse. But now she had seen the nature of the enemy with her own eyes, and she was ready to take another oath. "I will do anything," Elizabeth said aloud, "anything that is within my power, that helps bring down Nazi Germany."

Part II

By the Light of the Moon

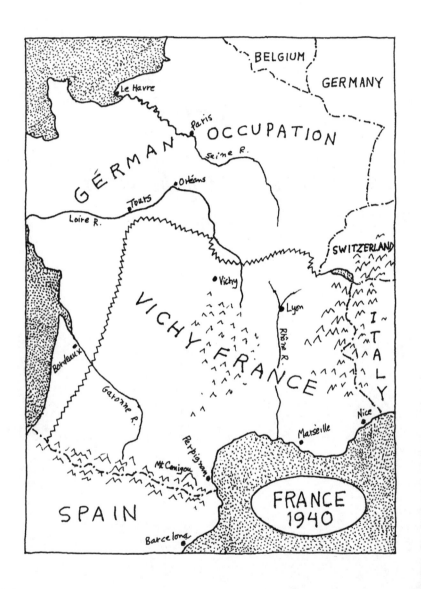

Chapter Fifteen

Aubigny-sur-Loire
June 14, 1940

He had almost to carry her up the worn marble stairs of Château Aubigny. She was physically and emotionally exhausted. Thank God she had found Jean-Luc, as strong as an oak, exactly where he was supposed to meet her if their world fell apart, as it most definitely had. In the distance Elizabeth could hear the soft thumping of anti-aircraft guns. German planes passed in waves, heading south, far above the puffs of smoke emitted by the French guns. All was lost, no question about that.

In the entrance hall of the château, *képis,* the pillbox hats that French army officers wore, were stacked on a Louis XV table, with so much gold braid on them that it was obvious that a congregation of French generals was being lodged at Château Aubigny. A *maître d'hotel* in formal dress led them into a high-ceilinged room, all white and gold, where Marc and Paula were engaged in conversation over a pot of tea.

"Elizabeth! Jean-Luc! Are you all right?" Paula asked, getting to her feet and coming toward them.

"We're all right, just exhausted, dirty and hungry, like most everybody else these last couple of days," Elizabeth said without thinking. She had not meant to imply any criticism of Paula and Marc. "I'm afraid I have put a few dents in your car."

"My car?"

"I took your car, got out of Paris just ahead of the Germans. . . ."

Suddenly Elizabeth felt her legs giving way, and together Jean-Luc and Marc caught her and deposited her on a sofa. "Do you remember that weekend on the pond?" She laughed, almost at the point of hysteria. "Who would have thought that we would all be together again in a year in the midst of the collapse of France?"

As if to emphasize her words, loud explosions rattled the windows.

"Well, Jean-Luc, for one, predicted all this," Marc said.

"But I never thought it would be over in a month."

"Perhaps we at last agree. You thought France was rotten militarily and I thought it was rotten politically."

"The two go together. What we have never agreed on is the remedy."

The two men glared at each other, and Elizabeth and Paula exchanged glances. Now the opinions of young men that had seemed academic at Laurel Hill, Virginia, had become matters of life and death. She could see in her eyes that Paula understood that just as well as she did.

"Where are all the generals?" Elizabeth said, to ease the tension. The two men had moved their heated discussion out onto the terrace. It occurred to Elizabeth that this might be the last time that Jean-Luc and Marc spoke to each other.

"Upstairs in the library," Paula said with a seriousness that was unlike her, "seeing who can sell France down the river the fastest. There will be much interest in that in Washington, I suppose. Peter is coming over shortly from the château that is serving as an American embassy annex to talk with the generals. Natcha is with him."

"I thought she had been evacuated to Bordeaux."

"And that's what Ambassador Bullitt back in Paris thinks.

But you know that Wardens don't have to play by the rules. Peter sent her to stay with me. . . . You've had a bad time, haven't you?"

"It shows, I guess."

"Yes."

"Paula, I saw German planes strafing refugees on the road. I . . ." and then she began to cry, her body heaving with sobs; and the once hard, cynical young woman who had become her friend rocked her in her arms.

"Poor baby, you weren't made for this."

"Do you know," Elizabeth said, wiping away her tears, "that's what Natcha said to me, and I said that none of us was made for this. We were just born at the wrong time."

A plane roared low over the château and there was another explosion.

"They're going after the bridges over the Loire," Paula said. "Once they're all down, the refugees will have to turn around and go back to wherever they came from."

"And what about you and Marc, Paula?"

"Oh, we'll be protected by the family's politics, but I'd rather not talk about that."

"Marc is wearing a black arm band. His father?"

"Yes. Day before yesterday. We rushed through the funeral, to have it done before the Germans arrive."

"Do you think they will occupy all of France?"

"I almost hope they do. If they don't Marc will go to whatever part of France remains under French control to work for a government that is cleansed of those elements that are responsible for . . . oh, you know the rest. I'll go with him, of course."

"The obedient wife?"

"Yes. It's hard to explain, but it's the only thing that has ever given any meaning to my life."

175

★ ★ ★ ★ ★

Elizabeth took a hot bath, and while Jean-Luc bathed she sat under the hair dryer in the newly decorated suite in which Paula had installed them. When her hair was dry she turned back the bed covers, let the robe she had found hanging in the bathroom fall to the floor, and lay down naked on the bed. When Jean-Luc came out of the bathroom she turned her head toward him. She saw in his eyes the same yearning she felt, in which sexual desire was mingled with a longing to be together somewhere safe, far from war and death. Then they made love tenderly, almost sadly, but ending for her with a spasm of pleasure so intense that it was almost pain.

Afterward they lay quietly for a while, and then finally she spoke. "What is wrong, Jean-Luc?" She looked into his eyes. "Well?"

"I worry about you."

"You must not do that. You must, for me, worry about yourself."

"I have to do what I am doing. You do not."

"Once you said to me that you could not live with yourself if you did not do what you could to help defeat the Nazis. After I saw men and women and little children lying in pools of blood on the highway, the inhuman look on the faces of the German pilots and tank commanders, I knew I could not live with myself if I did not do the same."

"I wish you had been spared that."

"I do not. Now I know. . . . Jean-Luc, once you told me that you and Marc met at a university flying club. Why did you two want to learn to fly?"

"Marc because it was a romantic thing to do, me because I had this idea of volunteering as a pilot to fight in Spain against Franco. But the instructor said I did not have the reflexes for it."

"Thank God. You would have been up against those fanatics—highly-trained fanatics—that I saw strafing the highway."

"I too think it was for the best. I could be of more use in journalism, warning of the threat of Hitler. But obviously I and the others who saw the threat were not successful, or France would not have been overrun in a matter of weeks. I still cannot quite believe it."

"When the war is over will you go back to journalism?"

"I truly do not know, Elizabeth. You have made such a change in me, that all kinds of things seem possible."

"I . . . I have made such a change in you?" She was astounded. She who had always been subservient had changed the life of this brilliant strong-willed man? "In what way?"

"Since I have known you life has become a joy, something to savor, to follow from day to day, wherever it leads. You may think I am serious and single-minded now, but you should have seen me before. I did not know joy."

"But why me? I can sense—indeed it would have been inevitable—that there have been a number of women in your life, but I also know that since we came together we belong to each other to the exclusion of all others, and that it will always be so. But why me, why someone so unlikely as a girl from a small town in Virginia?"

"How can one ever know, Elizabeth? It is like asking why I love my native land of Catalonia. Perhaps because, like it, there is something in you that is wild and free."

"Jean-Luc," she said, blinking away tears, "I have never been so touched in all my life."

While she dressed, Jean-Luc stood at the window, still in a bathrobe. "Elizabeth, come here. Look who Peter is talking to." Down on the lawn Peter Warden was conversing with a small elderly man in uniform and riding boots. "That is General Weygand, the commander-in-chief of the French armed forces."

"The general looks exhausted, and I suppose he is."

By the time they had finished dressing and walked downstairs, the generals had all departed in a convoy of cars taking the French government once again out of reach of the advancing Germans. This time they were headed for Bordeaux.

"What does Weygand think? There's no reason I shouldn't tell you exactly what I put in the telegram I just sent to the State Department. We're all friends, and friendship is now one of the few things left that has not lost its worth. . . ."

"Wait a moment, Peter, before you go on," Elizabeth said, raising her wine glass and looking into Marc's eyes, "I want to remind you all that the last time we six were together—St. Hubert's Day last year—Marc proposed a toast, and I would like to repeat it now: *à l'amitié* . . . to friendship."

Jean-Luc was watching her closely. Did he understand that she was trying to keep Marc, whose political views she feared, with them as a friend?

"*A l'amitié.*" The glasses clinked around the table. She also feared for all of them. As she took a sip of wine, Elizabeth breathed a silent prayer that they all might survive this monstrous war.

"Well, what Weygand said," Peter went on, apparently a little embarrassed by Elizabeth's outpouring, "was that the decision had been made to move the government to Bordeaux. They had beat down a proposal by that young upstart new general, Charles de Gaulle, to retreat into Brittany and evacuate as much of the army as possible to French North Africa to fight on. Weygand thinks Reynaud, who backed de Gaulle, will have to resign as Premier. I agree he's finished."

"And then what?" Jean-Luc asked, his attention totally focused. He was the most intense man Elizabeth had ever met, the most fascinating and—she acknowledged with a little shiver of pleasure and disbelief—he was hers.

"Although Weygand did not put it in so many words, that would leave old Marshall Pétain—the hero of the first war— the de facto head of government, since he is deputy premier. Weygand seems to think that Pétain—despite his eighty-four years—would be able to negotiate an honorable peace with Hitler."

"The ultimate foolishness," Jean-Luc said.

"Or perhaps the first step back toward sanity in France," Marc responded sharply.

"History will tell. But I can tell you, de Gaulle will not be part of any such arrangement. If that happens he will leave France to organize resistance to the Nazis from overseas."

"How do you know that?" Peter asked.

"He told me so himself."

"Yes, but when?"

"This afternoon. I saw him as he was packing to leave for Bordeaux at the house of some mutual friends with whom he has been staying."

"In any case," Peter said, breaking a stunned silence, "I will be there to witness. I've orders to follow the French government to Bordeaux in the morning."

"So I will end up in Bordeaux after all," Natcha said, "and Peter won't have his wrist slapped for having hid me away at Aubigny-sur-Loire."

It seemed to Elizabeth that Natcha had lost the bruised, exhausted look that she had had the last time she saw her in Paris, had regained that delicate, breath-taking beauty. As Jean-Luc had remarked that first day of the German offensive, at least now they all knew where they stood. The waiting had been the worst part.

"Peter," Elizabeth said, "I've told you what happened on the road here. You must be very careful in driving to Bordeaux. Take back roads. *Luftwaffe* pilots can't tell the cars of diplomats of neutral countries from the air."

"We'll be careful. We are only taking the same risk as the members of the French government and the other diplomats."

"Yes, Maurice?" Marc said to the *maître d'hotel*, who bent over and whispered something in his ear.

"No, I will not come out to speak to the German colonel. If he has something to say to me he is welcome to come in here."

A profound silence fell on the little dining room that Paula had lavished so much money and good taste on.

The colonel was a man of fifty, his silver hair cut in military fashion, immaculately uniformed and speaking almost perfect French. Marc did not rise to greet him.

"My condolences on the death of your father, Monsieur le Marquis."

"You are well informed, Colonel, but not so well as to know that the d'Aubigny family has not used its titles since 1793, when both my ancestor and the last King of France lost their heads to the guillotine. What may I do for you?"

Even in the dim light from the candles on the table, Elizabeth could see that the colonel's face had turned crimson. In her first seconds ever in the presence of a German officer, she had already acquired some perhaps useful knowledge. This man who had learned his French so well, who was a distinguished-looking member of the master race, could be devastated with a few carefully-chosen words.

"Monsieur d'Aubigny," the German said, searching to find his footing again, "we have occupied the village of Aubigny-sur-Loire, and my division commander has asked me to assure you that, now that hostilities have ceased, there is nothing to be feared from the German army. He is aware that your father was not unsympathetic to the Fuehrer's belief that only discipline and order can save European civilization."

"I share with my father the view that France's notable lack of discipline and order are largely responsible for my country's humiliation, but you should understand that I will never say or do anything that implies that I or my family acquiesce in the occupation of France by foreigners."

"If I may say so, Monsieur, the foreigners whom you should be more critical of are the English, who led you into this war and then abandoned you."

"Colonel, you do not need to lecture me about the English. One of my ancestors died by the swords of English occupiers of France as he fought to protect the person of Joan of Arc. I do, however, take your assurance that your troops will behave themselves in Aubigny-sur-Loire. And now, good night."

The German clicked his heels, turned about and marched out of the room.

"Well, at least they know how to do that properly," Jean-Luc said. "Well done, Marc."

Marc nodded his head in acknowledgment. Peter was laughing silently. Elizabeth stared in astonishment, first at Paula, who was looking admiringly at her husband, and then at the young man with the golden-red curls whom she had never taken very seriously. Apparently, within him there was a strong core of beliefs. But that was not necessarily to the good. They would almost certainly find themselves on opposite sides in the struggle to come.

After dinner Elizabeth and Jean-Luc walked in the

moonlit grounds of Château Aubigny. The sounds of war had given way to somber silence, but she supposed that with dawn the German planes would return.

"Do you remember that night on the pond when you asked if you could kiss me?" she said, almost in a whisper. "You so surprised me that I said yes, even though we had just met."

"What made you think of that?"

"I have been thinking about all our times together. I guess it kind of reassures me to know that we have had a past. I do not know why, but it somehow seems to make it more likely that we will have a future together—even though for now it is in the recently expanded Third Reich."

He took her hand in his large strong one. "Are you afraid?"

"Yes. That's what the Germans want, of course, to keep everyone too frightened to oppose them. Well, it will not work with me. I will conquer my fear when the time comes."

He looked into her eyes. "Yes, I believe you will."

"And we will survive the war."

"If we are to go on we must believe that."

"After we have won the war—and we will win—I think I would like to have a child. Would that please you?"

"Yes, I would like that . . . and a house in the country."

"And me in the kitchen mopping the floor, pregnant. It sounds so dull until you know you cannot have it, and then it sounds like paradise. When the war is over. . . . But now, we have other work. What do you want me to do?"

"Do?"

"As Miss Peach. I am not only your *amante*, remember, but also an agent of yours in Orchard Net."

"I think the first thing we need to do is to try to get out from behind enemy lines. I did not anticipate being caught like this, not expecting the Germans to move so fast."

"Nobody did. It probably surprised even them."

"Perhaps we could mingle with the foreign diplomats moving south to join what is left of the French government in Bordeaux. That might give us some protection, and there we would be close to the Pyrenees and my native land. We could wait safely there to see how this debacle ends. We cannot make any sensible decisions about Orchard Net until we know that."

"I suppose, under the circumstances . . . Oh, *merde,* why did all this have to happen?" She sighed. "No use complaining, though. You have to play the cards you are dealt." She pulled him down onto a bench. "And my hand includes the card of Jean-Luc Cabanasse, which trumps everything."

Elizabeth ran her hands over his face, kissed him ardently, opened her mouth to his.

"Could we go make love?" she whispered.

"Again?"

"Is there a French law, monsieur, against sex more than once on the same day?"

Chapter Sixteen

Paula came out into the great cobblestoned courtyard of the château, in a silk dressing gown over red pajamas to see them off. She ran the fingers of one hand through her tousled hair, while with the other hand she held a cigarette to her lips.

"*Le Bon Dieu vous protège.* If ever there was a day when a little divine protection was called for, I guess this is it. I did not wake Marc. He may need all the sleep he can get for what is coming in the next few days."

Peter and Jean-Luc stood beside a black embassy Buick. Elizabeth would drive Paula's green sports car, and Natcha, who was saying her own goodbye to Peter—just in case—would ride with her. Natcha had drawn little American flags with crayons on sheets of paper, and these she had pasted inside the windshields of both cars.

"I'll bring back your car when I can, Paula," Elizabeth said.

"Don't bother. Just get yourself back one day."

Paula kissed her on both cheeks, and Elizabeth could detect on her the sweet smell of sex. She too had taken her man in her arms and given him that blessed thing which was the best defense against the anxieties of a world gone mad.

"I'll be back, don't worry. I have too much to live for."

There seemed nothing more to say, and the four of them got into the two cars and drove off. It was barely dawn. In the rearview mirror Elizabeth could see Paula standing motionlessly on the staircase that led into the château. Was she wondering, as Elizabeth was, would they ever see each other again?

The occupying forces had apparently not yet reached the area. Although they occasionally saw a German tank in the distance and Luftwaffe planes passed constantly overhead, there were no German soldiers in the little villages they drove through. Indeed everything seemed oddly normal.

"That's Poitiers on the horizon," Elizabeth said. "We are making good time. If nothing happens to slow us down, we should make Bordeaux by the middle of the afternoon."

"If one of those German planes doesn't peel off and come after us."

"The Germans don't do things without a purpose, Natcha, and that would serve no purpose. Now if we got in their way, that's another matter. . . . That's why we have to stay off the main roads."

"It sounds logical, but every time a plane passes overhead I cringe."

"What will you do when you get to Bordeaux?" Elizabeth said to take Natcha's mind off their situation.

"I imagine the embassy will try to send me to America. They have brought a ship into Bordeaux to take away any Americans in France who can get there. But I won't go. Peter needs me."

"I think you and I and Paula all have men who need us. They wouldn't send me home either. But suppose the Germans occupy all of France?"

"Then I guess there wouldn't be any American embassy, and then . . ."

"But if any kind of French government survives?"

"Then, of course, Peter must stay. And so will I, no matter what the embassy says."

"They could order you home, Natcha."

"Peter will just have to get a little apartment and keep me in secret, like a mistress." Natcha laughed. "I rather like that idea. I try to make things spicy for Peter, and I can be very naughty." She laughed again. "Peter is so serious."

"That's what Peter's father said to me, and he said he hoped you were a woman of spirit. I'll write him—when there's mail service again—and tell him you are. You'll like Eustace."

"What about you, Elizabeth?"

"I'm staying with Jean-Luc, of course."

"Peter's told me something of what you're doing. Don't be alarmed. He tells me everything, no matter how secret, and he knows I would never repeat anything."

"I'm not concerned. I know I can trust you and Peter absolutely."

"The Nazis killed my parents, and I just want you to know that if there's ever any way I can help . . ."

"I know you would."

"You should also know that Paula may have guessed something. She said she didn't want to speak to you directly, but she said I could tell you that if you ever need help you can count on her. If it involves something Marc wouldn't approve of, then Marc won't know about it. She said . . . Elizabeth what's that up ahead in the road?"

"It looks like a motorcycle . . . a motorcycle with sidecar . . . and there's another just off the road. . . ."

Elizabeth looked in the rearview mirror, in which every minute or two she checked to see that the black Buick was still behind them. But the narrow country road had just taken a wide curve, and the car carrying Peter and Jean-Luc was lost

186

to view. As they approached the two motorcycles Elizabeth saw, with sinking heart, German uniforms. Well, she said to herself, you claimed that when the time came you would find the courage to do what had to be done. So find it.

"Natcha," Elizabeth said, trying to control her voice, "you're the wife of an American embassy official, and I'm a friend of yours."

"You certainly are that."

"I mean what we say to the Krauts. My name is Francine Dupont."

Elizabeth had three pieces of identification: her American passport, her French identity card, and a fake identity card in the name of Dupont, Francine, profession hairdresser. She dared not use the first two. The Gestapo presumably had good enough intelligence to know the name of the woman with whom Jean-Luc Cabanasse lived.

"Bonjour, mesdames," the young German lieutenant said, a slimmer, younger carbon copy of the officer who had visited Château Aubigny the evening before. "This is a war zone you know. You should not be here. Very dangerous. Where are you going exactly?"

"Bordeaux," Natcha replied instantly, to Elizabeth's relief. "I am the wife of an American diplomat, and this is my friend Francine Dupont, a French citizen."

The German officer could not conceal his surprise. "May I see your papers?"

Natcha took her diplomatic passport out of her handbag and handed it to the lieutenant. The three German soldiers looked on, obviously comprehending nothing.

In the rearview mirror Elizabeth saw the Buick emerge from the woods and then come to a sudden stop.

"This seems to be in order. My instructions specify that the diplomats of neutral countries and their families are free to travel, but I must warn you again that you are in a dangerous war zone."

The Buick was now approaching at high speed. The four Germans looked up as the car came to a sliding stop. Peter Warden jumped out. But where was Jean-Luc? There was no one else in the car.

"What is going on here? Why have you detained my wife?"

The German officer looked at the diplomatic tag on the big black car. "Excuse me, excellency, but my orders are to stop all cars—diplomatic excepted, of course—that have tag numbers from departments north of here. The car in which your wife is riding does not have diplomatic license plates, but regular French plates with a Paris number. And may I see your passport?"

Peter handed over his diplomatic passport.

"Very good. And now madame, your papers, please," the German said, turning to Elizabeth.

Elizabeth took out her false identity card, thinking that she had had her second lesson on how to deal with Germans. They went by the book. A French policeman would have verified that he was dealing with a bona fide foreign diplomat and waved them all on.

"Hairdresser?" The lieutenant looked from Natcha to Peter. "A hairdresser is a personal friend of yours?"

"Actually," Elizabeth said, "I am the hairdresser and personal maid to the wife of the American ambassador. The ambassador and his wife are also on their way to Bordeaux, and *madame l'ambassadrice* asked Second Secretary Warden to take me with him."

She was betting that this young lieutenant did not know that Ambassador Bullitt had not left Paris or that he had no wife. The German officer took a sheaf of papers out of the motorcycle sidecar and examined them.

"My instructions specify that French employees of foreign embassies no longer enjoy diplomatic privileges, given the state of war that exists between the German Reich and France. You will have to return to Paris."

"Can you not make an exception, lieutenant, for a member of the American ambassador's personal staff?" Peter said.

"We do not make exceptions, excellency. All French people must return to their homes. We cannot devote resources to supporting a wandering refugee population."

Lesson number three, Elizabeth thought. They don't make exceptions. "But how am I supposed to get back to Paris?"

The German officer shrugged. It wasn't his problem. "The train from Poitiers, I suppose . . . when it starts running again."

"And how am I to get to Poitiers?"

"You can walk. It is only ten kilometers."

"Surely," Natcha said, "I can loan her my car."

The lieutenant shrugged again. "If you wish. I will provide a safe conduct, including authorization to draw gasoline, if necessary, from any German military unit. We want people back in their homes. I will take down your Paris address, madame, and in a few days the authorities will verify that you have returned to your residence. If not . . ."

As Elizabeth drove away, watching the black Buick in the rearview mirror disappear in the opposite direction, she suddenly thought of Jean-Luc, and in her relief broke into laughter. Of course. They had seen the roadblock and stopped so that Jean-Luc could get into the trunk of the car. He was probably now as safe as in any place he could be—though even that wasn't very safe. Lesson four: do not let anything distract you from what you have to do. If you want the one you love to survive, then don't give a thought

189

to him when you are in action.

She looked at her flushed face in the mirror and smiled. Then she spoke aloud to herself, as she had done that night after witnessing the massacre of the refugees: "Sarah Elizabeth Vail, you are going to be good at this game, you are going to get back to your lover, and we are going to win this war." Brave words, but words that she needed to believe in.

This time when Elizabeth approached Paris, there were no masses of people moving with their belongings to block the way. The highways were deserted except for German military trucks bringing in the army of occupation. She had come back along Route Nationale 20, and the only signs of the passage of the refugees were bullet-riddled cars and overturned carts and carriages along the side of the road. The Germans, always efficient, had already picked up the dead bodies and hauled them away: it was bad publicity. What had become of the refugees she had no idea.

At the Porte d'Orleans an armored car half blocked the street, and for the third time she was stopped by a French-speaking German officer.

"Your papers."

Elizabeth produced her false identity card and the safe conduct she had been given.

"Ah, you are being returned to your residence. Do you have a special permit to operate a vehicle?"

"I did not know there was such a thing."

"When you reach your residence you are to garage this vehicle. Only persons with a serious need for a vehicle, such as doctors and nurses, are allowed to drive in Paris now. When the authorities come to verify your arrival your vehicle will most probably be requisitioned."

The officer then put a sticker on the windshield, where the

American flag had been earlier, authorizing the operation of a vehicle for the day of Saturday, June 15, 1940, only. Always efficient.

She drove straight to Paula's building, unlocked the garage and put the car back in its space. Maybe that would keep it from the Germans. Wouldn't Mathilde the concierge be surprised that it had appeared out of nowhere. Now the problem was where she was going to stay. She couldn't stay in Paula's apartment. She didn't trust Mathilde. She couldn't go to the address on her safe conduct. When the Germans went there to check on her they would find that it was the address of her grocery. Her false identity was now compromised. There was only one thing to do. Elizabeth made the long walk to Montparnasse.

The streets were still nearly deserted except for German soldiers, with whom a few young Frenchwomen were already fraternizing. Posters showing a smiling German soldier with two smiling French children were pasted on walls, along with a notice of the hours of curfew. Most depressing of all was the presence on every public building of huge red Nazi flags with the black swastika. One even flew from the top of the Eiffel Tower.

She climbed the stairs of the drab apartment building at 31 bis Rue Campagne Première, off the Boulevard Montparnasse. After hesitating, she knocked on the door of the apartment where Alain and Nicole lived as quietly as possible, as Marcel Lefevre, commercial traveler for a company making printing inks, and his wife, Madeleine.

"Yes?"

"It's me, Elizabeth."

Two locks were turned and Alain's eye appeared at a crack in the door, and then a chain was loosened.

"Come in quickly."

As she stepped into the room, petite, pretty Nicole emerged from behind a curtain that hung in the doorway to the next room, a large gun in her hand. *What kind of life have I gotten myself into?* Elizabeth thought.

"I wouldn't have come here, but I have to have a new identity right away."

"What's happened?" Alain looked alarmed.

"It's a long story."

"Then I'll go fetch a bottle of *gros rouge* and three glasses, and let's hear it."

Elizabeth told what had happened during three eventful days, in as calm and steady a voice as she could manage. She could see that they were watching her intently, wondering if she had the nerves for the kind of work that lay ahead.

When she had finished, Nicole said, "You were quite right to come here. As soon as they visit that address you gave them, Francine Dupont's name will go on a Gestapo arrest list."

"The problem with a new identity card tonight—and it's almost curfew time—is that we have to have a photograph," Alain said, pulling on his short beard. "We can't use the old one. The photograph is attached to the card with grommets, so it can't be removed without destroying it."

"I have a photo in my bag." Elizabeth took out an especially flattering fashion photograph that Max had made of her. She had meant to give it to Jean-Luc, but so much had been going on that she had forgotten. "You can just cut out the head." It seemed a shame.

"There, all done," Alain said, pressing a counterfeit rubber stamp down onto the card. "Now we need to give you a name, a very common name. How about Marie Robert? Easy for a policeman to forget. And a profession. Obviously, 'hairdresser' was not a very good choice. What would be better would be a profession that would explain why a woman was traveling on trains."

"Sales representative, cosmetics," Nicole said. "We would have to make up a sample case for you, but that adds to the authenticity, and cosmetics is something a policeman wouldn't know enough about to question you closely."

"Sounds good, and I do know about makeup."

"And, Elizabeth, you have a message," Nicole said, getting up.

She returned with a sheet of paper on which characters were printed in pencil in three-line groups, the triad of the one-time pad. Elizabeth read the clear-text bottom lines.

"FOR APPLE AND STRAWBERRY. REYNAUD APPEARS FINISHED. PROBABLY WILL BE REPLACED BY MARSHAL PETAIN. SOMETHING DECISIVE CAN BE EXPECTED IN NEXT DAY OR TWO. WHEN THAT IS KNOWN WILL CONTACT YOU RE NEXT STEPS. IF YOU ARE IN TOUCH WITH PEACH SAY I MADE IT SAFELY IF UNCOMFORTABLY TO MY DESTINATION. PEACH TO JOIN ME AS PLANNED AS SOON AS I CAN FIND A WAY. WILL ADVISE. MANGO."

On Monday morning, Elizabeth went out to buy some flowers for her room in the modest but comfortable hotel where she had lodged. She also planned, to buck up her morale, to have as fine a lunch as was still available in the *quartier*. In the hotel lobby a crowd was gathered around a radio. She pressed up as close as she could, just in time to hear an old voice say, "It is with a broken heart I tell you today that it is necessary to stop fighting." After a few more words the voice faded away.

"What does it mean?" she asked the man standing next to her.

"It means that the honor of France, which has endured for a thousand years, has just been thrown on the trash heap of history by Marshal Pétain." The man was crying.

So, France had finally surrendered, and her private war could now begin in earnest. Elizabeth felt a tremendous sense of relief.

Chapter Seventeen

A month later an old Renault truck rolled down the highway, empty wine barrels rumbling in the back. Roger Legros, vintner of Sainte-Maure, hummed a popular tune to himself. In his blue work clothes, a beret pushed down toward his eyes, the ubiquitous Gauloise dangling from his lower lip, he was the perfect picture of a French peasant. A well-to-do peasant, however, with a large paunch and a bulbous red nose from enjoying, as God intended, the good products of his own 120 hectares of rich land, land that happened to straddle the demarcation line between Nazi-occupied France and unoccupied Vichy France. Legros usually spat on the ground after pronouncing the word Vichy.

Elizabeth was seated beside him on the worn leather seat, in clothes bought by Legros' wife at the weekly Sainte-Maure market. The story was that she was Marthe, Legros' daughter, who had traveled with her father to Paris and back on his delivery of twelve barrels of wine—the Boches didn't mind giving out a little gasoline to see that their occupied capital was well-supplied with wine—to acquire a few things for the household from the black market. That is what Roger Legros had said, with a wink, to the office manager at the wine merchant's.

"We did not do badly, did we, *ma fille?*"

"Five checkpoints and not a hint of suspicion."

"The efficiency of the Boches is matched only by their stupidity. I would have spotted you, but I knew they would not, so it was not worth the trouble to warn you."

"What did I do wrong?"

"First, you are wearing a wristwatch. Unheard of around Sainte-Maure. Second, your stockings are well-fitting and without runs. They should be of heavy cotton and drooping a bit. Third, although you have given yourself the appearance of having been working in the fields, your hair is freshly washed. Related to that is the fact that you do not—if you will excuse me, mademoiselle—smell as though you come from a farm."

"Thank you, Roger. I greatly value all you have done for me."

"These things are important. The Vichy police are much more likely to see them. They are mostly country louts like myself. I want you to succeed. We may end up with our backs to a wall, facing a firing squad, but, *sacre bleu,* we are either French and free or we are nothing."

My goodness, he doesn't even know that I'm not French, she thought. He just takes the way I speak French to be a Parisian accent. With what lay ahead of her, it was good to know that her French would not give her away.

The sun was setting as they passed through the village of Aubigny-sur-Loire, and she could see the golden turrets of the château above the dark woods that surrounded it. Wouldn't Paula be astonished. But the château was closed, and the d'Aubignys had moved to Vichy where Marc's old patron, Pierre Laval, now minister of justice in the Vichy government, had secured him a senior post in the administration.

Peter and Natcha had also moved to Vichy, where an American embassy had been opened in the capital of that rump of France that Germany had not occupied. It had been chosen because of its many hotels, all empty, with no one— under the circumstances—taking the waters.

From Aubigny they turned south to Sainte-Maure, a few kilometers beyond which lay the Legros farm, known to the Orchard Net as Pear Tree. By the time she had finished the bowl of soup offered by a suspicious Madame Legros, as scrawny as her husband was well-fleshed, night had fallen.

By the dim light of a lantern they walked down the rows of vines, now beginning to show tiny grapes, Elizabeth pushing a bicycle.

"The main thing to remember is to stay to the farm roads, where your appearance, now that we have made a few corrections, will cause no notice. At the end of this field is my hay barn, now in another country. Spend the night there. If you start out at dawn you should be able to make Châteauroux before noon. There is a train south every few hours. Just leave the bicycle at the train station. I will donate it to the cause."

Elizabeth kissed him on both cheeks. "Thanks for everything, Roger."

"Hey, be careful. Out in the country you do not kiss people like that unless you are related or you went to school together."

"I will remember that."

Elizabeth slept in a pile of straw, awakening not once during the night; but at first light she was immediately wide-awake, her mind clear and focused. Perhaps she was also a natural for the secret war as for dancing and making love. She smiled at this thought and took comfort in it. Well, Sarah Elizabeth, here you go, she whispered to herself, either to the arms of your lover or to prison. You had better be a natural!

That dawn the Loire valley was covered by a heavy fog,

and she pedalled down the country lane, her valise and smaller case strapped to the back of the bicycle, without meeting even a farm cart until mid-morning. On the main road to Châteauroux there was little traffic, the division of France into two parts having shut off the normal flow of commercial traffic from Tours.

She came into Châteauroux just as the fog was lifting, and she felt for the first time naked and exposed, as though everyone on the streets was looking at her. Across from the train station where she left her bicycle, there was a public bath. She paid for a stall and took a much-needed shower, changed from farm into city clothes, and within an hour was on a train to Lyon. She had, in the disrupted situation of a divided France, a compartment to herself.

"Your papers, madame."

Elizabeth handed over to the rather seedy-looking Vichy policeman her forged identity card prepared by Alain in the name of Marie Robert. This was her first test.

"But this is an old document of the former regime. Why have you not obtained a new identity card from your local prefecture in Avignon?"

"Because I have just come from the occupied zone only yesterday. I was caught in Paris when the fighting began, and only now was I able to get permission from the Boches to return to my husband and little baby."

She deliberately used the word "Boche", the worst thing you could call a German, and she thought she detected a slight smile beneath the gendarme's wispy mustache. He was not, at least, a born collaborator.

"Madame, may I ask what you were doing in Paris, if you have a husband and small child in Avignon?"

"As it shows on my identity card, I am a sales representative of the house of Lanvin. I visit dealers in perfume and cosmetics in the provinces."

"Lanvin?"

"A Paris fashion house of great renown."

"Ah. Nevertheless, I have orders to hand over to the Lyon police for further examination anyone coming from the area of the demarcation line who does not have a well-documented reason for traveling."

"Well-documented? What about this, monsieur?" She got up, took down her leather case from the overhead rack, and opened it to reveal an array of powder compacts, lipsticks, perfume bottles and makeup brushes.

"Well, I do not know about . . ."

"What color is your wife's hair, monsieur?"

"Brown," the gendarme said, too startled to do anything but answer her question.

"And her complexion, dark or light?"

"Oh, light, very light."

"Then may I offer your wife these samples from the house of Lanvin? I can assure you she will be most grateful to you."

After the gendarme had left with his little bribe, Elizabeth lay back in the plush seat with a sigh. She could feel perspiration running down her sides. If someone who had learned cosmetics on the stage and at *Vogue* became that nervous over a cover story given to a provincial policeman . . . Nevertheless, it was a start. It was the beginning of becoming a professional.

By the time the train pulled into the Lyon station it was already dark. She readied herself for another examination of her papers, but there wasn't even a policeman in sight. The platform was soon emptied of arriving travelers and those who had come to meet them, except for Elizabeth and a woman who stood beneath a light at the far end of the platform. The woman came toward her. She was young, with large brown eyes and a sad, serious face.

"It has been a hot summer," the woman said.

"The orange trees will blossom early this year."

"I am Orange."

"Peach."

They both relaxed.

"Come. My car is in the station parking."

The car was a tiny two-horsepower Citroën, a *deux-chevaux,* as the French affectionately called them, and it looked like a sardine can on wheels. They drove off through the twisted streets of old Lyon, turning repeatedly. She could never have retraced the route, and that was perhaps intended.

"You are the first visitor Orchard has sent me," the woman finally said.

"And this is my first mission," Elizabeth replied. They exchanged sympathetic glances.

"I am the only representative Orchard has in Lyon for now, so we do not have a lookout. Keep that in mind. More will join later when they find out what the Nazis are really like. For now the German troops are on their best behavior, but that will not last. Then we will get recruits."

"You were recruited by Mango?"

"Yes. What an attractive man. I could have become interested. . . ."

Elizabeth said nothing. What could she say? She wanted to ask the woman why she had been the first to join Orchard, but she had already gone beyond the limit of what it was permissible to talk about.

They turned in the drive of a bungalow in a quiet middle-class residential area and entered the house from the rear.

"Welcome to the Orange Tree."

"You live here alone?"

"I do now. The Boches killed my husband. We had decided to put off having a child. I will regret that for the rest of my life." This bleak statement was made with quiet simplicity. "Would you like something to eat?"

"Some bread and cheese would be nice."

"There is plenty of room here. I will put you in the back bedroom."

The woman brought a tray with bread and cheese and a pitcher of red wine. As soon as she had finished her simple supper, Elizabeth went to bed and, emotionally exhausted, fell immediately to sleep.

She awoke to a gray morning. There was a pleasant little garden in back of the house, with a grape arbor shading the windows. A tabby cat in the arbor was looking down on her, and for several minutes they stared at each other. Then the cat jumped down to the window sill and disappeared. How she wished the war was over and she lived in a little house like this with Jean-Luc. She twisted and turned in bed with desire for him. Today was the day. Oh, if only she didn't make some mistake and get arrested for traveling on false papers. And who knew what risks he was taking?

There was a knock on the door, and Orange entered with a steaming mug of café au lait and a croissant.

"I will drop you off at the station on the way to work." The woman did not say where she worked, and Elizabeth did not ask.

By the time they reached the station it was raining heavily. The woman escorted her to the platform with an umbrella, which Elizabeth did not have. They kissed on both cheeks, like sisters or old school friends.

"Good luck," the woman said.

"Bonne chance à vous."

Then this brave, sad young woman, whom she would probably never see again, disappeared into the fog and rain.

★ ★ ★ ★ ★

Somewhere between Vienne and Valence the sun began to shine. They were entering the Midi, the land of the straight-down sun. She could feel her heart beating faster. Before this day was over . . . If only . . . nothing went wrong. She was so close. Within an hour olive trees began to appear, and then palm trees and banana plants. In the distance she could see the Palace of the Popes rising above Avignon.

In the Marseille station she had a hasty early lunch and boarded the train for Nice. A genuine traveling salesman, with two large sample cases, shared the compartment with her and eyed her from time to time over his newspaper. The towns sped by: Toulon, St. Raphaël, Cannes, Antibes. She took lipstick and a compact out of her handbag and renewed her makeup.

Nice was visible now, strung out along the deep blue Mediterranean. She thought of her excitement the other time she had come into Nice by train, with Paula and Marc and Leonore. . . . What a long time ago that seemed. Only ten months had passed, but in those ten months the whole world had changed.

When she descended from the train at Nice there were two policeman looking closely at everyone who got off, but they paid her no attention. They were looking for someone else. Now what did she do? The platforms were crowded with people getting on and off several trains, and she had no description of the person who was to meet her.

A man was watching her from the entrance to the station bar, but he was certainly not her contact: short and muscular with huge chest and biceps, balding; and he wore a tightly-fitting flashy suit with wide stripes. He looked like a pimp. But then the man crossed the platform to where she was standing.

"It has been a hot summer," the man said, wiping his face with a silk handkerchief he had taken from his breast pocket. He grinned, showing widely spaced teeth. An amiable pimp.

"The orange trees will blossom early this year."

"Well, let's get going then," the man said, picking up her two bags.

He escorted her to a black, brand-new Panhard and opened the door for her. He turned out of the parking area and drove fast and skillfully through downtown Nice.

"How did you know who I was?"

"Easy," the man said and grinned again. "They told me to look for the most beautiful woman who got off the train."

She laughed. "Why, thank you."

"You been here before?"

"Once."

"It's the only place to live. If my father had not got TB I would be shivering in Moscow now."

"You are Russian?"

"I reckon I am more French than anything at this point, more French than these half-Italians around Nice. But my name is Malakoff, Serge Malakoff. The climate did nothing for my father though. He died and left my mother with three small kids. She had to take in washing. I swore I was not going to live like that. I guess I have done pretty well for myself. How do you like my new car?"

"It's very nice." What on earth was going on?

"What kind of identity card you got?"

"The old kind."

"We will have to get you a new Vichy one fast. Manny will take care of that. You get caught with bad papers and you will end up in Fort de la Revère. You would not like that, I can tell you. I spent nearly a year there before I bought my way out."

"What had you done?"

"Unauthorized removal of forty thousand francs worth of money orders from the post office."

"Oh."

They circled the old port of Nice and headed out along the Lower Corniche that follows the shore from Nice to Menton and the Italian border, the same route she and Jean-Luc had taken to the marriage of Paula and Marc at the Beaulieu *mairie,* and all that followed, she thought with a smile, and still continues. She had decided not to ask this Russian-French gangster where they were going. It would show weakness. He had the password that Jean-Luc had sent by coded message to Paris, and that was the best assurance she was going to get.

Just before they came to the crossroads at Villefranche where the road leading out to Cap Ferrat and the Villa Warden split off from the highway, Malakoff—if she could believe his story—suddenly turned inland on a narrow road leading up the escarpment that rose above them, so suddenly that she suspected he might be trying to lose anyone who might be following them. He drove the road so fast, changing gears every few seconds, that it was like rising in a balloon, the port of Villefranche, Cap Ferrat and Beaulieu shrinking ever smaller beneath them. Within minutes they were on the Middle Corniche, halfway up the escarpment.

After a few turns they drew up in front of a truckers' stop. There was so little room to build anything on the sheer face of the cliff that the building where they had stopped was half-supported by concrete columns sunk into the escarpment and hung perilously out into space. One side of the building seemed to be an automobile repair shop, with a gasoline pump, the other half had painted over the door in black letters "Bar-Restaurant". On the other side of the road was a row of decaying villas in the little space between the road and the next rise in the escarpment. This was definitely not the Riviera that she had once heard Leonore describe as "the most important fifteen miles of real estate in the world".

"This is it?"

"It has its advantages," Malakoff said.

They got out, and he led her through a bead curtain into a smoky room, where some truck drivers were noisily finishing off a late lunch of stew amid half-eaten *baguettes* and half-empty carafes of red wine, while those who had finished were gathered around a pool table with glasses of milky-green pastis. They passed through the room, down a corridor and out into a glassed-in kind of sun porch thrust out into space above the Mediterranean, where four men were also finishing a late lunch. From the head of the table Jean-Luc—larger and stronger in life than even in memory—rose and came toward her. What was she supposed to do?

She had no chance to decide. He took her in his arms and kissed her on the mouth. "Elizabeth, I've missed you so much." She sensed that this was half-meant for her, the most he could do under the circumstances, and half-meant to state to those around the table that the two of them were to be considered one. It was just what she would have hoped for.

A big man, in stained white clothes with a white chef's *toque* on his head, stood up.

"Elizabeth, my friend Jean Raimeau, the owner of this establishment and *chef de cuisine extraordinaire.*"

"Madame has eaten?" the chef inquired.

"I have, but . . ."

"A little reinforcement might be in order?"

"Yes, I think so."

"While the menu has been devastated by these truckers, I think I might be able to produce a *contre-filet* and some *pommes frites. Ca va?*"

"Ca va." Suddenly she was ravenously hungry, and a plain steak and french fries sounded like the most divine meal imaginable.

She looked around the table at the sympathetic faces surrounding her, and she felt as though she had come home. It had been more than a month since she had been brutally separated from Jean-Luc outside Poitiers. She had gone through so much since, feared so much, almost lost her nerve once or twice, but now . . .

"Elizabeth, may I introduce . . ."

"Emmanuel Kuhn," an elderly man in suit and tie, with thick glasses and hair cut so short as to stand up in spikes. "Retired professor of architectural draughtsmanship at the College Commerciale de Nice. I live in the villa just across the way, the one with the concrete dwarfs on the gate posts, now a rooming house, not very elegant but comfortable enough, and cheap."

"Emmanuel is in charge of documentation."

"What Jean-Luc means is that I forge documents."

"Armand de Vaucluse," said an impeccably tailored middle-aged man with a high forehead and manicured nails. "I am a lawyer who does not usually frequent truck stops, but from time to time, when I have business in Monaco, I lunch at this one because of the known excellence of chef Raimeau's cooking."

"Armand keeps us informed of what is going on behind the scenes in governing circles in Nice and elsewhere in the Alpes-Maritimes. And Serge, who you already know, is my bodyguard."

Malakoff, entering the room with a bottle of Scotch from the bar, raised his glass in acknowledgment.

They laughed, the chef brought Elizabeth's *contre-filet* and *pommes frites* and more red wine, and they talked until the sun was sinking into the Mediterranean. Then Jean-Luc and Elizabeth took their leave and went up to a bedroom over the garage. It was a large room with an iron frame bed painted white, an armoire, a table with a pitcher on it, a mirror and a couple of chairs. She opened the big window that looked down on the Mediterranean and the coastline from Nice to Menton. Lights were beginning to come on. He came up beside her and put his arm around her.

"If you look down where that big yacht is anchored, that's the Villa Warden."

"I would rather have this room up here with you, above a car garage than the Villa Warden." She stroked his face. *"Tu es fatigué."*

"I guess I am pretty tired. We have had some busy nights recently."

Then they got into bed and he held her naked body from behind.

"Jean-Luc, could we wait till morning. I'm exhausted."

He did not reply, and she turned over. He was sound asleep.

Chapter Eighteen

She was awakened by a knock on the door. Jean-Luc sat up instantly, reached into the drawer of the bedside table and took out a pistol.

"Who is it?"

"*C'est moi*, Raimeau. The boy from Marseille has arrived. He wants to talk to you."

"I will be right down." He was out of bed in one swift movement.

She laughed. "Now that's a sight."

"What do you mean?"

"Standing there naked as the day you were born, brandishing an automatic pistol." She meant to keep things light, but what she had felt with that knock on the door was cold fear.

He laughed then and put the pistol away. "Well, you never know. I am sorry about this. I had other plans."

"So did I."

He was quickly into a striped sailor's shirt, canvas pants and a pair of espadrilles. Really, she thought, you are the most gorgeous man alive.

"I will be back as soon as I can."

When he had gone Elizabeth sat up in bed and, hugging her knees, watched the sun come up over the Mediterranean. She was sure now that this was home, a strange kind of home perhaps, but the only home she was able to have. So, she had better start getting her life in order. Just as in a new house in happier times, she would have been measuring for curtains and deciding what pots and pans would be needed, here she would have to plan how she and Jean-Luc could have at least something of a normal life at the same time they played their dangerous game.

She got out of bed and picked out the prettiest dress from the meager selection she had brought with her. Then she opened the case of Lanvin samples, went to the mirror and made up with as much care as if she were about to be photographed for the cover of *Vogue*. Before going downstairs she put on some expensive perfume.

She passed the doorway to the glassed-in private dining room, where Jean-Luc, Raimeau and old Monsieur Kuhn were discussing something with a young man she had never seen. Jean-Luc looked up and registered surprise. He had expected to return to her naked in bed. She blew him a kiss, pushed open the swinging door and passed into the kitchen.

Raimeau's wife was already at work preparing vegetables for lunch. She was close to forty, with a trim figure and frizzed red-dyed hair. She wore a lot of bright red lipstick, her eyes were heavily lined with kohl, and she exuded sexuality.

"*Bonjour, Margot.*"

"*Mon Dieu*, is it you? You look like a movie star."

There had indeed been quite a transformation. While traveling she had made herself as plain-looking as possible.

"I want to look good for my man. We have been apart for more than a month."

"Ah," Madame Raimeau said knowingly. "Shall I fix you something special for lunch?"

"Could you fix us a picnic?"

"*Bien sur.*" She shrugged, as if this was the simplest request. "Let's see . . . I have some pâté of rabbit, some cold chicken, asparagus, a little potato salad, and then perhaps a fig tart. That with a *baguette* and a nice bottle of Côtes de Provence and . . ."

"Oh, Margot, stop, stop."

When she returned to the dining room, Kuhn and the boy had gone. When Raimeau saw her he said nothing more than *bonjour* but his eyes opened wide. So did Jean-Luc's.

"Well, I had better get to work," Raimeau said, still staring at Elizabeth as he went out the door.

"You look good enough to eat."

She smiled and raised one eyebrow but said nothing.

"Coffee and croissant?"

"Yes, please." She slid into a chair. He kept looking at her. "Oh," he finally said, "Kuhn brought your new identity card."

"Madame Elisabeth Fournier." She looked up at him. "So we are married, Jean-Luc Fournier."

"It might be useful in certain situations. Be careful when you sign your name to spell Elizabeth in the French way, with an 's'. The rest of the group, who all live here, have their real identity cards, of course, but they also have false ones. We always use the same first name on both cards. It helps avoid slipups in conversation. . . ." He kept staring at her. "I was coming back upstairs."

"You surely did not think that, after a month, I was not going to have you, did you?"

"But I must go look over the terrain at Fort de la Revère."

"I know, and I am going with you."

"That might not be . . ."

She gave him one of those dead set looks with which she had seen a gorgeous Russian model at *Vogue* reduce men to speechlessness. "I said I am going with you."

★ ★ ★ ★ ★

Fort de la Revère was a dark mass of stone atop the escarpment. Built for military purposes, then turned into a prison, it was currently being used by the Vichy government as a place of detention for a large number of interned British, Polish and Belgian soldiers and airmen.

"There is little security," Jean-Luc said. "They sometimes even let groups of internees go into the village to buy things, even give them ration cards. It should not be too difficult to spirit away one or two at a time. But just to be on the safe side I thought we ought to explore the terrain all around the fort, to make certain there are no surprises. But first how about some lunch. I am starving."

They had parked the little closed van they had come in, of the kind used in France by plumbers and electricians, in a grove of pines just off the unpaved road below the fort. He took out the picnic hamper, and they walked deeper into the woods. When they came to a little break in the trees, where a patch of sun fell on the fragrant bed of pine needles, they spread a blanket. He peeked into the picnic hamper.

"Wait, Jean-Luc," and she drew him to her, "there is something we have to do first. . . ."

"I thought to save that for dessert."

"Well, you will just have to change the menu, because, to put it bluntly, I simply cannot wait any longer. Now undress me."

As he knelt removing the last of her underclothes, she reached up and took him by the neck, brought his head down between her thighs. For a long time she lay there with her eyes closed, gripping his hair with both hands, all her being reduced to the feeling of what his mouth was doing to her. It was delicious. Then, still holding him by the hair, she brought his mouth up to her nipples, and when she knew that she could not last much longer, to her mouth. "Now I want you inside of me."

Afterwards, she lay beside him and caressed his face, tears of joy in her eyes. "It had been such a long time." They lay together, Elizabeth drowsy with satisfaction. Only hunger kept her from falling asleep.

"Why, it is a picnic fit for Louis XV and Madame Pompadour," Jean-Luc said, after the contents of the hamper had been put out on the checked tablecloth. In addition to the pâté, chicken, asparagus and potato salad, there was a bouquet of raw vegetables, two stuffed tomatoes, a sauce for the asparagus, another for the vegetables, cornichon pickles, a jar of mustard, and a *pot* of sweet butter. Both the *baguette* and the fig tart were still warm.

After they had taken the edge off their hunger, and after two glasses of wine, Elizabeth said what was in her heart. "I thought I would die of loneliness all those weeks, and then the constant fear. It was hard, Jean-Luc."

"For me too it was hell, being without you. I worked myself far into the night, every night, until I was so exhausted I could sleep."

"Sleep, yes. So difficult not to stay awake, thinking always of all the worst things that could happen. Jean-Luc, you said the last time we were together, at Aubigny—how long ago that was—that I had changed you. I was so moved that I could not reply, and afterwards there was no time. I just want you to know that without you, I would now be . . . but you know. . . ."

"It was you who made the choice to dare."

"Do you think I would make a good journalist, maybe a foreign correspondent? We could make a team. What do you think?"

"I think you, who have succeeded at everything, could do

anything. Once I told you that you could conquer Paris. That now seems a child's step."

"Thank you, my darling. But first we must win a war. So tell me something about our comrades."

"All right. Kuhn was just a teacher of architectural drawing at the local commercial school, but he is quite well off. He has played the stock market successfully all of his life. I think he lives at that rooming house across from the truck stop just so he can have his meals with Jean and Margot. Quite a gourmet, even though he's thin as a rail. He's also made himself a master forger. Being Jewish, he has much to lose."

"What about the lawyer?"

"Armand de Vaucluse comes from some minor noble family in Normandy. His grandfather came to the Cote d'Azur, like Serge's father, like so many people—that is why the English first came—in hopes that the warm, dry climate would help his TB. The grandfather died, the family stayed on. Armand moves in all the right social and official circles, and that makes him very valuable to us. You did not recognize him?"

"Should I have?"

"He is the Warden family lawyer here. He drew up Paula and Marc's marriage contract and was at the reception at Villa Warden. He probably remembers me, though he has not said anything. He certainly remembers you, but then what man would not?"

"Oh dear. Can we trust him?"

"Kuhn vouches for him. Armand's father and both uncles were killed by the Germans on the Western front in the last war."

"Do you trust Kuhn?"

"Yes."

213

"How can you be sure?"

"I cannot. At some point you have to decide, I will trust this person. Otherwise, what is the use? If you cannot, finally, put your faith in individuals then you have nothing left but the state to believe in. That is what Hitler—and Pétain and his kind—would like for us to do, become robots marching at the orders of the state."

Elizabeth was thinking now what she must say, before they left this place, to this very serious man she loved so much.

"The Raimeaus?"

"They are what makes France what it is: hard-working, sensual, stubborn, tied to their native soil, not about to accept a France that is a puppet of the Boches."

"And Serge Malakoff? What could conceivably motivate a gangster like that to join the resistance?"

"Simpler than you might imagine. There are two gangs in Nice. The rival gang to Malakoff's have thrown in their lot with Vichy, so Malakoff's gang has no choice but to join the other side. We can count on him—there are profits to be made—as long as the equation stays the same."

"And you put this team together in the month since France was defeated?"

"It was the best I could do."

"The best you could do." She laughed. *"Mon Dieu,"* and she buried her face in his lap. She left it there, letting him stroke her hair, while she chose her words.

"Jean-Luc, I love you as much, I suppose, as a woman can love a man, and beyond that I admire and respect you. You are risking your life for what you believe in, and you are of a very small minority of Frenchmen who are willing to do that. . . ."

"Somebody has to plant the seed. Our ranks will grow."

"You are admirable in all respects, but—if I may say so—

you are a man and share a male illusion."

"Ah. What might that be?"

"That the dragon must be slain before you can ride away with the maiden. This dragon may take some years in the slaying."

"True."

"Women, on the other hand, want stability, a home, warmth and love."

"And?"

"And I am not prepared to put aside my life with you until the war is over. I will stay with you, fight with you, but on condition that we live our life together at the same time that we do these other things. I will make this life my home." She was breathless now. "And another thing. I must go with you on every mission, unless there is some good reason for my not being with you. There is nothing that can separate us now but this war, and that only by killing us. If that is to be, better to die together than alone."

"I can accept that."

"Then we need not speak of it again."

Several days passed in that astonishing perfection for which the French Riviera has become legendary, blue skies laced with traces of high cloud, the sea a deep blue streaked with icy green, the temperature so close to that of her skin that she could not even feel the air around her. She was the happiest of women, happier perhaps than if there had been a cottage in the country, a child soon to be born, curtains to be bought, pots and pans to be chosen for the kitchen.

What she could do she did, putting vases of flowers and fragrant dried herbs around their room over the garage, making herself, in clean starched cottons, fresh and desirable. And was it not something fine to be by the side of the man you loved, committed to the overthrow of tyranny; and had she not said the day that they had truly fallen in love, that she wanted to live a life of risk and danger? And then she remembered what Paula had said as Elizabeth was overseeing the packing of Leonore's trunks for the trip to Paris: that she should be careful what she asked for, because she might get it.

The Raimeaus' *bistro* was closed on Sundays, when there were few truckers on the road; but this Sunday there was a private luncheon in the back dining room, which was not all that unusual. This time, however, it was not a wedding, anniversary or baptism that was being celebrated. Around the table were six conspirators, including Margot Raimeau, still in her apron. The first course was sea bass grilled over charcoal, on which stalks of fennel had been thrown, the second a leg of lamb stuffed with rice, olives and pistachios.

Elizabeth was seated at one end of the table between Armand de Vaucluse, the aristocratic lawyer to the rich and powerful of the Côte d'Azur, and Margot, cook and hostess at a truck stop. And what a lively conversation they had! Armand and Margot argued over politics, told bawdy jokes, and discussed the qualities of certain wines; and Elizabeth had been in France long enough to join in. It seemed that— and she hoped it was true—their commitment to a common cause was more important to them all than their very different backgrounds.

"We've had a visitor from Marseille," Jean-Luc, at the other end of the table, said, "from Fig Tree, who says the line is open all the way to the Spanish border, what we've been working for. Let's hope it is so. Not much of an escape line but, if it works, we will have demonstrated it can be done."

"It is a beginning," Josette said, "like yeast, to make the bread grow."

"Mon vieux," Raimeau said, "you had better check out your line, like a fisherman along the river bank."

"Elizabeth has taken the line from Paris here, and it worked."

Well, yes, it worked, Elizabeth thought, but what does it consist of? A couple with British intelligence in Paris; a vintner, whose land near Tours straddles the demarcation line between Nazi-occupied France and Vichy France; and a young war widow in Lyon. Lose one of those and you've got no line. She could only admire Jean-Luc for the bluff he was carrying off with so little resources. But wasn't that how it was done? Bluffing your way through, proving it could be done, until those who had the money and men would believe in you and commit to the struggle.

"But what about the line from here to the Spanish border?" Raimeau said. "Have you ever run anyone over it?"

"No. The only two British airmen we've brought out were openly through Marseille, but that was before the British destroyed the Vichy fleet at Mers-el-Kébir and diplomatic relations between Vichy and Great Britain were broken."

"Then you had better check out the line from here to the Spanish border."

"I intend to . . . Elizabeth and I."

No one protested at this idea, even looked in her direction. She was deeply pleased to be treated as an equal.

"What cover?" old Kuhn asked, speaking up for the first time.

"Locksmith, from Toulon. I'm having it painted on the side of the van. One of Serge Malakoff's associates, a real master at picking locks, I must say, has taught me enough over the last month for me to get by, and supplied me with all the tools of the trade . . . at a grossly inflated price."

217

"What about Elizabeth," Armand asked, "what is her cover?"

"I have an identity card," Elizabeth said, "as the wife of Jean-Luc Fournier. The story is that we are going to a funeral in Perpignan."

Chapter Nineteen

Marjorie Dufay burst into laughter. "A locksmith? Jean-Luc, spare me. You, the most sophisticated Frenchman I know in overalls and carrying a toolbox. What is this all about?"

"This outfit gains me entry almost anywhere, like the man who reads the gas meter, but that is too easy to check on."

"You are something else," the woman said in English with a midwestern accent. "Well, come on over and sit down then, and let's talk."

Marjorie Dufay led them to the other end of the long room with a glass wall framing the old port of Marseille. She was tall, with shoulder-length red hair, and wore black slacks, a white silk blouse and a heavy silver bracelet.

"Shall we have a pastis?"

"By all means."

"Before we begin, I take it your friend is not just someone you picked up off the street," Madame Dufay said, as she mixed drinks, "despite that dress that looks like it came off a rack in the open-air Saturday market."

"Elizabeth is my courier."

Elizabeth laughed at the remark about her tacky dress, which was made in a humorous way, but she sensed jealousy. She had also realized from the way Marjorie Dufay lightly kissed Jean-Luc on the lips when they came in the room that at some point in the past they had been to bed together. She had always assumed that there had been a number of women in Jean-Luc's past. How could it have been otherwise? He was to women as catnip to cats. She did not care about his past, for she was serenely confident that he was now hers alone.

"Well, *salut,*" and Madame Dufay raised her glass.

Elizabeth took a sip of the cloudy green liquid tasting of licorice, as strange to her at first as a Gauloise cigarette had been. She looked around her. The parquet floor was covered with Oriental rugs, the terrace beyond the glass wall was lined with orange trees in tubs, and the green marble fireplace was flanked by two Matisses. Paula would have felt right at home.

"So, the boy got the message to you that we are ready both here and in Perpignan. We have even done a trial run. As you know the armistice agreement provides that the Vichy regime has to turn over any German national to the Nazis on demand. The Gestapo has already quietly moved into Marseille. They are operating out of a downtown hotel.

"The first person they began inquiring about was an anti-Hitler German newspaper editor who was hiding out here. We arranged a visa for him from the Brazilian consulate, my courier passed him on to Perpignan, and they took him across the border into Spain. I have word that he has already sailed from Lisbon. So, there is one more that Hitler will never put his hands on."

"Who did you use as a courier?" Jean-Luc asked.

"A gangster's girl. Do not raise your eyebrow. I know my town. I have become a real Marseillaise. I realized that when Gaston died. I was about to pack up and go home, and then I thought, that's crazy. What would I do in Des Moines? You can't keep a girl down on the farm once she's seen Marseille, and I have been here ten years.

"Anyway, if you have money in this town and want to get

things done, sooner or later you have to turn to the mob. They use their girls all the time as couriers. They carry stolen goods, or money or even a gun to someone who is executing a contract for them. The girls do what they are told and keep their mouths shut. They do or they get the hell beat out of them."

Madame Dufay looked at her watch. "Jean-Luc, I have a friend who has a proposition that I think may interest you. Would you talk to him if he came over?"

"What kind of proposition?"

"Putting out a clandestine newspaper."

"I have to be very careful."

"I understand, but I can vouch for him. We have moved in the same social circle for years. He owns a daily paper, which now has to follow the Vichy line, of course. He thought it would be amusing to use the same presses to produce a clandestine paper telling the truth about Vichy."

"I am not so sure. . . ." But Elizabeth could see interest written all over Jean-Luc's face.

"Well, I guess I will have to be more explicit. Claude and I have been having an affair for quite some time, a discreet affair. I would not want to hurt his wife, who is a very nice person, but they are just not matched. If you will agree to see him, he is right down there on his yacht, which is moored next to mine. I can call to the concierge to fetch him. He does not need to know you by anything but your first name."

"All right, then."

"Good. Now I suggest you two change out of those costumes. Jean-Luc, you will find some of Gaston's clothes in an armoire in the back bedroom. And, Elizabeth, you can put on something of mine. We are about the same size. If you want makeup it is on a table in my bathroom."

Elizabeth returned to the room in slacks and a loose-fitting knit blouse, her hair, now growing long again, tied back, makeup applied. Marjorie and Jean-Luc, who was wearing the kind of rough nautical clothes that one wore along the southern coast of France, were laughing over something. Marjorie looked up at Elizabeth, looked at Jean-Luc and shook her head.

"I understand," she said, as though Elizabeth was not even in the room, "that this is where you have finally come to port. I could see even in that outlandish getup, with no makeup and hair hanging straight down, that she was a fine-boned beauty. But she is, in fact, a beauty of world class. *Mes félicitations, cher ami.*"

Elizabeth should have felt like a kind of prize animal on display, but it was subtler than that. What Marjorie Dufay, who simply did not mince words, was saying, she believed, was warm and generous. If she could not have Jean-Luc then she would wish him Elizabeth. This was very far from the ways of Laurel Hill, Virginia.

"So there you have it," Claude Faucher said. "I am not going to play the Vichy game, though my paper and my radio station must, if they are to stay open. I have enough employees who think as I do to put out a clandestine paper in the wee hours of the morning. What I need is a network to gather information on what is really going on in Vichy, a network to distribute our little paper, and a first-class journalist to edit it. Marjorie tells me I may have all three of them in you."

Jean-Luc seemed to be studying the toes of his espadrilles. Elizabeth studied Claude Faucher, a tall, powerfully-built man who could not have been more than forty-five, but whose hair was snow-white, thick and bushy, contrasting with skin burned mahogany by the sun. When he entered the room Jean-Luc had made a slight bow to Marjorie Dufay, as if to say that she had not done badly herself.

"It seems to me," Jean-Luc said, looking up, "that it is a bit early to establish an underground press. Vichy is only a month and a half old. Who knows how things are going to unroll?"

"So we make sure they do not. Right now everyone is just happy the fighting is over, and that a symbol of France, old Marshal Pétain, is in charge. They believe that all we have to do is follow his idiotic slogan—work, family, country—and everything will be all right.

"What nine out of ten fail to understand is that Vichy, led in reality not by old Pétain but by that arch-traitor Laval, is falling all over itself to collaborate with the Nazis, and that our food supplies are being shipped off to Germany—why else would rationing already be necessary? It is exactly the moment to start spreading the truth, catch Vichy off balance before it even has a chance to get its feet on the ground. The truth, Jean-Luc, the truth. It is far more important than blowing up bridges and assassinating Germans."

"I have always believed that."

"Then will you join me?"

"I have other tasks that must be done first. But after that . . . perhaps."

"Fair enough. I will not ask what these other tasks are, but you might be interested to know that my presses are also turning out identity cards and ration stamps for the Vichy government."

Jean-Luc and Elizabeth drove on westward through Arles, Nîmes, and Montpellier, towns that had existed when Provence was Provincia Romana within the Roman Empire. In Béziers they had lunch on the vine-shaded terrace of a working-class café and then continued on to Perpignan. Now the snow-capped Pyrenees could be seen in the distance.

"I have always wanted to see where you came from, Jean-Luc."

"Of course I was brought up in Paris, but my father was determined that I know my origins. We made the pilgrimage to his village every summer. I even learned Catalan."

"Can you speak it now?"

"Pretty well. Besides uncles Martin and Roger that I have told you about, I have a dozen cousins of various degrees at Coustouges. From the edge of the village you can look down into Spain. That is where I went the day war was declared and we were having lunch at La Rose de la France. I wanted to see if my relatives would be willing, if France fell, to smuggle people into Spain."

"Jean-Luc, do you realize what today is?"

"It is—*Mon Dieu*—it is September 3. The war began one year ago today—and when the Germans struck, France lasted less than six weeks. I am not surprised to find myself where I am. I rather expected it. But I never would have imagined you beside me, with a false identity card and a pistol in your handbag."

"Well, here I am. And I am pretty good, Serge says, with the Beretta. He calls it a lady's pistol. We have had several practice sessions with it. . . ."

"You had better put that pistol under the seat. There is a roadblock ahead."

There were two tough-looking gendarmes at the roadblock, and one of them raised a red paddle for them to stop.

"Gray card, green card and identity cards, messieurdames."

Jean-Luc handed over the van's insurance and registration papers and the two identity cards. The gendarme looked at them and then at the license plate. "Toulon, eh? You are a long way from home, monsieur. You have business in Roussillon?"

"My grandmother in Perpignan died. We are on our way to the funeral."

"Grandmother died, eh?"

"Here is the telegram informing me."

The gendarme glanced at it. "*Alors,* on your way then."

They drove around the roadblock and continued on. Soon church spires and then the walls of Perpignan came into view.

"Where did that telegram come from?" she asked.

"Our agent in Perpignan."

"Who is?"

"Dr. José Girona."

"You have known him long?"

"As long as it is possible to know anyone. Dr. Girona is a gynecologist. He delivered me. That was in Barcelona. But when Franco seized power he fled to France and decided to settle in Perpignan, where he could still speak Catalan."

Dr. Girona's *cabinet médical* was behind the cathedral in an old mansion shaded by giant magnolias that had been divided up into doctors' and dentists' offices. He received them in a room adjoining his office that he had turned into a library, its walls lined from floor to ceiling with books in Catalan and French. A tray with decanter, three glasses and a plate of almond cookies had already been put out on the table.

"May I offer you an *apéritif?*" He poured a little into each glass. "*A bas les Boches.*"

"*A bas Vichy,*" Jean-Luc replied.

"*A bas Franco,*" Elizabeth was emboldened to say, hoping that it would not seem presumptuous for one who had not yet made any real sacrifice.

Dr. Girona gave her the kind of warm look that those who are fighting for a cause against great odds, give to one who has

225

offered to put what they have at risk.

"*Salut,*" the doctor said, and the three of them clinked glasses.

"Well, José, all goes well?" Jean-Luc asked.

"Well enough." The doctor leaned back in his chair and seemed to be gathering together and organizing his thoughts. Dr. Girona was a small man, in late middle age, with his receding gray hair cut short, dark eyebrows framing chestnut-brown eyes, a prominent nose, a wide mustache and not much chin.

"Yes, well enough. You heard about the German we got out?"

"Yes. You saved his life. Who is your courier?"

"My nurse."

"Are you completely confident of her?"

"My dear Jean-Luc, after you have delivered several hundred babies together, questions of confidence do not arise."

They laughed, and suddenly Dr. Girona was no longer a stranger to Elizabeth.

"Soon we will begin work in earnest," Jean-Luc said. "There are a large number of interned Allied soldiers and airmen being held in a fort above Beaulieu. We will try to get some of the airmen out first. They are desperately needed back in England."

"Everything depends, of course," Girona said, "on Franco remaining neutral. But for a while at least, we should continue to be able to obtain transit visas to cross Spain by train."

"That will not help our aviators much. They have no passports, of course, and hardly any would speak either French or Spanish."

"In those cases, we will have to take them across the Pyrenees at Coustouges."

"Where we are headed now, to make sure everything is in readiness."

"Once they are into Spain," the doctor said, "they should try to reach the British consulate in Barcelona. The consul will then take them in his official car to Madrid, and an embassy car with diplomatic tags will take them on to Gibraltar."

"How will you get them to Coustouges?"

"The same way you are going to have to go. The road was bad enough before, but with the heavy rains this spring it is no longer passable for cars. Do you ride horses, Mademoiselle Elisabeth?"

"Yes."

"Now you will have to adjust to a mule."

Elizabeth laughed. "I learned to ride on a mule."

"You will have to garage your car at Amélie-les-Bains, Jean-Luc. I will give you the name of a man there from whom you can rent mules."

After they had finished with their business, the conversation turned to other things, and Elizabeth was astonished at how much Jean-Luc knew about so many things, ranging from botany to Romanesque architecture to bullfighting. Dr. Girona was enjoying himself so much that he insisted that they have supper, prepared by his housekeeper, in his apartment above his office, and spend the night. It was one in the morning before they retired.

She was very glad the road was impassable to cars. A sure-footed mule was much to be preferred to a car on this rocky road, not much more than a track, along a precipice with a sheer drop of hundreds of feet. At noon they stopped beside a waterfall and spread the cloth in which the lunch prepared by Dr. Girona's housekeeper had been wrapped. They were in a forest of cork oaks, their bare trunks stripped of their bark.

"You can strip the bark after about ten years," Jean-Luc said, "and it takes another ten years for the bark to grow back. You have to be sort of patient to be in the cork business. In the meantime, the people of Coustouges let their pigs run wild in the forest and fatten up on acorns from the cork oaks. They also keep goats. About all they can produce up here, besides cork, is cured hams and goat's cheese."

"Can they make a living that way?"

"Not much of one, but it is a good cover for smuggling,"

"Then you were not joking when you told me—when we first met—that your family had been smugglers for hundreds of years?"

"Not at all. If my father had not got some education and moved to Paris, I would probably be doing the same thing. The way my father went into the art business was by selling Catalan wood-carvings brought him by people from around here. I suspect most of them were stolen from churches in Spain."

"What are your uncles and cousins like?"

Jean-Luc pulled the cork from the bottle of wine and cut off pieces of bread and cheese. "They seldom bathe or shave, and most of them cannot read or write, but they are good people to have around when you are fighting Germans. They carry guns a lot, and always a knife. The women are pretty fierce too."

"What an adventure this is for me."

"Well, *chérie,* you said you wanted a life of risk and danger. This is only the beginning."

The village of Coustouges, on a desolate wind-blown ridge high above the valleys of France on one side, and the Spanish plain on the other, was home to ravens and eagles. My God, Elizabeth thought, how exciting it is to know that this is where the man who I have made mine comes from. It is from here that he draws his strength.

Saddle-sore, they rode their mules, iron shoes clopping on big paving stones into the little square, surrounded by no more than a few dozen ancient houses. The village seemed deserted, but then a heavy-set man with grizzled hair and several days of dark beard, stepped out from between two houses, a pair of binoculars hanging from his neck, a double-barreled shotgun pointed directly at them.

"Oncle Martin."

"Jean-Luc, you should know better than to arrive here without warning."

"Ah, so. And how was I supposed to warn you who have no telephone, no telegraph? Send a boy with a message carried in a forked stick?"

"You always had an impertinent mouth. And who is that woman?"

"Mine."

"Ah. Well, then do not just sit there like idiots on those mules. Get down, get down. We are not without hospitality at Coustouges."

They were not, indeed, without hospitality at Coustouges. That evening the entire Cabanasse clan was summoned to dinner at Uncle Martin's. Fourteen or fifteen in all crowded around a long table of rough planks, which looked as though dinners had been served on it for some hundreds of years.

The cousins, wide-eyed at this blond woman that Jean-Luc had acquired, had been introduced to her one by one. But when the time came to sit down, Uncle Martin and Uncle Roger who were, to Elizabeth's amusement, newly-shaven, sat her down between them. Then three dark-haired young women, in black dresses and smelling earthy and female, served the first course.

229

"Sausages," Uncle Martin said, taking out a wicked-looking knife and cutting thin slices, "one of pork with fennel, one of pork with red pepper, the last and best of wild boar. Shot him myself, a big ugly tusker with red eyes. Did you know that wild boars have red eyes, like they have drunk a liter of brandy?"

"No, I did not know that," Elizabeth said. The room was filling with smoke from an olivewood fire, over which a whole piglet was being turned.

"Olives," Uncle Roger said, offering her the bowl. "Green, green-cracked, with garlic, black in vinegar, black with red peppers, and the little shriveled ones they pick up from the ground, the best of all."

"Goat's cheese," Uncle Martin said. "Three kinds. The first three days old, soft as butter, the second three months old—the one I prefer—the third three years old. Hard as a rock, but some people like it."

"How's business?" Jean-Luc, sitting across from Elizabeth's place of honor, asked, apparently greatly amused at his uncles' courting of her.

"Could not be better. The price of cigarettes brought in from Spain is four times what it was before. If the war goes on for a long time we may just become rich. . . ."

"But we would rather be poor," Uncle Roger said, "and have the Boches brought down. Five of our young men were conscripted, Jean-Luc, and you know that my son François was killed by the bastards."

"Yes, I know. May he rest in peace, Uncle. And we *will* bring them down."

A dessert of *crème caramel* was served, a glass of plum brandy, and the guests filed out. With some pride Elizabeth recognized that this had been a very special, a formal occasion, a tribute to Jean-Luc, but also a tribute to her. They were given an olive oil lamp and bade good night.

Their bedroom was in a loft. "Where I slept every summer from age eight to sixteen," Jean-Luc said. "I see they have put a new straw-filled mattress on the bed."

"On which I am going to make love to you. I intend to possess your past as well as you in the present."

And then they did make love. The mattress was new, but the ancient rusted springs made so much noise that she got the giggles. She was deeply happy.

Elizabeth awoke at first light and, leaving Jean-Luc sleeping on the straw mattress, quietly dressed. She climbed down the ladder from the loft, passed through the sleeping house smelling of wood smoke, crossed the little village square and climbed to a point where she could watch the sun spread across the Spanish plain. There lay the way to freedom for many, if she and Jean-Luc did their job well.

She turned and walked back down into the tiny village. The clouds that had hung over the mountains on the French side all the day before had dispersed, and almost the whole horizon was filled with the cylindrical cone of a vast mountain. Jean-Luc was coming up the path from the village toward her.

"That mountain," she said, without any greeting to him, so startled was she by what she saw, "what is it? It dominates everything, like Vesuvius or Fuji."

"More than that," he said. "It is Canigou, the sacred mountain of the Catalans, for as far back as there is memory in my race. Even now on St. John's Day, at the summer solstice, we build a great bonfire on the summit that can be seen by all of us who live within sight of the sacred mountain."

"The mountain is sacred to you, then?"

"Yes."

There was no irony at all in his voice. How delightful, she thought, to discover that the person you love is something quite different, something more, than what you had imagined.

Chapter Twenty

In early December Elizabeth made her ninth trip to Perpignan. Six of the first eight had been almost routine; two had some scary moments, one because a young British airman had panicked during a police check, the other because the gangster's girl who had handed over a Polish officer to her in Marseille had tried to extort money by threatening to create a scene. She had handled both those situations, but this time was different.

"Are you feeling all right?" she asked the small man with grayish-blond hair, scrunched deep down in his overcoat, like a rabbit in its burrow. She asked because she did not think he was.

"Oh, yes, I am just fine," he said. He spoke French well enough, but no one would fail to notice the German accent.

She turned and looked out the train window at the coastal landscape she had come to know so well. It was one of those brilliant, barely chilly days that the Midi offers well into the new year. She very much wanted to get this transfer over with. Then she and Jean-Luc had agreed to take Christmas off to relax and consider what they did next.

"I would have liked to visit Marseille," the man said.

"Perhaps after the war. Today that is the last thing you want to do. Today we are going to Perpignan."

"What happens when we get there?"

"Have you already forgotten? We will go to a public park and sit down on a bench. After a minute or two I will leave. A few minutes later a woman will sit down beside you. You will leave with her, and she will take you to the train station and accompany you as far as the Spanish border. Once you are admitted into Spain you are on your own."

"Yes, I remember now."

They fell silent then, and Elizabeth reviewed in her mind how they had reached this point, on a train coming into Perpignan. It had begun with a radio message from Alain in Paris saying that they were sending a box of prize fruit, but delicate, requiring very special handling: code name Apricot.

They had taken Apricot off the train at Nice. He had been traveling on forged papers that Kuhn said would never have passed serious inspection, but then Manny Kuhn was a perfectionist. What Apricot had to say was enough to send shivers down the spine of the bravest *résistant*.

He had been a code clerk at the German embassy in Paris, also filling in for the embassy cashier when he was on leave; and this had been the situation up until just before France declared war on Germany on September 3, 1939. On August 29 he had been accused of embezzlement of official funds, relieved of his duties and confined to his quarters in the embassy. During the confusion of September 3 he had simply walked out of the embassy and gone into hiding.

When the Germans occupied Paris, the Gestapo issued orders for Apricot's arrest. They were not interested in the embezzlement but in the fact that he had seen every secret telegram that had passed between the German embassy in Paris and Berlin for the three years preceding the war. Apricot figured the Allies might want to assure that he got free of Hitler's clutches with all that he knew.

★ ★ ★ ★ ★

As the train shuddered to a stop her fears dissolved. It was action now, with no time for thought. They passed through the station and out into Perpignan in the late afternoon, each carrying a small valise. Then they walked, without incident, to the little park that she had come to know well, with its moss-grown fountain, paths of orange sand flowing around islands of neglected shrubs. They sat down on a bench.

"Well, good luck."

"You are just going to leave me here?"

"Yes."

"What if no one comes?"

"Someone will." She didn't even want to think about what would happen if Marianne, Dr. Girona's nurse, should fail to show up. These were the chances you took when those who were willing to resist were so pitifully few.

"Goodbye, then," and she got up.

"Goodbye, and thank you."

She turned and walked away in the direction of the station. There she bought a ticket for Nice, and then went to the bar for a much-needed brandy. The timing had been good. The train for Nice was leaving in twenty minutes. She had a second brandy, the train left exactly on time, and she had a compartment to herself. As night fell the train reached full speed on its way to Nice where there would be a change of trains, and then only a few more minutes of travel to Beaulieu and the safety of Jean-Luc's arms. She lay down on the seat, put her coat over her and went to sleep.

"Madame." A hand was shaking her shoulder. She sat up slowly, coming out of the drugged sleep that follows the release of tension. The train was standing still.

"What is it?" she asked of the uniform of a policeman that came into focus above her. "Where are we?"

"Marseille, madame. Your papers, please."

Elizabeth fumbled in her handbag and brought out her identity card.

"Fournier, Elisabeth. You will have to come with me."

"But why?"

The heavy-set policeman, probably one of the Corsicans who composed the bulk of the police force along the Mediterranean coast of France, as the Irish did in New York, shrugged.

"I have no idea."

"Where are we going?"

"Police headquarters."

"I have some questions to ask you, madame," the man who had introduced himself as Inspector Gervais said, playing nervously with a pencil, as if it were he who had questions to answer. This helped a bit to relieve her own fears, compounded by waiting an hour for this interview in a tiny room lit by a bare bulb. He was a human being too with his own worries.

Then another man in a raincoat and a dark felt hat, entered the room. This seemed to make the inspector even more nervous. Without exchanging a word, the man in the raincoat drew up a chair beside the inspector's desk and sat down, leaving his hat on. The inspector opened a file on his desk.

"Do you recognize this man?" the inspector asked, passing her a photograph. The photograph was of Apricot.

Elizabeth swallowed to moisten her mouth and, in a barely audible voice said, "No."

"That is strange, because three times last week you visited the apartment in Nice where this man—I have no idea what name you know him under—was staying. Each time you showed the concierge an identity card made out to Elisabeth

Fournier, card 176383. That is the number on the card we took from you. So why not tell the truth?"

She frantically searched for some answer that would extricate her from this ominous situation. "Yes, I visited him. I did not know him by any name. We just went to bed together."

"Are you telling me you are a prostitute?"

Elizabeth nodded her head. Maybe it would work.

"We did not find a doctor's certificate, which prostitutes are required to carry at all times, in your handbag or valise. Do you have it on you?"

"No. I was coming back from visiting my mother in Perpignan. I saw no need to carry it."

Inspector Gervais played with the pencil some more. He was a middle-aged man, soberly dressed, with a neat graying mustache. She realized that he looked more frightened than nervous. Why? It was she who should be scared out of her wits, and she was.

"It is not a bad story," the inspector finally said, "but you are lying. When a woman visits someone under police surveillance three times in a week, naturally we want to know more about her. So we looked up the application for identity card number 176383. It was issued to a fisherman in Nice."

She said nothing. There was nothing to say.

"Therefore the card you were carrying must be counterfeit. Travelling with false papers is a serious offense, Madame Fournier—if that is indeed your name. It could put you in jail for several years, but it need not if you tell us the whole truth.

"On the other hand, if you do not, you are in much worse trouble. The man you visited is a German citizen who committed a serious crime under German law. Under the terms of the armistice agreement, we must turn over, on the demand of the German authorities, any German citizen on French territory. The only reason we did not arrest your friend earlier is that someone helped him travel from Paris to Nice with false papers. We were waiting to see if we could identify his accomplice, and it seems now that we have.

"Unfortunately, this German criminal has vanished. If we do not apprehend him, it will be a serious embarrassment for the government in Vichy, the police commissioner in Nice will probably be fired, but you will be in the worst trouble of all. So I suggest you tell the whole truth now, otherwise. . . ."

A police sergeant entered the room, whispered something to Inspector Gervais and handed him what looked like a passport. The inspector opened it, looked up at Elizabeth and then looked back at the passport.

"After thirty years on the force, I am seldom surprised, but I must admit that this time I am. The photograph on the French identity card of Elisabeth Fournier, who claims to be a prostitute, is of the same person as in the photograph in the passport we found in the lining of your valise, an American passport in the name of Sarah Elizabeth Vail. One hardly knows where to begin."

The man in the raincoat finally took off his hat. He was a very ordinary looking person, with mousy-colored hair. He leaned over and conversed in whispers with the inspector.

"Clearly," Inspector Gervais said, "this is a matter for serious investigation, Mademoiselle Vail—and I assume that is your true identity—one that cannot be undertaken tonight. I am going to transfer you to the Marseille detention center, where you will be photographed and fingerprinted. You will spend the night in a cell there, and tomorrow you will be taken to another location for interrogation. And let me give you a sincere piece of advice. Do not try to lie. It would be a serious mistake. Just tell the truth."

The whole time the inspector had been speaking she had

been staring at the black boots protruding from the trousers of the man in the raincoat. She felt like screaming. They were going to turn her over to the Gestapo!

"It's true," she blurted out, "I am an American citizen."

"It is a little late for that to be of any help to you," the inspector said. "You chose to assume a French identity, and we will just leave it that way. If asked, I have not seen the passport of Sarah Elizabeth Vail and know nothing about her."

She was taken to the detention center in a car driven by a policeman while she sat in the back handcuffed to another policeman. She was so frightened that she could think of nothing but that she was doomed. It was the worst situation imaginable. She was about to be handed over to the Gestapo for having helped a German citizen escape with secret intelligence of inestimable value to the Allies. No matter how much she cooperated, they would never let someone who knew that the Gestapo in Vichy France had failed in this major case— indeed, she was responsible for that failure—ever go free. After she had told them everything, they would kill her.

At the detention center she was taken to a large room where dozens of people milled about. Her handcuffs were removed and she was turned over to the sergeant in charge. The two policemen who had brought her then left, and the sergeant told her to sit on a bench with others waiting to be photographed and fingerprinted. She looked around the drab, dimly-lighted room that smelled of human bodies and alcohol. It was a mixture of petty criminals, men who had been fighting, others so drunk they couldn't stand and eight or ten young women who were obviously prostitutes.

A policeman came into the room and bellowed, "All right, girls, let's go. The van to take you to the hospital for your exams is here. When you are finished you will be brought back here for the rest of the night. Maybe losing a night's earnings and probably getting beat up by your pimps will teach you some respect for police regulations. When we say carry an up-to-date doctor's certificate that is what we mean."

The young women started moving toward the door. Elizabeth looked around the room. The sergeant she had been turned over to was nowhere to be seen. Her heart was beating wildly. A half hour before she hadn't even known that prostitutes were required to carry certificates. Maybe it was a good omen. Until she was photographed and fingerprinted no one in the room had the slightest idea who she was. She had nothing to lose and her life to gain.

She stood up. No one paid any attention. She watched the slinky walk that becomes second nature to prostitutes and imitated it as she crossed the room. Still no one paid any attention. Then she was through the door and going down the stairs in a clatter of high heels.

They were herded into the police van and immediately there began a chorus of complaints against the police in the foulest language. But Elizabeth was not listening. Her mind was concentrated on just one thing: when they got to the hospital, what?

They were there in five minutes, and the two policemen turned them over to a gray-haired, big-bosomed head nurse.

"Follow me," the nurse said and led them through swinging doors into a corridor painted pale green and smelling of antiseptic. "Sit down there," she said motioning toward a long bench painted white. "We will take you one at a time," and she turned to leave.

Desperation told Elizabeth that the time to act was while the head nurse was still there.

"Got to go to the toilet," she said in the best imitation of a

Marseillais accent she could manage.

"You just hold it back, sister. I am not letting whores who forget to get their medicals use my toilets. You all probably have something."

"So you want me to bleed on your floor."

The nurse gave an exasperated snort. "Where is your handbag?"

"The cops stole it."

The nurse snorted again. "Now I guess I am supposed to supply you with a sanitary napkin."

The nurse disappeared into a supply room. Through the porthole in the swinging door to the lobby Elizabeth saw the two policemen who had brought them, smoking cigarettes and talking.

"Here. And when you come out of that toilet it had better be as clean as when you went in. Go all the way to the end of the corridor and turn left. You will see it."

What Elizabeth saw when she got to the end of the corridor and turned left was a lighted sign: STAIRS. She went quickly down the stairs and found herself in an area where janitorial supplies were kept. At the far end of the room was another lighted sign: EXIT. The next minute she was out in a dark alleyway, walking fast. She came out on a street deserted except for a man under a street light trying to read something on a piece of paper.

"Monsieur, which way to the Old Port?"

"Just follow this street. You will run right into it. But it is a pretty long way."

"What has happened?" Marjorie Dufay said in an alarmed voice, as Elizabeth almost fell through the door into her arms. "You are as white as a sheet and you have been crying."

"The crying got me up here. Your concierge absolutely refused to ring you at one o'clock in the morning, until I started bawling."

"And what is that in your hand?"

Elizabeth looked down in astonishment at the object wrapped in blue paper clutched in her white knuckles.

"A *serviette hygiénique*," and she let it drop to the floor.

"Well, you can explain that later . . . I guess. You are scared out of your skin, aren't you?"

Elizabeth nodded her head and began crying again. "Marjorie, they would have killed me—after they had finished interrogating me."

"Well, you are safe here, I can assure you," and Marjorie Dufay, holding Elizabeth's arm firmly with one hand locked and chained the door with the other. "I think you need a good stiff cognac."

"Yes, please." Elizabeth collapsed on the sofa and took a big swallow of the cognac that Marjorie brought her, coughed, sighed and began to relax.

"So, tell," said the tall, warm-voiced woman in a flowered silk nightgown.

"I just delivered someone very important to the Nazis to Perpignan. By now he should be in Spain. But on the way back they took me off the train at the Marseille station. I was interrogated by the police with someone from the Gestapo present, and they were going to turn me over to the Gestapo . . . but . . . but I managed to escape. They discovered my identity card was fake, they even found my American passport that I—stupidly—had sewn in the lining of my valise. Now I am without any papers at all."

"American passport?"

"This is absurd. Why are we two Americans speaking French to each other?" Elizabeth said in English.

"I thought, when Jean-Luc brought you here, that you

weren't French. My guess was Belgian. But American? You don't have a trace of American accent."

"I've worked at it."

"Then who are you?"

"My name is Elizabeth Vail, and I'm from Laurel Hill, Virginia."

Marjorie shook her head, lit a cigarette and took a swallow from her glass of cognac. "Incredible. Well, Elizabeth Vail, you're in big trouble. From what you've told me the Gestapo and their Vichy toadies will have a dragnet out for you all over southern France. And if I let anything happen to you, Jean-Luc will kill me. We must move immediately. Do you mind if I involve Claude Faucher?"

"Whatever you think is best. But at this hour of the morning?"

"Oh, he's just in the bedroom. I'll fetch him."

When bronze, white-maned Claude Faucher, in pajamas and dressing gown, had heard her story repeated he said, "I see the seriousness of the situation, but I think we can outwit the Boches. I will have a sympathetic photographer from my paper take your photograph in the morning, and since I print identity cards for those gangsters in Vichy I can give you one with a number that we can be sure no one else has. But before we take the photograph we must change your appearance radically. Marjorie?"

"I say we cut her very blond hair off short and dye it a color that is believable with her coloring, perhaps a very dark red, almost chestnut. And since her eyebrows are almost black and in striking contrast to her hair, we could bleach them and then dye them the same dark red as her hair. My hairdresser is the best in Marseille. I will have her come up here and do it. She can dye hair so that your own husband would not know it is dyed."

"Is yours?" Claude asked Marjorie.

"What do you think?" Marjorie replied with a laugh.

"In that case, if I may make a slightly indelicate suggestion, her pubic hair should be dyed also. If she is stripped and searched, it will give a reassuring note of authenticity."

"Oh, you French," Marjorie said. "But you are right of course. So we have given Elizabeth a new identity, but her features are not unremarkable, whatever we do. How do we get her to Beaulieu with the least possibility of police checks? They will be circulating her photograph."

"I have trucks delivering magazines we print going in that direction at all hours. She can ride with one of our drivers, one on our side, and armed." He saw the tears of gratitude welling in Elizabeth's eyes. "The Gestapo will not have you, *chère Elisabeth,* believe me."

Chapter Twenty-One

At dawn a gray van stopped momentarily in front of a bar-restaurant on the heights above Beaulieu and then moved on down the road toward Monaco, leaving Elizabeth standing in the road. She turned and watched the sun rise out of the Mediterranean and emerge from the mist that lay over sea and shore. Then she crossed the road and climbed the metal stairs that led to the room above the car repair shop.

Somehow Elizabeth felt that she was a stranger, her own personality erased and not yet replaced by that of the person she was to become. To the Gestapo Elizabeth Vail was dead, but not in the way they would have preferred. She knocked on the door. She would have to get a new key.

"Who is it?" She thrilled at the sound of Jean-Luc's voice.

"You can put away the gun. *C'est moi.*"

The door opened. "Elizabeth?"

"No. Mariette Goubert."

"What have you done to yourself?"

"It is a long story. But it works doesn't it? For a second or two even you were not sure it was me."

As he turned from closing the door behind them she hooked an arm around his neck and kissed him long and hard, leaving a slash of scarlet across his mouth.

"I will explain everything in a little while," she said, taking off the soiled raincoat she had been wearing and tossing her beret and a woman's magazine onto the table, "but first I thought you would like to see more of the new girlfriend you have acquired. The magazine is for you, from Claude Faucher."

"*Marie-Claire* is for me?"

She laughed. "You will see why later."

She stepped in front of the mirror and began removing the clothes that Marjorie Dufay had brought her, clothes to match the new appearance created by her cut and dyed hair. She unbuttoned the cheap sweater and skirt and let them drop to the floor, then black lace bra and panties. She studied herself in the mirror, in nothing but garter belt and dark stockings. She looked tough, brassy, common, and quite sexy. She ran her fingers through her red hair and turned toward Jean-Luc.

"Well?"

He smiled. "You pay attention to detail, I see."

"One cannot be too careful."

She came to him and unloosened the belt of his bathrobe and slipped it off his shoulders.

"It is time for you to get to know your new girlfriend better," and she walked to the bed and stretched out on it. "I am yours, and do not be too gentle. Mariette likes it a little rough."

They made love fiercely, her legs wrapped tightly around him, until they could no longer. Then they lay spent, looking into each other's eyes.

"I only did that to excite you," she said. "For you I am still your Elizabeth when we are alone. But with anyone else I am going to be acting all the time. They are not going to catch me again."

"They caught you?" He sat up and looked intently at her.

"The Gestapo almost had me. Jean-Luc, if I had not had

incredible luck I could be dead by now." Then she told him the whole story.

"You are trembling," he said, holding her in the safety of his arms, in the most welcome embrace she had ever had.

"If I had not been so determined, I would have burst into tears when I came in the door, but they are not going to make me cry and they are not going to catch me again."

"No, they are not going to catch you, because you are finished as a courier."

"I will not permit that, Jean-Luc. I signed on to do a job, and I will not let the others see you showing favoritism to me."

"I am not showing favoritism," he said, with anger in his voice. "I would not do that, no matter how much I love you. If it were Josette or any of the others, I would have said the same thing. On top of everything else, you have made fools of the Vichy police and the Gestapo by walking right out of the Marseille detention center. They will be looking for you everywhere. Now what about that magazine?"

"Do not try to change the subject."

"The subject is closed. *Tu as compris?*"

"I understand." He was probably right, but the subject was closed only for now. She got out of bed and brought him the magazine. "Shake it."

He shook it and a sheet of paper fell out.

"*Le Résistant*, Volume 1, Number 1."

"Copies of *Marie-Claire* for southeast France are printed at Claude's newspaper plant at Marseille. Somewhere in the process of distribution this sheet was inserted into 10,000 copies. But it is only a temporary measure. After a few times the authorities will start seizing entire issues of magazines. Claude wants Orchard's help in setting up a regular clandestine distribution network."

"This is very exciting, Elizabeth. I promised Claude I would consider this once the net was better organized, which I think it now is. As an old newspaper man, how can I resist? Ink is in my blood. I would like you to work on this project. It may turn out to be the most important thing we do."

"And that way I will not be able to bring up the subject of resuming courier work again."

"Ah, but you agreed that subject was closed."

She said nothing. It was not the time to argue.

"I am meeting Armand and Josette this morning to discuss several matters. They are sort of my brain trust. Come along with me, and we can talk over Claude's proposal."

Where they were to meet Armand de Vaucluse came as a surprise to Elizabeth, but for privacy it made good sense. They had taken a big iron box of an elevator to the top of the Nice citadel, a great upthrusting of rock that had been the last stronghold of the Niçois in time of war for more than two thousand years. There you either held out or died to the last man, woman and child. Not much had changed she thought, but one would not have guessed it in the peaceful park which now crowned the citadel. A few old men were taking the morning sun, leaning on canes, and a few old women were walking or carrying their miniature dogs. No one would have guessed that the world was more violent and inhumane than ever it had been.

"Elizabeth, what is wrong?"

"The horror of it all," she said, and then the tears at last began to flow.

"Come," he said and took her to a bench on a belvedere overlooking the Old Port of Nice on one side and the long curving beach and the grand hotels along the Baie des Anges on the other. A bank of oleander bushes shielded them, and

248

then she broke down into sobs.

"What is it, Elizabeth?"

"There is something I have not told you." He wiped her eyes with his handkerchief, and she drew in a deep breath.

"I got a letter through the network a while ago, from a friend of mine at *Vogue*. It has haunted me every night since. There was a model there, a Polish girl, very beautiful and delicate. But Poles are considered an inferior race by the Nazis and to be used as they see fit. Yvette was reserved exclusively for German generals, and when the Gestapo officer who was to insure this found that she had been with her French boyfriend . . . he became so enraged . . . he drove his dagger into her brain. When they were taking me away from the Marseille police headquarters I thought, it will be even worse for me. . . ."

She had managed not to throw up at the telling of Yvette's death, but in a way she had. This vile matter within her had arisen. She would never again keep anything from Jean-Luc. Already she felt better in his tight embrace.

"That is why you are finished as a courier," he said at last, his voice trembling.

"What do we do now?"

"We fight, we keep on, we do not let these monsters take over the world."

"To do that we must stay alive."

"Yes."

"Which means that I too have a say in what risks you take."

He said nothing, and she knew that there would be stormy times ahead for them on this issue.

They were half an hour late when they reached the little café looking down on the Old Port. It took that long for Elizabeth to regain her composure, let the red leave her eyes, reline them with the kohl that went with her new persona. It was such a warm November day that Armand was sitting outside on the café terrace. He did not comment on their lateness, not even on Elizabeth's altered appearance. He was acting professionally, she thought, and from now on so shall I.

"What news, Armand?" Jean-Luc asked.

"News? Not much. Marshal Pétain has decided that we lost the war to the Boches because we were not pure of heart and that we deserved defeat. France must now do penance until her sins have been washed away under German supervision."

"What do you make of that?"

"Either Pétain has gone completely gaga, or it is Laval playing to the Catholic right, not all of whom are behind Vichy by any means. Some are beginning to think, as I have from the beginning, that General de Gaulle in London offers the best hope of redeeming France's honor."

"Other news?" Jean-Luc asked, giving no indication that he knew de Gaulle.

The lawyer regarded the thin gold pocket watch on the table beside his coffee cup, turned it with a finger.

"A big uproar at the Préfecture. Apparently something has just happened that has greatly annoyed the Boches. They have come down hard on our masters in Vichy, who are looking for scapegoats up and down the line."

"What happened?"

"Unclear. By the way, I take it Apricot made it safely into Spain."

"As far as we know."

This is, Elizabeth thought, the way one talks in the secret war. Unclear means clear.

An Algerian boy in a dirty apron brought them two coffees. She put sugar in hers and stirred it, looked out to sea. It really was a splendid late autumn day. Fishing boats were moving with their night's catch from various points on the horizon toward the entrance to Nice's *Vieux Port*.

"Let us return to de Gaulle," Jean-Luc said. "You really think he could become the rallying point for us?"

"I am convinced of it. Did you hear his call to arms over the BBC on June 18, the day after Pétain threw in the towel?"

"Some of us," Jean-Luc said, glancing at Elizabeth, "were making our way through German lines on that day."

"Well, I heard it. It was just what needed saying, that France had lost a battle but not the war. That very day I decided I would resist. . . . But then, you are committed to working with British intelligence."

"That was before the German offensive," Jean-Luc said, and for the second time that day Elizabeth heard a touch of anger in his voice. "I thought that France might collapse completely and that the only way to fight on might be with foreign support."

"In that you do not differ from de Gaulle."

"If I thought a French-led resistance movement was a serious possibility, I would of course put the network that we have developed at its disposal."

"Then do it," Armand said. "Your joining the cause would send big waves."

"But how? We have no way to communicate."

"The general has sent someone to organize Free French resistance within France," Armand said. "De Gaulle apparently has heard of you. He would like you to meet his representative."

"Where?"

"A small town in the Dordogne, where this person has established the first Free French cell. You could be there and back in, say, three or four days."

"Can we be sure this is not some kind of Vichy or German trick?"

"I believe it to be authentic, but of course . . ." and Armand turned up his palms and shrugged, a French gesture that meant one could never be completely sure of anything.

"All right, I will go."

"And, under the circumstances," Elizabeth said, looking Jean-Luc in the eye, her voice firm, "with both bodyguard and radio operator."

"Yes," Jean-Luc said in an equally firm voice, "I will take Serge and François, the radio operator at Nice airport, who is one of ours and has some leave due."

There was nothing more to be said. Jean-Luc had met her demands, but she would not be going with him.

"Now," Jean-Luc said, "I would like Elizabeth to describe to you a very interesting proposal she has received for distributing an underground newspaper. In fact, the first issue of *Le Résistant* is already out."

As she walked through the streets of the little town of Villefranche-sur-Mer, Elizabeth felt exhilaration. The magnificent weather went on week after week, with sparkling clear skies, the nights chilly but the days still warm. Perhaps, when the war was over, she and Jean-Luc could live on the Côte d'Azur. It would be hard to return to Paris and the rain and gray skies. . . . But most of all she felt exhilaration because this was the day she might hear from Jean-Luc.

There was a half-hearted attempt at Christmas decoration in some of the shops, but there was little to buy. The luxury foods that were so much a part of Christmas in France were absent: the foie gras, the pineapples, caviar, champagne, all gone. Basic foods were rationed now, as the Germans took more and more for themselves.

She stopped and checked her makeup in the mirror of a weighing machine, and then she took off her coat and hung it on the hook on the side of the machine. She stepped up on the platform and put in a coin. A rectangle of cardboard dropped into a cup. On one side was a picture of a movie star, on the other her weight was stamped. Amazingly, staying with Jean and Margot, who had easy access to the black market, she hadn't gained an ounce. Good. She was going to try to keep her model's figure. Beneath her weight on the card was a fortune: "You will soon visit old friends."

Elizabeth put her coat back on and checked her makeup once more. Then out of the corner of her eye she thought she saw the image of her features repeated, some optical trick. She turned her head. Her photograph was pasted to the wall. She went up to it and read snatches before turning away and walking quickly toward the port, phrases ringing in her ears: ". . . wanted . . . terrorist activities . . . reward . . . alias Elisabeth Fournier . . ." She felt the inner pockets of her coat, one of which held a set of radio crystals, the other her slim little Italian pistol.

On the nearly deserted quay of Villefranche a sailor leaned against a bollard. He wore tight canvas pants, a striped knit shirt and a beret, and a cigarette dangled from his lower lip: an American cartoonist's image of a Frenchman. The sailor approached her.

"Any peaches in the shops?"

"Unfortunately, not this year."

Without another word he helped her down into a rowboat tied to the bollard. As she was rowed out to the yacht, floating on the still water of the Villefranche roadstead like a big white gull, Villa Warden came into view. There, on the cliffs of Cap Ferrat, she and Jean-Luc had become lovers. Little more than a year had passed, but had any woman ever lived a more tumultuous year? It had been a year of danger and fear but, above all, a year of great happiness.

Marjorie and Claude were leaning against the rail, in bathing suits.

"Welcome aboard, Elizabeth," Marjorie said, kissing her on both cheeks. "It's fabulous, isn't it? And the week before Christmas. Would you like a swim before lunch?"

"You really mean to swim?"

"The water is warmer than the air," Claude said. "You will love it."

They swam and it was lovely, and afterward they were served lunch in a sun-filled dining room in the yacht's stern. As they were having dessert there was a knock on the door, and a man, whose white hair and bronzed skin matched Claude's, entered.

"We have a message." The man handed Claude an envelope and went out.

"Michel was for many years a radio operator on transatlantic liners," Claude said, tearing open the envelope. Elizabeth's heart was beating fast. "We are lucky to have him.

"It is, Elisabeth, from Mango. 'All went well. Have important news. Will come directly to Villefranche. Arriving late Friday afternoon. Love to Peach.' "

Elizabeth let out the breath she had been holding in. "Friday? But that's today."

She watched Jean-Luc's approach through big marine binoculars. In the stern of the rowboat his silhouette was dark against the sunset, still, almost serene, she thought. The oars of the boat sent ripples of red and gold across the surface of the water.

When he stepped onto the deck she held him quietly for a

few moments. Once more they had come together, were both still alive and free. How many more times would this be possible, how many more times before someone made a fatal mistake, before one of their ever growing number turned traitor?

They sat together on deck, wearing sweaters now, Elizabeth snuggling up against Jean-Luc. There was no lack of foie gras and champagne on Claude Faucher's yacht.

They talked of other things for a while, but then the time came for Marjorie to ask, "What can you tell us, Jean-Luc?"

"Would you be willing to work for de Gaulle?"

"I have come to think he is our best bet," Claude replied. "If they had listened to Colonel de Gaulle in the '30s on modern warfare, the Germans would have got a bloody nose in May, instead of cutting through France like a hot knife through butter."

"The British have proposed to turn over our network to him," Jean-Luc said, "if those of us in the network agree. I think most of them would feel as you and I do. It is a good net. We have twelve fruit trees in our orchard now."

"It is a good net," Elizabeth said with pride, "because you foresaw what was going to happen before anybody else and acted first."

"You can count me in," Marjorie said. There was no need for Elizabeth to say anything. She went where Jean-Luc went.

"De Gaulle is particularly interested in starting a clandestine press, to counter all this propaganda—and it is believed by most people—being put out in Pétain's name by Laval."

"Laval is a newspaper owner himself," Claude said. "He knows what he is doing. De Gaulle is right. We have to counter him."

"If we can make a success of *Le Résistant* in the south of France," Jean-Luc said, "then we could expand circulation to the German-occupied zone."

"Very difficult, that."

"I have been thinking about it. All we would have to do is smuggle the plates of the paper across the demarcation line. For months Apple has been traveling around Northern France as the representative of a firm manufacturing printing inks. He has lined up a dozen printers who are willing to co-operate."

"Excellent. Marjorie and I are sailing over to Corsica for Christmas and New Year's. But as soon as I am back in Marseille, I will get *Le Résistant* on its feet."

It was only after they had dined and gone to their cabin, where they made love and were lying quietly, that Jean-Luc said, "Elizabeth, I have something else to tell you, something that Marjorie and Claude need not know."

Her body stiffened. "What is that?"

"De Gaulle is considering asking me to be the head of all Free French operations in southeast France."

"Oh, no."

"I do not have much choice. As of now I am the most experienced person in resistance work in the area. It is a question of duty."

"All operations? Does that mean spying and sabotage as well?"

"I do not have the experience or the training to get directly involved in those aspects, but I would be responsible for co-ordinating all types of resistance activity."

"I see. That will mean that you will know more than anyone else, which will make you the Gestapo's number one target. Jean-Luc, we promised each other that we would survive this war. You continue like this and you will not."

"Unfortunately, that is not all."

"What else could there be?" And she knew that there

was bitterness in her voice.

"De Gaulle wants to meet me before making a final decision. I am to fly to London for the meeting. I would be gone only a few days. . . . I told them I must be back for Christmas."

"Fly to London? Are you crazy? There are no planes going to England except German bombers."

"The British are sending a plane over by night. I would return the same way."

"When?"

"Tomorrow night."

Behind the tears and recriminations that followed, they both understood lay only love. In the end Elizabeth knew that she had no more choice than Jean-Luc.

They said goodbye on the yacht, as they did not want to take the chance of being seen together. He was headed for the train station, she for the bus station, where she would take a bus to Jean and Margot's truck stop. Elizabeth promised him she would make certain a fine Christmas dinner was waiting for him there, and she smiled and held back the tears. She knew, however, that she might be seeing him for the last time.

When she was ashore Elizabeth went to a café-bar and called ahead to make sure everything was all right. Everything was fine, Paul the waiter, who answered the phone, said. She said that she would get something to eat before coming up.

When she got to the bus station she saw Paul, who was holding what looked like her valise. He motioned her out onto the sidewalk.

"What is it?" she asked in alarm. "What has happened?"

"The police raided our place. I think they were looking for you. They searched your room."

"They will not find anything there."

"They have taken Jean and Margot to Nice for questioning. I do not think they suspect them of anything. I believe they just wanted to find out more about you. At least I hope so. In any case you cannot go back to our place. It is under surveillance around the clock. I have brought your things."

"Where will I go?"

"I cannot speak to that." He began to back away from her. "We should not be seen together. I may have been followed."

Elizabeth looked around her. Across the street was a cheap hotel. She went in and registered. Once in her room she sat down on the bed, in a daze. Now what did she do? More important, what was to be done about Jean-Luc? There was no way of knowing exactly when he would be back, and they had left it that he would make it back to the truck stop as quickly as he could. He would walk right into a trap. She must get a message to London.

And then she realized with a sinking feeling that that would be impossible. François, their radio operator, had not come back with Jean-Luc, but had stayed behind for several days, she didn't even know where, to have repairs made to the radio. Marjorie's radio was on Claude's yacht, which had already sailed for Corsica. The next nearest radio would be with Orange in Lyon.

She pulled out the silk screen that held down the powder in her compact and dumped the powder out on a piece of newspaper, unfolded the tissue that lay hidden beneath. On it were written transposed numbers of telephones for use in only the most serious emergencies. This was one.

She put one set of numbers in the proper order and wrote it down on a piece of newspaper. Then she went down the stairs and out the door. It was only a short distance to the train station, where she wrote down the times of trains to

Lyon, looked in all directions and then slipped into a telephone booth.

"*Allô.*" Thank God, she was at home.

"It's Anne here," and before the woman at the other end of the line had a chance to say anything, Elizabeth added, "would you believe that I found six cans of peaches? I'll bring you some when I come. Would you like to go to the cinema tomorrow?"

There was a silence and then the reply, "That would be nice."

"There is a film that sounds good at the Odeon. Let me see," and she paused as if she were looking at a newspaper. "The matinee is at 4:35."

"Fine. Look forward to seeing you tomorrow. My love to Pierre."

When she got back to her hotel room Elizabeth lay down on the bed. She was trembling. There was very little time to get a message to London. And what about herself? She couldn't stay with Orange in Lyon, and it would be most unwise to return to the Côte d'Azur. And then she remembered the card that had her weight on it. She had kept it to remind her to keep slim. She reached into her handbag and took it out: "You will soon visit old friends."

Chapter Twenty-Two

By rail it is only two hundred kilometers from Lyon to Vichy, a journey that takes, even with frequent stops, barely three hours. Normally the compartments would have been crowded, but it was Christmas morning. Those who had the means, and the necessary permits to visit relatives for the holidays, had already arrived at their destinations. Elizabeth once again had a compartment to herself—and her thoughts and fears—as she literally rode into the lions' den.

"Joyeux Noël," the conductor said, handing her a chipped glass engraved SNCF, the initials of the French national railways, and a chocolate-filled croissant. The glass was hot and she wrapped her cold hands around it, put her nose into it.

"Hot spiced wine. How very kind of you."

"It's not much fun to travel alone on Christmas Day."

"No, it's not. Would you like a cigarette?"

"Thank you."

"Why not sit down for a minute. You cannot have much to do. There is hardly anybody on the train."

"Thank you."

As the conductor lit the cigarette taken from the pack she had held out to him, she looked out the window. Snow was beginning to fall into the tracery of bare tree limbs against the sky. Cawing crows sailed mockingly alongside the train. On the Côte d'Azur the sun was no doubt shining, the gulls wheeling above Villefranche and Beaulieu.

The conductor, tall and bent and with a droopy mustache, reminded her of pictures she had seen of Léon Blum, the socialist premier of France that Leonore had railed against at Laurel Hill on the day that she had met Jean-Luc and Marc. Then she had understood nothing. Now she understood a great deal, and Jean-Luc was a leader of the emerging French Resistance and Marc was *chef de cabinet* to Pierre Laval, Vichy's chief Nazi collaborationist. How decidedly odd life was.

"You are going to Vichy," the conductor said.

"Yes."

"Are they doing the right thing there?"

"You mean . . . ?"

"I mean Vichy is supposed to be the capital of France now, and they tell us that we just have to do what old Marshal Pétain says, and it will all work out in the end. Is it true?"

"No."

"Then what should we do?"

"Resist."

"How?"

Elizabeth hesitated, and then she remembered something Jean-Luc had said, that you had to decide at some point to trust people. If you could not do that, then you had nothing to believe in but the power of the state. That is what the Germans had done.

"How? You could help me."

"Vous êtes résistante, madame?"

"Oui."

"Then what may I do for you?"

A thrill ran through Elizabeth's body. She had literally risked her life and liberty by saying the French word for yes, and this employee of the French railways, with no doubt a family to support, had taken his own risk. One more Frenchman had committed himself.

"I need to get in touch with at least one of these two persons," she said, writing their names on a page torn from a notebook. "One is the wife of an American diplomat, the other the wife of an official of the Vichy government. I do not know where either one of them lives, what security checks there are, whether I could safely visit them. Could you . . . ?"

"Leave it to me, madame. Now I should return to my duties. When we arrive, just stay in the waiting room of the station, as though you were taking a train out."

The conductor could, of course, turn her over to the Vichy police the moment they arrived, not even knowing that there was a price on her head. She should have been much more frightened than she was, but she had heard from Jean-Luc in London; and this gave her courage. She had read the message in pencilled capital letters three times, committed it to memory, rolled it into a ball and tossed it into a wood fire at the house of the young war widow she knew only as Orange:

"MANGO SENDS TO PEACH. YOUR MESSAGE RECEIVED AND UNDERSTOOD. STAY WITHIN REACH OF ORANGE TO WHOM I WILL SEND SPECIFICS OF WHERE AND HOW WE WILL MEET. ONLY DAYS. NEW ASSIGNMENT FOR ME, NEW LIFE FOR US. ONLY BE BRAVE AND ALL WILL BE WELL.

The taxi, snow chains clanking, passed through the town of Vichy, France's premier watering place. Until July the dozens of hotels had stood empty, their business ruined by the war. But now Vichy was bustling again, with the entire government crammed into hotels and apartments and private houses. They left the town by a road lined with villas half-hidden by trees, turned through iron gates and drew up before a large nineteenth-century brick villa surrounded by snow-covered pines.

The maid who answered the door said madame was expecting her and led Elizabeth down a carpeted hall to a library. Natcha arose from a chair before a log fire, a book in her hand. For several seconds she stood staring at Elizabeth, not speaking.

She looked older, in horn-rimmed glasses, her streaked blond hair now light brown and plainly cut. In a sweater set and tweed skirt she could have been the wife of a prosperous American lawyer. Only the beautiful bone structure of her face recalled the glamorous Natasha Ravitsky.

"Elizabeth!" She cried out and came forward and took her in her arms. There were tears in her eyes. She rocked Elizabeth back and forth as though she were a child. "I've been so terribly worried."

"Worried?"

"You're in serious trouble, aren't you?"

"I guess you could say that."

"Well, you're safe now. The residence of an American diplomat is considered American soil. The Vichy police can't come in here."

"How did you know I'm in trouble with the police? From Peter?"

"Peter's in Washington. Come sit down by the fire."

Natcha picked up some papers from the rug beside her chair. "I just received this from him this morning," and she handed Elizabeth two sheets of paper. The first was a telegram:

DEC. 24, 1940, 11:30 P.M. FROM DEPARTMENT OF STATE. SECRET AND URGENT. FROM WARDEN FOR CHARGE D'AFFAIRES. PLEASE MAKE EVERY EFFORT TO LOCATE AND PUT UNDER EMBASSY

PROTECTION AMERICAN CITIZEN ELIZABETH VAIL. SHE IS CLOSE PERSONAL FRIEND OF MYSELF AND MY FAMILY. IF NECESSARY I BELIEVE PRESIDENT ROOSEVELT WOULD INTERVENE PERSONALLY. I ASK THAT YOU SHOW THIS CABLE, AS WELL AS YOUR OUTGOING, TO MY WIFE, WHO MAY BE ABLE TO HELP IN SOME WAY. REGARDS, PETER. HULL.

The second sheet was a telegram from the American embassy in Vichy to Washington. Two sentences leaped off the page: PETAIN AND LAVAL REGARD THIS AS A CASE, I AM TOLD BY DIRECTOR GENERAL OF FOREIGN MINISTRY, SO SERIOUS AS TO INVITE GERMAN INTERVENTION. I TAKE THIS TO MEAN THAT, IF VICHY DOES NOT ACT, GERMAN AGENTS MAY WELL ABDUCT MISS VAIL AND DEAL WITH HER IN THEIR OWN WAY. . . .

"Is it that bad, Elizabeth?"

"It's that bad."

"Are you all right?"

"You mean do I feel well? Oh, I'm fine, just tired, and with a bad case of nerves."

"Well, you can relax now. You can stay with us as long as necessary. What about Jean-Luc?"

"He's in London, but he'll be back in a few days."

"But how can he possibly . . . No, don't tell me. I don't want to know."

Now was not the time to tell Natcha that when she heard from Jean-Luc, she would be leaving the safety of the American embassy to join him and risk her life again. That could wait.

"You've certainly changed your appearance. I hardly recognized you. You look very French."

"That's the idea. . . . Tell me, Natcha, if Laval knows the Germans are after me, so must Marc, and I suppose Paula."

"If Paula knew she would have been in touch with me. I doubt very much that Marc knows. According to Peter, a single person on Laval's staff handles security matters, which Laval is very secretive about. You know. Knowledge is power. And in the foreign ministry only the director general is privy to such matters, on Laval's orders."

"Well, they may find out sooner or later anyway. My picture's on a wanted notice that's been pasted on walls. There's a reward for turning me in."

"Oh, my God, no, Elizabeth."

"How is Paula?"

"She's OK, but the marriage isn't."

"Another woman? Another man?"

"Strangely enough for Paula, it's politics. She's developed a real hatred of Laval, which isn't hard to do. But I guess Marc adores him. Would you like to see her?"

"Very much. We'll have to keep all this from her, of course."

"Yes. Among other things, I'm not supposed to see secret telegrams. I'm not even an American citizen. I have only a Polish passport."

"Have you heard that the Gestapo murdered Yvette?"

"Yes. The loathsome beasts. If I had stayed in Paris and not married Peter, as a Pole the same thing might well have happened to me. Except that before being prostituted to German generals, I would have killed myself. . . . Well, this is a jolly conversation. Look, I'll go call Paula. Marc's in Paris with Laval who has meetings with his German masters. I'll ask her to come to dinner. I have a first-class cook. I'll have him fix a special Christmas dinner, and we'll drink lots of wine and gossip till all hours, like the old days in Paris."

"That would be wonderful. . . . Natcha, I don't want to get Peter into any trouble, but I'm expecting a message from Jean-Luc that I would like to receive here. It would be delivered very discreetly."

"Any risk is on my shoulders. If it weren't for Peter, I would probably be in the underground with you. Oh, how I hate those swine."

"Then if I might have your driver mail a postcard for me. It will be innocent-looking, but there will be a code word in it meaning that I am staying with you."

"Of course. I'm dying to ask about what you are doing, but I won't. I just hope you are causing a great deal of trouble for the Boches."

"That much I can tell you. We are."

Elizabeth took a leisurely bath and washed her hair. Then she put on an evening skirt and blouse and makeup, all borrowed from Natcha. When she came down, Paula had already arrived and was sitting by the fire with Natcha.

"I came early," Paula said, hugging Elizabeth. "I couldn't wait any longer to see you. You're as gorgeous as ever. I even like your red hair."

"Well, with more subdued makeup of Natcha's, at least I look less like a streetwalker than when I arrived. You're looking good, too, Paula." And she did, as always superbly groomed and dressed, but she also looked tired and tense.

"Oh, how wonderful," Paula said, looking from one to the other of them, "to have Christmas dinner with the only two real friends I've ever had." There were tears in Paula's eyes, and Elizabeth could feel tears stinging her own eyes.

A shiver ran down Elizabeth's spine, as she remembered that last day on the mountain above Laurel Hill. Then she had declared that Paula, Jean-Luc and Marc were her friends;

and that day she had, for different reasons, been kissed by each of her new friends. Then, with Peter and Natcha, they had become three couples, for whom now all innocence had been lost; and now three women separated from their men had, for different reasons, shed tears. Dear God, Elizabeth said to herself, do not let this end in tragedy.

"Well, then," Natcha said, turning away from them, "I think we should have some champagne opened. In fact, I believe we still have some 1936 Dom Pérignon left."

"Super."

By the time dinner was over, a magnificent meal of foie gras baked *en brioche,* breast of guinea hen and a strawberry soufflé, and they had retired to the library with yet more Dom Pérignon, they were all a bit drunk—and rightly so. Natcha had wandered off to the powder room.

"Well, Elizabeth, I guess I've had enough to drink to ask you," Paula said. "You're still in the underground with Jean-Luc."

"Yes."

"Are you two in a lot of danger?"

"You're too good a friend for me to try to hide the truth. Yes, we are."

That was all Elizabeth was prepared to say. She had steeled herself to resist Gestapo torture, although she very much doubted that she would be able to; but certainly alcohol would not loosen her tongue.

"I would like to help."

"I don't see how you can."

"Would you accept a million francs?"

"A million francs? You can't be serious."

"It's nothing to me, but I would like to help."

"And Marc?"

"That's my problem."

"Well, yes, a million francs would do a lot."

"Then here," and Paula reached into a large velvet evening bag and brought out a thick brown envelope. "There are one hundred 10,000 franc notes inside."

"I will see that they are put to good use."

Natcha had still not returned from the powder room. There was obviously collusion between her two friends.

"Would you like to talk to me about your own situation?" Elizabeth asked. Their situations, she felt, had almost reversed from what they had been in America. What she had been through had put her on an altogether different level of sophistication from Paula.

"Well, it's not very good."

Elizabeth said nothing.

"Do you remember that afternoon on the pond . . . in Virginia." Paula's voice was trembling. "Jean-Luc and Marc had gone to pick up some things, and you and I talked."

"Of course I remember. It was the beginning of my life."

A burning log collapsed in a shower of sparks, and Paula got out of her chair and sat on the floor beside Elizabeth's.

"And do you remember that I said sex was OK but I wasn't sure I was capable of love."

"Yes."

"Well, maybe I was right. But I went ahead and fell in love with Marc, and I thought, well that's all right, a Paris apartment and a château in the Loire valley, that will be fun and, if it doesn't work out, then we can fall out of love and each go off and do something else. But it doesn't work that way does it?"

"No."

"Well, now I'm trapped. I told you when we last talked in Paris that I thought that being an obedient wife might be my salvation."

"Yes, I remember well."

"So it might have been, if this goddam war hadn't come along. Marc is a very dependent person, you know, a weak person, which is OK when the going is good. But now. . . . When his father died I thought maybe he would transfer his need for support to me, but instead he has found a new father figure in Pierre Laval."

"Is Laval all that bad?"

"Elizabeth, he wears white ties."

Elizabeth could not help laughing.

"And he looks like a toad."

She laughed again. "Some very fine people have been ugly."

"Laval is an evil man."

This time Elizabeth did not laugh.

"They like to say in Vichy that the Germans make them do the awful things they do. It's a lie. The Germans couldn't care less what Vichy does as long as it ships out huge quantities of food to Germany and maintains law and order. Among the first things the Vichy regime did was pass laws against the Jews, not as bad as in Germany, but bad enough. Marc had a hand in it."

"Why?"

"It was an obsession with his father. Elizabeth, what should I do?"

"You could go back to America."

"Unfortunately, I'm still in love with Marc."

Then Paula put her head in Elizabeth's lap and began to sob. Elizabeth stroked her dark hair but could think of no words of comfort that would not be dishonest.

Four days later a boy arrived at the door with a letter that he would deliver only to Madame Warden. An annoyed maid led him to the library. Natcha opened the envelope and told the maid to wake Elizabeth, who was having one of the many naps she took while still in a safe place, to release all the tension that had built up within her over the last months.

"Well, there you are, Peach. It seems you have a message from Mango. I won't ask what that's all about."

Elizabeth opened the inner envelope, read the message and handed it to Natcha. It was as good a way of breaking the news as any.

I AM ARRIVING EARLY MORNING DEC 30. PEAR WILL BE WAITING FOR YOU FROM SIX THAT EVENING AT STATION FROM WHICH YOU LAST LEFT PEAR TREE. TAKE EVERY PRECAUTION. OUR FINAL DESTINATION NOW PARIS.

It was a stark message, which even if it had fallen into the hands of the Germans or the Vichy police would have made no sense. She understood every word of it. Jean-Luc was being landed in France by the British before dawn on the twenty-ninth. He would be taken to the farm of Roger Legros, vintner of Sainte-Maure, near Tours. She was to take the train from Vichy to Châteauroux, where Legros would be waiting for her with his truck. Then she and Jean-Luc would proceed to Paris.

"This is from Jean-Luc, of course."

"Yes."

"You are going with him into the German-occupied zone."

"So it seems."

"Elizabeth . . . I don't have the right to say don't, but given your situation . . ."

"I have no choice, Natcha. This is my fate."

"Then God go with you. If ever I can help . . ."

"I know."

★ ★ ★ ★ ★

There was not a hitch. The train came into Châteauroux a little after seven. Legros was leaning against a lamppost, a Gauloise firmly affixed to his lower lip. He gave no sign of recognition, but turned and disappeared into the darkness. Elizabeth followed him. Less than an hour later they were at the Legros farm. Legros drove the truck into the barn, and then by lamplight they made their way through the vineyard, vines now bare of leaves, and crossed into Nazi-occupied France. And here, Elizabeth said to herself, my fate will be decided.

Madame Legros was standing in the kitchen door and behind her Jean-Luc, in a black turtleneck sweater and brown corduroy pants. She literally threw herself into his arms, kissed him on the mouth, all over his face. Monsieur and Madame Legros, being French, looked on approvingly. Then Madame Legros said that she thought a local dish might be in order, which turned out to be a *fricassée de poulet,* a big fat chicken cooked in white wine and cream, with little onions and mushrooms, followed by a green salad grown under glass in winter by Monsieur Legros, and then some of the famous goat's cheese of Sainte-Maure.

Later in bed Elizabeth said, "Do you think it will be just as good at fifty?"

"What will be just as good?"

"What we just did, silly."

"Well, I certainly count on it."

"So do I, because I intend to be alive at fifty, and beyond. But why Paris?"

"Two reasons. The first is that I have been found out in the south of France as well."

"How?"

"Just good police work, it seems. They noticed the name

271

Fournier, which was on your false identity card, on a lock-smith's van. No Fournier in the Alpes-Maritimes with a license as a locksmith, which requires police approval. And then they traced the van to Jean and Margot's place—they were not detained, by the way. So, it's better for us to avoid the south. Armand will take over the network.

"But more importantly, de Gaulle thinks the most important thing I could do, with my background, is to start a clandestine press in Paris."

"It will be very dangerous, Jean-Luc."

"I know. I only wish . . ."

She put her hand over his mouth. "Once you commit yourself to the Resistance, wishes are not worth a sou."

On New Year's Eve Elizabeth passed for the third time through the Porte d'Orléans into Paris, riding in the cab of a truck carrying a load of wine, with Roger Legros and his tall handsome assistant, an olive-skinned Mediterranean with long black hair and several days' beard.

In her mind she felt the great iron doors, which in past centuries had shut in the city of Paris at night, close behind them. The snow was deeper than at Vichy, and its surface was marked only here and there by the tracks of some vehicle headed to one of the military headquarters listed on signs in German. The sidewalks were deserted too, except for a few German army and French police sentries, stamping their feet against the cold.

Chapter Twenty-Three

Paris
May, 1941

But all things change with time, Elizabeth thought, putting on dark glasses and pulling up her skirt to receive more of the sun on bare legs, declared to be fashionable, now that stockings were unobtainable. The stark fear that had nearly overwhelmed her the day they entered Paris was still there, but she now kept it confined to one dark corner of her mind. It had been a long, hard winter, with growing shortages of food and fuel and electricity. But now, with the chestnut trees in bloom in the little park across from the sidewalk café they frequented, you could almost think yourself back in Paris the way it was.

"*Vous désirez, madame?*"

"A pastis and a pack of blues."

"Ration stamp?"

She tore off a tobacco ration stamp, beautifully forged in London, and handed it to the waiter. With the warm sun at last returned to Paris, she had ordered a pastis out of nostalgia for the Côte d'Azur, and to pass an idle half hour until Jean-Luc arrived. Not all things changed with time, she reminded herself, certainly not her love for Jean-Luc, her passion for him.

They had moved slowly and carefully to establish identities. Alain and Nicole had warned them when they arrived that the life of an agent in Paris was usually brief: too many

Germans and too much security apparatus. The slightest slip and they would find themselves in Fresnes prison.

She had exchanged her red-dyed hair, which had grown longer, for a soft brown, and Jean-Luc had grown a beard. Not all that much difference for her, she had told him, as she was used to and liked having her face scratched by two or three days' stubble when they made love. He had acquired a little bookshop in the Latin Quarter, and she had found employment as a photographer's assistant. What irony there was in this, after she had made the great decision of her life not to go back to Amos Leach's portrait studio but to dare Europe.

Two German officers passed in the crowd of students on their way to classes. They always came in pairs. They would not sit down. They frequented certain cafés where they could be in sufficient number to ignore the hostility that surrounded them. Across the café terrace a fat little man in dark glasses bowed toward her. Perhaps because she had been thinking about photography, she immediately recognized Max Bonnet, the *Vogue* photographer. It would be wiser to talk to him and give him some kind of story than let him leave wondering, telling others he had seen her. And she must do it before Jean-Luc arrived.

Elizabeth put down some coins on the saucer and went inside, as though she were going to the toilet. This was the way one learned to act. At the bar she bought a draft beer, went back out on the terrace and sat down with Max, to make it appear as though they had arrived together.

"What a surprise, Max."

"A bigger surprise for me. I heard you were in the Midi."

"I was for a while."

"Why on earth would you want to come back to the occupied zone?"

She had no answer for that one. "And I heard you went into hiding."

They were sparring now. Neither of them had removed their dark glasses.

"I did for a while. I guess I panicked. My mother is Jewish, but that's not a matter of record. So far they have not really done anything to the Jews except seize their property. How's Jean-Luc?"

"We separated some time ago."

Max smiled. "You have changed your appearance."

"But you recognized me."

"How could I not. Have I not photographed that profile a hundred times?"

"What are you up to, Max? I heard the Germans would not let *Vogue* reopen."

"True, but more to it than that. Me, I am doing free lance work. I make a living. No matter what, people want photographs. You are a damned good photographer, Elizabeth. Interested in a job?"

"Like what?"

"Listen, you have no reason to worry about me. I am on your side. How could I not be? I do not want to know what you and Jean-Luc are doing—and you can spare me stories about having broken up. But when I saw you sitting over there with a pastis, I thought, that's it. There is the other half of the equation."

"You are being very mysterious, Max."

"Well, let me enlighten you."

She waited in a doorway of the tree-lined street down which Jean-Luc came each noon to meet her at their habitual café. As he approached she stepped out of the doorway, linked her arm in his and led him across the street. He showed no more surprise than if he had expected this. That, too, one learned to do.

"Why not have lunch somewhere else today," she said.

"I would not mind a change."

"In fact it may be time to switch. Bad idea to follow the same routine for too long. I was recognized by someone there. Max Bonnet."

"So he has surfaced. What did you do?"

"I talked to him. He is kidding himself that he will be all right because he is only half-Jewish. I did not tell him anything about us, of course, but he has guessed. He had plenty to tell me."

"You trust him, Elizabeth?"

"You do not need to worry about Max. Where would you like to have lunch?"

"I know a place not far from here, a little café-bar, a houseboat on the Seine."

"Sounds nice. Tell me, what do you know about Otto Abetz?"

"The German ambassador to France?"

"Yes. But first, if he is ambassador to France, why is he here in Paris and not down in Vichy where the French government is?"

"Under the armistice agreement Paris is still the French capital, but the Germans keep finding reasons why Pétain and company cannot yet move back. In fact, Hitler wants to keep them down south, maintaining law and order in the unoccupied zone and shipping food to Germany, not up here in Paris causing problems. Germany does not need an ambassador to France. Abetz's job is to be the small carrot that accompanies the big Gestapo stick. He speaks excellent French—his wife is French—and he spends a lot of time sponsoring cultural events for the German-French Friendship Society and the German Institute."

"So I have heard. Frau Abetz is looking for a female photographer."

The houseboat on the Seine was the perfect place to have lunch on this beautiful May day. A table was put outside beneath an awning on the stern where they could be alone.

"Absolutely out of the question."

"Jean-Luc, you could at least hear me out."

"All right, but it is not going to change my mind."

She put her light-skinned hand on his dark one: Scotch-Irish and Catalan. She found the contrast exciting and sometimes watched their lovemaking in a mirror.

"Do you remember when you took me off courier work because I was compromised?"

"Yes."

"And I said that I would not be shown favoritism, and you got angry and said you treated me just like anyone else in the organization."

"Yes."

"Well I accepted that then, and you must accept it now. Listen to me as if I were just anyone in your organization. Jean-Luc, it is a golden opportunity."

"Go ahead."

They paused while lunch was served: a fish soup ladled out of a tureen over thick slices of bread, a spring salad and a carafe of the house white.

"I am constantly amazed at what the French can do with the pitifully few things that are on the market," she said. "This is excellent. Now, about Frau Abetz.

"Max occasionally does some work for the German embassy, and they asked him recently if he could find a good female photographer. Frau Abetz finds it disconcerting to have male photographers barge into her exclusively female gatherings, teas and lectures. But the ambassador insists there be photographs of every event that he can send back to Berlin to show what a great success he is in Paris.

"I know I could get the job. Max would recommend me, I have already established my credentials as employed at a photographic studio, the man I work for would be delighted to have the money. My photos are, if I may say so, of a quality that will give the Germans no cause for complaint, and finally, there are virtually no female photographers in Paris. The few good ones were foreign and they have all left."

"I see serious objections. The people that accept Abetz's invitations are the same people who saw your face on the cover of *Vogue*, saw you at the viewing at Paula's apartment of the photographs of Elizabeth Vail, a name currently high on the Gestapo's wanted list."

Elizabeth reached into her handbag and put on a pair of ugly black-rimmed glasses.

"Where did you get those?"

"At an optician's. I thought they might come in handy some day. They are just plain glass. When I worked for *Vogue* I wore very dramatic makeup. What you see now is only a halfway job. I can make myself so mousy you would not believe it. Nobody is going to recognize me."

"Max did."

"As Max said, he has shot my profile alone a hundred times. He has seen me from every angle, with and without makeup. Anyone who has seen me only once or twice will have carried away an image—I guess I am going to have to say it—of striking beauty. As for the Gestapo, yes, they are looking for Elizabeth Vail, a citizen of a powerful neutral country. That is why that wanted poster made no mention of my real name. And that information will not have been shared with the German embassy, where the Gestapo are not welcome. Abetz was appointed directly by Hitler."

She drank some wine and leaned back in her chair, enjoying the warm glow the wine had brought on.

"Suppose you did get the job taking photographs for Frau Abetz. That does not provide us with intelligence."

"I would be supervised by Ambassador Abetz's social and appointments secretary, who also handles his wife's calendar. She is French—has to be to know correct form in Paris society—but she comes from a German-speaking family in Alsace. Now that Hitler has absorbed Alsace into Germany, she is technically a German citizen. Abetz treats her as one, but Max says he thinks her sympathies lie with France."

"That still does not get you close to German embassy secrets."

"Oh, but it does. The social secretary works in Abetz's inner office, with secret documents flowing back and forth all the time. Max says the security is lax, with the German security services not around to impose discipline. And the German embassy is the one place in Paris where the Gestapo cannot look for me."

"I will have to think about it. Does not the idea of doing what you propose send chills down your spine?"

"Yes."

She took another sip of wine and watched the light from the Seine pass in ripples across the underside of the awning. She had won, and now she was really frightened. She was wanted by the Gestapo for spiriting out of France a timid little German code clerk known to her only as Apricot, who had taken with him the secrets of the German embassy in Paris. Now she proposed to gain access to those secrets herself.

★ ★ ★ ★ ★

She awoke at dawn, after a night of unpleasant dreams. Through the tall windows of their apartment above the bookshop she could see a piece of the sky, limpid and calm. It would be another beautiful spring day in Paris, a paradise for a young woman in love. Yet every move she made in this city she adored was stalked by fear, and every day the web of deceit that she was weaving became more tangled, until one day she must surely catch herself in it, along with the man she loved. She turned in the bed and touched Jean-Luc.

"What is it, Elizabeth?" He too was awake.

"Just hold me," she said, her voice trembling. "I am so terribly afraid." And then she began to cry and told him what she had held back for so long. "Most of all I am afraid I will break down and give everything away."

He held her and stroked her hair. "You will not break down. Every step of the way you have been just fine. If I had ever seen the first hint that you were losing control of yourself, I would have taken you out of Resistance work immediately."

"Maybe I am OK, but right now I feel like a country girl from Virginia who is in way over her head."

"You won't fail. Still, I would not have let you do it, but you trapped me. When I asked myself if you were someone else working for the Resistance, would I have said yes, I knew I would have, the possible rewards so outweigh the risk."

"Remember, it was my idea. . . . Jean-Luc, I tell myself every day that 'I wish' is a useless phrase for us and all of our kind, yet how I wish we could have had our first two years together—it has been almost that long since we met—in time of peace. By now we would have traveled places together, developed common interests. I would probably have become pregnant."

"And we might even have been able to find that little place in the country."

"Jean-Luc, promise me we will survive this monstrous war."

"We will survive it."

"But only by being on our guard twenty-four hours a day. Sometimes I feel I barely know you."

"I understand, but at the same time we are sharing something very special, something so deep that those who have not experienced it cannot imagine it."

"I know. Jean-Luc, I want you to promise me something else. When the seed that you have planted becomes a whole vast field of grain, when the handful of us who have dared to resist the Nazis become thousands and thousands—and that day will surely come—you will leave France with me. There is no necessity for you to stay on until the last German has been driven from French soil and you lose your life in the process, as you almost surely would."

"When that day comes, yes, I will leave France with you."

"Good. But understand that I will not release you from that promise."

"I understand. Now are you going to tell me what happened? Last night all I could get out of you was that you had been hired by the German embassy."

"I will tell you after we make love. It is the only thing that restores my courage, and besides I want you."

Afterwards she did feel calm, almost serene. She could go on now. She would do her very best for him. She would take every precaution. They would survive, and if they didn't, well, that was their fate.

"Yesterday afternoon, about four, I had a call at the studio from the German embassy. My police clearance had come through. So that worked."

"Just remember, Elizabeth, your identity card will always be a threat. There are two young women of about the same age in Paris, both wearing glasses, their hair cut the same, the same number on their identity cards, and the same name, Odette Pichegru. If the real Odette is ever picked up by the police, she will claim to work at your studio. It is the best I could do, but it is not very safe. It will always be your most vulnerable point."

"Understood. Well, anyway, I went immediately to the German embassy, and I was hired on the spot. It was as easy as I expected. They did not have much choice. I was interviewed by the social secretary, Mademoiselle Baumann, very cool and efficient. Then I had a conversation with Frau Abetz. She was mainly interested in my understanding that I should be as unobtrusive as possible when I took pictures. I even had a few words with Ambassador Abetz."

"Stay out of Abetz's way as much as you can. He is supposed to be both shrewd and suspicious."

"Then I went back to Mademoiselle Baumann. I signed a contract between the embassy and the studio, arranged for billings, was given a list of Frau Abetz's social events for the coming month, and a German embassy identity card. I would say it went pretty well."

"I would say it went perfectly. De Gaulle should know of this right away. This is your rendezvous day, isn't it?"

"Yes. Two o'clock in the little park next to St. Germain-des-Pres."

"I will do up a message for you to drop off at your rendezvous. We will need to give everyone code names. You will be . . . Periwinkle and I will be . . . Tortoise. Abetz is . . . Oyster and the German embassy is Oyster Bed. Frau Abetz is Seagull and Mademoiselle Baumann, should something develop there, Plover. And General de Gaulle will be Starfish."

★ ★ ★ ★ ★

She entered the park at exactly two, checking first to make sure a copy of *Signal*, the German French-language newspaper, was not caught in the branches of the bush beside the gate. That would mean that the rendezvous was to be aborted. There were other precautions. No telephone calls or postcards to arrange a rendezvous. You just showed up once a week. If there was no information to exchange, so be it. Each week it was a different Left Bank park, a different day, a different hour.

Nicole was already seated on a bench, a folded newspaper beside her. Elizabeth sat down and put her newspaper beside Nicole's. The first to leave would pick up the other's paper.

"Smoke?"

"Thanks."

She lit the Englishwoman's cigarette for her. "How's Alain?"

"Bearing up well."

"And the network? Any problems?"

"Yes. We've had a loss. A courier and two British airmen were taken off a train near the Spanish border. The airmen have been interned. We don't know what they've done with the courier. I hope they haven't treated him too badly. The Vichy police have him, not the Gestapo. There's not much he can tell them except operational methods. The only person he knows is his group leader, and then only by code name. What do you have for me?"

Their conversations were brief and businesslike. The less time they spent together the better.

"Two items. A coded message for radio transmission to London and an article for *Le Résistant*. And you?"

"Oral only. The next issue of *Le Résistant*, two thousand copies, will arrive Saturday evening by train, two trunks to be picked up at the baggage room at the Gare St. Lazare after seven o'clock. They're in the name of Louis Dupont."

"That's it then?"

"Just one other thing, Elizabeth. How do I seem to you?"

"Seem? As usual. Why?"

"I'm afraid of having a breakdown. My nerves are in a terrible state. I haven't said anything about it to Alain. He has enough on his mind as it is. But it's the month after month of pressure, and I can't stop myself from thinking about what they will do to me if I'm caught. You hear the most bloodcurdling stories. . . ."

"I know."

"I thought I was the professional and you were the amateur, but if I could only remain as calm as you always are."

"Don't be deceived by appearances, Nicole. We are all experiencing the same thing."

"Promise me one thing, Elizabeth. You see me every week. If it ever looks to you that I am really on the edge of a breakdown, you must tell me. Because then, for Alain's sake, for the sake of the organization, I would have to take myself out of operations, ask to be sent back to England."

"I promise." She put her hand on Nicole's. "But that's not going to happen."

Chapter Twenty-Four

As she was being driven to the Longchamps racecourse, Elizabeth mused on the ironies of life, not the least of which was that someone who hated Nazi Germany with all her heart was being chauffeured about in a German embassy car. Another was that the cancer that had first eaten Germany, and now threatened to devour all of Europe, perhaps all the world, had first become real to her at Longchamps, nearly two years ago to the day. On that day the world had gone to war.

On that day Natcha had been taken away in tears, fearing for the lives of her parents in Warsaw, fears so soon justified. On that day she and Jean-Luc had fallen in love. That day she had cheered on the d'Aubignys' winning horse. Now she was returning to photograph the German conquerors at play. She opened the folded sheet of paper that Mademoiselle Baumann—they were now Thérèse and Odette to each other—had given her, a scenario for the afternoon of August 28, 1941, containing a list of Frau Abetz's guests, times, places and a sketch-map of Longchamps. All very German.

Elizabeth had grasped early on what was wanted of her. She was always on time, silent, efficient, producing crisp photographs taken from the right angle, at the right moment. She had made herself into a machine at the embassy's service. The Germans liked that. With Thérèse she had attempted nothing further than a few of the kind of mildly sarcastic remarks that a Frenchwomen would almost inevitably make about German culture. Thérèse allowed herself nothing more than a slight smile, but the smile was there.

She had dared no more because Jean-Luc's message to de Gaulle had elicited an immediate terse response: RECALL TORTOISE HOW YOU BEAT THE HARE. STARFISH. That was all. Jean-Luc had commented that it took a man very sure of himself, and of them, to say nothing more.

At Longchamps everything seemed the same, but it was just an imitation of the real thing. The boxes were filled with German officers, right-wing aristocrats, collaborators and war profiteers; the stands with German soldiers and sailors— and professional racetrack bettors. At least that hadn't changed.

She got some good shots with her Leica, very unobtrusive that, of the first race. As the horses came down the stretch, she had captured the intentness and enthusiasm on the faces of Frau Abetz's female guests. Then she took a few shots of the women chatting and reloaded for the second race.

There was a commotion in a box above them. Three men in dark suits had entered the box and were speaking to the fashionably-dressed women occupying it, when one of the women let out a scream and collapsed. Two of the dark-suited men caught her and took her down the aisle past the Abetz box. Tears were streaming down the woman's face. It was Paula.

The third man ran quickly down the steps to Frau Abetz. "What has happened?"

"*Madame ambassadrice,* the vice-premier of France has been shot."

"*Mon Dieu!* Shot dead?"

"No, madame. He is being operated on even now, with another member of the government who was also hit. The doctors say that both will survive."

"Thank God. Who was it? Terrorists?"

"Monsieur Laval was at Versailles reviewing the first French volunteer troops on their way to Russia to join with Germany in the struggle against Bolshevism. Then one of them stepped out of the ranks and fired three times at Monsieur Laval at point-blank range."

"A communist, no doubt."

"No doubt, madame."

"That is all?"

"Unfortunately, no, madame. The third bullet killed one of Vice Premier Laval's aides, the Marquis d'Aubigny. It is his widow, as you may imagine, whom we have just notified."

"Where did you take her?"

"To the hotel where the d'Aubignys were staying."

"Then I shall go to her immediately. Odette?"

"Yes, madame."

"This is none of your affair, but you have an embassy car and there is no one else to do it. Would you please go directly to the embassy and ask Thérèse to compose an appropriate telegram in my name to be sent to Madame Laval in Vichy."

"Yes, madame."

On the way back from Longchamps an entire motion picture of memories ran through Elizabeth's head, and it ended with a sequence in which, on a terrace above a pond, Japanese lanterns overhead, she had danced for the first time. It was with Marc d'Aubigny, and it was then that she had discovered that it was pleasurable to be held by a man.

There was turmoil in the German embassy. The ambassador went immediately to Gestapo headquarters to discuss tightened security for the Vichy leaders. Frau Abetz had returned from the hotel to report that she had been received with some coldness by the Marquise d'Aubigny, who had told her that she was leaving that very evening for the family château at Aubigny-sur-Loire, and had no intention of returning to Vichy—ever.

By the time Frau Abetz arrived at the embassy, Thérèse Baumann had composed a suitable telegram to Madame Laval, with some help from Elizabeth, who found herself suddenly almost a member of the German embassy staff. Frau Abetz gave it hasty approval and rushed off to her apartments. She and the ambassador were to dress for a formal dinner.

"Thank God this day is over, for me at least," Thérèse said, lighting a cigarette. "There will be telegrams flying back and forth all night between the embassy and Berlin, and tomorrow will be living hell. I could use a drink. Want to join me, Odette?"

"Yes, I could use one too. I was there when they took d'Aubigny's widow away, tears streaming down her face."

Elizabeth was appalled at what she had just said. She was using Marc's murder and Paula's grief to begin the entrapment of a woman who, as far as she knew, had done no one harm. This was the way the Nazis forced you to fight; either that or bend your neck to the yoke.

"Why do I work for the Germans, after all I have told you . . . ?"

There was a long silence while Thérèse Baumann, Elizabeth was sure, considered whether to go on. They were both slightly drunk: four or five cherry brandies in a smoky bar in a basement, with nothing to eat but some little Alsatian sausages.

"Because—and you must speak of this to no one, Odette—I want a very big favor from Ambassador Abetz, a favor that can be asked for only once, and I am waiting until he feels he owes me such a great favor, and such a moment has not yet come. . . ."

"And what is this favor?"

"My fiancé is a prisoner of war in Germany. . . ."

When she reached the street where they lived, Elizabeth was surprised to find the lights on in the bookshop. It was nearly nine o'clock. Jean-Luc was sitting on a stool at the back of the shop, apparently working on accounts. He got up and came to her, took both her wrists in his large hands.

"You have heard?"

"Yes."

"And that Marc was killed?"

"Yes. Paula was at Longchamps. I saw her being taken away."

Jean-Luc reached over his head and turned off the green-shaded light. And then he held her and absorbed her sobs into his body. "It's not easy for me either. We were on opposite sides, but Marc was my friend."

"Did we do it? I could not stand that."

"No, Elizabeth, it was not the Resistance. I have had people coming in all evening with details. The assassin has a fascist background. The suspicion is that there's a power struggle on the far right."

"Can we go up now? I am totally exhausted. I would like a shower, and then if you could fix an omelette . . ."

"Of course."

". . . and then I have something important to tell you."

The killing began on August 28 with the death of Marc. One week later a German naval cadet was gunned down in a Métro station. Three captured agents of de Gaulle were executed in retaliation, and the next day the German commandant of Paris announced that for every German killed a number of hostages would be shot. That same day, over Jean-Luc's strenuous objections, Elizabeth boarded a train for Aubigny-sur-Loire. It was a matter of honor, wherein one does not count the cost. Marc d'Aubigny would have understood well.

She got off at the Aubigny station, where the train paused for only a few seconds, looked all around her, as though she were searching for someone who was supposed to meet her. Everything seemed normal. Carrying a shopping basket, she began the five kilometer walk to Château Aubigny. It was a fine late summer day, the fragrant honeysuckle in bloom along the fence rows, and she became so lost in pleasant memories from the past, that she arrived at the château gates, standing open, with no sense of time having passed.

Elizabeth had a story prepared for the servants, but before she reached the steps of the château she caught sight of Paula in the distance. She was in riding clothes strolling along the edge of a pond overhung by willows. A pair of swans swam gracefully alongside her.

"Elizabeth? It is you?"

"Yes, it's me."

"You've so changed your appearance, that if you had said 'no', I would have believed you. . . . Come walk with me," and she linked her arm in Elizabeth's.

"I've come to be with you for an hour or two, at least. It's all I can do. Things are starting to turn really ugly, and in a week or so travel may be impossible for me."

"I'm glad you came."

"It sounds so banal, but I want you to know how sorry Jean-Luc and I are. We cried in each other's arms for Marc."

"Thank you." Paula squeezed Elizabeth's arm. "Now don't say anything more, or I will start crying."

They walked along the pond's edge in silence for a while.

Elizabeth was pleased and a little surprised, at Paula's calm, almost serene, expression.

"What will you do now, Paula?"

"Stay on here at Château Aubigny. It's my home now, and I feel an obligation to care for it. Surprised? Well, there's a special reason. I'm pregnant."

"How wonderful."

"Yes. A year ago I would have thought 'how awful'. But now it seems the Aubigny line may not expire after all. I'm glad that Marc knew about it before he was killed. The doctor thinks it will be twins, so there's a good chance there will be a boy to carry on the name. I'll stay on and manage the estates and raise my children. I won't remarry. I will remain a d'Aubigny. I owe Marc that too.

"So, you see, things did work out after all. It may seem a tragedy, and I suppose it is, but marrying Marc saved me from the kind of dreadful, empty life my mother lives. If Marc had lived—and this is going to sound horribly cold-blooded—we probably would not have had a happy marriage, probably would have separated eventually. And Marc had been drawn into things that would have brought lasting disgrace on the name of his family. This way . . ."

"You never flinched from the truth, Paula, and I always admired you for that. But if you stay on, what happens when America enters the war against Germany, which is almost bound to happen, sooner or later?"

"You forget, Elizabeth, I'm no longer an American citizen. When I signed those papers before I married Marc, I became a French citizen and automatically lost my American citizenship. But however this all ends, I'm safe. Even should the Germans win the war—God forbid—I would be all right. After what happened, the German ambassador's wife came to my hotel to tell me that Marc was a martyr to the cause. It was all I could do not to throw up."

They had reached the end of the pond, beyond which was the dark, ancient forest of Aubigny. They sat down on a bench, and the two swans waited expectantly for scraps of food that were not forthcoming.

"It will be lonely for you here, won't it?"

"Chère amie," and Paula lowered dark-shadowed lids over her green eyes and adopted that ironic tone that Elizabeth had once so dreaded, "when I said that I did not plan to re-marry, I didn't mean to imply that I was going to become a nun. I have my apartment in Paris, far from this provincial scene. I could not live without men in my life. . . . Now, enough of me. What about you and Jean-Luc? Still risking your lives?"

"Yes. If it were not for that I would be living in paradise."

"Even with the danger—and I know the fascist pigs—I envy you. If there is ever any way that I can help . . . For in-stance, my apartment in Paris is still always at your disposal."

"Thanks, Paula, but I don't trust your concierge."

"Mathilde? She's not there, took up with a German ser-geant. They're running some kind of black market racket. The apartment is just standing empty now. The Boches wouldn't dare requisition the apartment of the widow of a martyr to their sacred cause."

On the first of September, the second anniversary of the German invasion of Poland, there was much jollity in the German embassy, champagne was served, and Ambassador Abetz gave a little speech and offered a toast, complete with "Heil Hitler!" Then everyone was told to take as long for lunch as they pleased. Elizabeth, who happened to be there, was included in the festivities; and she and Thérèse Baumann went off to lunch together.

As they were having coffee, for it was a black market restaurant, Thérèse suddenly burst into tears.

"What is it?"

"I am leaving Paris, Odette. I am going back to Alsace."

"But why? Your fiancé . . . Ambassador Abetz . . ."

"My fiancé is dead. The Red Cross just informed his family. A typhoid epidemic in the prison camp from a polluted water supply. The filthy Boches. So, you see, there is no reason for me to stay on in Paris."

It was now or never. "Yes, Thérèse, there is a reason. You are well placed to strike a blow for France against the Nazis."

"What *are* you talking about, Elizabeth?"

"Would you be prepared to work for the Resistance?"

Two weeks later a courier delivered a parcel from a parachute drop which had consisted mainly of dozens of a new weapon, the Sten gun, but including other items, one of which was a small package to be hand-delivered to Jean-Luc. Inside were two miniature cameras disguised as cigarette lighters, rolls of film, an instruction book, and a coded message.

While Jean-Luc was decoding the message in their bedroom, Elizabeth lay on the bed and read the booklet. The camera was for photographing documents. When the film in one camera had been used up, it was exchanged for the other camera with fresh film, using some variation of the old newspaper exchange in a park. Developing and printing should be no problem. While her boss was out photographing a wedding or baptism, she could do it in the studio darkroom.

Jean-Luc came across and sat on the bed. "It's too bad we have to burn this. It's something you would have wanted to show your grandchildren."

"Why? What does it say?"

"FOR TORTOISE. WHEN PLOVER HAS SYSTEM WORKING PROPERLY, PERIWINKLE SHOULD FIND SOME EXCUSE FOR TERMINATING EMPLOYMENT AT OYSTER BED. SHE IS TOO VALUABLE TO OUR CAUSE, IN MY OPINION AND THAT OF SEA OTTER, TO RISK HER ANY FURTHER. PLEASE EXPRESS TO PERIWINKLE OUR PROFOUNDEST GRATITUDE FOR WHAT SHE HAS ACCOMPLISHED. STARFISH."

"Who is Sea Otter?"

"Winston Churchill."

A week later Elizabeth exchanged cameras with Thérèse Baumann in the Luxembourg Gardens, and she was impressed with how steady the Alsatian woman's nerves were and with the elaborate precautions she described for assuring that she was not caught. And then when she developed the film, forty frames of German documents, all stamped "Secret", she realized that "Plover" might turn out to be one of the best sources yet available to the Allies.

"I do not read German very well, but these would appear to be very important documents," Jean-Luc said, looking up from the magnifying glass through which he had been examining the film, "including the names of a number of French citizens working as German agents. What a coup you have made, Elizabeth."

"Then I am glad." But what she was thinking was that one night, sooner or later, a *Résistant* would step out of a doorway with a pistol and leave a traitor dead. That was what she had really done. Born at the wrong time. . . .

"I think we need to take extraordinary precautions to protect Plover," Jean-Luc was saying, "including not letting her be seen with a soon-to-be ex-employee of the German embassy."

"Then how are we going to exchange film?"

"There is a university student who helps distribute *Le Résistant*. She has ice water in her veins. At your next rendezvous with Nicole, take her with you. Then take her to your next meeting with Plover. After that, drop out completely. My university student can take over. That way the films can pass from Plover to Nicole without either ever having seen the other."

"Then what happens to the film?"

"It gets sent down the Orchard line to Annecy, where we now have agents, two sisters. One of them will cross the Swiss border at night, through a forested area, and deliver the film to the British consulate in Geneva."

"Then I am being retired?" she said, surprised to be a bit indignant.

"My dear Periwinkle, as de Gaulle and Churchill said, you are too valuable to risk any further on this case. Now, how do you propose to break with the German embassy?"

"Thursday I will tell my boss at the studio that I am going to return to my hometown of Nantes where I am to marry my childhood sweetheart. That afternoon I have some work at the German embassy, and I will tell Frau Abetz the same thing."

"Good. And then the second Odette Pichegru will simply vanish from the earth. By then I will have a new identity for you. When all this is wound up, I think we deserve a weekend in the country."

Early one Saturday morning in late September, wearing country tweeds, Elizabeth and Jean-Luc boarded a local train at the Gare St. Lazare for the town of Poissy, a few kilometers from Paris on the edge of the St. Germain forest. He carried a picnic hamper and she a small valise. At Poissy a Monsieur and Madame Albert Marchand, according to their papers, went into a café across from the train station and emerged from the rear of the café with two bicycles. They then proceeded to pedal off into the countryside.

It was a warm day, the road was deserted, and they cycled side by side. Along the edges of the road a few blue asters peeped out from grasses going to seed, and the shadows of slow-moving fluffy clouds passed across fields and forest. It could have been rural Virginia in early autumn. After seven kilometers they turned into a narrow, unpaved road and soon came on a cottage with a kitchen garden, a vine, beginning to turn color, shading a terrace, and a pile of logs, the winter's fuel, dumped out beside the terrace.

"What is this?" Elizabeth asked, getting off her bicycle, sensing immediately that it was something special.

"Our weekend place."

They crossed the little lawn, grown up in weeds, and the terrace plastered in leaves. Jean-Luc turned a key in the lock of the front door, and they stepped inside.

"Our weekend place?"

He began opening the shutters, and light flowed into a room with a big stone fireplace, bookcases filled with books, sofas and chairs covered in flowered fabric, two big brass reading lamps.

"Like it?"

"Well, of course. It's just as I imagined our little place in the country after the war. Too bad it is only for a weekend."

"For every weekend we can get away from Paris. I have rented it for a year."

"Oh, Jean-Luc." Her eyes filled with tears.

"We pledged each other to survive the war and have a child or two and a place in the country, but why wait for a place in the country? It may even help us survive. If things

become bad in Paris—and sooner or later they are bound to—
I thought perhaps we could escape here, as Albert and Cécile
Marchand. In the meantime, enjoy it."

"I will, I will," and she held him close.

"Excuse me, monsieur, may I come in?" a voice called
from outside.

Jean-Luc turned. "Of course, Monsieur Chauvet."

A farmer in boots and corduroy appeared in the doorway,
a shotgun on a strap over his shoulder. In one hand he was
holding a dead rabbit by the ears.

"This must be Madame Marchand."

"Yes."

"Pleased to meet you, madame. Excuse me if I do not
shake hands, but they are all bloody. Would you be interested
in this rabbit I have just shot? It would make a fine lunch."

"Indeed I would," Elizabeth said.

"My wife could come over this evening with some milk
and butter and eggs, if that might interest you too."

"Yes."

"Well, I will be going then. I will leave the rabbit outside."

"Thanks, and goodbye, Monsieur Chauvet," Jean-Luc
said.

"What was that all about?"

"Monsieur Chauvet owns that farm beyond the fence. He
looked out for this cottage for the owners, a Jewish couple
with a jewelry business in Paris, who had the good sense to
escape from France just ahead of the Germans. Chauvet is
collecting the rent on their behalf, he says, but it goes right
into his own pocket. He will also provide us with food at inflated prices, no ration cards required."

"Can he be trusted?"

"He can be trusted to do nothing to lose him this unexpected windfall I am providing. The Gestapo will have to get

up very early in the morning to entrap him."

"The crafty French peasant."

"Exactly. What he knows he knows very well. What he does not know he does not know at all. Although it is only thirty-eight kilometers away, Chauvet told me that neither he or his wife have ever been to Paris."

"This is where you have been recently on little mysterious trips?"

"Yes."

"Jean-Luc, has anyone ever told you you are brilliant?"

He shrugged, laughed, looked a little embarrassed. "As I told you when we first met, I descend from a long line of smugglers. One learns how to do these things. Shall I clean the rabbit?"

"You can leave that to me. Country girls from Vail County, Virginia, know how to do that kind of thing."

While she cooked the rabbit, Elizabeth watched Jean-Luc, stripped to the waist, splitting logs for the fire. "Well, my dear, I shall certainly have you tonight," she said half-aloud. That every day of happiness you had might be your last made those days infinitely precious.

Chapter Twenty-Five

Elizabeth looked up from the book she was reading, got up to put a log on the fire, took a sip of wine from the glass she had left on the fireplace. Jean-Luc continued to read, and she watched him lovingly. Their weekends in the country were now what she lived for. She felt as though long married, and the war could have ended for all it impinged on their little rural retreat. She sighed. The war was not over, and they would be taking the first train in the morning back to Paris to open the bookshop and resume their clandestine life. She looked at her watch.

"Would you like to try the BBC?" German jamming was usually effective in Paris, but at Poissy it was often possible to listen to at least part of the news from London.

"Sure, why not." He yawned and stretched. She walked across the room and turned on the radio.

". . . massive Japanese air attack on the American naval base at Pearl Harbor in Hawaii, and simultaneous attacks by Japanese planes on British installations in Malaya and Hong Kong . . ." The voice faded away in a splutter of static.

"What happens now?" she asked when she had recovered from the shock of what she had heard.

"If America enters the war, then . . ." He was on his feet, pacing the room. "And they will. Japan must have a commitment from Hitler to declare war on America. If he does, then maybe we can say the tide has turned. The Germans failed in their attempt to bomb England into submission, Rommel is stymied in North Africa, winter is beginning in Russia, and the German armies risk being trapped there like Napoleon's. If the Americans enter the war . . . The resistance in France will grow fast, now that there is hope."

"And, *cher ami,* the danger to us will grow. Our newspaper *Le Résistant* will become even more a thorn in the side of the Germans. We have already lost two members of the distribution network, and we know they were offered their freedom by the Gestapo if they returned to the network and led them to resistance leaders. They refused, but how many others have been caught and have agreed to cooperate? We do not know. Jean-Luc, it is time you turned the *Le Résistant* network over to someone else. You know that the only way to survive in this business is not to continue in the same activity for too long. Those who do are always caught in the end."

"You are right. The fabric is wearing thin. I will ask London to start looking for my replacement."

"Thank you, *chéri.* I have been wanting to say what I just said for a month or more. And as long as I am lecturing, I am going to remind you that when it looks as though the Allies have won, you and I leave France."

"I have not forgotten my promise."

"In the meantime, Jean-Luc, be extra, extra careful. . . ."

"It is you that I worry about."

"Yes," she said, "I have some rather bad charges on my police record, do I not?" She too worried about this a lot. If she were ever caught . . . she knew so many things. . . .

When they returned to Paris early on Monday morning everything appeared normal. Browsers at the bookshop reported that the latest issue of *Le Résistant*, 3000 copies, had been fully distributed without incident; and just before noon the university student who served as the cutout between Mademoiselle Baumann and Nicole—Plover and Strawberry, as she knew them—dropped by to say that the ninth exchange of film had taken place. Elizabeth gave her the coded message that Jean-Luc had written for transmission by Alain and Nicole, asking Free French headquarters in London to replace him as head of the *Résistant* network. They were one step closer to surviving the war.

On Thursday Germany and Italy declared war on the United States. Elizabeth told herself that surely now the tide had turned, also told herself that she had been overly apprehensive. She went out to the market and bought some artichokes. Then she turned down a narrow alley that led to a black market butcher's to buy a couple of lamb chops to go with the artichokes for lunch. As she entered the alley she noticed a man leaning against the wall, reading a newspaper. That was not natural. She turned around to see a large car enter the alley, blocking it completely.

She started to move forward, but the man had dropped his newspaper and was coming toward her, while the car, moving slowly, approached from behind. A door opened and a man dropped lightly to the cobblestones. The two men closed in on her, and she was tossed into the back seat of the car with so little effort she might have been a sack of laundry. As the door was closing she saw the artichokes spilling out onto the pavement.

But not even the terror she felt diminished her powers of observation. The man who drove the car had a German enlisted man's kind of haircut. Her captor wore a leather coat. The street that they turned into was the Rue de Saussaies, where the Gestapo was installed. Once before in Marseille she had escaped the Gestapo. Now, what chance did she have?

She was taken into a plainly-furnished room, without any of the trappings of terror, and put down in a chair before a man sitting behind a desk. He shared with the Gestapo man in Marseille a blandness, a lack of personality. In ordinary life he would have been a nobody. But now he had power.

"Mademoiselle Odette Pichegru, I believe," the man said looking down at a paper. "Well, is that your name or not?"

Elizabeth's mind was a blank. She had no idea what to answer. If they had discovered that identity then they probably already had Thérèse Baumann under arrest. It really didn't matter what she said. Her fate was sealed.

The man came around the desk and stood over her.

"Well?"

She had no voice with which to answer him. She was already one of the dead.

"Answer!" the man screamed, and still her ability to observe did not fail. The power that the Gestapo had given this nonentity was not working and had provoked in him a kind of hysteria.

He drew back his arm and struck her across the face with such force that she was thrown to the floor, her head hitting with a sickening thump. The room went around and around, but she did not lose consciousness. When she was fourteen she had fallen off one of the Wardens' horses she had been exercising. Eustace had sent the family physician, Dr. Beauchamp, to look after her. The first thing old Beauchamp had asked was whether she had blacked out. That would be a sign of concussion.

She raised herself to one knee, knowing that her mind was trying desperately to retreat into a safe past. A fist slammed into her eye, and she lay on the floor, still conscious, and she could feel blood running out of her nose. Perversely she wanted to defy this man, and she raised herself again. This time he kicked her in the mouth, and this time she could not get up. She lay on the floor feeling a loosened tooth with her tongue. All she wanted was for it to be over with quickly, but that would not be.

"So, you think it is amusing to distribute the so-called newspaper of terrorists, do you, Mademoiselle Pichegru? To-morrow we will interrogate you in a systematic way, and you will tell us everything. We will begin like this. . . ." And then he brought down his heel on her hand with such force that he got what he had wanted: she screamed in pain.

Two Gestapo sergeants carried Elizabeth away, for she was incapable of standing, and dumped her in a bare cell. There was a cot with a filthy mattress, smelling of the bodies of other victims who had passed this way. She managed to climb up onto it and lay there, trying, in her pitiful state, to make her mind work. Distributing a newspaper?

In the darkness of the cell a tiny light began to glow. Was it possible that they had picked her up thinking that she was the original Odette Pichegru, whose name and identity card number she had used in penetrating the German embassy? The real Odette had distributed copies of *Le Résistant* for the network. In that case . . .

"Here," the woman, wearing some kind of German military uniform, said, "clean yourself up. What a disgusting mess you are."

Elizabeth sat up, took the offered bowl of warm water and clean towel, dabbed at the dried blood on her cheeks. Her whole face pulsed with pain. One eye was swollen nearly shut, her upper lip was like a sausage.

"Now come on. You're going to take a little trip."

So, this was it. Her only chance, if it was one, was to main-tain her identity as a university student who had done nothing more serious than distribute copies of a clandestine news-paper. That was serious enough, but compared with what she had really done . . .

The car in which she traveled from the infamous building on the Rue de Saussaies had blackened windows, and she had no idea where she was being taken. After a few minutes she was helped down from the car in an underground parking garage, put in an elevator that went up five . . . six floors. Then she was led down a corridor with blue-flowered wall-paper, doors painted white with polished brass numbers. She guessed it was a luxury hotel.

The man who opened the door did not appear at all Ge-stapo. He was short and stout, about forty-five, with blond hair that was beginning to turn gray. His face assumed a look of outrage and concern.

"Please come in," the man said in German-accented French. "Sit down, please," and he helped Elizabeth onto a sofa. "This is intolerable behavior and will be reported. Would you like some coffee and croissants?"

"That would be nice."

The man rang room service. He looked at her again and clucked his tongue. "While we are waiting for your breakfast you may want to go into the bathroom and freshen up. You will find lotion and alcohol. I do apologize. Later I will have a doctor look at you. Another unfortunate jurisdictional problem, but it has now been resolved."

She had not the slightest idea what he was talking about. Her appearance in the bathroom mirror was even worse than she had expected, but no worse, she told herself, than Vir-ginia mountain women—and she had seen them several times—beaten up by their men coming home drunk on a Sat-urday night.

Ravenously hungry, she ate two croissants with butter and

jam. She supposed a healthy appetite was a good sign.

"I am Major Waag," the man said gently. "It is Mademoiselle Pichegru, is it not?"

"Yes." She did not know whether this was the right thing to say, but it seemed her best bet.

"You will not be going back to where you were. We are a bit more civilized here. But I will have to ask you to show a spirit of cooperation."

Elizabeth said nothing. Her eyes were fixed on the saucer to her coffee cup: "Lutetia". The Hôtel Lutetia was the headquarters of the Abwehr, German military intelligence, archrivals of the Gestapo.

For the next four days Elizabeth was questioned at length, always patiently and quietly, by Major Waag. As he said jokingly, it passed the time while her face returned to normal, and he did not want her to leave until then. It might be thought that his organization had had something to do with her condition. Yes, he had said, "when you leave."

She actually looked forward to her sessions with Major Waag in his light-filled, well-appointed suite. There was always coffee or a glass of wine and a morsel of something to eat. The rest of the time she was confined to a drab servant's room under the eaves. Her meals were left outside the door by a maid. The Major did not want even the hotel staff to see her condition.

Alone in her room she was often in tears. If Jean-Luc had not himself been picked up by the Gestapo, he would be worried sick about her. Only in her captivity did she realize how profoundly she loved him. Whatever she said or did she must not betray him. This could well be some elaborate hoax perpetrated by the Gestapo and the Abwehr working together.

Was it possible that neither organization knew that an

Odette Pichegru had worked for the German embassy? If they really thought she was the student Odette Pichegru, how had they connected her with the bookshop, which they must have been watching when they seized her?

On the fifth day there were no more questions. With her breakfast tray came a package containing new clothes, a winter coat, assorted cosmetics, and she was invited to have lunch with Major Waag in his suite. During lunch they discussed French Impressionist painting, one of the major's enthusiasms. Only with coffee did he get down to business.

"Mademoiselle Pichegru, I have a proposition for you that will allow you to get up from the table and walk out of this hotel in freedom. Whether I agree or not, I can accept that you have been involved in distributing this clandestine newspaper out of a sense of patriotism, and I am sure that you would like to see that the least possible harm comes to your compatriots in the network when we break it up—as we inevitably will. I can assure your freedom. My orders are to see that the distribution of *Le Résistant* in Paris ceases. I have no interest in filling up the jails with misguided French students. Certainly those running the network will be jailed, but that need be all."

Major Waag paused. "More coffee? That's how I would do it. If I am not able to seize the leaders of this network and shut it down, however, then the case will be turned over to the Gestapo and they will pursue it with their usual methods. Those of your compatriots who have already been identified—quite a few, actually—will be rounded up and forced to talk. Everyone will go to prison, and the leaders of the network will almost certainly be executed. The breakup of the network is inevitable, you see, the only question is how it will be done."

"What do you want of me?"

"We have reason to believe that you and the bookshop owner with whom you live are more important in the organization than these students we catch stuffing newspapers into mailboxes. We want you to identify for us who is in charge of the network in Paris and who outside of Paris is printing this paper that is being distributed all over France in so many thousands of copies."

"I do not know who the people at the top are."

"I am willing to accept that. I am asking that you use your ingenuity to find out who these leaders are, and find out quickly. Then you and your friend are free to resume a normal life, and no one will ever know what role you played."

"And if I refuse your offer?"

"Then I will have no choice but to turn you back over to the Gestapo, and things will resume where they left off."

Ten minutes later, after being introduced to a young Abwehr lieutenant who would be her contact, Elizabeth walked out of the Lutetia. It was a cold raw day, and dark clouds hung low over Paris.

She went into the *brasserie* where she and Jean-Luc usually had lunch and asked the proprietor if she could use his phone. The German military authorities had forbidden not only long distance calls but even local calls from public phones, but restaurants and bars often would look the other way for good customers.

"Pegasus Books."

"Albert, it's Cécile. I thought you were joining me at our usual place."

"*Ma foi,* I forgot."

"Well, just drop everything and come right over."

Thank God, they had developed a routine for just such a situation. Jean-Luc's phone would be tapped, but by the time the Germans had figured things out . . . She ordered a drink, and her hand shook as she brought the glass to her lips.

Five minutes later he came through the door in a raincoat and felt hat, carry a large shopping basket with a bunch of leeks sticking out the top. Underneath would be two pistols, radio crystals, a variety of blank forms, ration stamps, a million and a half francs in banknotes and the identity cards of Monsieur and Madame Albert Marchand. He followed her down the corridor that led to the toilets and they went straight out the service entrance. It had begun to sleet. They walked quickly in the direction of Gare St. Lazare.

"Where have you been? What's happened? I was absolutely frantic."

"I was abducted by the Gestapo."

He took her by the arm, his face etched with concern. "What have they done to you?"

"They beat me, but nothing really serious." She wanted him to be clear about that. "Before they could do anything serious, the Abwehr claimed jurisdiction. They think they have turned me around. But we cannot afford to play that game. I will explain later."

They crossed the Seine over the Carrousel bridge. At the end of the bridge they turned and looked back. Anyone following them could only come this way, but there were no pedestrians on the bridge. To make absolutely sure of not being followed, they went in one door of the Louvre department store, decorated for Christmas, and out another door, and repeated this maneuver at the Galeries Lafayette. An hour later they were on a train for Poissy. Now, at last, she could find comfort in his arms, feeling less like his lover than a small child who wants to crawl in bed with a parent to be assured that it all was only a bad dream.

Only seconds before the train left the station two loud,

slightly drunk, traveling salesmen entered the compartment; and Elizabeth and Jean-Luc sat silently for half an hour, listening to the salesmen's fatuous talk, until the train pulled into Poissy. Then conversation was out of the question. Sleet mixed with freezing rain was falling heavier now, and as they rode along the country road, illuminated only by the lights of their bicycles, their coats became coated with ice. But at last they arrived at the cottage.

She sat silently while he made a fire, poured two large glasses of cognac, and then she threw herself sobbing into his arms.

"Jean-Luc, Jean-Luc, I cannot go on like this. I am not strong enough for this."

"What did they do to you?" He held her tight, stroked her hair. The wind howled outside, sleet rattled against the window panes.

"Some pathetic little man from the Gestapo, who I am sure has always been mocked by women, took it out on me. He punched me and kicked me in the face. But then I was transferred to the Abwehr, where I was treated very gently. They know me as Odette Pichegru, but if they are aware of our operation in the German embassy they gave no hint of it. I was very, very lucky, but the next time . . . I was sure they would quickly discover that they had not turned me around. The beating I took well, I think. But if I were rearrested . . . torture and degradation . . . I'm not at all sure. I might give Plover away. . . . So, I lost courage and made you flee."

"Any of us might give way under torture, and Plover is more important than any number of copies of Le Résistant. We cannot show our faces in Paris again . . . at least until the Germans are driven out. Then I will bring you back."

"You are not doing this just for me?"

"Yes, I am. I said that I would treat you like anyone else in the network, but now I know I am not strong enough to put our cause above ourselves."

"Strong without human feelings you can go to the Nazis for. What do we do now?"

"Get out of the occupied zone entirely. I would like to go back to my native land, see the peak of Canigou again, be with friends . . . continue the fight, of course."

"Then I am with you."

The next morning Jean-Luc and Elizabeth began their slow and tortuous clandestine return to the south of France.

Chapter Twenty-Six

Mont Canigou
April, 1942

When she awoke it was deep night and the snow had stopped falling. Of the fire nothing remained but a pink smudge in the blackness, but perhaps that was nothing more than an image left on her retina from staring at the fire. She closed her eyes, and the images of the bright day danced before her. When she opened them again the pink glow was gone, if it had been there. A gray shape appeared at the window, like a large animal, paused momentarily, and then disappeared into the night. But perhaps that was an illusion too. There was not a single light on the mountain, and she imagined that the snow was deep enough to muffle sounds outside. That was only a thought, for there were no sounds; the silence was as complete as the darkness.

She knew he was in bed with her. She could feel the heat radiating from his body, but she did not move. She did not want him to touch her, to desire her; she just wanted him there. She felt very secure, sinking down into the snow and silence and warmth.

She awoke with a start. It was full day and the lodge was bright with reflected light from the snow. It was a strange place. The walls were made of the trunks of trees stripped of their bark, and drops of rosin had come to the surface and crystallized, where they sparkled in the brilliant light like thousands of tiny diamonds. The glass eyes of mountain sheep and goats, whose names she did not know, sparkled too in the stuffed heads mounted on the walls. Everything was so clear and bright that it seemed the lodge was above not only the tree line but above the atmosphere: a place for the use of gods not mortals.

Now she could tell from the temperature at her back that he was no longer in bed; nor was he in the lodge. There was not the feel of another human being inside the walls. She did not know where he had gone, but it did not matter. He would be back. She looked out from the covers, across the shellacked pine floor strewn with the pelts of animals, to the window where she thought she had seen a live animal during the night. The snow on the mountain was as deep as she had imagined. On the horizon other mountains, all snow, ice and bare rock, glowed pink in the morning light. Reluctantly she put out her bare feet onto the cold floor, but she had to pee.

When she was done she paused before the bathroom mirror. She regarded her naked body, her face, her short blond hair, that had been restored to her by cutting off the last dark ends of dye. She was beginning to age. There was not a single feature that she could have pointed to, but there was a change, slight but undeniable. He had come up behind her, wearing a fur-lined jacket, and their eyes met in the mirror.

"What is it, Elizabeth?"

"I am dying, Jean-Luc, that's all."

"What do you mean by that? You have escaped death."

"Oh, the Gestapo. Yes, I have escaped death for now, but I have just realized that you can only postpone it. When I say I am dying I do not mean, I hope, anytime soon. But as soon as one is fully grown, the dying begins, doesn't it? You are not allowed to stand still, not even for a year. I saw that in the mirror for the first time this morning. . . . And then the months, the years are passing by, stolen by this awful war, as I grow old."

"That is absurd. You are perfection," he said, enclosing her in his arms.

"And ten years from now, twenty?"

"Ripeness is all," he said.

"That is from the point of view of he who tastes the fruit. What about the fruit that is shriveling up?"

"You will die all right, of pneumonia, if you do not get some clothes on."

"Are you afraid of dying, Jean-Luc?"

He looked at her in the mirror, startled. "Yes, sometimes very afraid. Sometimes I think that what I have committed myself to must, as part of that commitment, kill me. . . . And then the worst is that we would be lost to each other."

"Do not say things like that. . . . You are right, I had better get dressed."

As she put on her clothes, rough hunters' clothes, corduroy and denim, not all that clean, she said, "There was a large animal sniffing around here last night, unless I was dreaming."

"A wolf. Its tracks are all around the lodge."

"It came right up to the window."

"By now it will be far away. Strange that you should see it. I come from Canigou and have never in my life seen a wolf. The few wolves that are left on the mountain have to use all their cunning to survive."

"Like us, Jean-Luc."

She laced up her boots, put on her black beret and buckled the cartridge belt slung low on her hips, checked the safety catch of the pistol hanging from the belt.

"Do I look sufficiently ferocious to impress our new recruits?"

313

"That is not what will impress them. You have never been more beautiful, Elizabeth. And with that tan you have from sun on the snow, and with your hair bleached even blonder, they will stare at you open-mouthed."

She laughed. "Good. I want them to envy *le capitaine* his woman, as women envied me in Paris when I introduced you."

She went to the window and looked up to the snow-covered peak, where even in late spring a foot or two of snow could fall overnight. Yet the mountainside below was already washed with the golden-yellow of the blossoms of Spanish broom. Down there they had another rendezvous in an hour, one of those encounters from which, one day, one or both of them might not return.

They were waiting for Jean-Luc and Elizabeth, a dozen men and one woman sitting around a fire, left to die down now that the sun was up and the snow in the tops of the pines was sliding off and falling with soft thuds onto the forest floor. She knew them all, mostly tough Catalans armed to the teeth, relatives of Jean-Luc's or trusted friends of relatives. She knew them all, except for two. One would be the printer sent from Marseille by Claude Faucher to open a new press for *Le Résistant* in the Pyrenees. The other was an old man who must be the forger that . . .

"Oh, my God, Manny Kuhn!"

"C'est moi, Elisabeth."

"But why you?"

"Things were getting a bit hot for me in the Nice area. . . . I will tell you about it later when I have recovered from riding a mule up a mountain. When I was teaching architectural drawing in the commercial college in Nice, I would never have thought to see the day. . . ."

"The others in the network?"

"All right so far, but heads down for the time being. Oh, Armand said you might be interested in this. I cannot imagine why."

The old man, still wearing a suit made for life in the city, took out of his pocket a piece of paper and handed it to her. It was a recent clipping from the Nice newspaper: "Our readers will be pleased to know that the Marquise d'Aubigny, widow of the martyred hero of France, who has honored us by choosing her family estate on Cap Ferrat for her confinement, has given birth to healthy twin boys. . . ."

Elizabeth knew why Armand had sent the clipping. He had drawn up the legal documents for Paula's marriage, at which she had been maid of honor, though that had remained unacknowledged in his Resistance role. Well, good for you, Paula, Elizabeth said to herself.

"Any messages?" Jean-Luc asked of the piano player, as all radio operators were known in the Resistance. This operator, dropped off by submarine on a beach near Perpignan, was English, with just enough French to get by.

"Two messages, one I have deciphered, the other is from Starfish in your private code." He handed Jean-Luc the message from the person all knew to be *le capitaine*'s superior in London, but only Elizabeth knew to be General de Gaulle.

"Where did you send and receive from last night?"

"Six kilometers west of here. The mule slipped on the ice and damned near fell off the mountain with my radio."

"Still, we have to do it. I do not need to tell you," Jean-Luc said, "that you operate from the same place for a few weeks and you are dead, even up on Canigou. The Gestapo is providing the Vichy police with the technical means to pinpoint radio signals. Down in Perpignan they would have you in two nights. . . . Manny, welcome. We are honored to have someone of your talents among us."

Jean-Luc was masterful, a born leader. Once again Elizabeth thought how good it was to be able to admire and respect
the man you loved. Those who followed his orders, she knew,
felt the same admiration. Each possible approach to the
hunting lodge, the property of a big Paris industrialist,
unused since the war began, was guarded day and night by
one of the Catalans. The woman *résistante*, Minou, a secretary in Perpignan police headquarters, was their most valuable asset of all. She was, among her other duties, the
translator for business between the Vichy police and the un-
dercover Gestapo agents.

"It seems," Jean-Luc said, looking up from the first message, "that someone important to the Free French has been
taken by the Vichy police and wounded badly enough to be
confined to the Perpignan hospital. When he is well enough
to travel he will be turned over to the Gestapo and transported to the occupied zone for interrogation. That, of
course, is information that London has from us, from you in
particular, Minou," Jean-Luc said to the young woman who
worked in police headquarters. "The question from London
is can we free him before this happens?"

Jean-Luc looked in turn at each of them seated in a circle
around the embers of last night's fire. He, Elizabeth knew,
would make the final decision, but he always heard everyone's opinion first. Then he would act.

In the end Elizabeth and Jean-Luc had alone undertaken
the freeing of the French general who had defied the Vichy
regime and tried, at almost the cost of his life, to bring his
troops into the Resistance. She had simply marched up the
steps of the Perpignan hospital in a nurse's uniform provided
by Dr. Girona's nurse, who was still escorting Allied airmen

into Spain. Dr. Girona had spent several hours instructing Elizabeth in every detail of hospital routine. Armed with this knowledge, Elizabeth had made her move just as the nurses' shifts were changing.

"I do not know you, do I?" the nurse in charge of the floor said, looking over her glasses.

Elizabeth showed her papers, elegantly forged by Manny Kuhn. "Substituting for Nurse Archard, who is not well." This too had been arranged by Dr. Girona.

"Ah. You know your duties, I suppose."

"Yes. At eight o'clock I am to . . ."

"Never mind," the nurse in charge said, "but for the next half hour I want you to stay on the desk here. I have an errand to run."

"Very well."

It could not have been better arranged if she had planned it herself. As soon as the nurse in charge disappeared down the stairs, Elizabeth followed Dr. Girona's directions to the general's room. He was sitting up in bed, a bronzed, mustached man of about fifty, smoking a cigarette and playing solitaire on a lapboard beneath a gooseneck lamp.

"*Bon soir, mon général,*" she said, and he looked up at her in surprise, obviously not used to being addressed in this way. The hospital nurses probably did not even know who their patient was.

"I have come to . . ."

"Not to give me another enema I hope."

"No, I have come to take you away."

"Ah. The Gestapo, I see, have learned some subtlety," and the general crushed out his cigarette. "I wondered when you would come."

"No, general, I am from the Free French, and we must move quickly. Can you?"

"Pretty much recovered," the general said, but he got out of bed with difficulty, put on bedroom slippers and, with her help, a dressing gown.

"This is not a Gestapo attempt at even greater subtlety, is it? Because if it is, you should know that your masters are not very good at that."

"We can discuss that later. Come quickly."

Dr. Girona's directions were beautifully precise: three turns, an elevator, a door that opened to a platform where hearses waited to take dead bodies from the hospital. A hearse was waiting. Half an hour later the general was deposited in a farmhouse; an hour later the hearse had been returned to the funeral establishment that had lent it.

Another hour and she and Jean-Luc were dancing in the night club of a beach hotel. Since the Vichy regime had banned dancing as decadent, such places were crowded every night. This brief period of freedom violated their own rules of security, but if you didn't have a little fun now and then the business they were in would eventually drive you mad. And releasing the general had been so easy, too easy, she knew. The next time, or the next . . .

She awoke very late, clear-headed but with a throbbing headache. They had danced and drunk cognac and made friends for the night with a black marketeer and his girlfriend, who had a lot of good stories to tell about the techniques of bribing Vichy officials. It was well past three before they went up to their room, and then they had made love for a long time, slowly and wantonly. It must have been nearly dawn before she sank into a sleep so deep that even the Gestapo could not follow her in her dreams, as more and more often they did.

The weather was so fine that lunch was served on a terrace above the deep blue Mediterranean. After lunch they went for a walk on the deserted beach. After a quarter hour a tiny figure appeared in the distance, coming toward them, growing into a young woman, who stopped, turned and waited for them to reach her. Then they walked along together in the direction from which she had come, following her footprints in the sand being eaten away by the incoming tide.

"Well, it worked," Minou said. "They are totally baffled as to how the general was spirited away. The Gestapo are furious, the Vichy police commissioner is being held responsible, and the head floor nurse has been put under arrest."

"What happens now?" Elizabeth asked, trying to suppress the feeling that their long run of luck was coming to a close.

"The Gestapo chief said in the end—the meeting I was interpreter for lasted nearly two hours—that it was clearly treachery on the French side, and the commissioner had forty-eight hours to find the traitor."

They walked on in silence. Elizabeth knew that Jean-Luc and Minou were thinking the same thing as she. The most obvious suspect was the slight young woman who, as interpreter, knew everything that passed between the Gestapo and the Vichy police.

"I wish," Minou said in a quiet voice, "that I had never studied German at the lycée."

"You think they suspect?" Jean-Luc asked.

"How could they not? They will certainly question me when I return to work this afternoon."

Elizabeth looked into Minou's luminous blue eyes and felt like screaming. How many innocent persons had she and Jean-Luc, in the name of the cause of freedom, put in the path of the German war machine. She thought of the Stukas strafing the Tours road, she thought of Plover passing secrets from the German embassy in Paris and what her fate would be if caught. I can't take much more of this, she thought.

"Are you afraid?" Jean-Luc asked.

"Of course," Minou replied, "although I think I can evade their questions . . . that is unless they let the Gestapo question me. Then . . . I am not a strong person . . ."

"Would you like us to get you out? We have an escape route across the Pyrenees to Spain."

"I cannot do that. My mother is all alone, and I am her sole support. . . . Go now. We must not be seen together, and you should be back up on the mountain before dark."

They watched Minou walk away down the beach until she disappeared around a curve in the shore.

"I was proud of what we did," Jean-Luc said, "but now I feel only shame. I may have merely traded one life for another. Back in London, of course, they will say a Free French general is more important than some young girl . . ."

"Please, stop, Jean-Luc. I do not want to hear anymore."

He turned and looked at her with that sadness in his dark eyes that she had seen only a few times before, but that she knew was the sign that he was withdrawing to the world of his ancestral village. He was preparing himself for death. She was not.

"If it comes to that, we will have to free Minou, that is all," she said with a calmness that was not feigned.

"How?"

"Our two bodyguards. Instead of accompanying us back up the mountain, we set them to watching the Perpignan police headquarters. If Minou is in serious trouble, they will take her somewhere else, and you know where that somewhere else will be."

"The Gestapo."

"Yes, and neither you or I can live with that."

"Then what do we do?"

"As I said, if it comes to that we free her."

"That can only be done by force, and you said that . . ."

"I remember what I said. Jean-Luc, I am prepared to kill to save that girl from torture."

It was as if a cloud that had shadowed his face had passed on and left his sad eyes filled with light. He drew her to him and held her tightly.

"It could mean our own lives."

"I understand."

She knew what her Catalan lover was thinking: better to face death than dishonor. She could but agree, and trembling in his arms she felt great happiness.

"Now we must move quickly," Jean-Luc said. "Your idea is a good one, but while Pedro and Joaquin are tough and brave they are not very bright. They could not carry this off alone. I will go with Pedro to put police headquarters under surveillance, and Joaquin will take you back up on the mountain. Have Terence get on the air. If they take Minou away, we will follow them and find out where. Then I will go to Dr. Girona's and use his radio to tell you where to send the men to attempt the rescue. I will be waiting for them."

She could not protest the danger. How could she after what she had just said?

The two young bodyguards, with several days of beard, were lounging on the hotel terrace drinking beer but keeping the beach under close observation. They quickly reviewed the plan with them, and Jean-Luc left with Pedro in one car and, after two hours, Elizabeth and Joaquin in the other. All she had allowed herself with Jean-Luc was *"garde-toi,"* take care of thyself.

Joaquin drove out of Perpignan toward the shape of Canigou on the horizon, violet in the late afternoon sun, through flat fields of vines, with an occasional manor house of a vineyard owner, surrounded by high walls and hidden by dark cypresses. Elizabeth occupied the other front seat and held Joaquin's Sten gun on her lap. As the road curved through a wooded area between two vineyards, they ran headlong into a police roadblock.

Joaquin skidded to a stop, muttering oaths in Catalan. Elizabeth, as she had done once before, shoved the Sten gun under the seat. But this was much worse. She realized she had no idea what kind of car papers the bodyguards carried. For all she knew the car was stolen. But there was no polite request for papers. One of the policemen approached their car with revolver drawn.

"Get out."

With those two words spoken in French, Elizabeth knew it was all over. The man who had spoken was clearly in charge, tall, blond hair, pale blue eyes. These were Germans.

"Where is your friend?"

"This is my friend," she said, nodding to Joaquin.

One of the other counterfeit policemen was searching their car and discovered the Sten gun.

"Come, Miss Vail, I mean Jean-Luc Cabanasse." The man glanced at the Sten gun held out for his inspection. "This young man is a nobody, probably your bodyguard. We hoped to have you and Cabanasse both, but you decided to travel separately. By now, however, we probably have him as well. Please get into my car."

The man turned and said something to the other two in German. They shoved Joaquin into the back seat of his car and roared off down a track into the woods. A few seconds later there was a single pistol shot. She drew in her breath with a gasp. They had killed Joaquin, no doubt with a shot in the back of the neck, the favored Gestapo method of execution. The man beside her showed no emotion. He looked at his wristwatch. He probably would need to mention the incident in some report. Elizabeth felt herself descending into hell.

The car, with Elizabeth and the Gestapo officer in the back, and his two underlings up front, turned off the road to Canigou and down a long drive that led to one of those rather sinister manor houses hidden behind their walls in ancient dark trees. Two men in civilian clothes, but obviously military, opened the rusted iron gate for them, and then the Gestapo officer and she mounted the steps to the crumbling old house, once quite grand.

Two men inside the entrance hall, with a curving staircase and decaying frescoes, gave the Nazi salute. They passed into a large, well-lighted room cleared of all furniture but a table serving as a desk, several chairs and a safe with two combination locks. She turned her head, and her descent to hell was complete. Minou was bound, naked, to a high-backed chair, by wires around her arms and legs and neck. Her face was badly battered, and her mouth was sealed with adhesive tape. The Gestapo man ripped it off.

"I believe you know each other."

"I did not tell them anything," Minou said in a dry, weak voice.

Elizabeth was too horrified to speak, and nothing she could say would make the slightest difference. Yet, Minou, who had said she would not be able to resist, had. One does not know, the calm part of Elizabeth's mind said, what courage one has until it is put to the test. But this was only the beginning. On a small table beside Minou were arranged a set of household tools: hammers, pliers, saws, a drill. She was sickened by the realization that these were improvised instruments of torture.

The Gestapo officer went to the door and locked it, took off the French police uniform jacket, revealing a gray shirt with wide military suspenders over a powerful frame. He hung the jacket on a chair and flexed his muscles, like someone who is about to engage in strenuous physical exercise. Then he unlocked the safe and took out a thick file.

"Please sit down. What we have to do now is a matter for the three of us alone." He paused, cracked the knuckles of each hand with the other. "Let me explain, as we do not have time to waste, Miss Vail, also known as Elisabeth Fournier, Mariette Goubert, Odette Pichegru, and most lately, Cécile Marchand. You see we have the whole story, after considerable bungling, which I do not need to tell you about. That is why I was assigned full-time to your case. It is quite a tribute to your abilities."

You egotistical ass, she thought; but what she thought made no difference. Minou was staring at the man like a fly caught in a web watching the spider approach.

"You clearly have a very great deal to tell us. You are, in fact, such a fine catch that my orders are to have you delivered immediately to Germany, where we expect a long and fruitful interrogation. However, my orders also state that there is one piece of information that is needed immediately, because it is possible that great damage is being done daily to the Reich. . . . Why did you penetrate the German embassy in Paris, where as I also do not need to tell you, the German security services have not been—until now—allowed to go?"

"I have no idea what you are talking about."

"*Bon.* If that is the way it is to be, then let us get right to the point. Berlin wants you delivered 'pristine and intact' I believe the words were, which presents me with something of a dilemma. But we do have your friend over there, who was provided by the French police as my interpreter—not that I need an interpreter with my excellent French. I have no instructions to leave her pristine and intact."

He walked over to Minou and put his thumbs against her eyelids and pushed until she winced, he picked up a pair of pliers and pinched one of Minou's nipples with them.

"I am sure you understand. Either you tell me what I want to know or I will slowly destroy your friend in front of your eyes: nails, flesh, eyes, and one by one every bone in her body broken."

It was growing dark now, and the bars of light through the shutters were fading. The German turned on a floodlight and pointed its beam on Minou. He did not want Elizabeth to miss anything.

"And if I tell you?"

"She will go free, unharmed, except for a few bruises inflicted by an overzealous member of my staff. You have my word of honor as a German officer."

"But not myself."

"There I have no discretion, Miss Vail, but you can save your friend."

Yes, she thought, looking into Minou's terror-stricken eyes, and that will put in your place Thérèse Baumann, who I deliberately led into the path of monsters like this.

"Shall I proceed or not? It is your . . ."

The room reverberated with a pistol shot. The Gestapo had taken another victim. But no, the Gestapo officer moved quickly across the room and reached for his gun belt hanging from a chair.

There was an explosion of automatic weapon fire and the lock flew off the door. Two Catalans burst into the room, Sten guns pointed at the Gestapo officer's chest. He raised his hands above his head. Jean-Luc stepped into the room, taking in the scene at a glance.

"Thank God, Elizabeth. Have you been harmed?"

"No."

"Luis, release Minou and find her some clothes. Pedro, empty the safe of all papers and put them in the van. I want the Germans tied up securely, all weapons taken, any radio smashed, vehicles disabled, but nobody killed, understand. We do not want to give any excuse for hostage-taking."

And then Jean-Luc addressed the Gestapo officer, pale and trembling, his hands still held high. "Major, you are very lucky that we arrived just when we did. If you had done serious harm to that young woman, nothing I could have said would have restrained my men from dealing with a torturer of women in their own way."

Chapter Twenty-Seven

She poured a cup of black market coffee from the pot on the stove and stood for a while watching from the kitchen window the shadows of big fluffy clouds pass across the plain below. She had been in France for nearly three years. She was with the man she loved, and together they had done a brave and good thing, and she felt cleansed by it and glad to be alive. But she also knew that what she and Minou had gone through would affect them for the rest of their lives. When the war was over they would never quite be able to lead normal lives. Their souls would always bear invisible scars left there by Nazi Germany.

"Coffee?" she called to Jean-Luc in the next room.

"Yes, please."

She found him staring out the window at the peak above, where only pockets of snow remained in the bare rock. What were his thoughts? He turned and took the cup from her.

"How is Minou?"

"She is still sleeping. I undressed her and put one of my nightgowns on her. She is going to hurt like hell when she wakes up. That I remember very well from my brief visit to Gestapo headquarters in Paris."

"Any broken bones?"

"I do not think so, and she is lucky. She is such a delicate little thing, not a big strapping woman like me."

Then in a rush of words she could not hold back, Elizabeth

told Jean-Luc what he had saved Minou from. She also told him of how Joaquin had died, something that she had held back the day before, knowing that that too would have caused the Catalans to kill every German in their reach. After she had finished her grim tale, he held her close while she sobbed.

"There, *c'est fini*," she said. "It is the only time I will ever speak of it."

"Minou must never fall into German hands again," Jean-Luc said. "I will send her into Spain with the next escape party."

"How many?"

"Two British airmen and a Belgian major who has been in hiding ever since May of '40."

"If Minou agrees to go, we will have to support her mother."

"God knows, Minou deserves anything we can do for her."

"And she, for her part, owes you her life—and more. Tell me what happened after we parted at the beach. How did you know I had been taken too?"

"By the time we got to police headquarters Minou had already been taken away, we found out from a friend of hers who sometimes picks up our messages for her at the café across the street. She was waiting there hoping someone from our group would show up. She did not know where Minou had been taken, but she did know that the Gestapo chief, Major Wiesel, had his headquarters in an old manor house near Thuir.

"I went to Dr. Girona's and sent a radio message to my men to come down off the mountain—all of them—and meet me at Thuir. When they got there, they said you had not come back to the lodge nor had they met you on the road. Since I had come up the same road from Perpignan and not seen your car, the only explanation was that you too had been taken. So we went to Major Wiesel's headquarters and took out the guard. The rest you know."

"But how did you do it with only one shot fired?"

"There were thirteen of us and six of them. It was nearly dark, and Catalan smugglers know how to move silently. The men had brought along a couple of ladders and we scaled the wall and took them by surprise, and your Major Wiesel did not move quite fast enough. He would have tried to put a pistol to your head and hold you hostage. That was what I feared."

"What will he do now?"

"Precious little." Jean-Luc laughed. "He not only had captured the most wanted *résistante* in France and then lost her, but his entire ultra-secret files are now in Resistance hands. I have Manny, who reads German perfectly, reviewing the files. Major Wiesel will be lucky if he is not shot."

"The only thing that still worries me, and very much," Elizabeth said, "is that if the Gestapo knows that I penetrated the German embassy in Paris, Thérèse Baumann is at great risk. She may have already been arrested."

"I can assure you she has not been arrested, and Ambassador Abetz is not going to let the Gestapo loose in his embassy unless they can show some very strong evidence of treachery inside to Berlin. They have just lost that possibility."

She shuddered. "You mean making me talk."

"Yes."

"And how do you know she has not been arrested?"

"She is still sending out secret German documents to London. You remember that private message I got from de Gaulle just before all this happened? I have been waiting to show it to you. I think you will be pleased."

Jean-Luc went to his desk, unlocked a drawer, and brought her the deciphered message.

"EYES ONLY AREA COMMANDERS. HITLER'S ARMIES ARE EXTENDED TO THE LIMIT AND WE SHALL SOON BEGIN TO ROLL THEM BACK. KEEPING ALWAYS IN MIND EVENTUAL ALLIED LANDING, RESISTANCE IN FRANCE IS NOW TO ENTER ACTIVE PHASE. YOU SHOULD BEGIN IMMEDIATELY TO FORM AS MANY MAQUIS AS PRACTICABLE IN YOUR AREA. YOU WILL BE SUPPLIED WITH WEAPONS AND OTHER NECESSARIES BY PARACHUTE DROPS. DETAILS FOLLOW IN REGULAR CHANNEL. VIVE LA FRANCE.

"PERSONAL FOR TORTOISE. PLEASE INFORM PERIWINKLE THAT WE HAVE RECEIVED ENOUGH PEARLS FROM OYSTER BED TO MAKE A NECKLACE. PERIWINKLE AND PLOVER HAVE BEEN AWARDED FRANCE'S HIGHEST MEDAL FOR VALOR, WHICH I SHALL PRESENT PERSONALLY WHEN I RETURN TO FRANCE. STARFISH."

"How is that for a girl from Laurel Hill? You are to be decorated with France's highest medal for valor."

"Well, I am proud of course, and greatly relieved that Thérèse Baumann has survived—so far. But if anybody but Thérèse deserves a medal it is that courageous girl asleep in the next room. Jean-Luc, what is a 'maquis'?"

"It is a word borrowed from the Corsicans. Maquis is thick underbrush, and it is where bandits hid out in Corsica. The word is now being used in France for armed resistance groups operating out of headquarters in wild areas, in the forests or mountains."

"Like us."

"Yes, except that we have been mainly involved in helping

Allied airmen escape into Spain. Now, it seems that we are to prepare to fight."

"And what does that mean for us?"

"I will have to travel some, setting up Maquis in various places."

"Jean-Luc, de Gaulle believes the tide has turned. You promised that when it became clear that the Germans would be beaten, we would leave France."

"We are not there yet."

"Perhaps not, but when the time comes, I have every intention of holding you to your Catalan word of honor."

"I am well aware."

"Jean-Luc, if you get yourself killed, I will . . ." She laughed. "Then there would not be much I could do. Just be very careful, for me, *chéri.*"

One of the Catalans, who guarded all approaches to the lodge, had killed a pair of pigeons with one shot, he had bragged, as they crossed in his gun sight. Minou had cleaned and cooked the dozen pigeons that he had brought with the first cherries of the year, a dish that a great Paris restaurant would not have been ashamed to present, as Elizabeth told her.

"It is a local specialty. The first cherries in France come from around Canigou, and it is our custom to send a basket from the first picking to the President of the Republic."

"I assume you will not be sending a basket to the chiefs of the Vichy government."

"It is a thought . . . with a bomb inside. When the card is opened, *'Cher Vice-Premier Laval',* and then boom!"

"I am glad that you can joke now." Elizabeth reached across the table and squeezed the girl's hand. "How do you feel?"

"Not bad. How do I look?"

331

"About like I did three days after the Gestapo beat me up in Paris, nothing left but some blue and green new moons where those black bruises were."

She reached across and took both of the girl's hands in hers, and the two women's eyes filled with tears.

"Enough of that," Elizabeth said, wiping away her tears. "When Jean-Luc returns day after tomorrow, we are going to put together an escape party to Spain, and you are going with it."

"No, I am not going."

"If it is your mother, there is no need to worry. We will provide for her."

"It is not that, but I am not going to leave."

"Now you listen to me, Minou. You cannot show your face again in the Pyrénées-Orientales until the Germans are driven out."

"I know that. I intend to stay and fight with your Maquis. You thought I was asleep, but I heard what you and Jean-Luc said. Please say you will have me. That first time we met, I thought that is the most glamourous, the strongest woman I had ever encountered. You were wearing Catalan hunter's clothes, and you had on an ammunition belt with a pistol, and a beret, and with your blond hair and bronze skin . . . Are you really American?"

"Yes."

"I would wish to be like you."

Elizabeth had never been idolized before, and she felt herself blushing.

"You see, Elizabeth, this is my chance, my chance to be something different from all my relatives for generations and generations. I have such yearnings . . . But I am very shy. I want to be like you."

"Do you have a boyfriend?"

"No, and well, I suppose that is part of it. When I saw you and Jean-Luc together . . . You see, I am still a virgin."

"So what?"

"But . . ."

"How old are you?"

"Nineteen."

"Are you in love with anyone?"

"No. I do not even know how to talk to men."

"Well then, Minou, wait until you are in love. It will come. Just between us two women I was very shy and more than a little afraid of men, and I was a virgin until I met Jean-Luc— the only man I have ever known in that way. Age? Twenty-two. And if you would like to be part of our Maquis, it would be our privilege to have among us the woman who made it possible to free one of the handful of men who saved the honor of France from being lost entirely."

The first full moon of June rose over the range of mountains beyond the River Tet. It was on nights like this that the survival of the Maquis that had sprung up in all the wild places of France depended.

"There she is," one of the Catalans said, "our elder sister."

Elizabeth looked up at the moon and understood what this youth who could barely sign his name meant. After one had lived in isolation on Mount Canigou for a while, the moon and the stars and the mountain itself became sacred. In three weeks' time, at the summer solstice, the Catalans would, despite the Vichy ban on fires at night, light their bonfire somewhere on the peak of Canigou. Nothing could break this tradition that went back no one knew how many centuries.

"It is so beautiful," Minou said, "but strange, particularly if you have always lived in a town. No sound, no light, just the moon and the mountain. How much longer?"

Elizabeth looked at the illuminated dial of her watch. "It should be here within the next half hour."

"Elizabeth, do you remember when we talked about love?"

"Do not tell me you have fallen in love."

"I think I may have."

"Oh. Who is he?"

She could barely make out Minou's face. They were sitting in a field from which the spring wheat had just been harvested, and the air was fragrant with the smell of the cut wheat. A nightingale began to sing.

"The Englishman."

"You have fallen in love with our piano player?"

"I think so, but it is hard to tell when you have never been in love before. We take walks together, and talk. Last night he kissed me."

Elizabeth smiled. How well she remembered her own confused feelings that weekend on the pond at Laurel Hill when she had first awakened to men.

"What language do you speak?"

"A little French, a little English. We do not need many words."

"No, it does not take many words. . . . Listen."

It was the faraway hum of a plane's engine. The British Lysander would be flying down the valley of the Tet, following the reflection of the moon on the river. Soon it would reach the town of Prades, where it would veer southwest. The field in which they waited was outside the tiny village of Serrabone, far enough up a remote valley to discourage a police raid, but not far enough to risk the plane crashing into the mountain.

The sound of the engine altered pitch. The plane had

changed course. At the far end of the field Jean-Luc turned on his flashlight, followed by Elizabeth and the others, five lights down one side of the field, four across, to make the standard "L" for drops. The plane came in low, made its turn, and by the time the two parachutes had opened, like two large pale moons, was on its way back to England.

It took them nearly an hour to load the contents of the two large metal cannisters onto the waiting mules: Sten guns, ammunition, hand grenades, two radios, flares, a box filled with French currency, another with forged identity cards, work permits and rations coupons. There was a bottle of English gin for the piano player, chocolate, coffee and a small packet for Jean-Luc. It would take the rest of the night to bring their supplies back to the lodge.

They slept late the next morning, and over coffee Jean-Luc opened the oilcloth-wrapped packet. Inside was an envelope addressed to Tortoise and another for Periwinkle. Inside her envelope there was no note, only a string of pearls.

"I shall wear these as a charm," she said, "every day until we are safely out of France." She was deeply touched.

"I had heard that the general knows how to treat ladies." He tore open the envelope addressed to him.

"This is incredible. How could this . . ." He handed her a single sheet of heavy notepaper, on which was written with a broad-nibbed pen, in a handwriting she knew well:

"Dear Jean-Luc and Elizabeth,

If this reaches you, which I am told may be possible, I want you to know that Natcha and I will be taking a few days' holiday in the little coastal resort of Collioure near the Spanish border, beginning June 15. It is my understanding that you are now somewhere in the Eastern Pyrenees. If you could meet us safely in Collioure—and only

if—it would give us great pleasure. We will be staying at
the Beau Rivage.

> Love from us both,
> Peter."

It was, for Elizabeth, a grand entrance, and also in its
way the best of disguises. The tall, powerfully-built Mediterranean man on whose arm she entered the Hôtel Beau
Rivage, turned, as always, every feminine eye. Yacht
broker, major black marketeer, agent of some foreign
power? In any case, this was no place where the Vichy
police were likely to come.

She wore the single good dress, a Schiaparelli that had survived their armed retreat from the salons of Paris to the slopes
of Canigou. While Jean-Luc was at the desk inquiring of the
Wardens, Elizabeth confirmed in the rococo-framed mirror
that never had she looked better: blond hair, dark eyebrows,
tanned, slim and muscular, all the elements of her youth
translated into a woman who had found herself in a life of
passion and danger. Well, enjoy it for tonight, she said to herself. Despite your great escape, any night may be your last.
But yet, would you trade this for an ordinary, safe life? *"Non,
jamais!"*

A woman in green satin that matched her eyes had come
up beside her, her image smiling ironically from the mirror.

"Paula," she said in a whisper to the woman's image,
"what are you doing here?"

"Tell you later. I've sent Jean-Luc to our table on the terrace, where we can be out of the public eye."

The last color was leaving the sky over the Mediterranean
as champagne was brought to the five of them in a discreet far
corner of the hotel terrace. The old harbor of Collioure and
the fort beyond were fading into the night. The champagne

was opened and poured and Jean-Luc raised a glass.

"I would like to propose a toast. To Marc."

"To Marc," Peter said, raising his glass, "who first pledged a toast to our friendship and never once betrayed that pledge."

Paula drew in her breath sharply, let out a small sob. That was all. Peace had been made.

"Why am I here, Elizabeth? Because I was about to go out of my mind. You have no idea what giving birth—to twins no less—is like. Don't do it. What follows that is even worse. Fortunately, I've found an excellent wet nurse, Italian, of course. They seem to have all this milk. And then I have the Wardens' old family doctor in Beaulieu going around to the villa once a day. So . . ."

"So what now?"

"I'll raise the kids for Marc, in my own way. I won't go back to the occupied zone, though. I've had my fill of Nazis. Particularly now that America is in the war, I don't want to leave—I'm French after all—and make things difficult for my boys afterwards. God, would you ever have expected to hear me sounding responsible?"

"We're all doing things we wouldn't have expected."

"Elizabeth, you don't know how much I admire you. Just don't get yourself killed, or Jean-Luc, who if he were not yours I would make the world's greatest play for."

"I'm doing my best. . . ." Their hands touched. "Oh, what a surprise this is. I hadn't expected to see any of you again until this awful war is over . . . maybe never see you again. What good luck."

"It's not luck, Elizabeth," Natcha, who until then had been silent, said, looking over her shoulder at the two men leaning against the balustrade, sipping their champagne and

talking. "We've planned this very carefully. Do you remember that day at the Longchamps racecourse when the
war began?"

"How could any of us forget, least of all you?" Elizabeth
remembered that day in such precise detail that it was like a
film being rerun every time she thought of it.

"I think, for all of us, it was the beginning of a life together
that would never have been but for the war. We would have
gone our separate ways, done things that seemed glamourous
or exciting, but which ultimately we would have recognized
as banal. But war has spared us that disappointment. It was
our good luck to live in these times."

A shiver ran down Elizabeth's spine. How often in the beginning she had thought what bad luck it was to be born in
these times, but now Natcha had put into words what had
long been growing in her subconscious: it was not how long
you lived, it was how intensely you lived. And it was the war
that had given them that. More champagne was poured by a
solicitous waiter.

"I, certainly, was headed nowhere very interesting,"
Natcha continued. "Fashion editor for even French *Vogue* is
perhaps good for a decade, and then you've swapped your
youth for something very ephemeral. I guess I understood
that when I decided to marry Peter. . . ." She looked over her
shoulder again at the two men at the end of the terrace. "And
suppose there had been no war? Can't you see serious Peter,
trying to prove that his advancement in the American foreign
service was due to his hard work and not his vast fortune? And
no matter what, he would have been advanced until he was
ambassador to France like his grandfather, or something
comparable, and we would have both been bored to death.
But now . . ."

"Natcha," Elizabeth said with a frankness that came from

living constantly with danger, "the last time I saw you, at Vichy, you were, I thought, settling down to the kind of matronly role that you might have had with Peter had there been no war. But now you are even more the exotic half-Polish beauty that so fascinated me at Longchamps." She realized she had been pondering this from the moment she had seen Natcha on the hotel terrace at sunset. "What has changed?"

"Peter's interest in me. I think it took him by surprise. It certainly took me by surprise. I had rather reconciled myself to . . . a more sedate life than I suddenly find I have." Natcha was blushing.

Paula laughed softly. "It seems the war also promotes frank talk, which I for one have always been in favor of, as I don't need to tell you."

"It's because," Elizabeth said, "you know that if you don't say what you really feel then the chance may not come again." She spoke from a kind of knowledge that she would not even try to convey to Paula and Natcha.

"I guess we can credit what has happened between me and Peter to the war as well," Natcha said. "And that brings us to why we are here this evening, Elizabeth."

"Tell." She was luxuriating in this exchange of female confidences that she had been deprived of for so long.

"Not long ago the British approached us in Washington, wanted to know if we would be willing to send and receive messages from their agents in France, and those of the Free French, through an officer in our Vichy embassy. If so, this officer would be known to no more than two or three senior persons in the American, British and Free French intelligence services, and would never receive any recognition for his work. Six months ago we would have turned the Brits down, but we are getting seriously fed up with Laval and company—at last—so we agreed."

"Peter?"

"Yes. You know what appealed to Peter most? That he would receive no recognition, that no one would ever know what he had done, would never be able to say, 'It was only because he is a Warden.' From that moment on Peter has become a changed man, and suddenly I was no longer Peter Warden's wife, I was a woman. . . ."

"*Chère amie,*" Paula said, "you don't need to tell me the price of being born a Warden. I've certainly paid my dues. I'm happy for you."

"So that's how Peter knew that Jean-Luc and I were in the Pyrenees?" Elizabeth said.

"Yes. We had to see you, once we knew. Anything that we can do to help the Resistance . . . You can communicate through the Orchard Network. We exchange messages with London through Orange."

Elizabeth felt the hair stand up on the back of her neck at hearing an old friend use so casually code names on which lives hung, like that of Orange, the young war widow in Lyon whose real name she still did not know.

"I want to help too, Elizabeth," Paula said.

"You have."

"That was only money. I want to do more. Like Peter, I want to do something that no one will ever hear of, will ever say of, 'It is only because she is a Warden.' Now that I have established my selfish motive, will you give me an assignment?"

Elizabeth understood that Paula's mocking tone was meant to hide behind, should she be rejected because she had nothing to offer except as a Warden, and she knew that she must not let that happen.

"There are more and more Allied prisoners captured in

North Africa escaping from the Italian prison camps where the Germans have sent them. Many are making their way across the border into the Côte d'Azur area. We have no place to hide them. . . ."

"What can I do?"

"The regime would never think of, would never dare to, search the Villa Warden on Cap Ferrat."

"It goes without saying that it will be made available. Who am I to contact?"

"There is a couple who run a restaurant-bar and truck stop on the Moyenne Corniche, Jean and Margot Raimeau. From their place you can look down on Villa Warden. I can put you in touch. You understand the risks?"

"I understand that one morning I went into Aubigny-sur-Loire and found twelve young Frenchmen—two of whom I knew—hanging by their necks in the village square, because a German soldier had been shot by the Resistance. I know that two weeks ago my Jewish friends in Paris were made to put on a yellow Star of David. They say it is so that it will be easy to pick them up when the time comes to take them off to Germany and kill them."

"I understand," Elizabeth said, her voice trembling a little. And she understood too that Marc had played a role in the beginning of the persecution of the Jews in Vichy France.

A large platter of seafood had been placed in the middle of their table, and Jean-Luc and Peter had put down their glasses on the balustrade and were coming to join them.

"I'm sure you will agree," Natcha said in a low voice, "with the Polish saying that there are secrets, top secrets, and then secrets among close female friends."

Chapter Twenty-Eight

"It is eleven o'clock," Dr. Girona said, consulting his gold pocket watch. He looked around the small group that made up their council of war this November morning, as though he expected some reaction, but all he received was blank stares.

"It has indeed been a day of dramatic events, but they are only the continuation of . . ."

Again no one responded. "At the eleventh hour of the eleventh day of the eleventh month . . ."

"Ah," Terence said. "How could we have failed to note it. Twenty-four years ago to the hour . . ."

"November 11, 1918," the doctor resumed, "Germany surrendered, and the war to end all wars came to a close. Now we know it was only act one. . . ."

Jean-Luc filled their glasses again from the bottle of Spanish brandy Dr. Girona had brought, cut some wafer-thin slices from the sausage that had accompanied the brandy.

"Shall we drink to this day being the day the third and final act began?"

Jean-Luc held out his glass and the others clinked theirs against it. "To victory!"

Three days of suspense for Elizabeth were over. Vichy, Germany and the whole world had been taken by surprise by the American and British invasion of Vichy North Africa. How would the Germans react? By protecting their southern flank, of course. At dawn on November 11 division after division of German troops had rolled across the demarcation line and begun occupying Vichy France. The period of greatest danger for the Resistance—for her and Jean-Luc—had begun. Within a few hours Mount Canigou would be encircled not by the hesitant Vichy police but by the Germany army and the Gestapo.

"Well, Jean-Luc," Dr. Girona said, "we have sliced the problem as fine as you have just cut that sausage, but we have not answered the question of what we do now."

Elizabeth got up and put another log on the fire. Outside clouds had settled on the peak of Canigou. By evening there would be snow.

"I think we stay put for the time being," Jean-Luc answered. "It will be weeks before the Germans have their military occupation fully in place, and until then they will have no time to spare for the Resistance."

"But once they have got things nailed down," Terence said, "the Gestapo will be free to act right out in the open. I reckon one of the first things they will do is try to locate our radio that broadcasts from different locations on the southern slope of the mountain. The Vichy police do not dare, but the Germans can assault the mountain with a whole battalion if they think it worth their while."

Minou snuggled up against Terence's side, her back to the fire. The question of her relationship to their radio operator had been long settled. Terence, who it turned out was a graduate of Oxford and a poet, blond and blue-eyed, had come to Elizabeth to ask formally if he might move into the lodge's second bedroom that Minou occupied, as though Elizabeth were Minou's guardian. Perhaps in a way she was, and permission was granted. A nineteen-year-old Frenchwoman who had been through what she had experienced could seek happiness wherever she chose, but Elizabeth was touched.

"And the other Maquis?" Manuel, a cousin of Jean-Luc's and the acknowledged leader of their Catalan contingent, asked.

"They should stay in place for now. We must see what happens in North Africa. If the Allies succeed, then they will want from us, at this point, not an armed uprising but intelligence on what measures the Germans are taking to fortify the southern coast of France."

"So now we move on to espionage," Elizabeth said, and Jean-Luc gave her a sharp look.

She had immediately regretted the edge of sarcasm to her voice, but she was reaching her limit in allowing him to put off the day of their departure from France, because always the Resistance, General de Gaulle, or his conscience, demanded yet one more task of him. They had done enough. In her time with Jean-Luc she had known much tension, often exhaustion, loneliness when they were apart, and always fear for him, fear for herself; but most of all she had known happiness. Now, for the first time, she was unhappy, and she knew that her unhappiness could easily turn to bitterness.

And then, like a pleasant dream unfolding, the tide of war did turn. First Rommel was defeated at El-Alamein, Vichy French resistance to the Allied invasion of Algeria and Morocco collapsed, the Russians counterattacked at Stalingrad; and that morning when they turned on the BBC they heard that the French had destroyed their fleet at Toulon rather than let it fall into German hands.

She and Jean-Luc had been sitting around the kitchen table with Terence and Minou, drinking coffee and discussing what delicacy Minou, their cook by acclamation, would prepare for lunch.

"Well," Terence said, turning off the radio, "Pétain and Laval have lost North Africa and now their fleet, their last two cards to play against the Boches. Now they will have to dance to the German tune for sure."

"They already have," Elizabeth said. "I could not bring myself last night to show you the pictures from that roll of film Manny Kuhn sent us." She sighed. "But I suppose I must."

She went to her makeshift darkroom and took down the prints that she had hung up to dry.

"These were taken with a hidden camera at an old military camp at Rivesaltes, a few kilometers north of Perpignan." She laid out on the table the pictures of men, women and children being herded into the boxcars of a train, their faces blank with terror.

"According to Kuhn the Vichy police rounded up between three and four thousand Jews and transported them to this camp at Rivesaltes. They have been sent from there, a train-load at a time, to Paris. What happens after that nobody seems to know."

"They would prefer not to know," Jean-Luc said. "They will be transported to Germany to their deaths, just like the Jews rounded up in Paris in July. It is too bad Vichy broke off diplomatic relations with America over the North African invasion. We could have sent these pictures to Peter Warden."

"By now Peter and Natcha should be back in Washington, or more likely Laurel Hill," Elizabeth said. "At least *they* are safe." She almost burst into tears at the thought that she and Jean-Luc could have been there with them.

Minou threw down the picture she had been looking at with a gesture of disgust. "One expects this kind of thing of the Boches, but for Frenchmen to let themselves do this, it makes me sick."

"We must find another way of getting these pictures out," Terence said. "We cannot do anything for these poor devils now, but maybe after the war the French involved in this, starting with Laval, can be prosecuted. For now all we can do is win the war as fast as possible, and when it is all over, I will wager that we will all agree that November, 1942, was the month when Hitler's fate was sealed."

She knew that Jean-Luc, who had foreseen so well the course of events, must agree, but he said nothing. She knew why, and it was at this moment that she decided to act. Immediately she felt a great weight lifted from her.

"Jean-Luc, let's go for a walk. I could use some fresh air. This business has made me ill."

He frowned. "I have messages to send, Elizabeth, and then I need to visit the Maquis at . . ."

"Come, Jean-Luc," she said in a tone that did not allow for further protest.

They walked along a familiar path that wound through the fragrant fir forest, with views opening up of the plain and the Mediterranean under a cloudless blue sky. It was very warm.

"Another St. Martin's summer. The first time that I heard that that was the French expression for Indian summer was the day we went to Château Aubigny for the horse show. Three years ago, almost to the day. We stopped along the way. Do you remember what we did?"

"We had a picnic."

She took his hand. "That too, but what I remember most is making love under the open sky, just as we did in the woods beneath Fort de la Revère."

"You have a good memory for such things."

"They mean a lot to me. Do you know how many days it

has been since we last made love?"

"No, not exactly."

"Sixteen. That will not do, Jean-Luc, but you are always tired and preoccupied, and I have been tense and nervous . . . and depressed. They say in our business that sooner or later everyone burns out, and when they do they are not doing those who depend on them a favor by continuing."

They had stopped by a little waterfall. A beam of sunlight fell on the pool beneath the fall, the masses of ferns, the floor of moss, turned a brilliant emerald green by the sun.

"You think I am burned out?"

"Let me ask you a question instead. Do you agree with Terence that this is the month when the tide of war changed, when we first could see that victory is assured?"

He looked into her eyes but said nothing.

"Jean-Luc, I am calling in my pledge. We are leaving."

"But at this critical moment who will lead . . ."

"Terence can take over from you. He is very good and his improvement in French in the eight months he has been with us has been phenomenal."

"But, what will de Gaulle . . ."

"Jean-Luc, *tout simple,* I am holding you to your word of honor."

"In that case I have no choice."

She let out a sigh of relief. "Thank God!"

He took her in his arms. They were both shaking.

"Now that that's settled, I want to make love. Take off my clothes."

"No precautions?"

"Now that we are leaving, if I get pregnant, that's just fine."

When they were both undressed, she lay down on the bed

of moss and joyously opened herself to him. They had, after all, survived.

"So, what have we here?" Jean-Luc asked, lifting the lid from the copper pot, inhaling the fragrances arising from it. Elizabeth smiled. After men had made love they were always hungry. Men? She was ravenous.

"Kid goat cooked with wild mushrooms picked in the forest," Minou replied. "Your Catalan boys find them for me, along with the herbs."

"After the war," Terence said, "Minou and I have thought about opening a restaurant somewhere around Collioure. My father is a wine merchant in London, so I could handle that side of business."

"After the war", Elizabeth thought, was the phrase one heard most often among people in the Resistance. What it meant was, "if I survive the war". While she and Jean-Luc had been gone, their young friends had been spinning fantasies about what they would do if they survived. And from the flushed look on Minou's face, they too had taken the opportunity of being alone to enjoy each other.

"Any messages, Terence?" Jean-Luc asked.

"One from Tangerine."

"Paula!" Elizabeth exclaimed. "What does she say?"

"She has two British officers, escaped from a camp in Italy, at her estate on Cap Ferrat. She plans to take them as far as Marseille herself, where she will turn them over to Fig."

Paula and Marjorie Dufay would get along fine, Elizabeth thought, both rich, hard-boiled Americans. But it was difficult to imagine the Paula that she had introduced to Jean-Luc and Marc, the morning after Paula was expelled from Vassar, as a woman who was risking her liberty and even her life to help Allied prisoners escape. What changes the war had made in them all.

"Also, Jean-Luc," Terence said, "a short message for you in your private code."

That evening, after Minou and Terence had gone out for a walk of their own, Jean-Luc handed her a scrap of paper.

"FOR TORTOISE. WE ARE HAVING SEVERE PROBLEMS WITH OUR ESCAPE ROUTES THROUGH SPAIN. NEED CATALAN SPEAKER WITH FULL KNOWLEDGE OF OUR SITUATION TO TRAVEL ROUTE TO BARCELONA AND SURROUNDING AREA AND SECURE THE ROUTES. ARE YOU WILLING AND CAN YOU GET THERE? STAY INDEFINITE. STARFISH."

It was like a gift from heaven. She looked at Jean-Luc across from her in a chair beside the fire, nursing a glass of Spanish brandy. In the semi-darkness she supposed he could not see the tears in her eyes. Now the last obstacle to their departure had been miraculously lifted. She rolled up the piece of paper and tossed it into the fire, as was done with all the private messages from de Gaulle, once they had been read.

"When shall we leave?" she asked.

"Tomorrow early, if that is possible. I will turn control over to Terence tonight."

"I will start getting ready now," she said.

"We will have to go by way of Coustouges on muleback. We dare not try to make it by train or road with Germans now swarming everywhere."

"Good. I would like to see your uncles Martin and Roger again." She laughed. "I really like them."

That night Elizabeth went to sleep in Jean-Luc's arms, after contemplating for some time what a miraculous day this had been, a day in which everything, at last, had turned out right. She had set the alarm for dawn.

When the alarm rang she was already awake, anxious to get started. She retrieved her nightgown, in a ball at the foot of the bed, where it had ended up after they had made love again during the night. She sat up, pulled the gown over her head, put her feet down on the cold floor, just as the gunfire erupted. Sten gun, she thought clinically. Our people. She had learned to use one in a remote ravine on the mountain, knew the characteristic sound of its fire, had even lobbed a couple of live grenades from behind a boulder, to experience what that was like. Then there was firing from some heavier type of gun, then Sten guns again, several of them, then silence.

For a split second she regretted that they would not be going anywhere this morning, but to think anymore about that was to risk not going anywhere, ever. Jean-Luc was, of course, on his feet, a gun in his hand, lighting a lamp. They went out into the main room, where the fire of the night before still glowed. Terence and Minou were already there, both armed, he in pajamas, she wearing nothing but a bath towel. The war of Jean-Luc Cabanasse and Elizabeth Vail was not yet over.

"You would have been proud of us, Captain," one of the newly recruited Catalans said in broken French. "This German army patrol car drove right up to where the road ends. Even with the lights painted blue we saw it coming from a long way off. We let it start to turn around and then we opened up. Got three of them. The one left fired a few shots in our direction, and then we got him too. The Germans will not be sending any more patrols up Canigou anytime soon. You can bet on that."

"No," Jean-Luc said evenly, "they will send enough force

All Through the Night

up Canigou to blow us all off the face of the earth. Now we all have to get out of here. Tell Manuel to assemble his men, all the equipment, the mules. We will be damned lucky if they do not put planes up against us. Now go!"

The man stood open-mouthed for a moment, dumbfounded at this outburst rather than the praise he had expected, then saluted and took off at a run.

"And, of course," Jean-Luc said to the other three, "they will take hostages, ten or twelve for every German killed, and shoot them."

The line of mules moved all morning along the forest path beneath the peak of Canigou. No planes appeared overhead. Perhaps the Germans had not yet discovered what had happened to their patrol. By noon they had arrived at the top of a ridge where the path divided, one branch leading to the remote mountain village of Valmanya, the other descending to Amélie-les-Bains, and then ascending again to Coustouges and the Spanish border.

"Here is where we part, Terence," Jean-Luc said. "They will welcome reinforcements at the Maquis of Valmanya, particularly when they find out you have a radio transmitter."

"I propose a toast," Terence said, taking a bottle out of a pannier on a mule's back. "To a safe journey, a speedy victory over the Boches and a reunion at my and Minou's restaurant in Collioure."

There were no glasses, so they each drank from the bottle in turn. Then Elizabeth and Minou embraced. They were both crying.

"Minou, do not let anything happen to Terence. And take care of yourself. . . ." She was too choked up to say more.

The four of them kissed, Jean-Luc kissed cheeks with each

of the Catalan men, and he and Elizabeth mounted their mules and set out.

"*Garde-toi!*" Minou called. Elizabeth turned and waved, and then they were out of sight of the others.

They rode for the rest of the day, meeting no one. Then they stopped to rest and eat some bread and sausage and wait for the full moon to rise. At the last full moon they were waiting for an air drop in a field outside Serrabone.

When the moon was well up they mounted again and, tired and saddle-sore, continued on. By ten o'clock they had reached the top of the last ridge and could look down on Amélie-les-Bains where a few lights burned.

"They do not even bother with a blackout there," Jean-Luc said. "Certainly there is nothing of any strategic value around here, but there will at least be some kind of German contingent at Amélie, so we will have to be careful. The bridge will be guarded for sure."

"How do we cross the river?"

"This path we are on is an ancient one. It was here before there were any bridges, and it crosses a few kilometers above Amélie, where the river is shallow enough to walk animals across. Then the path continues on to Coustouges, and by the time the sun comes up we should be far enough up the mountain that we are unlikely to run into any Germans or Vichy police."

"Then can we sleep for a couple of hours? I do not have much energy left."

"Sure we can, and just remember, all we have to do is reach Coustouges and we are safe. From there we can just walk over the border into Spain."

"Let's go then."

They reached the river just as the clock in Amelie struck twelve, and crossed to the other side easily. The water was only knee-high and the bottom covered with loose gravel.

"Now we have to cross a highway," Jean-Luc said. "It is after curfew now, so we could be arrested."

Within a few minutes the paved surface of the highway was visible, gleaming in the moonlight.

"These mules' shoes are going to make a lot of noise on the pavement," Jean-Luc whispered, "so we should tie them here, and go check first to make sure there is nobody about."

They walked softly to the edge of the road. In one direction the moonlit road was empty. In the other—and then she saw it. A car was parked in some trees on the other side of the road. Suddenly they were standing in headlight beams.

"Ne bougez pas!" a voice rang out. A gendarme stepped out of the darkness. "You are under arrest for curfew violation. We catch a lot of people here. Let's see your papers."

They handed over their identity cards. Curfew violation couldn't be all that serious, but a hundred feet away stood two mules with panniers containing Sten guns and hand grenades. If those were found their false identities would quickly be discovered, and then . . .

"You are doubly unlucky, Monsieur. You come from this district and you picked a very bad night to break curfew. Come with me."

The gendarme shined his flashlight down the road and other headlights came on. An engine started and a truck moved down the road toward them. It was a German army truck.

"Get in the back with the others," a German sergeant said in execrable French.

In the back were two German soldiers and a half dozen young men in civilian clothes, obviously local men. Jean-Luc got up into the truck as he was told, and they exchanged anguished glances before the truck rolled away.

"What is happening?"

"I am really sorry about this, Mademoiselle," the gendarme said. "If I had known that this was what the Boches had in mind, I would have called in sick today."

"What do you mean?" she cried, the truth already on the edge of her consciousness.

"Some Maquisards up on Canigou ambushed a German patrol and killed four German soldiers. The German commander ordered forty hostages taken from among young men already in jail, but there were only thirty, so they decided to make up the balance with curfew violators. I am really sorry that things turned out this way."

For a moment Elizabeth thought she was going to faint, but then she pulled herself together.

"What happens now?"

"The Maquisards either surrender themselves today or the hostages . . . are shot at dawn tomorrow. I am terribly sorry. The stinking Boches. Under the circumstances I will not arrest you for breaking curfew. Would you like a ride into town?"

"No, I live just across the river. We waded over, as you can see. I will go home now."

"Maybe the Maquisards will turn themselves in or . . ." He did not finish his sentence. They both knew that nothing like that would save the hostages.

"That will not happen, but could you give me one piece of information, Monsieur? Where are the hostages being held?"

"In a small hotel, a distance of two kilometers, between here and Amélie—no one is taking the waters now, of course, and all the hotels are empty, so . . . But there is a German army squad posted there, so do not even consider . . ."

"No, I am not a fool. Besides what could a single woman

do? There is nothing left but to go home. I am sorry for Jean-Luc, but it is not like we were engaged or anything. Still, what lousy luck, huh?"

"Sure you will not accept a ride into town?"

She shook her head. Then the gendarme drove off, leaving Elizabeth standing alone in the middle of the moonlit road.

Chapter Twenty-Nine

She stood there for some time, looking down at the moonlit hands she held out in front of her. What could she, alone, do with these hands? She could think of nothing. Once before, on the day the Germans had strafed the refugee column on the road from Paris to Tours she had felt dark despair, but she had slept in the forest that night and her confidence had returned. She had not done badly since. Maybe, Sarah Elizabeth Vail, she said, addressing herself as she always did in moments of crisis, your ancestors who crossed the ocean and settled in the Appalachian mountains have supported you all this way. But now, what can they or anyone else do for you? You, a human being all alone, must decide what comes next. This is the most important, possibly the last, decision of your life. You can accept what has happened, get on a mule and make your way up the mountain to Coustouges and freedom, and hope you are carrying Jean-Luc's child, which is statistically unlikely, but it would be something to fling in the face of a cruel, indifferent universe. On the other hand, you can attempt to free Jean-Luc, and almost certainly add your death to his, to no avail. Now, you must choose.

After this conversation with herself, Elizabeth let her outstretched hands fall to her sides. Her choice, the only one possible, had been made. She turned and walked back down the path to where the two mules were tethered. She tied the reins of one to the tail of the other and led them across the road, their shoes clicking on the asphalt, and up the path that led to Coustouges and Spain.

Of the two mules, she knew that Belle would remain quiet—and there must be quiet—but Myrtle was another matter. Already she was beginning to act up and might soon neigh. Elizabeth pulled down Myrtle's head with one hand; and with her other hand she pinched the mule's nostrils. Well, maybe her ancestors hadn't abandoned her entirely. . . .

When Myrtle had quieted down, Elizabeth took out an oil-cloth packet from a pannier, stripped off her filthy corduroy and leather battle dress until she stood naked beneath the moon. Then she unwrapped the clothes that she had brought for the day that she and Jean-Luc would enter Barcelona as representatives of Free France.

She put on panties and garter belt and silk stockings and the last of her dresses, the Balanciaga, seams torn, spotted with grease, but still good enough for what she had to do. The most difficult was the makeup, applied by flashlight shining blindingly into her compact mirror, applied with studied crudeness, nothing like what she had learned at *Vogue*.

Then Elizabeth began walking down the narrow, moonlit, asphalted road to Amélie in her stockinged feet, her shoes in one hand and her handbag in the other. And as she walked through the dark woods, night birds crying, she thought of all the times together with Jean-Luc, who had opened the wonders of the world to her, beginning on a pond in Virginia. How different it could have been. Now she was walking down an obscure road in southwest France to her death. She did not doubt it, and with all her heart she wanted it not to be. But what must be must be, for she had made the only choice that she could.

357

And then she saw through the trees an electric-blue neon sign: a palm tree and the sinuously twisting letters, "Le almier." The name of the little hotel where the hostages were being held was "Le Palmier", the Palm Tree. The letter "P" had been broken off, and the rest of the neon sign flickered as though it were about to expire as well. It had no doubt been left on to guide the Gestapo execution squad that would arrive shortly before dawn.

"Halt!" A helmeted German soldier stepped out of the bushes along the hotel's garden wall, a submachine gun held level. A second soldier emerged and turned a flashlight beam on her.

Elizabeth froze, and then something so unexpected happened that it was almost supernatural. She was standing on the stage of the theater at Laurel Hill College as the curtains opened. Below her were row upon row of faces in the semi-darkness, and she was caught in the stage light's beam, terrified, every line she had learned forgotten. But then out of her mouth had come the words of a woman of ancient Greece, a dagger hidden in her gown, ready to defy even the gods. She had not returned to her own body until the curtain closed, awakening to applause.

"Come on now," she said, "what's this all about? You'd scare a girl to death."

"Why are you out after curfew?" the one with the submachine gun said.

"Yes, why?" the one with the flashlight echoed.

Thank God, they speak some French, she thought as she composed her reply.

"I'll tell you why. Because my boyfriend and I had a fight, and he left me outside a nightclub the other side of Arles-sur-Tech to walk back to Amélie, that's why."

"Nightclubs are illegal."

"*Dites-le-moi,* and the nightclub full of German soldiers."

This produced a pause, and then the flashlight one said, "Can you explain why you are in the vicinity of a military installation?"

"Because the road goes past it, you dope."

"You had better watch how you address a member of the armed forces of the German Reich."

"Oh, go screw yourself!"

"That does it. We are taking you to the sergeant of the guard."

"OK, OK, just let me get my shoes on." Elizabeth bent over and put on the black high-heeled pumps she had been carrying.

They marched her through the hotel entrance, past a startled sentry, up the stairs of the hotel Le Palmier; and the one with the submachine gun knocked on the frosted glass door of the concierge's office. Act one, scene one, was over. She was inside.

"So your friend dumped you at a black market club and left you to walk back to Amélie alone, a gorgeous babe like you? He must be crazy," said the German sergeant who spoke French, and not bad French. He was greatly enjoying showing off his linguistic skill to the others in the smoke-filled room where they had been playing cards. "And you want us to take you into town."

"You have two vehicles out front. Why not?"

"What can you pay?" one of the soldiers asked.

"I told you, the bastard left me without a sou."

"Well, then?"

Four pairs of eyes were focused on her. She let what she hoped was a sultry look from her over-made-up eyes pass slowly across each of their faces.

"In any case, we aren't taking her to town," the sergeant said. "The captain would have the hide off my butt." He paused, calculating the risk. "But we do have some trucks going into town in the morning, if you want to spend the night."

Yes, she thought, quite dispassionately, because she was on stage, outside of her body, trucks that are coming to take away the bodies of those executed.

"I still can't pay."

"There's always barter," the sergeant said. He got up and came to her and cupped her breast in his hand. "With merchandise of this quality, we might have a deal, including a cot for the night."

"I suppose I could visit with one of you for a few minutes," she said.

"Then that is me," the sergeant said.

"Wait a minute," one of the soldiers said. "All of us."

"Forget it," she replied scornfully. "I would rather walk to town."

"Two," one of the German soldiers said, picking up the cards. "We will cut for it."

She shrugged. "All right, but you will have to make it quick. I am not a charity."

The door flew open. A German officer strode into the room.

"Attention!"

The sergeant and his men drew themselves up ramrod stiff, eyes straight in front of them.

"What is going on here?" the officer said in perfect French, glancing at her. She understood. He wanted her testimony. "We have a most delicate mission tonight, and you bring a woman in here? Explain yourself, sergeant!"

"It is not as it seems, my captain. Our sentries picked up

this woman lurking around the perimeter."

"Lurking, my ass!" Elizabeth said in her best lower-class French. "I was walking down the road."

"After curfew," the sergeant said, looking not at his superior but at the wall in front of him.

"I explained that to you," Elizabeth said in a purring voice, and then burst out, "Ask them, captain, what they wanted me to do in exchange for just a ride into town!"

"I do not need to, mademoiselle," the captain said in a very correct tone. "It is quite obvious. It is also obvious that we cannot provide you with transportation into Amélie, least of all with the trucks in the morning. Nor can you spend the night here. You must leave now. I will give you a curfew pass, but I expect you to leave immediately, on foot, for Amélie."

As the captain spoke Elizabeth, removed from the role she was playing, studied him. He reminded her of Major Waag, who had saved her from the Gestapo in Paris; an upper-class German with proper manners, in a uniform, she knew from her time at *Vogue*, that had come from the finest of tailors. His sandy hair and mustache were perfectly cut. His hands had never known manual labor and, possibly, like Major Waag, he had such interests as French impressionist painting. He probably abhorred the work he would have to do this night. But it made no difference. What must be must be.

"Can I at least use your bathroom to freshen up? I have had a bad night," she said.

"Of course," the captain replied. "It is on the first floor. But do not go to the second floor. That is off limits."

She put her handbag down on a low table beside the door, reached into it with trembling hands, fumbled about, brought out a lipstick.

"I will take only a minute."

Then she went out the door, closed it behind her, and ran

with all her strength up the stairs. As she reached the first floor landing there was an explosion that shook the entire building, as the grenade in her handbag exploded.

"God forgive me," she whispered, but she had no more time to think about what she had done. Down the stairs to the floor above came the thundering of feet, as dozens of young men ran for their lives. Then, there on the landing, she stood facing Jean-Luc. Their eyes met for only a second, both knowing that to hesitate was to die.

The next instant they were running down the last flight of stairs, bringing up the rear of the fleeing hostages, on past the blown-out door of the guard room, from which clouds of acrid smoke billowed, down the front steps and out into the garden, the hostages fanning out in all directions, pouring out the gate, scaling the garden wall.

Bullets sang past them like a swarm of angry bees. But then they were through the gate and out onto the unlit road, across it and into the woods, where they fell flat onto the ground. The German soldiers rushed forward to the gate, their submachine guns pointing out into the darkness, but there they stopped.

"We've made it," Elizabeth whispered. Jean-Luc did not respond. She put her hand on his shoulder, warm and soaking wet. By the glow of floodlights that had finally been turned on in the hotel grounds, she could see enough to strip off his shirt and find the wound in his upper left arm from which the blood was spurting.

"No, no," she cried aloud, "don't leave me, don't let me lose you." Tears poured down her face. But then cold fury seized her, fury not only at the Nazis but that such things could be. If death was to take him, it would first have to struggle with her.

She tore a stocking loose from her garter belt, twisted it

into a rope, wrapped it around Jean-Luc's arm and tightened it with a piece of tree branch. The flow of blood dwindled and stopped. Now what?

"Madame?"

Elizabeth looked up into the dimly-lit face of a boy of about sixteen.

"What is it?"

"You must come with me."

"Who are you?"

"I was one of the hostages. Jean-Luc is my friend. He said when the Boches shot us we would hold hands to give each other courage, and we would die like patriots. Are you Elizabeth?"

"Yes."

"Come, then."

"But where?"

"Elizabeth . . ." It was Jean-Luc's voice, barely audible.

She put her ear close to his mouth. "What, my darling?"

"Tell him to take us to Dr. Vernet."

"Your blood type?" the dark lean face above her inquired.

"What do you mean?"

"What I mean is do you know your blood type?"

"O."

"You are quite sure about that? There is no time to check."

"Yes, I am sure."

"If you are a universal donor, then it is possible we may be able to save his life."

The doctor began taking apparatus out of a drawer, not slowly, just deliberately. "I have wasted a certain amount of time on you. When I saw you I thought, she is done for." He motioned with his head to her blood-soaked dress on the terrazzo floor. "But when I got your clothes off you did not have even a scratch on you. It is all his blood."

"I know. I tried to make a tourniquet with a stocking, but I did not know . . ."

"Not a bad job. You saved his life, to this point at least."

She felt a stab of pain in her arm. "Are you taking blood?"

"Yes, and I am going to have to take a lot, if he is to live. Afterwards, you will be very weak for a while. Now close your eyes, and keep them closed. Try to remain calm."

She felt, or she thought she felt, the blood draining from her body, blood that would soon be flowing into his. Oh, Jean-Luc, live, live.

"Oh, thank God you were here, doctor." She knew she was becoming a bit delirious. "And thank God Jean-Luc knew you were our agent in Amélie, and thank God the boy knew how to find your clinic, and thank . . ."

The last thing she felt before she lost consciousness was Dr. Vernet's hand on her wrist, searching for the pulse.

"He will live," Dr. Vernet said. "In fact, he is probably in somewhat better shape than you. I had to take a great deal of your blood. But that was all he needed. The wound to his upper arm is in itself superficial, a few millimeters to one side or the other and I would have called it a scratch, but within those few millimeters is a major artery, almost severed."

"Then my blood saved his life."

"Without any question, that and the tourniquet you made with your stocking."

"Where are we?" she asked.

"In the attic of my house, behind a sliding panel that hides two small rooms. Your friend is in the other. You should be safe here, for a few days at least. This is where I conceal the British aviators and others that you send us on the escape route through Coustouges to Spain."

"Why did you do it?" She had a childlike curiosity, in her light-headed state, about everything that had brought her to this strange point in her life.

"Do what, take you in?"

"That I understand, once you joined the Resistance, but why did you join?"

"My old colleague, Dr. Girona, recruited me."

"That meant trusting him with your life."

"Yes, and one does not do that in this part of the world except with close relatives or with schoolmates who have become as close to you as brothers. Girona and I, he from Catalonia and I from France, went through the medical school of Montpellier together, one of the oldest in the world. It dates from the twelfth century, and in the entrance to it there are marble plaques listing its professors from the earliest times. The very first were Jews. Perhaps I am repaying them a bit by what I am doing."

She thought about that, studied the dark, narrow face of the man who had, in fact, saved Jean-Luc's life. He reminded her, with his bristly moustache and pointed ears, of a fox, a wise, kind fox.

"But you are saving lives. I have just killed five men—at least I suppose they are dead—to save the life of the man I love. And now the Germans will take even more hostages to replace those who escaped when the grenade went off. That is what I have done. If I were Catholic, I suppose I would need a confessor very badly."

Dr. Vernet smiled. "Have you not just confessed, and is not the tribe of doctors very close to the order of priests? We both have great traffic with death. Would you like my absolution?"

"If that were possible."

"The Orchard Net, founded by you and Jean-Luc, has helped hundreds to freedom. I am sure you have done much more than I know of. As to the violence you have just committed, is there any other way, unless we are prepared to submit all Europe, perhaps all the world, to the ghastly rule of the Nazis? They leave us no choice but to submit or fight back. It is they who chose the path of violence."

"Yet . . . Because of me there will be even more hostages shot."

"Ah. It is otherwise. The German military command in Perpignan has announced that the terrorists responsible for the attack on the patrol have been hunted down on Mount Canigou and all killed. Therefore, the hostages have been released."

"That is not true."

"Do you imagine the German commander would want it known in Berlin that a young woman from the Resistance has overpowered a German military unit and freed forty hostages? That does not mean, of course, that he will not make every effort to apprehend that young woman. She must go to some place safe as soon as her companion is able to travel."

"But where?"

"Coustouges. I have been in touch with Martin Cabanasse, the head of the clan. In two days time he will be sending an armed party to take you there. I would not want to be in a German patrol that encountered them on the way."

First there was the sound of feet on the attic stairs, then lights being turned on, the face of Dr. Vernet's housekeeper looking down into hers. Elizabeth glanced at the wristwatch that she never took off. Three-thirty in the morning.

"What is it?" she asked apprehensively.

"A *grande rafle*, at dawn."

A big police roundup. "French or Gestapo?"

"Gestapo."

As soon as she heard the word Gestapo, Elizabeth sat up and put her feet on the floor.

"Dr. Vernet said you must come down quickly. He is getting out the car."

She was on her feet now, turned to go into the other cubicle where Jean-Luc slept on a narrow cot identical to hers—like a monastery, he had said—but he was already in the doorway.

"You heard?"

"Yes."

Within five minutes they were in Dr. Vernet's waiting car, its engine running. They no longer had any possessions to gather up, no false identity cards, no weapons. This time, Elizabeth said to herself, we either get away for good or it's all over. One or the other.

"This is a bit risky, you understand," Dr. Vernet said, as they sped along the road that followed the river north, "but I do not see much choice. At dawn the Gestapo will begin a house-to-house search of Amélie. The roads out of town are already sealed off, but by our police, and they are used to my leaving town at any hour to preside over a birth or death. So, with a little luck . . . I will say that you are the children of someone at death's door up on the mountain."

"Why the *rafle?*" Jean-Luc asked.

God, was she glad to see him himself again: calm, analytical, tough, gentle. Her hand rested lightly in his. Women of the world, envy me—if we stay alive.

"Why? They found two mules tethered in the woods alongside the road we are about to go up, if we get past the roadblock. Panniers full of interesting items: Sten guns, hand grenades, a variety of false papers, etcetera. So says my informant in the police who alerted me to this morning's *rafle*."

The roadblock was not a problem, particularly when Dr. Vernet produced a bottle of fine Cognac for the police at the barrier, his usual Christmas gift a little in advance.

It was still dark when they reached the little town of St.-Laurent-de-Cerdans, from where the road up the mountain to Coustouges was not much better than a track. At the livery stable, the party from Coustouges was just saddling up to begin the journey down to the valley to rescue Jean-Luc and Elizabeth.

"So, the journey will be a great deal shorter," the bearded leader of the party said, another cousin of Jean-Luc's, it seemed. "So much the better. There are German patrols all over the mountain. They must be onto something. We should get moving."

There was something very reassuring in the economical way the six men moved, turning aside Jean-Luc's attempts to help with his arm still in a sling, something very reassuring in the solid metallic sound of carbines being loaded, in the sight and smell of the large dark-brown mules, stolidly waiting to be harnessed, their breaths billowing in the cold air of the lantern-lit stable.

A boy came running into the stable. "Three German patrol cars coming up the road from Arles."

"How far away?" the leader of the party asked.

"Ten minutes."

"We must move out then. From here on they will have to travel on foot," and white teeth showed in his black beard, "particularly since we have taken all the mules."

From the top of the first ridge they looked back on the town of St. Laurent below. The three German patrol cars were drawn up in the square in front of the church, and then they began to move.

"Mon Dieu," the leader of the party said, "they are going to try to drive on. The crazy Boches. Can't they see the snow-storm coming off mother Canigou?"

And then the snow began to fall, sticking fast, and within a few minutes covering the mountainside in a sheet of white. By the time the mule train passed through the gate of Coustouges it was ankle-deep. For two whole days the snow fell, until it was a meter deep, totally isolating the village.

On the third day the sun shone down from a deep blue sky on a sparkling white world. It could be several days, even a week, before they would be able to leave for Spain, once again accompanied by Jean-Luc's kinsmen; but from the little sun porch where she was setting the table for lunch, one could see Spain. Jean-Luc was sprawled in a broken-down wicker chair with a glass of red wine.

"What do I smell from the kitchen?"

"A casserole of roast chicken with potatoes, carrots, dried mushrooms and rosemary."

"You have done that while I have just been sitting here idly, drinking wine and looking out the window?"

"Jean-Luc, have you ever before been idle in all your life?"

"Not really."

"How does it feel?"

"It makes me nervous. There is much to do."

"Thank God for this deep snow. Whatever you think has to be done cannot be done in Coustouges, and you cannot turn back. Ahead of us lies, well, who knows. I know I have missed my period. Maybe it is what I have been through in the last few days, but perhaps . . . In any case we will now live another life, our own life . . . at last."

"Thanks to you. Thanks to you I am alive today. You are a very brave woman."

"No, and I cannot be proud of what I did, but Dr. Vernet helped me to understand that sometimes, particularly if you are born into times like these, there are no choices that one can be proud of. I did what I felt I had to do. Now it is over. Jean-Luc, it has been a long voyage from Laurel Hill to Coustouges. . . ."

Too moved to go on, she poured herself a glass of wine from the bottle on the table, wiped away the tears in her eyes with a napkin.

He raised his glass. "To you my love, my valiant Elizabeth, who has everything to be proud of. Did not I tell you that first weekend at Laurel Hill that you would lead an extraordinary life?"